DEADLY
Mementos

A Keith Carson and Sara Porter Mystery

Leslie Bendaly

iUniverse, Inc.
New York Bloomington

Deadly Mementos
A Keith Carson and Sara Porter Mystery

iUniverse books may be ordered through booksellers or by contacting:

iUniverse
1663 Liberty Drive
Bloomington, IN 47403
www.iuniverse.com
1-800-Authors (1-800-288-4677)

ISBN: 978-1-4502-3323-1 (pbk)
ISBN: 978-1-4502-3322-4 (cloth)
ISBN: 978-1-4502-3324-8 (ebk)

Library of Congress Control Number: 2010908673

Printed in the United States of America

iUniverse rev. date: 7/7/2010

To
Mom

Acknowledgements

Where to begin? Perhaps several years ago when I took a mystery writing course with Peter Robinson during which he gave one of my assignments a kind comment. That was sufficient encouragement to drive me forward. That piece became the seed for this novel, and is embedded in the following pages.

Many friends have championed this work and made it better. Thanks to: Joan Homewood who has believed in Deadly Mementos from the beginning and has supported me unfailingly with her many skills from editorial to marketing and most importantly her enthusiasm; Dean Robinson, whose meticulous nature and enquiring mind make him an amazing copy editor; Judy Robinson who energizes me with her friendship and wit; my first agent, Leona Trainer, and Dale Jeffries, good friend and energetic supporter, to whom the baton was passed when Leona retired; Staff Sergeant Chuck Konkel who took time to chat about policing in Toronto; friends like Margaret and Patrick Farley who asked to read the manuscript and cheered me on; my sister Nan who is always there and keeps me laughing and of course Elie, Chip, Nicole and Jason who are my constant cheerleaders.

Thanks too to iuniverse's phantom editor whose invaluable feedback made this a much better novel.

Prologue

Kathryn McPherson was about to make the last decision of her life. She acknowledged the fact not with regret but with relief. After a few moments of contemplation, she struggled to prop herself up against the pillows. She didn't intend to make her last decision lying down. In all of her years of decision-making, this was the first decision she could remember approaching without absolute certainty. Decision-making had always been easy for her. She had known just what had to be done and did it. Clients considered her focused and decisive; staff and friends called her unbending. Competitors and enemies were more likely to suggest ruthless.

Even this morning's decision, the one she now labeled her second last decision, had been easy. She had fought the good fight. She found martyrs to be highly annoying and didn't intend to be one. She would never speak again, never walk again and, most importantly, never accomplish anything again. And she was determined that the weak-faced sycophant who passed himself off as a nurse's aide would never demean her with one of "our" baths again. That decision had been made instantaneously. This one took greater analysis.

She had waited until she knew she would not be disturbed. The hall lights had been dimmed for the night. The nurse, on her last check for the evening, had left the door slightly ajar, leaving room for a strip of ocher to fall through and across the bed.

The familiar box rested next to her on top of the bedcovers. With effort she ran the fingers of her left hand across its embossed top. For the first time she noticed that what had been a blue paisley pattern on brilliant white was now more green than blue on rancid yellow. Until this moment she had always seen it as it had been when she was a teenager, and she had asked her mother if she could use it to store her schoolgirl mementos. When had it started to fade? Probably about the same time she had, she thought with a touch of resentment. That was one of the few things in life she hadn't been able to control, though God and the best cosmetic surgeons in the world knew she had given it a damn good try.

She lifted the lid a crack. A musty odor emerged. As it reached her nostrils it became instead the overpowering smell of decaying flesh.

"You're not only dying, you're batty," she thought. But the odor was so strong and so real that a wave of nausea swept over her as it had done once in the past.

1

Sara slowly opened her eyes and quickly shut them again. In the fraction of a second that her lids were raised, a shard of sunlight jabbed through her left eye, finding the throbbing pressure that had lingered there all night and taking it to new heights.

She rolled over toward her husband's side of the bed for comfort, stretching out one leg in search of his sleeping body. Instead it found only smooth, cold sheets. Her memory was up to its cruel tricks again, letting her momentarily forget, and then thrusting the truth at her anew.

She took several deep, slow breaths. Managing her emotions had become a full time job. "Think about something else," she reprimanded herself out loud. What was it she had been thinking about each time she awoke during the night? A puzzle of some sort had been nagging at the back of her mind. She had made repeated efforts to grasp the pieces but each time, just as she knew she was on the brink of the solution, she was pulled back into sleep.

She stretched out farther, forcing herself to claim the entire bed. Her progress was stopped when her foot hit something heavy resting on top of the covers. At first she thought perhaps she had left her briefcase on the bed. But it didn't feel right. Then she remembered. That darn box. She had had one wealthy relative. One shot at an inheritance and what did she end up with? A hatbox full of Aunt Kate's mementos.

She tried opening one eye again. No darting pain this time. The box sat there waiting. For what, she didn't know, but it commanded her attention. It didn't feel like a gift. More like something imposed upon her that demanded action of some sort.

Its appearance certainly held no power. It looked tired. A touch of brilliant blue lingered in the corners of the underside of the lid, but the matching blue that would have washed the outer walls had not been able to hide from time. Greenish yellow age-stains blotched the entire surface. The lid, its corners split, sat precariously and ineffectually on top of the heap of memorabilia that had outgrown its container.

The smell of coffee coaxed Sara into an upright position. One of the few things she and Richard had agreed on toward the end of their marriage was that a coffee maker in the bedroom was a small but precious luxury. Instead of setting the alarm clock at bedtime, they set the coffee maker. Propped up in bed with a cup of magic brew, as Richard called it, was the only civilized way to enter the day. Add the *New York Times* on a Sunday morning and life was rich. She wondered whether Richard was at this moment sharing their morning ceremony with Diane Brooks.

As she pulled herself from bed, the dull pain returned to her left eye, letting her know that it wasn't through with her yet. The room was cold and she pointed herself toward the white terry cloth robe that hung over the corner of the bathroom door. As she moved across the room she avoided looking toward the full-length mirror that reflected her naked body. She glanced toward the balcony instead. The maples growing on either side gave Sara the feeling of being perched in a tree house. She greeted the day from there as often as possible. But not today. Autumn had brought a crispness to the air that would demand she wear more than a robe, and the bright sun would tease her headache into full-blown action. A breeze rustled through the leaves, tugging the less tenacious from their branches and laying them gently on the wicker furniture. She would have to bring the furniture in soon. Richard had always done it earlier than this, but doing so would acknowledge the end of summer. Perhaps in another week or so.

Back in bed, cradling her mug of coffee, she thought about getting up and getting ready for work but reached for the box instead. The wispy threads of the puzzle that had teased her all night long hovered at the edge of her mind. After a few sips of caffeine and with determined concentration she had almost grasped them, but the sharp ring of the phone sent them scurrying. Her hand jerked and black coffee splashed the front of her white robe. *Damn.* She reached for the phone knocking over an empty wine bottle in the process. Had she finished the whole bottle? The chardonnay hadn't even been that good.

As she picked up the phone she made a small bet with herself that it was Tony Hamilton wanting her advice on whether it would be safe to skip the meeting called by their boss at Morrison and Black. Tony's mind tended to wander at will and cornering it in a meeting room was always a torturous task for him.

"Hi Sara. I didn't wake you, did I?"

"No. Of course not." Her tone suggested she had been up for hours.

"What do you think about today's meeting?" She should have placed a higher bet.

"Personally, I think it will probably be a waste of time. Ken will ask our opinion about something and then do what he has already decided to do.

Politically, you'll have to decide for yourself. Ken takes his meetings very seriously." Was she sounding as negative as she felt? She hoped not.

"So you're going?"

"Some people might be able to get away without showing up but I'm afraid I'm not one of them."

"I don't get why Ken has it in for you. You work bloody long hours, all of them chargeable. He has to appreciate that."

Chargeable hours were normally the only determinant of success at Morrison and Black. You could get away with handing clients poor advice and even behaving in ways that many would call unethical as long as your chargeable hours were high. Sara prided herself on not only producing more than anyone else in the firm but also on being ethical and the best in the business. Yes, she worked bloody long hours. If she wanted to self-flagellate, the long hours she had worked for years would make the perfect instrument. Those hours are what had cost her her marriage and apparently gained her nothing. Something she preferred not to dwell on.

Tony was still talking. She tried to tune in. "Why don't you try being nicer to Ken? You know that old adage about catching more bees with honey than vinegar, or something like that."

She knew he was right but she just couldn't say the things that were required as entrance fee to Ken Morrison's inner circle. She couldn't bring herself to laugh at his crude jokes or praise his vicious business coups.

"Now you're sounding just like Richard," she said. "He used to tell me that I might as well quit working so hard because my lack of kissing up negated any kudos I might be earning."

"Anyway, I'll see you at the office?" asked Tony changing the topic. He had been a friend of Richard before she had met either one of them, and he skirted conversations that referred to Richard. She assumed he didn't want to risk the appearance of taking sides.

"Yes, I'll be in. A bit later though. I think maybe I'll spend some time browsing through my inheritance."

Tony chuckled. He had heard about her legacy. "So have you found any diaries that you could sell for millions? Your aunt must have had the scoop on every major artist in North America in the second half of the century. I doubt there are many who didn't either have works hanging in one of her galleries or had cozied up to her trying."

"I wish." Sara picked through the box with one hand as she talked. "I've got disintegrating corsages with little more than their stems intact, prom invitations, thank you notes, theatre ticket stubs and engagement announcements from the old *Telegram*. Most of this stuff is over sixty years old. I really don't get it."

"Maybe there is nothing to get. Perhaps this box of memories was important to her and she wanted someone to have them."

"You met Aunt Kate. Did she seem the sentimental type to you?" Sara didn't wait for an answer. "This stuff is insipid. Aunt Kate hated insipid."

Sara managed to get Tony off the line by promising to meet him for dinner. She reached for the Tylenol, whose home had moved from the medicine cabinet to her bedside table, swallowed two with a gulp of cold coffee and turned back to the box.

The more she picked through its contents the more the souvenirs seemed to have nothing whatsoever to do with the Kate McPherson Sara knew. Kate had been a woman with flare. Her business acumen combined with her instinct for fine saleable art led to successful galleries in Toronto, Boston, and New York. Kate had definitely created the woman she had presented to the world, and Sara couldn't imagine why she would leave these remnants of her former self to anyone.

As she looked again at the piece that rested on top she remembered what she had been puzzling about during the night. This item seemed out of place. While most were old, the papers yellowed and curling, this piece, torn from the *Globe,* and dated just last month, sat fresh and unmarked on top of the pile. It was the death notice of Judge Theodore Jamieson. As she lifted it from the precarious mound of personal history, the rest of the mementos that had been piled high in the box slid onto the bed.

Jamieson, Theodore Sandwell, suddenly at his home, September 8, 2009, in his 80th year. A much respected member of the bench for the past 30 years, Judge Jamieson will be much missed by family, friends, colleagues and the community at large. In 1995, his receipt of the Order of Canada recognized his many contributions to Canadian society.

Lovingly remembered by his nephew, Patrick Jamieson of Toronto, his niece Susan Jamieson Stanwick, her husband George Stanwick, and their children Sophie and Brian Stanwick, all of New York City. Services will be held at Timothy Eaton United Church, September 11 at 10:00 a.m.

The date of his death made the addition of this clipping to Aunt Kate's box even stranger. Aunt Kate had died on September 9. Presuming the announcement had been published the day after his death she must have torn it out only hours before she herself had died. How ironic.

The jagged piece of newsprint had taken a corner of a neighboring announcement for an unknown "Jones, Ralph" with it. Would Mr. Jones be pleased to have his memory preserved amongst the life stuff of a stranger?

She knew the judge had been a friend of her aunt. She remembered Kate attending his Order of Canada ceremony. But why tear out the announcement and put it in this box of keepsakes? At first glance it seemed that the next most recent item was a postcard from Sara's parents on a trip to Greece in 1978. It appeared Kate had abandoned her need to archive her life about that time. There was nothing representing the opening of her galleries in Boston or New York; there was nothing about her receiving the Woman of Influence award that she had so cherished; there was nothing about the judge receiving the Order of Canada. Why then this? And above all, why leave the darn stuff to her?

She had just picked up her now cold mug when the phone rang once more. She thought it was probably Tony again and answered with a casual, "Hi there."

"Hi Sara, it's Dina."

Damn, damn, damn. There was no way this would be a good news call.

Ken's secretary didn't wait for a response. "Ken's got to go out of town this afternoon and wants to move the meeting to this morning. The board room in an hour?"

The slight inflection allowed her last line to pass as a question rather than an order. But the response was assumed.

Sara knew she would be there but answered, "I have a meeting at nine but I'll see what I can do to move it. Tell Ken I'll be there if I can."

It had become part of the game she played with Ken. Toe the line when necessary but fight to preserve some dignity in the process. She wasn't by nature a games player and at times she feared that in her effort to survive, she had begun to mirror some of her opponent's characteristics. It was at those times that she didn't like herself as well as she used to.

2

It was a day off for Detective Sergeant Keith Carson. Feet on his scarred coffee table, he sipped a take-out from Starbucks and perused the *Globe*'s financial section. His high tech stocks were still sliding but his old economy blue chips were doing just fine. As much as he hated to see any of his stocks go south, he felt some pleasure in seeing the old world holding its own.

The previous night he had picked up a six-pack, a steak and a Grisham novel he was determined to read before he saw the movie. He had no intention of leaving his apartment until the next morning.

He folded the newspaper, smoothed away any wrinkles and placed it carefully on top of the stack of discarded newspapers and magazines that grew beside the sofa. He debated whether it was time to start a second pile. Instead, he renewed his daily vow that the next time he went out he would remember to take the whole lot down to the recycling box that sat conveniently at the foot of the stairs to his flat.

A little music to read Grisham by and he would be set for the day. He flicked through his CDs. Dave Brubeck's jazz seemed too mellow, the Boston Philharmonic too serious, and Simon and Garfunkel much too nostalgic. He gave up on the CDs and moved over to the window instead. One slam with the palm of his hand against its frame and a two-armed shove upward and the window was open. The sounds of the street swept in. The Queen streetcar rattled past and Wing, the green grocer who owned the shop down stairs, shouted directions in Chinese to his two sons who were unloading the fresh produce they had trucked from the market. Baskets of potatoes, McIntosh apples, yellow zucchini, purple grapes, and orange pumpkins were off-loaded, relay style. A few impatient drivers, stuck in the backed-up traffic that the Lees' double-parked van had created, beeped their horns.

No music track ever produced could at one time stimulate and yet relax Carson the way the jumbled chords of the city could. What others heard as nerve-grating noise, Carson heard as an old, sometimes discordant, but always familiar melody that told him he was home.

At first he didn't hear it. He had turned down the volume on his cell phone and it took him a couple of minutes to differentiate its ring from the sounds of the street. Once he did, he knew immediately that his twenty-four hours of self-indulgence weren't going to happen. This would be no social call. He had spoken with his sister a half hour before and it was unlikely that anyone else would be making a personal call to him.

He jogged across the room, scooped up the phone from the floor beside an easy chair, and automatically fingered the talk button: "Yup, Carson."

As he had suspected it was the desk sergeant rounding up the troops. "Sorry Keith but your day off's not going to happen."

"What's up?"

"A woman was murdered in one of those big places in Rosedale."

What the sergeant meant was this was not another black kid shot, an Asian gang member stabbed or a street person with his head bashed in at a bus shelter. This victim had to have money or was close to someone who did and therefore would be receiving a lot of attention.

"OK. You'll send me the info?"

"As we speak."

Carson grabbed a jacket, his keys and wallet and was out of his apartment in seconds, taking the steps two at a time. "Damn," he thought as he streaked past the empty recycling bin. Tonight for sure. That is, if he even got home.

3

Sara drummed her fingers on the meeting room table unable to focus on the chitchat her colleagues used to fill the time. They all agreed that they spent too much time in meetings and, most frustratingly, too much time waiting for meetings to begin. She had a presentation to make to a prospective client in a couple of hours and it was far from being completed. Her stress was mounting. Her fingers moved from tapping the table to doing a drumbeat on her chin.

The room they sat in was smaller than the boardroom next door but still meticulously designed to remind anyone who entered that Morrison and Black was the most prestigious management consulting firm in the city. A red Persian carpet set off the dark hardwood floors. A collection of Canadian paintings that could rival anything at the Art Gallery of Ontario hung on the paneled walls.

Before every meeting, the consultants wandered into the room, all claiming their usual chairs and displaying the very resistance to change they complained about in their clients. Across from Sara's seat hung a Tom Thomson landscape. Stark spruce trees clinging to hunks of the Canadian Shield. It had become her place of escape during the frequently tedious meetings and she went there now. But one could even tire of beauty, she decided, and turned her gaze to the open doorway. She could see Dina's desk in the reception area just outside of Ken Morrison's office. Let's get going.

Sara watched as Dina picked up the phone and spoke quietly and too briefly to communicate anything other than something in cryptic code. As Sara expected, Ken's door opened immediately and he headed toward the meeting room. The routine was always the same. Dina would give the signal that everyone had arrived. Ken would walk briskly from his office, make quick eye contact with Dina as he swept around the corner of her desk, and start the meeting as he charged through the door.

"Good morning everyone. Sorry for having to reschedule this meeting at the last minute but I need to get moving on something and want your input before we do anything." His voice conveyed the energy of a busy, in-charge leader. Perched on the edge of the chair at the top of the table he pivoted his head in a smooth 180-degree arc, catching the eye of each of the consultants in turn and holding the gaze for just a moment. The act had the semblance of being personable but Sara, who had been around a good deal longer than the rest, knew differently. She had once heard Ken say that if you could pin someone with your eyes you could control them. When Ken's sweep reached Sara she ensured her eyes were otherwise engaged.

Ken brushed a hand over a dark temple that she was sure, had nature had its druthers, would be gray. He flashed perfectly manicured nails and a diamond ring in the process.

"I promise this will be short," he continued. "As you know, two new recruits have been hired and we need office space for them. A couple of cubicles will suffice. We can take a few feet from the reception area but that won't be enough. We also need to take some of the office space that is already occupied. Sara, your office is right next to the reception area and is a good size. It makes sense that we use it. That would give us enough space to create a third, fairly large cubicle for you. We might even be able to incorporate your window into it." He added the last sentence as though it were an unusually magnanimous gesture.

Sara's wasn't the only office that was adjacent to the reception area but apparently the only one Ken was targeting. Would this be unfolding differently if she hadn't stubbornly refused to make eye contact with him a few minutes ago? As petty as that seemed, she knew it was entirely possible.

What could she say? She had no good option to offer other than someone else's office and she could hardly do that.

No one protested but Sara understood. Shock at Ken's selecting the most senior consultant's space combined with a sense of self-preservation would prevent her colleagues from jumping to her defense. Ken Morrison gave and Ken Morrison took away. A hand on the shoulder when Ken was speaking to you signaled that you had been drawn into the firm's inner circle. Invitations to enjoy a Blue Jays game from the firm's box at the Rogers Centre or to dine with him and Dina at Scaramouche would follow. And then the plum assignments and hints at your being made junior partner. No one knew for sure why they had been favored, although colleagues spent many lunch and coffee breaks speculating about it. And no one knew for sure why the favoritism was suddenly rescinded. Morrison and Black's was not an environment that encouraged risk-taking. Only Tony Hamilton, politically oblivious and everyone's defender, ventured into the silence.

"But that doesn't seem quite fair considering Sara's workload. Sara needs her space. Why don't you take mine?" Tony suggested tentatively. He spoke to Ken but his eyes rested on his own intertwined hands resting on the table in front of him. His thumbs spun around one another as though self-propelled.

"That's admirable of you Tony but your space is too small and not properly located to be of help," Ken responded, using his "end of the discussion" tone.

So much for getting people's input, but for once Ken kept his promise. The meeting was short.

4

As Carson pulled off the Bayview extension, he passed his hand across his chin and remembered he hadn't shaven. Ah well, if a little stubble had worked for Miami Vice why not Toronto Homicide? The Inspector would certainly not agree. If he had to go down to the office, he would have to shave before Simpson spotted him.

Today, he was content to allow the GPS to direct him to his destination. Often he kept it turned off because it spoiled the fun of finding a place on your own. But add "Rosedale" to the word "hurry" and it spelled exactly what, in Carson's mind, the GPS had been designed for.

Before GPS, Carson never failed to lose his bearings in the streets that had been wound around the stately Rosedale homes. Most of Toronto had been neatly placed on an orderly grid but a few enclaves like Rosedale had declared their uniqueness by eschewing the norm.

The address the desk sergeant had given him was in north Rosedale. An area he could not afford to buy into but, sitting just below the railway tracks, it was a little outside of the mansion district.

Carson checked his BlackBerry for the address but didn't need the house number once he reached the street. The yellow tape cordoning off the property and the police cruisers lining both sides of the narrow street in front of it announced to anyone passing that something deadly had happened in that house. The Toronto police motto "To Serve and Protect" emblazoned on the side of a cruiser caught Carson's eye. Too late for the latter, he thought with a touch of regret.

Just as Carson parked, an unmarked, driven by Detective Harry Perkins arrived from the opposite direction and pulled into the curb nose to nose with Carson's derelict Mustang. Carson's own unmarked was in the shop.

"So how's Grisham?" Perkins asked as he heaved himself from the car. Carson had told him about his plans for his day off.

"Wish I could tell you."

"Serves you right for holing yourself up with a damn novel on your day off. Gone fishing, that's what you should've done. A little boat, a quiet lake, a case of beer, and too far away to get back here in a hurry."

If Perkins were asked to describe heaven Carson expected it would be pretty much the same.

Their destination was one of several houses perched above street level. It sat at the top of two short flights of stone steps. Waiting on the porch at the top was Detective Constable Dave Kirpatrick. Kirpatrick was new to the squad. Seen as an up-and-comer, he had been matched with Carson to learn the ropes. The young rookie was rocking back and forth from toes to heels. Carson had already learned that this meant Kirpatrick was either excited or nervous. Excited was Carson's guess. Your first murder investigation would do that to you.

The uniformed officer at the bottom of the steps recognized Carson and nodded his consent for the two to duck under the tape.

Perkins stopped at the top of the first flight of steps and attempted unsuccessfully to haul sagging trousers up over a stomach that could soon be classed as a beer belly. A few more baskets of chicken wings washed down with a couple of cold ones and he wouldn't pass his next medical. Perkins would go crazy on a desk job.

Perkins glared at the second flight before tackling it.

"Real keener, that one," he whispered, nodding toward Kirpatrick as Carson passed him taking the steps two at a time. Carson wondered whether he and Perkins had appeared as keen twenty-five years ago.

"Hey, how did you get here so quickly?" Carson greeted Kirpatrick.

"I was at headquarters and hitched a ride with a couple of the guys who caught the call. Forensic ident should be here soon."

"Good. Anything happening downtown?"

"Just a lot of noise about this one. The chief has been on to the Inspector. He told Simpson he expects us to have something before it hits the news."

"So much for that." Carson nodded toward the CTV news van that was trying to create a parking spot where none existed on the crowded street below.

He didn't ask Kirpatrick how he got the information. For a rookie, Kirpatrick seemed to have managed to connect very quickly into the squad's grapevine. But then Kirpatrick was a talker and chatted up everybody. He was sure to get something in return.

Once Perkins mounted the porch, Carson pushed open the heavy oak door. The entrance was several square feet of black marble and everything beyond it was intimidating white carpet. Carson began slipping off his loafers. Perkins sighed and bent down to untie one of his oxfords. Before either had finished a man appeared from a room at the end of the main hall.

"That's alright gentlemen. Don't worry about the carpet."

Perkins immediately did a quick retie and pulled himself upright but Carson continued to remove his shoes. He couldn't bring himself to tread on either the shiny marble or the pristine carpet with anything that had seen the outdoors. Kirpatrick glanced from one to the other and decided he best follow Carson's suit. A toenail poked through one of Kirpatrick's socks and he curled the toe under.

The man approaching them was slight and moved toward them with just less than a stagger, occasionally careening into a wall. Wearing wrinkled dress pants and a dress shirt, half-untucked, he looked as though he might have been on an all-night binge.

"Thank you for coming, gentlemen." He spoke as though receiving guests. "I am Alan Chadwick, the husband of the ah... deceased."

After introductions and condolences Carson suggested that Kirpatrick and Perkins accompany Chadwick to another room and wait for him there.

"We'll be in the study then," Chadwick said as he turned to lead the two detectives back the way he had come.

To the right, a constable stood on guard, ensuring that the message sent by the yellow tape stretched across the archway to the living room was respected.

Carson didn't believe in small talk when a murder victim was lying a few feet away. He nodded at the young man and moved his stocking feet as far into the room as the tape would allow. His toes sank into the plush carpet while his heels still registered the cold of the marble hallway.

The body of a woman in a pink housecoat and matching slippers lay rather elegantly, Carson thought, on the white carpet a few feet from a white marble fireplace. Close by was what looked like a snow globe, partially embedded in the deep pile. Carson remembered his mother having a snow globe which she put out each Christmas. It held a snowman that all but disappeared in the snow flurry that was produced when the globe was shaken. He and his sister would argue over whose turn it was to shake it. He doubted whether today's electronic kids would take any notice of it at all.

The contusion on the woman's head, clear even from the doorway, suggested that the globe may have been the murder weapon.

Carson spent a few more minutes observing the room. It was one of those rooms that one didn't expect to ever be used. Navy, uninviting furniture trimmed with gold brocade looked as though it was meant to be sitting behind a tasseled cord in a museum. At least a dozen other snow globes were crowded between the pieces of Lalique glass and Chinese porcelain that covered tables and filled two curio cabinets. Most globes held traditional winter scenes of snow-laden cottages, churches and Santas. At least one was a fall scene and

Carson assumed that when shaken, it produced miniature colored leaves rather than snowflakes. To his eye the globes did not match the room's décor but someone obviously had thought differently.

When Carson entered the study, Kirpatrick and Perkins were perusing a display of model cars. It appeared that the Chadwicks were collectors. Chadwick sat crumpled in a large, brown, leather chair. An empty whiskey decanter and half-full glass sat on the table beside him.

"May I offer you a drink gentlemen?" Chadwick still tried to play host but this effort was a weak one.

"Thanks, but no. Please tell us when you found your wife?" Carson took the lead.

Chadwick drooped forward and rested his head in his hands.

"I didn't exactly find her," he mumbled.

"I'm sorry sir," Carson continued. "Could you please sit up so we can hear you better? Did you say you didn't exactly find her?"

"Yes." Chadwick made an effort to sit up right.

"What do you mean you didn't exactly find her?"

"I didn't find her. I was there when she died."

"How did she die?"

Chadwick looked straight at Carson and paused a minute before answering. "I killed her. I threw one of her damn snow globes at her. I didn't mean to kill her. At least I don't think I did."

Carson, Perkins and Kirpatrick glanced at one another. Kirpatrick looked disappointed. Was it over that quickly?

"When did this happen?" Perkins stepped in.

"Last night some time. I don't know what time. Around eleven maybe."

"But you didn't call until this morning."

"That's right. I didn't see there was any rush. She was dead and reporting it wouldn't change that. And I doubted that I would gain any brownie points for calling quickly. I came in here for a drink and ended up just sitting here drinking for the night. I was puzzling over whether I had intended, at least for a moment, to kill her. I am an accountant and we accountants need things to make sense."

"Alright sir," Carson interrupted. "I would recommend you call your lawyer and don't say anything else until you make a formal statement. Maybe you would like to shower and clean up before we go down to headquarters?"

Perkins went upstairs with Chadwick. It was unlikely the man would climb out a window and escape but suicide was a definite possibility.

Carson and Kirpatrick found the kitchen and took Chadwick up on his suggestion that they try out his espresso machine while they waited. The man was obviously functioning on automatic pilot.

Kirpatrick shivered at his first sip. "I usually get a double double at Tim Horton's. This stuff isn't what I call coffee."

Carson downed his in a couple of swallows, rinsed his cup, and looked for a tea towel.

"Do you think he really did it?" Kirpatrick sounded hopeful that the response might be in the negative.

"Well, there's always the slight possibility that he is covering up for someone. But I wouldn't get your hopes up. It looks pretty clear-cut."

Carson himself felt a bit let down. Even though, Chadwick's statement was taken and the paperwork done, he might actually be able to salvage a bit of his day off, he would have happily traded it for some real detective work.

Carson had just finished placing their cups back in the exact spot he had found them when Perkins called from the front hall to say he and Chadwick were ready.

As they reached the hall, a tall figure came in the front door: smooth suit, smooth hair, and skin that attested to the fact that summer rays are no longer required for the perfect tan. Carson immediately felt his defenses go on alert.

Detective Brad Greally was tall, good-looking, and a ten-year veteran who saw himself as the next staff inspector.

"Greally, what are you doing here?' Carson attempted to make the question sound casual. He was sure he already knew what the detective was up to. He must have heard that Carson had caught the call and because of its location, knew the victim wouldn't be some kid playing big gang member. This would be a high profile case. Greally would look for a way to weasel himself in and that would mean squeezing Carson out. The latter, Carson was sure, would give him the most pleasure.

"I'm taking this one over," Greally announced, snapping his perpetual wad of gum.

Greally had worked faster than usual this time.

"Why don't you update me?" he continued as he approached Carson and nudged him down the hall.

"So what's happening?" Carson sounded as nonchalant as his rising blood pressure would allow.

"You didn't get a call from the desk sergeant yet?" Greally leaned into Carson's space bringing a cocktail of Juicy Fruit mixed with a heavy dose of Hugo Boss with him.

Carson shook his head in the negative.

"Well you will. I was just at the office and let Simpson know I've pretty well finished up the Jane and Finch case and could squeeze in another one. I gather you're pretty busy and could use some time off."

Greally spent an inordinate amount of time in the Inspector's office, which had not gone unnoticed by his colleagues. But, like his methods or not, they seemed to work.

"You might find a better use of all that extra time on your hands. The husband already confessed to the murder." Carson took a step back trying to escape the cologne zone.

Greally briefly registered disappointment but caught himself and quickly returned to his usual cockiness. "Well I'm sure that with a little work I can punch his confession full of holes and find whoever he is covering for."

Carson always forced himself to take the high road with Greally but he was finding the air a little too thin up there. Sometimes he found it hard to breathe. One of these days he feared he would join Greally down in the gutter and might have trouble climbing back out.

Perkins and Kirpatrick had already put Chadwick in the back seat of a cruiser. As Carson climbed into his car Greally called after him, "Hey man, enjoy the rest of your day off."

Perkins scowled and gave a slow shake of his head. Greally, oblivious, turned to chat up an attractive CTV reporter.

5

It had taken Sara longer than she had expected to empty her office. Whatever happened to that paperless office the techies had at one time promised? She had decided that it was a good opportunity to clean house and get rid of files that should have been discarded years ago. Tearing up files would also be a way to vent some of the anger toward Ken that had started burning a spot the size of a dime in her stomach. She tore each handful of paper several times before feeding it into the shredder. After an hour and a half, her hands were sore and covered with paper cuts, and she still had two years worth of documents to go through.

She was sick of paper and sick of Dina poking her red head around the door jamb every five minutes asking, "How're ya doin' Sweetie?" Sara stuffed the rest into cartons and lugged them to the storeroom where they would sit until her new cubicle was ready.

Fortunately Ken was out of the office. She wasn't sure she would be able to contain her anger if she saw him and she wanted to make sure that her head, not her emotions, determined her future.

It was early afternoon before Sara pulled back into her driveway. As soon as she got out of the car, her neighbor opened his back gate. He had obviously been watching for her.

Stephen Dempster was as close to a heron as a human could come. When he walked he lifted each long, spindly leg high. His body fat was nil and his too-long neck was topped by a sculpted head so small that there was barely room for the black beady eyes and the huge beak of a nose. He had been a senior executive in the oil industry but since retirement had taken up the occupation of neighborhood busybody.

"Sara, there's something you should know."

He was a little breathless. He had probably run down from his perch at the window on the second floor from where he kept watch over the street and all its residents.

"Hi, Mr. Dempster. Nice to see you." He was the "Mr." type of person. She had never heard him called anything other than Mr. Dempster and wondered what his wife had called him. Certainly not Steve or Demps. Perhaps Stephen but Mr. Dempster wasn't outside the realm of possibility.

"Sara, you really must be careful," he puffed, "now that you are living alone."

She had never discussed Richard's leaving with her neighbor. He had obviously noted her husband's absence and, for once, jumped to the right conclusion.

"There was a strange character prowling around the back of your house. I came out and challenged him and he said he was delivering fliers. He definitely wasn't delivering fliers. Who delivers fliers to the back of the house? And he was hanging around much too long. I don't have a full view of your back door, but I think he even tried it."

Here he goes again, she thought. He probably meant well but he ended up being a troublemaker. His mission in the spring had been to persecute anyone who tried to live an ecologically sound life by composting kitchen waste. He claimed the compost was nothing other than a feast for raccoons. The raccoon population in their one-block neighborhood had doubled in the last two years, he contended. Where he got his statistics she didn't ask. Next to come, he said, would be the rats. He soon had the neighborhood divided between pro-composters and anti-composters. The neighbor directly behind Sara, who was an early convert to the compost movement, now carried her deposits to the composter behind her garage only after dark.

Dempster's next crusade was against people who didn't cancel the newspaper when they were going to be away for a couple of days. Just asking for trouble, he said, letting the crooks know you are away. And worse still, attracting them to the neighborhood where they were likely to prey on the more careful households at the same time. He took it upon himself to collect any lonely newspapers left on front porches and would deliver them with a lecture when the residents returned. On one occasion he misread his evidence. Mark Robinson, who lived a couple of doors up, left in the morning with a suitcase and did not return at his usual time. He arrived home at midnight and was not happy to find no paper awaiting him. He knew exactly what had happened and pounded on Dempster's door until Dempster was not only awake but had called the police, believing if he opened the door he would be victim of a house invasion. How was he to know, Dempster argued, that Robinson had taken several old suits, packed in an old suitcase to drop off at a Good Shepherd mission that morning? He was just being a good neighbor.

And now it was flier deliverers. Sara really didn't have the energy to deal with this.

"Perhaps he was actually delivering fliers," she suggested. "I've heard that some of them dump half of their load into garbage cans so that they can get paid for the whole job and only do half the work. Maybe he was looking for a garbage can."

Even as she completed her argument she knew it was a waste of time. Working with Ken Morrison had taught her that repelling logic is an automatic reflex response in zealots and pig heads.

"Absolutely not. He was carrying a couple of fliers alright but, believe me, they were only a cover. After I challenged him he left that one by your door." He nodded his head toward a rolled-up sheet of colored newsprint that lay by the back entrance. "But I watched him. And he went right up the street and around the corner, likely heading for the bus stop, and never stopped at any other house. And I didn't get any flier. He was damn suspicious."

"Well, I'm sure it's nothing, but I appreciate your concern Mr. Dempster." She turned to take her briefcase from the car.

"Well if you aren't going to worry about yourself, I don't know why I should." He sniffed loudly and retreated. Back to his lookout, she was sure.

On the way home Sara had stopped at the dry cleaners. She managed to juggle her load of skirts, shirts, and pants encased in slippery plastic sheaths as she unlocked the door and set everything down on the mudroom bench. Before she closed the door she reached out and picked up the flier. It was from the local drug mart listing the specials of the week. She tossed it into the blue recycling box in the corner, gathered up her briefcase and things from the cleaners, and headed upstairs to her room.

She had told Dina that she had meetings outside of the office for the afternoon. She could have simply said that she was working at home but then Dina would be sure to find some reason to call. She didn't want to think about the office or her crumbling career.

Aunt Kate's box awaited her, its contents overflowing onto the bed. It was as though it were sitting there patiently waiting for her to return to finish a conversation that had been interrupted.

She had intended to change into jeans and then force herself to eat some lunch. Instead she set her packages on the chaise lounge and began rummaging through Aunt Kate's memories. Is this what is meant by the detritus of one's life, she wondered.

She decided to go through the box carefully. Much of its contents was not dated but if no one else had gone through the box, and it didn't look as though anyone had, it could be like an archaeological dig. The artifacts from various periods lying in layers of history waiting to be discovered and interpreted.

The items that had slid onto the bed had been just under Judge Jamieson's obituary. They looked as though they would have been collected in the seventies. An invitation to the wedding of a couple Sara had never heard of, the program for *Twelfth Night*, a production at the Stratford Festival, and a note from Maria Callas, dated November 1972, thanking Kate for the "extravagant" dinner party she had thrown for her when she was in town to perform at the O'Keefe Center.

Why had she stopped saving mementos in the seventies? Did her life no longer seem important enough to document or was she just too busy building her reputation and her galleries? Perhaps as one grew older, the present and the future became much more valuable than the past.

Three hours later, having at different stages removed her jacket, skirt, and stockings, and having drunk more than a couple of glasses of wine, Sara had arranged the box's contents in a dozen small piles scattered across the bed, the floor, a dresser top, and the seat of the high-back chair. On top of each pile was a sticky note with the year or years she guessed the items in the pile had been from. The earliest date she could find was 1938 and the latest 1978. Aunt Kate had been a fervent collector of personal memorabilia for forty years and then had apparently lost interest in documenting personal events until she added the judge's obituary, just before she herself had died.

Sara's bare legs were beginning to feel cold and she stopped to pull on an old pair of track pants and glanced at her watch. She was amazed at how much time had passed and was surprised to realize how satisfying the exercise had been. Someone else might not see the scattered piles as order but Sara knew a pattern was emerging. And a huge bonus was that she had thought of nothing else for the entire time.

She had perused a few of the mementos but mostly she had just tried to date and categorize. Some, however, had engrossed her. In particular, several newspaper clippings from the *Toronto Telegram* and the *Toronto Daily Star* in the early fall of 1948. The same photo of a young girl with long black hair and huge dark eyes appeared in each of the articles. Her back was straight, chin tilted, and eyes gazing upward as though anticipating things to come. It was probably a school photo. In spite of the less-than-perfect reproduction, reduced further in quality by the age of the paper, a certain beauty emanated from the pictures. The first article was headed, "Toronto Woman Missing in Cottage Country." Although the date had been left behind on the discarded newspaper, Sara assumed it was the first because the other pieces were headed: "Suspicious Death of Toronto Woman Shocks Community," "No Leads in Death of Toronto Woman," "Chief of Police Announces Coroner's Findings," "Jane Stewart Murdered," and finally, "Funeral of Murdered Toronto Woman Draws Many." Most of these had their publication dates intact and there appeared to have been a flurry of articles printed between September 7 and September 18, 1948. Later articles were headed "Still No Clues in Stewart Death," dated October 15 of the same year, and another on September 4, 1949, apparently the anniversary of her disappearance, screamed, "Police

Fail Jane Stewart."A later article, written in the fifties, was headed "Unsolved Murders in Ontario" and Jane Stewart's death was once again recounted.

Kate seemed to have been obsessed with this death. Perhaps Jane Stewart was a friend. Stewart was twenty-two when she died. They would have been close in age.

Sara examined a newspaper photo taken at the funeral. It showed a group of young people gathered on the steps of Timothy Eaton United Church on St. Clair Avenue. Well-to-do Toronto families were known to make up Timothy Eaton's congregation; Aunt Kate's was an easy fit. One of the young women in the photo could have been Kate. She was a brunette and quite tall, as was Kate.

The sudden slamming of the front door startled Sara but she immediately sensed who it was. The familiar heavy footsteps on the stairs confirmed her expectation. It was Chloe, pounding up the stairs as she had done for at least twenty of her twenty-three years of life. Sara had given up suggesting she "walk like a lady" years ago when it became apparent that ladylike gestures had not been included in Chloe's genetic map. Sara sometimes regretted having called her daughter Chloe. The incongruity of the tomboy traits against the ultra-feminine name perhaps accentuated Chloe's awkwardness. She had no doubt that because of her inability to fulfill expectations of femininity, Chloe had gone to the other extreme, opting for jeans and a leather jacket, and having her dark hair cut close to her head. Small diamond stud earrings had been her only concession to the feminine, but now that men were as studded as women, jewelry no longer defined gender in the same way.

Richard had worried about her even more than Sara had. He struggled with the conflict of not wanting his little girl to ever enjoy other men, but at the same time felt anxious when her friends started dating and Chloe still spent evenings at home. "No interesting boys out there?" he would ask teasingly, but he was really hoping for a sign that there were. Chloe would roll her eyes and feign boredom but Sara could see her discomfort.

Their concern was for naught. In first year of university Chloe brought Craig home one weekend and announced they were going to live together the next semester. That was two years ago and they were still together for the most part.

Chloe kept her key to the house and popped in regularly, sometimes briefly moving back into her room when she and Craig had an argument. "It'll do him good to have a cold bed," she had announced once and Richard had scooted from the room in discomfort.

Now Chloe appeared in the doorway dressed in green khakis, autumn leaves clinging to the bottom of her wet army boots. Sara thought of the beige carpet but opted to say nothing. She hadn't seen her daughter for a week and missed her.

"Wow! What a fashion statement," Chloe laughed, noting Sara's attire, the track pants on bottom and the silk long-sleeved blouse she hadn't got around to changing on top.

"My God, what's all this?" Chloe maneuvered the black boots around the piles of mementos on the floor.

She answered herself before Sara could speak. "I know. It's your inheritance from Aunt Kate, isn't it? What a riot." Chloe and James, her older brother, had already had a good laugh over their mother's windfall. "No diamonds at the bottom huh? My God, who would want to keep this stuff?" She leaned over to pick up a concert program from the 1946 pile. One of Chloe's most distinguishing characteristics was her tendency to speak with the speed of a runaway horse, never reigning in for a pause into which someone could slip a comment.

"Hey listen to this' The Benny Goodman Orchestra, for your listening and dancing pleasure. Sunnyside Pavilion, July 17, 1946.' That's kind of neat after all. Is that that place on the Lakeshore with the big swimming pool?"

Sara mumbled yes from under the sweatshirt she was pulling over her head, not worrying whether she was heard. In the area of communication, her daughter seemed to be completely self-sufficient, requiring not even the prod of a brief response for encouragement.

Interrupted from her task, Sara took the opportunity to check for phone messages while Chloe rummaged through the 1947 to 1949 pile.

"Wow! Did you know Aunt Kate wrote?"

Sara waved to her to be quiet as she replayed the last message. Her closest friend, Patty Levine, had just moved to LA and had left her new phone number. Sara jotted it down on the back of the envelope her bank statement had come in. Then she turned back to Chloe who had pulled off her boots and emptied a chair to curl up in it.

"This is spooky. Listen:

The stench assaulted her as she opened the door of the empty summer cottage.

'My God, there has got to be a dead raccoon in here,' had been her first reaction. After years of helping her parents open their cottage every spring she was used to finding carcasses of animals that had sought a sheltered place to die. But never before had she experienced a smell so piercing that it immediately carried a pain to her head.

Her companion's only response was to turn on a dusty lamp whose dull yellow light revealed the shape of a chair beside it. The chair had been draped with a sheet to protect it over the winter. Apparently oblivious that the chair was not meant to be in use, a shriveled body lounged in it. Its body fluids had oozed from it, releasing the odoriferous death announcement. A rat, poking its nose from under the chair where it had scampered when it had been interrupted, confirmed that the announcement had been received. White shiny spots glistened on the ankle where the rat had visited.

She could feel the dampness of the wood of the door jamb that supported her shocked body. She concentrated on the pattern made by the cracks in its blue paint. As the nausea subsided she found herself hypnotically focused, not on the horror, but the body's determined effort to deny death. The head was quizzically cocked to one side, red lipsticked lips parted as though about to challenge a companion's argument. Dark, shiny hair fell over the shoulders of a red silk shirt, a tanned arm was tossed casually across the broad arm of the draped chair, and legs hidden by black slacks were neatly crossed to one side. Toenails painted bright red matched the strappy sandals.

"God, she still has style," she thought, hatred suddenly overpowering any other emotion.

Sara felt goose bumps travel down her arms and she shivered.

"Was Aunt Kate ever published?" Chloe put the lined exercise book back in its pile. As usual she didn't wait for an answer. "Well got to go. Thought I'd just pop in to see how you are doing."

Now she waited.

"I'm doing fine, Sweetheart. Please don't start worrying about me." Sara knew Chloe hadn't missed the empty wine bottle from last night or the more than half-empty one from today.

Chloe asked casually while leaning over to tie one of the long boot laces, "Mom, don't you think you are drinking too much?"

"Chloe," Sara tried to keep her tone light, "Remember, I'm the mother. I tell you what's good for you. Not vice versa."

Chloe gave her a hug, "Love you Mom." And she was gone, clumping back down the stairs.

Sara forgot the messages that she had been about to return. She picked up the lined exercise book that Chloe had been reading from. The cover was a faded blue with the brand name Hilroy at the top. In the blank spot beside "Name," Aunt Kate had written Kathryn McPherson in a neat black script. The spot beside "Grade" remained empty.

Sara leafed through it to find the passage that Chloe had read. Some entries were dated, some not. A diary of sorts, the notebook contained several entries that were several pages long, describing a ball or a coming-out party for the daughters of the Toronto elite. Other entries might be only one line such as "That man drives me crazy!!!" or "Will I ever accept reality and get on with my life?" both dated "Summer 1948". The piece Chloe had read wasn't dated and had no heading. It was written on an angle diagonally across the lines rather than on top of them. The word "hatred" in the last line had been written over many times indenting the page and leaving its clones on several pages that followed.

She poured another glass of too-warm sauterne and reread the passage. The chills returned. She went to the 1948 pile and picked up the first article on Jane Stewart's disappearance. "Miss Stewart is five feet six inches tall, has dark brown eyes and shoulder length black hair. When last seen on September 9 she was wearing a red silk blouse and black slacks." Probably a coincidence. Lots of women had long dark hair and wore red blouses and black slacks.

Would Aunt Kate write a piece of fiction based on a murdered friend? The other explanation sat in the pit of her stomach.

As she closed the book something dark fell from its pages and landed on her knee. A lock of shiny black hair tied with red thread.

6

The young woman had the house to herself for the entire evening. Thank God. She and the man of her dreams had been living together for nearly seven weeks and had not been apart one evening. Love was wonderful but she needed her space, particularly when focused on an assignment.

She padded barefoot across the black and white tiled kitchen floor and put the carton of leftover Thai in the microwave. With her right hand she punched in two minutes on high and with her left pointed the remote at the television that was mounted under the upper cupboards. She was a news junkie and needed her fix. Lynne Rupert, the 11 p.m. news anchor settled into the 18-inch screen and told her that Prime Minister Harper was being accused of being too American and President Obama's ratings had dropped again.

She finished the Thai while leaning against the counter, half listening to the news and half contemplating Rupert's just-so demeanor. Her expression never changed. A little less than a smile, a little more than "I'm just reading what I'm given," Rupert had found an expression that worked for everything from tragedy to "good news" stories. Her hairstyle, the ingenuous tilt of her head, her perfect make-up, and the carefully modulated tone changed not even slightly from newscast to newscast. Only the words changed. The woman toyed with the idea that the Rupert she watched every evening was a computer composite of the real Rupert. That at least would explain the sameness. Not a bad idea for a plotline if she ever found time to turn to writing fiction.

The autumn wind slapped nearly bare branches against the kitchen window. This afternoon there had been a few leaves scattered on the lawn. By morning it would be covered. Red leaves from the stately maples on the front lawn were shuffled with the yellow ones from the neighbor's oak. She must remember to call Kenny, the lawn-maintenance fellow, tomorrow. It would be one of the last yard clean-ups of the season.

She licked the fork and put it in the dishwasher, debating for a moment whether it was full enough to turn on but decided not. She threw the empty carton into the garbage, flicked off the TV and moved back to the kitchen bar where she had organized her laptop and research material.

The two lovers had just begun to settle into this too-big but too-beautiful-to-resist turn-of-the-century home. Its noises and idiosyncrasies were not yet familiar. The house creaked as she supposed older houses did. In her adult life she had never before lived in a house that was older than herself. The wind vibrated the windowpanes until they whined and then whipped around the back to rattle the French doors in the den.

She was anxious to get back to work on her assignment. She had promised herself that she would have it done by the end of the week. It had started out as a pretty straightforward project that could be somewhat interesting but certainly not exciting. What she had found had changed all that.

The sweet scent of cologne interrupted her thoughts. It wasn't her Opium or the scent of her lover's Tsar. Too strong and too sweet. And why was she afraid?

The answer came to her with a stab of pain that was excruciating but mercifully brief.

7

Carson worked his way through Queen Street rush hour traffic, one hand on the steering wheel and one holding the mug of orange juice he hadn't had time to finish at home.

Another day, another murder. Toronto used to pride itself on its low crime rate, particularly violent crime. Its close proximity to American cities and the barrage of American news made comparison inevitable and Torontonians were proud, and perhaps just a bit smug, when they noted how much safer Toronto was. But things were changing. Had the city and its people rested on their laurels or was it simply inevitable that the gangs that taunted US cities would eventually burrow themselves into Toronto as well?

But this week's murders had nothing to do with gangs. Chadwick had made his formal statement and so far Carson hadn't heard that Greally had had any success in poking holes in it. Chadwick had given more details about the argument that had precipitated the thrown globe. He and his wife had been arguing over some decorating choices she had made for their Rosedale home and when she told him he didn't have the taste to decorate a double-wide in a trailer park, he threw the globe at her. "Imagine," he had said. "Her saying that when I am the one who collects Chinese porcelain and she collected those cheap snow globes and insisted on having them all over the formal living room."

That demeaning the husband was not an isolated incident but the proverbial straw seemed obvious, and yet it was unnerving how often Carson dealt with cases in which someone who had never shown violence before went over the edge. He often wondered whether there was something that could take him there.

Apparently today's case was, strangely, another Rosedale murder. Not a good week for the rich. Two other detectives had been called out last night and this morning's meeting would be a briefing to bring everyone up to date and to hand out assignments.

Carson pulled into the underground parking, found a spot and reversed and repositioned several times until he was sure it was equidistant from the vehicles on either side. Headquarters was being refurbished and as soon as Carson entered the building, he regretted the paint smell that permeated everything and destroyed the familiar. The smell of wax, of dust settled too deep in cracks and crevices to ever be routed, of old reports yellowing in their files, of the subtle odorous mark of each person who had worked here and of those who had unhappily visited. It had spoken of a history that had somehow been reassuring.

Carson headed for Inspector Simpson's office. The meeting would be held there as Simpson's corner of the building had been completed and the regular meeting room was in the middle of the renewal process. Kirpatrick met him at the elevator but was too absorbed in the morning paper to say more than "good morning." There had to be something of unusual interest in that paper. The angle of the tabloid paper Kirpatrick was holding and the low wolf whistle told Carson he was examining today's Sunshine Girl. The shot of a young woman sexily posed was a popular feature in one of the local dailies. It gave ambitious young things an opportunity to flaunt their attributes and it kick-started, according to the paper's marketing polls, a large percent of the city's males every morning.

When they reached the Inspector's office it was already crowded. The office's new décor was impressive. But the lighting hadn't been improved. The fluorescent tubes made everyone look hung over. Of course, there was a distinct possibility that many of them were.

The men and women stood sipping their first of many coffees of the day from styrofoam cups, admiring the Inspector's office and congratulating him on it. The scene had the feel of a house-warming party. Carson half expected the troops to start producing gifts and giving speeches.

Brad Greally was admiring a bright red and yellow abstract painting that hung behind the oversized desk. The Inspector, with the patience and charm of a good host, was telling Greally the story of how he and his wife had found the painting at an estate sale they had come across on a vacation in Vermont.

Perkins sidled up to Carson, nodded toward Greally, and whispered, "Ass kissing as usual."

Before Greally could continue the conversation, Simpson turned to the room, cleared his throat, and quickly slipped into his boss role with the ease of one who had been doing it for years. "Alright, is everyone here?" he called brusquely above the rumble of several conversations that would go unfinished.

"I think you all know what is at the top of our agenda this morning. In fact I'm making it the only item on the agenda. Don't expect a slam dunk like Chadwick case. Greally cleared that one up in a hurry."

Carson quietly exhaled air through pursed lips. It was the best way he knew of to let off steam quietly. What had happened to Greally's determination to prove that Chadwick was covering up for someone? Carson could easily answer his own question. This case was even higher profile so Greally had slammed the Chadwick case closed as quickly as he could.

Simpson continued, "I want as much manpower as possible on this one, hence more people than usual in this meeting.

"I expect you've all heard the broad details but let me give you a rundown of everything. Last night, a 911 call came in from a Richard Porter, at 11:17 pm, apparently panicked, screaming that the woman he had been living with, Diane Brooks, was dead and that she had been stabbed. We had a car there within ten minutes. That was McNair and Stephens," he nodded to the man and woman standing together close to the door. "I'll let you two add anything I miss.

"Diane Brooks was indeed dead and indeed stabbed. She was found in the kitchen. She'd apparently been sitting at the kitchen bar doing some paperwork. According to the coroner, she had been dead about an hour by the time Porter arrived on the scene, shortly after midnight."

McNair and Stevens handed out 8½ by 11 glossy, colored photos of the dead woman from several angles. Purple pants, white blouse, the back entirely blood-soaked, blond hair, maybe thirty years old, good figure, not beautiful but good features. Add lively eyes and warm lips to the corpse's face and she would definitely have been attractive.

At the edge of the picture was a narrow, dark slice of what Carson guessed to be a laptop computer. Her hand, still holding a pen, rested on a blank sheet of paper. What were her last thoughts before the shock and the pain? What words had formed in her brain, never to be communicated? The makings of a love letter or a grocery list? The dramatic or the mundane? It had always struck him that the mundane was the more poignant in death.

He had become conditioned to the horrors of violent death but the innocuous details haunted him long after a case was closed. The freshly made cup of coffee that would never be drunk; the reminder to buy bread for a lunch that would never be eaten; or the carefully pressed clothes for an event that would never be attended.

The facts continued to roll from Simpson, who obviously had immersed himself in this one, which was not his habit. In fact, he was often criticized for not being on top of the details of a case.

"That's what I have good men for," he would counter. "I'm the big-picture man here." His detailed knowledge of this case signaled its importance.

"According to Porter, he had been attending a company awards dinner.

Claimed he left the house at about six o'clock. There did not appear to be anything stolen. The French doors to the garden, however, had been forced.

"You probably recognize the name. Porter made a small fortune as a stockbroker. Has a good reputation and is well respected by investors, other brokers, and the community at large. He is very generous and recently donated a large sum to the museum. A couple of weeks ago, I was at an opening of a new room at the museum that has been named after him. I might add that he is also an avid supporter of the mayor and contributed significantly to his last election success.

"He had been living with Ms. Brooks only a few weeks. His wife, Sara Porter, whom he apparently left immediately prior to he and Brooks moving in together, works with Morrison and Black, the management consulting firm. McNair tells me Porter was devastated by not only the death of Ms. Brooks, but by the fact she was pregnant. Ms. Brooks was a freelance writer and daughter of Gerald Brooks, who founded Brooks Real Estate. You probably recognize the name. Her parents have been notified and are returning from Florida.

"What we have from forensics so far tells us little. An autopsy is scheduled for ten o'clock although the cause of death appears to be the knife wound. Oh, and no weapon was found. I think that's about it?" He turned to McNair and Stephens for confirmation.

"Yes sir, just about," said McNair, "except forensics dusted for prints and hasn't come up with anything useful. The handle of the French door to the garden was wiped clean. There are only three sets of prints in the kitchen – that of the deceased, Porter's, and, we haven't had time to check yet, but we expect that the third set are the housekeeper's."

"Any questions?" Simpson looked around the group.

"Any indication of this being a crime of passion?" Carson asked.

"Unlikely," Simpson answered. "The little we do have from forensics suggests a single clean knife wound. Almost like a surgical incision. Methodical rather than violent. There is no tearing of tissue or downward slicing, as there would likely be if someone had stabbed her in anger. Nor is there bruising around the wound which would have resulted had the instrument been driven hard into her back, as in a case of passion. The room was not disturbed. There are no signs of a struggle. The position of the body, the papers, and the laptop on the kitchen island suggest Ms. Brooks was working and unaware of, or unconcerned about, whomever was in the room with her."

"So at this point, we don't have any direction concerning motive. Not passion, not theft and no obvious potential enemies," Carson concluded.

Simpson nodded his confirmation.

Carson felt his internal engines revving. This case was going to require some serious detective work. Often the "whodunnit" was clear. It was a rival bike gang or the pimp of the girl who had tried to go it on her own. In those cases, it was just a matter of getting enough solid evidence for the Crown to make a case. Here they were starting from scratch.

A few other questions were asked, but useless ones, from Carson's perspective, like, "Can anyone confirm Porter's alibi?" People under pressure sometimes gave stupid alibis, but in Carson's experience, no one claimed to be at a dinner probably attended by at least forty people if they hadn't been there.

He looked around the room. Somehow, the guys like himself who had been around for a while, looked tired. No, that wasn't quite it. They looked out of place. In Simpson's old office with dingy walls and worn furniture, they had fit. They had looked in charge. The younger guys had been the ones who looked out of place. Now it was the young guys with their gelled hair and fashion-plate suits who looked at home. The older officers seemed depleted by the fresh surroundings, while the young people were enhanced by it. Carson searched for his own reflection in the glass of the print hanging on the wall beside him.

"Carson?"

"Yes sir?" The Inspector was handing out assignments. "Sorry, sir, I was – uh – just mulling over the case. You said something to me?"

Simpson stared at him a long moment, debating, Carson was sure, whether he should wing one of his signature sarcastic reprimands at him. The Inspector must have decided to pass out a pardon in honor of the new décor.

"Carson, as I was saying, I'm putting more manpower than usual on this. McNair and Stephens have the drive-by killings on their plate as well, so they will finish up the interviews with the neighbors that they started early this morning, and leave the rest to you, Kirpatrick, Perkins, and Greally. I want you two," he looked at Greally and Perkins, "to partner up for this one." Greally's partner, sick of the stress and long hours, had moved to auto theft, and Perkins' was on another training course.

"I've got to rationalize this amount of manpower, so I'm expecting results. Got it?" Simpson looked at Carson now.

"Yes, sir."

"I want all of you to report back here for a meeting at sixteen hundred hours. I have a meeting with the unit commander at eighteen hundred hours and I expect you to make sure I'm armed for it. I don't have to tell you that the mayor was elected on a clamp-down-on-crime platform and he intends to get re-elected. And I also intend to be here a few more years," Simpson added. "So people, let's get on with it!"

A half hour had been far too long for Kirpatrick to maintain silence.

As soon as they were dismissed, he began to make up for the lost time, and continued to talk as they got into the elevator. "Simpson seems pretty tough."

"Yes, he is. But he needs to be in his job."

"Has he ever given you a hard time?"

"Yeah. He suspended me once." Carson bent down to shine his loafers with a Kleenex.

"No shit. What happened?" Kirpatrick's level of interest escalated.

"The short story is I shot a guy who wouldn't drop the knife he was holding at his girlfriend's throat."

The unmarked assigned to them was still in the shop, so they headed toward Carson's Mustang. Kirpatrick had offered his car but Carson couldn't stand being in the passenger's seat.

"You killed him?"

"Uh huh." Carson's stomach muscles began to tighten as they still did every time he relived that moment. The drug-induced insanity screaming from the guy's eyes, the terror in the huge blue eyes of the girl, the smell of Chinese food from the restaurant downstairs, the girl's scream when he fired, the insanity in the guy's eyes replaced by a look of surprise, and then nothing at all.

"Were you suspended for long?"

"No, I was cleared in a couple of days but the Inspector didn't like the media the whole thing attracted. Turned out the guy was the son of one of our city councillors."

"Geez, you sure know how to pick them."

"That I do." Carson's mind darted to ex-wives.

"What's it like to kill someone?"

Kirpatrick's voice had changed from curious to awestruck. Thank God they had arrived at the car.

His old partner, Martin, who had taken early retirement, used to talk too much for Carson's liking as well, but at least he talked about his wife nagging him and the kids never appreciating anything. You didn't have to think in order to look like you were listening to him. An "uh-huh" and an occasional "tsk" were enough. And most importantly, Martin never asked personal questions.

"Let's check out Sara Porter first," Carson changed the subject as he unlocked the car. He felt tired and tried again to check his image, this time in the dirty car window. A gray face, with deep lines around the eyes and bags under them, looked back at him. The gray was compliments of the dirty windows. The rest had been earned.

He saw Kirpatrick eyeing the derelict '67 Mustang. When Carson bought the classic a few years ago, it was in pristine condition and he had cared for it fanatically.

The polishing stopped after an incident in the mall parking lot. He had taken his usual care, choosing a spot in the back end of the lot where shoppers seldom parked. Not only had he parked in the back lot but in the farthest corner in the last row. He was gone less than half an hour making a quick stop to splurge on a new Versace tie. Few at the office would appreciate it. To most people he knew, it would look no different from a twenty dollar Sears job. But that wouldn't lessen his personal enjoyment.

His second stop was to pick up a McDonald's number one, a Big Mac, fries and a Coke. He headed back to his car looking forward to eating his take-out while watching some television, and afterward finding a spot for his new acquisition on his already-crowded tie rack.

As he approached the back lot, the pleasure of the afternoon and anticipation of the evening were wiped away. A pick-up truck with more rust than paint was parked next to his Mustang and on an angle that carried its cab over the line into his spot, and just inches away from his bright red fender.

That goddamn cowboy. He took off at a run, paper napkins flying from his cardboard take-out tray. *At least fifty empty spots and he parks beside me.*

He kept telling himself he was overreacting until he reached his car and found he wasn't. He didn't even have to run his hand over the shiny red surface as he sometimes did just to check, or put his head on an angle to catch the light just the right way. The concave dint in the driver's side door was obvious, a glint of steel uncovered at its center. The hurt and disappointment joined and moved together from his stomach up into his throat. Tears welled for a second before the anger took charge. He kicked a bigger dint in the door of his Mustang, then turned and kicked his anger into the truck, frustrated that the additional damage made little difference. Finally, he yanked open his door forcing it to slam into the truck and threw himself inside, tossing the tray of food onto the passenger seat, spilling the Coke and fries. The Coke stains still marked the upholstered seat and it was likely that fries lay petrifying under it. Other than by the grace of an occasional rain, the car had not been washed since.

And so it was with everything in Keith Carson's life. They were either spanking new and lovingly cared for, or derelict.

It was why he had been married three times before he had given up on the institution. His wives could never understand how their amazingly attentive husband, who did everything possible to make them feel like a new bride long after the wedding, would suddenly become distant. For them the hurtful words of the first real quarrel were soon forgotten. For Carson, once the relationship was marred by a hurt, it could never be the same.

For the most part, he managed to hide the confused clutter of his life. It had been years since he had invited anyone to his apartment. If there was no one to note, even with just a look, the oddity of the few obsessively cared-for possessions, shining incongruently amongst the jumble of things neglected and abused, he wouldn't be forced to question whether his behavior was indeed creeping closer to the abnormal.

Seldom did anyone else ride in his car. Kirpatrick climbed into the passenger's side, first having to move a pile of newspapers and discarded hamburger wrappers to the back seat. As soon as Carson started the car, Kirpatrick rolled down his window and leaned toward it.

"Geez, Carson. This car is filthy. It smells like stuff is growing in here."

Maybe with his head hanging out the window he'd quit talking.

8

The city was stretching and yawning itself awake as Sara headed north on Yonge Street.

It was a crisp autumn morning and shopkeepers expectantly opened their doors and welcomed in the new day and the business it might bring. Green grocers dragged stands of produce onto the sidewalk, creating a series of still lifes. The new crop of shiny red McIntosh apples fought with pots of purple and gold mums for the focal point of the tableaus. Office workers, not quite ready for another day, hovered groggily at bus stops, their staring eyes sending "do not disturb signs" to anyone who might consider offering a good morning smile. Others hurried from coffee shops, late for work but clutching take-out cups of the essential elixir that was worth every look of reprimand they might receive for their lateness.

Yonge Street wasn't a meandering, easygoing street. It was a street with purpose. It shot straight north from Lake Ontario whose cold waters lapped at its foot, ran up through the middle of the entire city and on through towns and countryside to end in what some Torontonians might describe as the middle of nowhere. It was proudly touted by the city as the longest street in the world and the Guinness Book of World Records had endorsed the claim. Sara would have liked to keep on driving straight ahead, letting the street carry her to its end. But not today.

She had awoken with a plan. She wasn't sure whether she had actually formalized it before she had fallen asleep, fully clothed on top of the bedcovers, or whether it had emerged as she slept. She had had much too much to drink at dinner and her memory of the evening after Tony left her at the restaurant was vague. Every time she thought of last evening she had an anxious feeling that something had happened that she wouldn't feel good about if she remembered it.

What she did remember was spending the early hours of the morning absorbed in the world of the 1940s, or at least Aunt Kate's corner of that world. Sara had continued to wrestle with why Aunt Kate would will the odd collection of memorabilia to anyone. Other than the clippings about

Jane Stewart's death, most of the mementos were bland bits of nostalgia. They suggested a sentimental and frivolous young woman. Certainly not the woman Kate McPherson had worked so hard to create. Kate had never talked about herself as a young woman and had even deflected questions about her youth. Sara had always sensed that she had determinedly cut the younger Kate McPherson from her life history. Why reveal her now? If anything, she would have expected Kate to cringe at the idea of someone poking through these items.

And then there was the judge's obituary. New and seemingly out of place. But it wasn't out of place. Her aunt, or someone, had deliberately placed it there. The box had once again become important to her.

Sara wasn't sure at what point she had become convinced that her aunt had not just left her a box of stuff but had left her something to be completed. As fanciful as the idea seemed, Sara felt with certainty that Kate was asking her to do something that she could no longer do herself.

Kate McPherson was not one to leave things undone. Everything undertaken was to be completed and completed to the best of one's ability.

The thought took Sara back to when she was seven years old and sitting in her aunt's living room at the games table. Her feet dangled above the floor and the backs of her legs hurt from the pressure of the chair's edge. The table sat beside a window draped with heavy dark red velvet. When Aunt Kate opened the drapes farther, particles of dust floated through the stream of sunlight that had entered.

"There now you can see better," her aunt had said. At that moment Sara recognized for the first time that what adults presented as their motives were sometimes shams. Sara knew instantly that Kate had opened the drapes not to ensure that Sara had better light for her project, but so she could see her older brother and sister and some neighborhood children playing in the side yard. They had played Ring Around the Rosie, Hide and Seek and Simon Says, and their shouts and laughter could barely be heard in the cool, dark, sitting room.

She and her siblings, Kittie and Ronnie, had arrived at Aunt Kate's in great anticipation. Visits to their aunt were infrequent treats and there was an air of mystery about her large rambling Victorian home. The house had three floors and most intriguingly of all, two sets of stairs, one looming up into the dark upstairs hall from the main foyer, and one from the kitchen. When their aunt was in a particularly lenient mood she would let them run up one stairwell and down the other.

The visits were orchestrated as was everything in Kate's life. She would invite neighbors' children in to play with her nephew and nieces and lead them in games and scavenger hunts. Before they began their play she showed them the extravagant prizes that were awaiting the winners. Sara remembered one occasion there being a boxed set of The Bobbsey Twins books and roller skates that attached to your shoes. Kate encouraged competition and ensured the prizes were hard won. Before the children left, ice cream and cake were served. And once it was eaten, Kate announced that it was time for them to leave. She stood regally on the front porch and shook each child's hand as they recited what she had taught them on their first visit and expected them to remember: "Thank you Miss McPherson, we had a lovely time."

Visits began in the formal sitting room before the other children arrived. Sara and her brother and sister tried to display their best manners, although Aunt Kate frequently found their best terribly wanting. Instead of lunch she served them what she called tea, which they thought was odd since the serving tray held no tea but was laden with lemonade, tiny sandwiches, huge oatmeal cookies and butter tarts packed tightly with raisins.

On the afternoon that Sara so vividly remembered, she had spied a jigsaw puzzle on the games table and asked if she could look at it. The puzzle pieces were spilled onto the dark green felt top. Several of the tiny pieces had been fitted together. Sara could see that a lily pad was emerging. The top of the box that displayed the picture being pieced together was propped against its bottom. Sara was mesmerized by it.

"You like that picture, dear?" her aunt had asked.

At first Sara had just nodded her head, absorbed in her discovery, but then remembering that nodding would not pass Kate's definition of good manners, she had answered, "Yes, Aunt Kate, I think it's the most beautiful picture I've ever seen."

Aunt Kate never seemed happier than when she was teaching someone something, or perhaps flaunting her knowledge. Sara had never been sure which her true motivation was. But Kate had grasped this opportunity and had gathered the three of them around the table.

"This work, children, is a painting called 'Pond With Water Lilies.' It was painted by Monet, an artist who lived in France in the nineteenth century. He was a member of a group of artists who came to be called the Impressionists." Throughout her mini lecture she would stop to ask questions such as, "Have you ever heard of the Impressionists?" The answer was invariably a chorus of "No, Aunt Kate."

Sara had begun to feel embarrassed, not for herself and Kittie and Ronnie, but her parents, whom surely Aunt Kate would think were doing a terrible job of educating their children.

She had tried to politely interrupt the lecture both in an effort to protect her parents and to get permission to work on the jigsaw.

"Please Aunt Kate, may I try to put the puzzle together?"

"No, dear, it's much too difficult for you," Kate had smiled. Sara had noticed her aunt was using the smile she reserved for children and her cousin Edgar, whom she had heard Kate refer to as an imbecile. "Besides," she had added, "it's time to go outside to play. The other children will be here shortly."

Kate had headed toward the door, ushering Kittie and Ronnie ahead of her.

Sara had hung back, held in place by the colors of the picture. She wanted to move into the picture and sit by that pond and listen to the frogs she was sure would be hiding under at least one of the lily pads.

"It's not too difficult, Aunt Kate. Please may I try?"

Aunt Kate had stopped short at the door. Her voice changed from the patient nurturing teacher to the stern, impatient one. "No, Sara. I said it's too difficult."

Her aunt's tone had triggered a response in Sara that burst forth so quickly she couldn't stop it.

"It is *not* too difficult for me," Sara had retorted a little too loudly and much too firmly. Her hands had seemed to move to her hips of their own volition and a stamp of her foot had served as an exclamation mark.

Aunt Kate had walked briskly back to her and Sara had noticed that her nose looked pinched and white. She had remembered a group of people at her home once talking about her Aunt Kate and her father had said, "Whatever you do, never rile Kate. There'll be the hell to pay if you do." She had no doubt she had just riled Kate and she feared the hell that would surely come.

"Very well," Kate had said. She had grabbed Sara's arms so roughly they burned and hauled her onto the chair. "But just remember," her pointer finger jabbed at the air a few inches from Sara's nose, emphasizing each word as she spoke, "Never start something you can't finish."

Sara had spent the next several hours sitting at the table, her legs and bottom sore from its oak chair. Tears trickled down her face for the first few minutes. Then for awhile she became engrossed in the picture, feeling a small thrill when she had managed to find three small pieces that fit without having to push them too hard. But when she saw written on the box "1000 Pieces" the enormity of the task depleted her.

Aunt Kate had breezed in and out periodically, smiling cheerily and asking, "How are you doing dear?" Her manner suggested they were both perfectly pleased with the situation; Sara was spending the day doing exactly what she wanted, and of course Aunt Kate was happy to make that happen.

Ronnie now lived in England and Kittie in South Carolina and they seldom got together. But when they did, the two would inevitably recall that day. Sara remembered Ronnie's comment at the dinner table after Aunt Kate's funeral. "It was that day at Aunt Kate's that I realized how much you were like her. Neither one of you was willing to back down."

And then he added with a grin, "Your stubbornness has been getting you in trouble ever since that day. You'd think you would have learned your lesson."

But that wasn't the lesson Sara had learned. She had gotten to know her aunt very well that day and had felt a deep disappointment at the realization that you didn't always like the people you loved.

Now she reflected on the stubbornness Ronnie had identified. He was right. She was stubborn but she had rationalized it as sticking to values. She was too stubborn to back down when she disagreed with Ken. She had been too stubborn to work less when Richard had urged her to. How much was she like Kate? Kate had been successful but died lonely. Anxiety began to form somewhere in her solar plexus and she tried to quell it by turning her mind back to her day's agenda.

Before leaving home, she had developed a plan of sorts and jotted the steps on a yellow lined note pad that now sat on the seat beside her. One, visit the nursing home where Aunt Kate spent her last few months. She hoped to talk with Pauline Williams, Kate's favorite nurse's aide. Pauline might be able to tell her something about Aunt Kate's last few days. At least she might find out whether the judge and her aunt had still been in touch with one another.

The second to-do scrawled on the pad was to talk with Tony's father, Howard Hamilton. She knew that her aunt and the elder Hamilton had at one time been casual friends, and at dinner the night before, she had learned from Tony that his father had also been acquainted with Judge Jamieson and had attended Jamieson's funeral. He should have some first-hand knowledge about the judge and his death. He might even remember Jane Stewart's murder.

"Visit The Point" was the final note. Oak Point was where the McPhersons had spent their summers when her father and Kate were young. It was also where Jane Stewart had been murdered. She knew the McPherson cottage was still there but as far as she knew, it had sat empty for many years. Sara had considered calling her father to prod his memories of The Point but she knew she would receive only bluster and would accomplish nothing other than raising his blood pressure. The family cottage had been a sore spot with him. His parents had died when he was in his early twenties. He had been left the family home and Kate had gotten the cottage, which financially was more than equitable, but his happiest childhood memories had been created at the cottage. He had resented his sister closing it up and then refusing anyone access to it. It had hurt him that he couldn't take his children there to share his childhood with them. No, he would not welcome questions about The Point.

It was highly unlikely she would find anything useful there, but it would be a pleasant day trip. If nothing else, it would help keep her mind off other things. She knew that the parts of her life that were festering would heal faster if she quit picking at them. She would head up to The Point tomorrow or the day after.

Once she had organized her thoughts about Kate's mementos, it seemed easier to get her own life in order. The first step was clear. She would take a week or two off to get her head together and consider her career options. At this moment, resigning from Morrison and Black had no contenders for first place but perhaps she would feel differently in a couple of weeks.

What she would do for a living if she left she didn't know. She had no intention of living off Richard, although legally she knew she could. But it didn't matter. She was confident she would find a new career, if indeed that was her final decision.

She had sent Ken an e-mail letting him know she was taking time off. She knew she was leaving Ken shorthanded and previously would never have done so. In spite of his treatment of her, she felt a bit guilty.

Yonge Street traffic grew heavier as she drove further north. She took the 401 East exit and joined the bumper-to-bumper commuters headed to offices and factories. She might have been wiser to make her way through the city. Her destination, the Cardinal Long Term Care Facility, was only a couple of exits away and a little north of the highway but at this rate it could take some time. Normally, she would be weaving in and out looking for that opportunity to move even a car length ahead. This morning, she was content to go with the flow.

A half hour later Sara turned into the long impressive drive that led up to the Cardinal. It was a double drive with beds of late-blooming fall flowers down its middle. The elegant entrance assured guests that this was a place for those who could afford the very best. This was a home away from home, not a nursing facility.

The first part of the message was true. It was expensive. The second was false. But the beautifully decorated dining room with its sideboards and Queen Anne tables and chairs, the overstuffed furniture in the lounge and the French doors to a perfect patio, helped family members pretend it was just like home and so assuaged their guilt. Realists and residents knew better. She glanced into the lounge as she passed. Shriveled men and women in wheelchairs, many hooked to oxygen, gathered around a piano to listen to songs from the first and second world wars and made brave attempts to squeeze a little happiness from their painful final days. The smell of the dying elderly lingered under the antiseptic attempts to disguise it.

Sara waited for a few moments for the elevator but then realized she would have a long wait. She watched the needle stop at each floor and knew that caretakers were maneuvering more wheelchairs into the lift. It was always like this at recreation and meal times. She opted for the stairs instead.

The stairwell offered a familiar climb. Always in a hurry when she visited her aunt, Sara had seldom waited for the elevator. As she climbed, the feeling of guilt she had experienced frequently since her aunt's death settled in her chest. Sara was the only family member remaining in the city. Her parents had retired on the west coast where the milder winters allowed them to golf and garden a good part of the year. And so it was left to Sara to visit and keep an eye on her aunt. Preoccupied with work and life in general, days would go by without her even thinking of Kate. When she did, she would dash in for a quick visit between appointments. She would bring her aunt's favorites, caviar or smoked salmon, delicacies she was never served in the nursing home; deliver a quick update of any news she thought would be of interest; then make a stop at the nurses' station to check on Kate's condition. They were duty visits and she knew her aunt saw them for what they were. She hadn't always liked her aunt but had respected her immensely, and now wished she had told her how much she had admired her.

She arrived at the third-floor nursing station, somewhat less guilt-laden and only a little out of breath. Pauline Williams was filling out a report and looked up when she heard Sara approach. Her eyes immediately filled with tears and she stood up.

"I'm so sorry about your aunt. She was a good lady."

"Thank you, Pauline. She really was. But I know she could also be a handful. I appreciate the care you gave her."

Pauline was wiping the tears away with the back of a soft, dark hand.

"I wondered if I could talk with you for a few minutes?" Sara continued.

Pauline stepped back just slightly. Was it Sara's imagination or did she look wary?

"What did you want to talk about?" Pauline asked.

"I just wanted to chat about her last day. There are a couple of things I'd like to know."

"There really isn't anything to tell you. It was just another day. You know she couldn't really do anything and spent all of her time in her room. It was just a typical day."

"If we could talk privately, there are one or two questions I'd like to ask you. I promise it won't take long."

"I'm sorry, Mrs. Porter, but there really isn't any place to talk here and I'm just going off shift."

"Perhaps I could take you for a cup of coffee."

Pauline's arms had folded themselves across the full stomach that stretched her blue uniform to its limit.

"I'm sorry, Mrs. Porter, but I really can't. Veronica was on that day as well and helped out with your aunt. Perhaps she could answer the questions. She's off today but you might catch her tomorrow."

Pauline's usual open expression closed. Sara had been dismissed. She headed back downstairs, past strains of "Lili Marlene," and out into the fall sunshine that was beginning to draw the morning chill from the day. She was shocked and disappointed. Pauline had always been so helpful. Why was she avoiding talking with her?

Sara backed out of the parking lot and paused for a moment to open the sunroof. She wanted to savor the nice weather while it was here. As she searched for the button to open it she realized that in the two years she had owned the car she had never once opened the sunroof.

Her Volvo had begun to move slowly down the front drive when she heard the *slap slap* of sandals on pavement coming behind her. She looked in the rear-view mirror to see Pauline running after her, a red sweater over her blue uniform, a black plastic carry-all slung over her left shoulder and flapping at her side.

Pauline frantically waved her right arm. "Mrs. Porter, wait."

Sara stopped and lowered her window.

A puffing Pauline caught up to her, paused for a moment to catch her breath, slapped her chest with her right hand as though the motion would increase her oxygen intake, and leaned through the open window.

"Here." She offered Sara a pink telephone message slip. "Here's my address. I'll be home at four."

She turned quickly away and continued down the drive, no longer running but striding at a quick pace.

"May I give you a lift?" Sara called after her.

"No thanks. The bus stop's just at the gate."

The gate was a probably a quarter of a mile away and Pauline was still puffing.

Sara pulled along side her.

"I can drop you at the end of the drive?"

"No thanks." Pauline did not even look at her.

Sara pulled slowly away. Pauline wasn't ready to spend any time with her yet. Not even the couple of minutes it would take to drive to the gate.

9

He had parked his car across the road from the foot of the Cardinal drive. That way he wouldn't miss her coming out and if she noticed his car, she would have no reason to be suspicious of his being there.

He normally hated waiting. But lately he had had so much to think about that he cherished the moments between things.

Last night he had read that some people believe that each person is put on earth with the attributes to fulfill a specific purpose. Perhaps this was his. He had never thought much about such things before, but during the many evenings he had spent in planning, it had struck him that this venture required the two attributes on which he had always prided himself. Never being squeamish and always being helpful. Even as a child, these had been his greatest gifts.

When his mother had come down with what his grandmother called "a case of the nerves," it had been he who had immediately volunteered to care for his younger, diabetic sister. Directing the needle that carried the insulin through the skin and into her flesh hadn't been a problem for him. He particularly enjoyed it when it was her soft, white belly's turn to receive the injection. The only difficulty had been that ridiculous nurse who had insisted he practice on an orange before jabbing his sister. And then she had gone on about how she would never have believed a ten-year-old could have managed the task so well and with no hesitation whatsoever.

And it had been he who had saved Freddie Philips from going through life minus one-third of the pointer finger on his left hand.

He and Freddie had been building a tree house in Freddie's overgrown backyard. Any battle the grass had mounted against the weeds was long forgotten. Now plantain and dandelions covered the ground and wild cucumber crawled between them, entwining itself around the remaining pickets of a derelict fence and pulling itself tendril over tendril upward toward the sun.

In their search for tools Freddie had found a rusty hatchet discarded amongst the jungle-like weeds. Just what they needed to chop the long pieces of lumber they had carted from a nearby building site. He had explained to Freddie that they weren't really stealing the wood because the builder could just write off the cost of the missing lumber. He didn't actually know what that meant, but he had heard his uncle talking about the advantages of writing things off and it seemed like a good way to appease Freddie's conscience. Freddie, of course, would follow his lead anyway but things always moved more quickly when Freddie wasn't worrying about what Jesus would think.

He had been sitting on the ground with his back to Freddie, staring up at the tree and visualizing what their finished product would look like. Not too big, but big enough to put some things in. Maybe a small table to put a candle on, a sleeping bag, and a wooden crate to store his magazines. Freddie hadn't seen his collection of magazines yet and would say that Jesus wouldn't like them, but he would think of something that would make it alright.

The chop of the hatchet had just begun to develop a neat rhythm when Freddie began screaming. He had turned to see Freddie clutching his left hand with his right. Wonderfully red blood gushed from one finger. He had never seen blood pour from anyone before. As Freddie jerked his arm up and down in panic the blood made arches in the air before spattering the wood, the weeds and the dropped hatchet. He was mesmerized by the perfect pitch of the scream and the symmetry of the red speckled pattern that was painting itself on the green canvas.

When Freddie's mother ran out of the house and half dragged, half coaxed the hysterical boy toward the house, he had hung back. As he pondered the splashes of blood and their power to ignite such a feeling within him, he had noticed something in the middle of a clump of twitch grass. The finger, severed just above the first joint. He had examined it with fascination, at first holding the disembodied finger at arm's length and then bringing it closer for inspection. He shuddered. Not at the severed finger but at the dirty, cracked fingernail attached to it. Freddie really was a pig.

What had fascinated him most was the tiny hangnail. Innocuous on the living finger, it was now a defining feature worthy of contemplation. He had played with the hangnail, worrying it as he would one on his own finger. He had caught it between two of his own meticulous fingernails and tore it back a little to see if it would bleed. It didn't.

He used a fallen leaf to wipe the blood from the severed digit so that he could examine it more closely. Perhaps he could memorize every cell and every shade of color so that he could enjoy it later. The exact spot where the layers of skin ended and the flesh began, the yellowish pink color of the flesh, the tiny spots that must be blood vessels, and the gleaming white bone at the core.

He had thought about keeping it, but opted for heroism instead. A choice he had at times regretted.

He had wrapped it carefully in a not-too-dirty Kleenex, and waited for the medics to arrive to offer his gift.

"Here," he had said quietly to one of the men, "you might want this."

What presence of mind, they had said. And to think he had actually picked it up himself. Many, they had said, would not have been able to stomach it.

Now, he had to help someone else, a man he admired and who had many qualities of which he was fond. But *that* man was definitely squeamish. He was someone who could never have done what had to be done no matter the consequences. And the consequences could be devastating for all of them.

There was more yet to do and he felt elated that he was the one who had what was required to do it.

As the Volvo pulled out of the Cardinal driveway, he pulled into traffic behind it.

10

Carson felt conspicuous and exposed. He was used to the calculated, low profile that went with the detective business. In another area of the city, his derelict Mustang wouldn't have been noticed. But in this neighborhood, it didn't exactly blend in. Sedate BMWs, Mercedes, and Volvos of recent vintage sat in wide driveways waiting their turn to be driven. The lawn-maintenance trucks parked in front of a couple of homes and a station wagon with a sign in its rear window advertising Squeaky Clean Window Washers were the only exceptions. Just how clean were the window washers, he wondered.

The address they were looking for did not mark the most ostentatious house on the street but likely one of the most expensive. Apparently anxious to be released from Carson's microbe-filled car, Kirpatrick jumped out quickly before the car had come to a full stop and took two or three very deep breaths as he checked out the property.

"Doesn't look like there's anyone here," he decided. "No car."

A large three-car garage sat with all doors open. From this vantage point, it looked like it housed little at the moment. A couple of bicycles and a stepladder were propped against one wall.

"Well, let's find out." Carson headed for the front door, aware of the pair of eyes staring at them from the second floor of the house next door.

They tried the front doorbell and then knocked with authority. When they got no response, they went around to the back and went through the same procedure at the back door. Looking through the glass on the door didn't tell them much. The mudroom on the other side of the door provided more space than any family could possibly need to remove boots or even store a dozen kids' snowsuits. It looked like a space that was meant to be cluttered with boots, shoes, coats and sports equipment, maybe an open hockey bag with skates, pads, and smelly jerseys pouring out of it. Instead, the red Mexican tile floor was bare. One wall held several coat hooks. Only one was being used, by a yellow oilskin raincoat. Matching boots sat neatly below. A blue recycling box filled to the brim with newspapers suggested a household that subscribed to more than one newspaper and probably several magazines. A colored advertising flier lay on top. A copy of *The Economist* and one of *Vanity Fair* had been tossed in before the flier. A long bench, the kind that has a seat that lifts to access the storage space inside, stretched along the wall opposite the coat hooks. A few steps led up to the kitchen. The kitchen door was partly closed and only a corner of a large kitchen range was in view, but it looked like one that had been designed for gourmet cooking.

Kirpatrick shook his head. “Shit, that mudroom is bigger than my bedroom. What is it they say about life not being fair?”

As Kirpatrick gave the door one last knock that was closer to a bang, a breathless voice called from next door.

“Can I help you?”

The eyes had made their way down from the second floor in record time. Carson turned to see an elderly man carrying a calico cat under one arm.

“No thank you, sir. We’re looking for Sara Porter,” Carson responded.

“Can I ask what your business is?”

“No, sir, I’m afraid you can’t. I’m Detective Sergeant Carson and this is Detective Constable Kirpatrick.”

As he expected, the beady eyes lit up.

“I see. Stephen Dempster’s the name. Sara and I are close neighbors. If there is anything I can do —”

“No thank you sir, not a thing.”

“Well Sara’s not at home. She left a bit later than usual today and didn’t look like she was headed for the office either. Dressed too casually.”

“Thank you sir. We appreciate your help.” Carson headed back to the car with his partner close behind. Busybodies like Dempster irritated Carson. He wouldn’t give him the satisfaction of interviewing him now. They could always get back to Dempster later. Right now he was anxious to find Sara Porter. As the spurned wife, she had to be treated as a key suspect.

“Anytime,” Dempster called after them. “People don’t seem interested in doing their civic duty anymore.”

The old man was probably hoping for a compliment to compensate for not getting even one juicy bit of information, but Carson said nothing as they climbed into the Mustang.

That was probably one of the most useful things Carson had learned at the academy. How not to say anything. It had been drilled into them that it was OK, and often preferable, to say nothing even if in civilian life it would have felt rude to do so. He had learned that silence could be very powerful.

Dempster had followed them down the drive and stood watching as they drove away, giving them a wave like a host bidding farewell to his guests.

“Guess we made his day.” Kirpatrick was still new enough to the division to get a high from people's reaction to his status. "So it looks like there's no point trying to find her at work."

"Maybe, but with the new dress code, you never know what people are going to wear to work today. Besides, if she isn't there, we can talk with Tony Hamilton. He also works for Morrison and Black and is on the list as a close friend of both Sara and Richard Porter. And, if she isn't there, perhaps someone can tell us where we can find her."

They drove down a few tree-lined residential streets, each as affluent looking as the one they just left and found Mt. Pleasant Road, the busy four-lane street that would take them downtown.

Carson wasn't completely comfortable with the way the team was set up for this case. He was the senior man and so essentially he was the lead, but Simpson hadn't made that official. He had simply asked that the two teams head up the case together. Working the case with Greally was something he didn't relish and it made it more difficult if he didn't officially have the authority to make the calls. He had never taken to Greally. The man bragged about everything he did and constantly looked for ways to get the credit others deserved. And a couple of years ago the dislike had become personal. Carson stayed out of his way as much as possible.

Carson had made sure that he and Kirpatrick had locked up the key interviews: Sara and Richard Porter, their close friends and business associates, along with those of the murdered Diane Brooks. In that way, he at least had some control over the case. But it seemed that Simpson intended to ultimately call the shots. The pressure was obviously on. They had better make some headway fast.

It was close to ten o'clock and traffic was still heavy. What had happened to morning and evening rush hour? Bumper-to-bumper trips had become the norm any time of day, and any day of the week. Carson gunned the Mustang, and attempted to make headway by weaving in and out of the traffic. One taxi driver gave him the finger, and he guessed by the look a white-haired woman in a Mercedes gave him that she would have done the same had the finger been in her lexicon.

Once they reached Lakeshore Road, they headed east a few blocks into an area that had at one time been factories, warehouses, and old office buildings. It was now an exclusive business community. The Morrison and Black building was one of a string of buildings on the lake side of the road. Snippets of sun dancing on dark water could be seen briefly through the narrow spaces between the buildings as they passed. All of the buildings in this strip had been updated but their original character had been kept intact. There was no sign of a parking lot, so Carson pulled up in front, ignoring the "No Standing Any Time" sign.

Once again, Kirpatrick dove out of the car before it came to a full stop. He was already in the lobby, looking around, when Carson caught up to him.

"I thought they'd be in one of the downtown towers with the other big guys.

What's this bare brick walls stuff?"

"I think it's what you call trendy." Carson had pushed the button for the elevator and an old-fashioned wrought iron cage settled in front of them.

"You think this thing's safe?" Kirpatrick, for the first time, hung back.

"If not, we'll go down together partner. Come on, let's go." Carson jerked his head for Kirpatrick to join him.

The elevator opened into the reception area on the second floor. A girl, who he supposed was actually a young woman, looked too young to be working and much too small for the oversized desk. She presented a perfect smile and modulated greeting that communicated that, despite any appearance to the contrary, she was perfectly in control.

"May I help you, gentlemen?"

"Yes, we're looking for Sara Porter." As Carson spoke, a striking woman with bright red hair and what, under a two-piece mauve wool suit, promised to be a perfect figure, came out from the inner office.

"You're looking for Sara?" she asked. Eyes, that he suspected could smolder off duty, coolly scanned each of them from head to toe. Appraisal completed, they revealed no hint of the results.

"I'm sorry. Sara's not here today."

"When do you expect her back?" Carson took the lead.

"May I ask who's enquiring?"

"The police, ma'am. I'm Detective Sergeant Carson, and this is my partner Detective Constable Kirpatrick."

"You must be here about Richard Porter's … er –… girlfriend. We are all devastated. How awful." The lack of emotion in her voice negated any concern the words might have attempted to convey.

"Sara e-mailed to say she would be away for a few days," she continued.

Carson tried probing with, "Got that nasty flu has she?" Carson didn't know of any flu going around but there had to be some somewhere.

"I don't know what her problem is Detective. Sara isn't a suspect is she? That would be dreadful." More feigned concern. This time though he didn't read disinterest, but perhaps hope that it might be true.

"May I ask what your role is here, ma'am."

"Of course, forgive me for not introducing myself. You caught me off guard. We are not used to being visited by the police."

He'd make a handsome wager that this woman was never caught off guard.

"I am Dina Warner, executive assistant to Ken Morrison, our senior partner." She stood a little taller and raised her head just slightly as she made the announcement.

"I understand Tony Hamilton also works with the firm. Is he in?" Carson asked.

"Yes, I believe so. Let me take you into the boardroom and I'll find him for you."

She left them there with more bare bricks and a view of the lake. They watched three sailboats, rigging stretched taut by the crisp autumn wind, and sun bleaching the white sails whiter.

Neither heard Tony Hamilton enter the room and his soft "Good morning, gentlemen" came unexpectedly.

Hamilton closed the door behind him and they each took the chair closest to them. Hamilton sat across from them, the sun from the window causing him to squint occasionally. He folded his hands in front of him, thumbs clasped tightly over one another as though one were keeping the other in check. He reminded Carson of a psych prof he'd had at university.

Carson sensed some discomfort in the man but wasn't sure whether it was the physical discomfort of the sun in his eyes or something else. Carson suggested that Hamilton move to where he would be more comfortable but the man declined. The sun, he said, felt good. He didn't have a window in his office.

This guy couldn't be too high up the pecking order, Carson surmised.

"I suppose you are here because of Diane's – er – death."

Carson nodded.

"I couldn't believe it when I saw it in the paper this morning. Actually spilled my coffee all over the front page. We're all in shock. You hear about these things but of course it never happens in your own circle."

"Did you know Ms. Brooks well?"

"No, not at all really. I met her at a few social events that she attended with Richard. She seemed very nice and Richard seemed happy with her. I really don't know anything else."

"How do you know the Porters?"

"I met Richard at a youth hostel in Amsterdam. We were both spending a summer traveling through Europe. As two young guys from Canada we were blown away by the Amsterdam mores. Being able to buy hash in a bar seemed to be both the height of decadence and the height of sophistication. The people we had both been traveling with moved on and we stayed for a couple of weeks. We've been close ever since. I met Sara when Richard started dating her a couple of years later. It turned out that her family and mine had some connection and we hit it off. It was Sara who recommended me for the position here."

"Do you know of anyone who would have a motive to murder Ms. Brooks?"

"No, of course not. As I said, I didn't really know her."

"I understand Ms. Porter called in sick today."

"Yes, that's what I understand. I didn't speak with her."

"Does she take sick days often?"

"No, not at all. In fact she often works when she should be in bed. If there's anyone too committed to the job, Sara is."

"Did she seem ill yesterday?"

"No, although she was upset. The senior partner has been giving her a hard time."

That wasn't a line Carson was interested in pursuing, at least not at the moment.

Instead he asked, "How did Ms. Porter feel about Diane Brooks?"

Hamilton's thumbs unclasped and went into a spin.

"I don't know a great deal about how she felt."

Hamilton, Carson thought, must have a difficult life. He would never get away with lying to his wife if he had one and would make a lousy poker player. It wasn't the sun that was causing his discomfort.

He found the direct approach usually worked best with Hamilton's type.

"Something's bothering you, Mr. Hamilton. Why don't you tell us about it?"

Hamilton made a brief and weak disclaimer. Then he sighed and focused on his thumbs as he spoke.

"It wasn't anything I thought much about at the time. Besides Sara had been drinking quite a bit. And I'm sure it's nothing. But then when I read about the murder in the *Globe* and some of the details that were printed ..."

Relief battling against guilt, Hamilton went on to explain what had happened at dinner the night before.

11

It was quiet in The Lost Camel. The lunchtime rush was over and Sara's favorite window table sat empty, pale yellow sunlight resting on the chair closest to the window, keeping it warm.

It had been ages since she had been here. It was too far from the office to come during the week and days off had hardly existed for a couple of months. When she did take one it was to sleep.

She had been almost afraid to come in for fear of seeing an "Under New Management" sign. She didn't recognize anyone behind the counter. One of the women with a distinct Australian accent chatted with a fellow about her upcoming trip to England. But the menu board listed the cheese melts she remembered and the aroma of the coffee assured her that they still served the best latte in town.

While her sandwich was being prepared, Sara cradled the large steaming cup and watched Queen Street characters make cameo appearances in the café window. A very fat woman dressed in bright red with bleached blond hair piled high pulled a tiny Chihuahua on a bright red leash behind her. She looked as though she had set out to disprove the theory that pet owners looked like their pets.

Two painters in paint-spattered coveralls and work boots stopped for a moment to light up. The overalls were olive green and each daub of paint, some more faded than others, was an identical, uninspiring off-white. They must specialize in painting apartments, she decided. No special talent required, just make sure any evidence of the last tenant is covered, and in as little time as possible.

A blind man, with a full beard speckled with gray, dark glasses, a black turtleneck, a taupe beret, and a white cane that he swept in front of him moved by at a pace that suggested that this was home territory. A blue baseball cap appeared and disappeared frequently at the corner of the window frame. It seemed not to be going anywhere.

This was luxury. Sara had not thought of work, Ken, or Richard since last night's dinner. She calculated that that was at least fourteen hours. A record. And one which she intended to break.

Normally she had to fight to steer her mind away from stressful subjects. Today her mind felt lazy and stimulated at the same time, and showed no interest in ruminating over her problems. She had turned off her BlackBerry, ensuring that no one would intentionally or otherwise pull her back into the pit of anxiety that had become her day-to-day existence.

When she left The Cardinal, she had driven across the city to visit Tony's father. He was in his garden, wrapping his rose bushes in burlap for the winter. Sara had met Howard Hamilton at several events at Tony's home and he greeted her with a kiss on the cheek. She noticed he had a musky smell that reminded her of Tony. Perhaps it was in the genes. He wore his gray, straight hair quite long for someone of his generation. It was tucked behind his ears. His equally gray eyebrows were two clutches of wiry hairs that sprang in several directions. Thick lenses supported by gray plastic rims magnified watery gray eyes. A gray cotton shirt topped gray twill pants. Was he monochromatic by design?

He had insisted she have a cup of tea with him, and the weather had been just warm enough to sit at the green wrought-iron table in a corner of the garden.

She had spent a great deal of time trying to think up a plausible opener to the subject of Judge Jamieson, but it hadn't been necessary. When she asked how well he had known the judge, Tony's father had seemed not in the least curious as to why she would be interested in Judge Jamieson. Perhaps after eighty some years of life, nothing was curious.

He distinctly remembered when he first met Jamieson. He remembered it so clearly, he said, because Teddy Jamieson had been with her aunt. "Your Aunt Kate was the kind of girl," he stopped to correct himself. "I guess that's politically incorrect these days. The kind of young woman," he continued, "that a young man would not forget. She was distinctively beautiful. Huge dark eyes with unusual thick, straight lashes that she would use with great effect to either hide her eyes when she chose to be mysterious or to peek from under when she was being coy or flirtatious, which was most of the time. Her straight talk let you know, though, that being a flirtatious female and being totally in charge were not mutually exclusive. She would frequently tell people to 'Go to hell' when she didn't agree with them, and with a vehemence in her tone that suggested she meant it literally. It wasn't the kind of language expected of young ladies in those days." Hamilton laughed at the memory. "But she carried it off with panache. Yes, that's the best way to describe Kate; she had panache. But panache with a hard edge. I remember thinking that here was one woman I would not want to scorn."

Hamilton paused to add sugar to his tea. He tasted it and still not satisfied, added more, before he continued. "Pretty soon I was being invited to Jamieson's cottage at The Point in the summer. It wasn't really a cottage of course. More like a summer estate. The place was always packed with people. Teddy's family, his mother and father were both alive at that time, his brother Sebastian and his wife and son, Teddy's friends, the housekeeper and her husband, who was chauffeur and handyman, as well as their children and sundry other staff. It always used to amaze me how they managed to be prepared every weekend for an unplanned number of people. There was a standing invitation for any friends to drop in at the last minute and spend the weekend or, during the summer, perhaps stay for weeks. I guess it was the staff that had the headache. But they didn't seem to mind. In fact they seemed to consider it a privilege to serve the Jamiesons."

His eyes had left hers early in his story, and he gazed off into the distance, staying there after he had stopped speaking. She knew he had slipped back into his youth and for a moment she felt nostalgia for a time she had never experienced but unaccountably felt a longing for. She hesitated to interrupt his memories, and so sipped her tea and listened to the robins calling back and forth from one spruce tree to another. Shouldn't they be heading south by now?

Sara shuffled through the items from Aunt Kate's archive that she had brought with her and pulled out a photo. Her rustling reminded Hamilton that he had a guest.

She pushed the picture towards him. "I think I have identified my aunt and Judge Jamieson in this picture. Do you remember the others?"

He took so long to answer that at first she thought he had been unsuccessfully searching his brain for their identities. When he finally spoke, it was with assurance.

"Of course I remember them. This was the Group, as they referred to themselves. You've already picked out the leaders. The good-looking blond kid on Teddy's right was Harper, a bit effeminate I always thought; in fact Teddy often played his defender. Next to him is Jane Stewart, the poor girl who died so tragically."

Sara had thought it might have been Stewart, but hadn't been sure because the photo was faded and the young woman was looking away from the camera.

"And on the other end is a fellow by the name of Kendall whom I don't remember a whole lot about except he was the practical joker, always throwing people in the water and putting whoopee cushions on chairs. And the blond woman beside him was someone who appeared occasionally and her name escapes me. It's sad to think that Kate and Teddy are both gone."

"You aren't in the photo?'

"No, I was an occasional visitor. Most members of the Group either spent the whole summer with Teddy or their families had cottages of their own on the lake. I suspect most of them are gone."

"How did the judge die?" She tried to sound casual.

"I was at his funeral and, from what I heard there, I gather it was his heart."

A voice from the other side of the high privacy fence interrupted them.

"Mr. Howard?"

Hamilton twisted a paper napkin and stared down at the table for a moment before he answered.

"Yes, I'll be right there," he called.

"Excuse me for a moment. It's the handyman. I need an estimate on repairing the front steps. I'll just be a minute."

Sara was glad to have a few moments to formulate questions that would get at the information she wanted. The difficulty was she didn't know what she was looking for. When he returned she chose, "What do you remember about my aunt and Teddy Jamieson? Were they a couple?"

"Not officially, although Teddy was often your aunt's escort to formal functions. The rest of the Group, plus a number of what you might call part-time members, were always with them too. But there was something about the way they responded to each other that suggested a long-standing relationship. They definitely cared a great deal for one another."

"My aunt left a box of her mementos to me. There are several articles on Jane Stewart's death. That must have been a horrible experience for all of you."

"Yes, what can one say? Jane met a terrible too-early death. She was a close member of the Group. I think today's young people would say she was tight with the other Group members. Her death left its mark on everyone."

Hamilton's attention was caught by a gray squirrel, sporting a thick winter coat and sitting at the edge of an empty flowerbed.

"Ah, there he is. This fellow visits me every day. He's collecting his store of nuts for the winter and he has discovered that charming me is much easier than competing with the others for whatever nature may still be providing."

He drew three almonds from his pocket and held out his hand. Sara would have been nervous. She had heard that squirrels could be vicious and their bites particularly difficult to heal.

The squirrel darted forward, took the nuts one by one, found room for them in its cheek and then darted off. Hamilton watched the squirrel search for an appropriate storage place for its harvest and Sara took the time to do a mental review of the questions she wanted to ask. Two more to go.

"My aunt and Judge Jamieson seem not to have been in touch for many years. Do you have any idea when they reconnected?"

"No, but as you probably know, your aunt was at Teddy's Order of Canada ceremony and she and I spoke. I remember her saying how they were occasionally in touch and how good it is to know that good friendship is always there no matter how many years pass and that these are the people we turn to in the end."

"And that was in the early nineties, wasn't it?"

"One loses track of time but yes, it must have been. Your aunt was still actively running her galleries and it was just after *Toronto Life* ran that article on her as a woman of influence. I remember because we talked about it. She laughed about it but I could tell that for her it was confirmation of what she had been working for all her life."

"Yes, she did achieve her public goals. But I wonder whether she was lonely. I have this romantic idea that she loved Teddy Jamieson and that for some reason they didn't end up together and she was never interested in anyone else."

"That's possible. I believe they did love one another, at some level at least."

"Then why didn't they end up together? Did someone come between them?"

"It's possible."

She felt that Howard Hamilton had more knowledge to share but she didn't know the questions to tap into it. They chatted for a few more minutes, mostly about Tony, what a great son he was and how his father worried that he hadn't brought him up to be assertive enough. Sara could see that Howard Hamilton was lonely and that he would happily chat for the whole afternoon. She made an excuse and left, promising to visit again soon, though they both knew that was very unlikely.

Now, as she nibbled her way through one of the Lost Camel's spectacular cheese melts, she jotted down notes from her conversation with Howard Hamilton on the long yellow notepad. She wiped sticky fingers on several unsubstantial paper napkins and then pulled the clippings about the murder from her portfolio. She was drawn once again to the faded photo of the young victim. The murdered girl's strikingly beautiful portrait locked eyes with her for a compelling instant. Death had not completely taken Jane Stewart's power. Sara rubbed goose bumps from her arms and set the clipping aside.

She revisited the photo taken on the church steps at Stewart's funeral and examined it with new interest; she was now certain that this was Teddy and Kate's group. Just as Hamilton had suggested, there was a blond girl, not terribly remarkable; a fragile-looking but handsome young man, also blond, probably the fellow Hamilton had referred to as Harper; and the dark woman she was now certain was her aunt as she noticed for the first time a trait that was definitely Kate's. The young woman stood with her left hand on her hip but not in the usual fashion. The hand was bent backward so that the top of the hand, rather than the palm, rested on her hip. That pose was one of Kate's trademarks. The other two men were dark. She guessed the taller one between her aunt and Harper would be Teddy. She couldn't see the features well enough to go by them but the judge had been a relatively tall man and the other fellow was stocky and shorter than Kate. He must be Kendall, the prankster. Even in this solemn shot, there did appear to be something impish about him.

The young faces increased her curiosity and drew her back to the faded exercise book that had intrigued Chloe. It had served Kate as an all-purpose notebook. Lists of expenses: *stockings 69 cents, nail polish 25 cents,* were interspersed with to-do lists: *write a thank you note to Mrs. Jamieson for her hospitality, organize fall wardrobe and call Holts to book a fitting,* and brief notes that sporadically diarized snippets of Kate's life. Sara skimmed the pages looking for references to 1948. Several were headed "Summer, 1948."

Another just right day. Swimming and lawn tennis and then gin tonics and chatter on the veranda. We occasionally run out of the first but never the latter. Kendall does get trying at times, just too silly for words but he has a good heart and Teddy considers him a good friend so we all suffer good humoredly. (Alright I must fess up. My smile does occasionally slip a bit. Last night I threw his infernal whoopee cushion into the lake.)

And then a few pages later:

A rare few moments alone with Teddy tonight. We sat on the dock and watched a meteor shower. The air was cool. Autumn is creeping back. Teddy put his arm around me to prevent my getting a chill and I received a peck on the cheek as a good night. I must quit hoping for more than Teddy has to offer. Damn! Damn! Damn!

The last sentence was puzzling. What had Kate meant by "more than Teddy has to offer"?

Sara glanced at her watch. She had lost track of time. Pauline had said she would be at home at four o'clock. She had only twenty minutes to get to the other side of town. She quickly packed her yellow pad, pen, and clippings back into her small leather portfolio and rushed from the café. She was a short way up the street when she heard something drop. By the time she turned to look behind her, a blue baseball cap was bent over her pen. A small white hand with perfectly manicured nails offered it up to her. She took it with thanks and hurried on. The figure stood up, lifting its head to show the Blue Jays logo, and followed her down the street.

She found Pauline's address in an assisted housing project. It was tenanted by people who could not afford to fully support themselves. Many were on welfare; others, like Pauline, worked hard but struggled to make ends meet. Rents paid were based on income. Pauline probably paid more than many of her neighbors but certainly didn't get any more in return.

Sara parked at the back in a spot that she assumed was meant for visitors. It read - - - - t - r - - rk - - g. The rest of the letters had been worn or scraped away. The apartment was a fifties gray nondescript building with tiny balconies clinging, often precariously, to its sides. There was slight evidence that the balconies had at one time been blue, but they were now rusted so badly that when a tenant stepped out to shake a dust mop, a shower of rust was dislodged by the movement and the brown flakes floated to the ground like miniature autumn leaves.

Sara pulled open a grimy front door. The smells of living had accumulated for so long that they had broken from the confines of the apartments and hallways and now permeated the front lobby. Pungent East and West Indian spices merged with the smells of fried cabbage, baked beans and people.

Pauline lived on the twelfth floor. The elevator creaked slowly to its destination and Sara wondered how often it was inspected. It stopped with a jolt as the needle moved just past the twelve, and the doors opened reluctantly, offering her a dim hallway.

She started off to the right and then realized the numbers were going in the wrong direction and so turned and worked her way back past the elevator. The walls were scuffed and obscenities had been scrawled on them with black marker, pencil, and lipstick. The painters Sara had watched on Queen Street would need a lot of paint and a lot of time to cover the marks of anger, frustration, and perhaps plain boredom, left here. Someone had tried to wash off the graffiti next to Pauline's door, number 1265. They had managed to obliterate the words but left several dark smears on the pea soup walls.

Sara's knock was answered by a young girl of about ten with huge dark eyes set above chubby cheeks. Her hair was plaited close to her head and tied with pink plastic bobbles.

Sara introduced herself: "Hello, I'm Sara Porter. Is your mother in?"

"Yes, ma'am." The big eyes looked down at her pink sneakers and the soft voice was barely audible.

"Sissy, is that Mrs. Porter?" Pauline's voice came from behind a closed door down a short hallway.

"Yes, Mama." Sissy's voice was raised just slightly in recognition of the distance her response had to travel. Sara couldn't imagine it having penetrated the bedroom door but Pauline must have adjusted her hearing to accommodate her daughter's wispy voice.

"Well, let her in then, child," she called back.

"Yes, Mama." The girl crept slowly backward pulling the door with her, both hands on the knob. "You can sit in the living room if you like." Sissy looked up at her appraisingly. Sara must have passed, for Sissy added, "The blue chair is the best one. Daddy sits in it when he's home. He's not home now though so you can have it."

Sara accepted the offer and marveled that this bright cheery apartment could be just inches away from the dark hallway she had just left. Second-hand furniture had been painted yellow and cushions were covered in various shades of blue. A corner table was full of family photos, many taken in front of Caribbean homes or on Caribbean beaches. Windowsills were full of pots of flowering plants and herbs. Freshly starched white lace curtains framed them. The fresh scent of the herbs mingled with the smell of something sweetly spiced coming from the kitchen. How appropriate, thought Sara. She knew that Pauline was from Grenada, often referred to as the island of spice. Sara and Richard had holidayed there one year and had been charmed by the beauty of the island and its people. She remembered most vividly the story of a town in the north of the tiny island, called Sauters. According to legend, thousands of Carib Indians, who had been the first inhabitants of the island, terrified by invading Europeans, leaped to their death from a high cliff into the sea. The area had been called Sauters, from *sauter*, to jump, in French.

Pauline appeared, eyes heavy from sleep and dressed in a pink house dress. Her black sandals had been traded for fluffy red bedroom slippers.

"I'm afraid I'm cutting into your time off," said Sara, realizing how hard the woman worked and that her trip to work from here by local transit must take at least an hour.

"That's alright. My shift doesn't start until nine. Will you have a slice of Sissy's spice cake? She's a real good cook for a little girl, aren't you, Honey?" Pauline's arm slipped around her daughter's waist and pulled her tight to her side. Sissy nodded proudly.

The Lost Camel had more than satisfied Sara's appetite but she was afraid that perhaps Pauline had asked her daughter to bake because she was coming and so said that she would love some.

In spite of Pauline's hospitality, Sara sensed wariness in her eyes and in her manner. They made small talk about her aunt until Sissy arrived with a piece of cake that must have been a quarter of the entire cake and a large glass of lemonade.

"I was wondering about Aunt Kate's last couple of days. I guess to be more specific, I'm curious about a clipping that was on top of the pile of things in the box she left me."

Pauline said nothing.

"It was the obituary of Judge Jamieson. It had been cut from the *Globe* the day she died."

Pauline looked away into a corner of the room beyond.

"It seemed curious. I asked myself two things: one, where would she have gotten it? She wasn't able to read the paper herself, and two, why would she have torn it out?"

Pauline's eyes strolled slowly back to meet Sara's and rested there.

"I don't know why, Miss, but I know how. We have a volunteer, Mrs. Amos, who comes around visiting every day. She reads to the residents. She occasionally reads local news or maybe general interest like the heat wave that killed people in Europe this summer or how older women are dating younger men, things like that. But mostly she reads them the obituaries."

"The obituaries?" Sara communicated both surprise and distaste.

"Yes, that's what I thought at first. How morbid! In fact, I was going to suggest my supervisor speak to her about her choice of reading material, but then I realized that the residents like to hear them. Maybe it's because at their age they will inevitably hear about people they know or maybe it's comforting that others have gone before. Perhaps it's a sense that if they can do it I can do it. Whatever it is, they like it. Mrs. Amos would visit your aunt last and always left the paper with her. I never knew if she could read it herself but she would struggle to turn a page or two after Mrs. Amos left. She must have managed to tear the obituary out."

"And you have no idea why she would have done that."

"No, Miss. How would I know? You know she could barely speak and even if she could have she wouldn't be telling me why she did things."

"Did Judge Jamieson ever visit my aunt?"

Pauline's eyes darted back to the far corner of the room.

"I don't keep track of who visits the residents. That's not my job." A truculence that didn't suit Pauline had slipped into her voice.

Sara was trained in conflict resolution and had received many accolades for her ability to get people to open up even in stressful situations. She had always thought that it wasn't anything in particular that she did or said but more her manner that created a sense of safety. It certainly wasn't working this time. Sara decided to try empathy.

"Of course, Pauline. I wouldn't expect you to keep track of visitors. I know how busy you are and how good you are at what you do. I just thought you might have noticed him." Sara meant what she said. Pauline, in her mind, was an extraordinary caregiver. She had seen others sitting at the nurses' station chatting while residents bells rang and rang. People left sitting in need of bedpans, water or perhaps something even more serious. But Pauline was always running, and running with a smile. "I'll be there in just a minute, Honey," she would call in one door as she ran to another resident's aid.

Pauline, Sissy and Sara sat in silence, listening to the fridge hum loudly and then shudder into silence. Children chased each other down the hall, a man and woman shouted at one another and a door slammed loudly.

"Sissy," Pauline didn't move. "Go to your room and do your homework."

"Yes, Mama" The girl wriggled her way to the front of the sofa and slipped off it. She left the living room without looking at either of them, her footsteps as soft as her voice.

Pauline waited for the click of Sissy's bedroom door. Her eyes stayed in her corner retreat as she spoke. "You have the right to know but you must not repeat what I'm going to tell you. If you do, I will lose my job. I will lose my certification. I'll never be able to work again. Maybe I should have stopped her. It would have been so easy to stop her. It was harder to do nothing but the lady deserved respect. And I tried to show her respect."

"You mean that my aunt committed suicide?" The disbelief was evident in Sara's voice. Kate had always been a fighter.

Pauline nodded, still not looking at her.

"But how could she have? And how do you know? The doctor didn't know."

Pauline's eyes moved back to Sara, faster than a stroll this time but much slower than a dart.

"A couple of days before she died, the judge came to visit her. I was going into her room with some fresh linen. They didn't see me come in and I saw a bunch of pills spread out on her bedcovers and the judge was counting them and putting them into a little blue cardboard box that she always kept in her drawer. You know, the kind jewelry comes in.

"He was whispering but I caught the gist of it. He was saying that according to a friend of his who was a physician, she had plenty and did not have to worry about it not working. She was nodding and looking so relieved. I stepped back out of the room and I listened for a few minutes. I could only catch a few words. He was saying how they had both made decisions that once acted upon could not be changed, and it was reassuring that they supported one another.

"The pills looked like the alprazolam tablets she was given every night to help her sleep. She had probably been spitting them out and saving them up. I decided not to tell anyone. I know what I did was probably unethical, maybe even a sin, but she was such a great lady when she came to us and then with each stroke she lost more and more of her independence and dignity. A great lady shouldn't have to suffer the indignity of having someone else bathe her or take her to the bathroom. I saw the spark in her eyes fade every day. She had the right to choose."

Pauline's eyes moved slowly away again, this time traveling in the opposite direction to the window. They filled with tears.

The huge tears flowed over the rims and found the deep vertical crevices that her ready smile had patiently dug and let themselves be carried down the long dark face to the chin line from where they leapt onto her lap. Sara thought of Sauters and saw Carib Indians leaping to their death.

Pauline did nothing to stop the flow. She did not close her eyes nor dab at them with the tissue that was scrunched in her hand. She did not apologize. She just sat, perfectly erect, staring out the window waiting for the tears to complete their task of washing away her sadness and guilt.

12

The sun had been shining when Sara entered Pauline's building but as she left, a sudden shower descended carrying the fresh scent of ozone with it. She envied Pauline her cleansing. Sara had never been able to cry like that. She envisioned stopping in the midst of her dash to her car and standing here in the middle of the parking lot with the rain not just washing over her but passing through her and washing away all the pieces of debris that had accumulated and weighed her down. But she knew that as they washed away she would have to examine each. She opted to jump into her car and keep her mind busy instead.

The shower became a downpour just as she slammed her door shut. The kind of rain windshield wipers can't keep up with. She didn't mind a slow trip home. There was nothing awaiting her but her archeological dig and she had always found her car a great incubator for thoughts. She pushed in a CD of piano concertos and Tchaikovsky charged into her space. She quickly turned it off. The sound of the rain and the slap of the wipers were more soothing and conducive to thinking.

Strangely, she found the news of Aunt Kate's suicide not in the least disturbing. In fact she felt uplifted. The most distressing part of Kate's death had been the sense that it was something that had been done to her, as had so many things in the past year since her first stroke. The most defining characteristic of Kate McPherson had been that what Kate wanted, Kate got. She was always in control. To know that Kate had been the one in charge at the end was confirmation that, in spite of appearances, Kate had triumphed.

"Good for you Kate." Sara punched a clenched fist into the air, banging her knuckles on the sunroof in the process.

But what about the judge? Pauline had mentioned his saying that they had both made irreversible decisions. Did he commit suicide too? But why? He wasn't in Aunt Kate's situation. Tony's father had said he had died from a heart attack. If his irreversible decision wasn't suicide, what was it?

As she approached the Drug Mart she remembered she had planned to stop to pick up a few things on the way home. It was usually hard to find a parking spot but today the lot was nearly empty. People must be waiting for the rain to let up. She reached into the back seat for the Drug Mart's sales flier she had pulled from the recycling bin as she left home this morning. She thought she had noticed a special on tortilla chips and salsa, Chloe's and James's favorite snack. She was working on the theory that if the kitchen cupboards were not completely empty and held at least a few of her children's favorite foods, she might see them more often and for a little longer. Surely it would take at least ten minutes to down a bag of chips.

Not that she was likely to see James for even ten minutes any time soon. James was the adventurous one. He had chosen a university that had allowed him to be as far from home as possible and still be in Canada. Within a week of graduating from the University of Victoria, he was on a plane to Thailand. He planned to travel as far and as long as the money he had saved from waiting tables at the campus pub would take him. He called home every few weeks and Sara tried not to think about him in between, because when she did, every possible nightmare filled her mind. James lying ill with malaria on the floor of a little shack on a beach. James attacked and robbed and left for dead on a lonely road that was little more than a footpath. And worse, James arrested, wrongfully, of course, for drug possession, cowering barefooted and with torn shirt in a dank cell. In each scenario he was whimpering as he used to as a child when he would wake in the night, his legs aching. Growing pains, the doctor had said. She would lie down beside him in his bottom bunk, barely awake herself, rubbing his calves until he fell back to sleep.

She glanced through the flier again, waiting for the rain to let up enough to allow her to sprint into the store. She looked at the bottom to check the sale dates. The fliers were usually delivered a couple of days before the items went on sale. Perhaps she was too early. "Sale prices apply from Oct. 1st to the 7th." She reminded herself of today's date and read it again. Odd, the flier was over a week old. The knowledge set an uncomfortable feeling in the pit of her stomach. Perhaps she shouldn't have completely ignored Mr. Dempster. She supposed that even paranoid busybodies could occasionally be right. Well, she wouldn't think about it right now. She filed it in the back of her mind, recognizing that it was getting rather crowded back there.

Her cell phone beeped. She'd left it in the car all day so she wouldn't feel guilty not answering it. She might as well at least see who had been trying to contact her. Chloe, Tony, Chloe, Dina, Ken, Chloe, Ken, Chloe. Four messages from Chloe. She felt a mother's panic and quickly dialed Chloe's cell. Chloe answered on the first ring.

"Mom?"

"Are you OK, Chloe?"

"Yeah, I'm OK. As OK as I can be, I guess. But where have you been? I've been trying to reach you since this morning."

"What do you mean you are as OK as you can be? What's going on?"

"Mom, you haven't heard?"

"Heard what?" Sara's voice rose with concern and impatience.

Chloe was uncharacteristically silent.

"Chloeee!"

"Mom, it's about Diane."

"You mean your father's Diane?" Her neck muscles had constricted and she tried to keep the tightness from her voice, all the while asking herself why she or Chloe should care what happened to that woman.

"Yes, it's been in the papers and on TV, Mom. I can't believe you haven't heard."

"Chloe, for God's sake tell me in the very next sentence what you're talking about."

"Diane's dead, Mom. She was murdered."

Sara was responseless. She had nothing to say. She watched a woman holding a newspaper over her head splash through puddles as she ran for the Drug Mart door. She imagined the woman, at home, drying her wet shoes with paper towels and setting them on a radiator to dry. But then she wondered if they hadn't turned the furnace on for the winter yet whether the shoes would dry themselves overnight.

She forced her mind back to her own life. She would have to find something to say. She searched but her mind seemed totally empty. She borrowed Chloe's last word and managed to add a question mark to it.

"Murdered?"

She said the word but shock prevented its horror from registering. Sara's mind looked for other places to rest.

"Where are you?" she asked.

"I'm with Dad. He's booked into Sutton Place. The police won't let him back into the house yet."

The house. She and Richard had found that house together. They had thought that perhaps they needed a change after the children had left home. They both loved it and almost put in an offer. But then Richard decided that that wasn't change enough for him.

Richard. He must be in pain. In spite of everything, she felt an acute need to comfort him. To put her arms around him and tell him everything would be alright. Words came.

"Chloe, let me speak with your father."

His voice was husky from crying.

"Richard, I'm so sorry. I'm coming right over."

"No, that's not necessary, Sara. I'm alright. Diane's parents got in this afternoon and I have to go to the funeral home with them to make the arrangements."

Once again she had nothing of her own to say. She took his last two words and managed to scrounge two of her own.

"The arrangements? Of course."

13

His blue Honda Civic had followed her Volvo into the Drug Mart parking lot and pulled into the spot right next to her. He expected her to get out quickly and go into the store but instead she sat there. He could see her clearly through the rain-streaked windows, sandy blond hair falling over her face as she looked down to read something. Her hair was just long enough to touch the shoulders of the bright red blouse that had been his beacon all day long.

Waiting for her this morning, up the street from her home, he had been unsure. Perhaps he needed to restrain himself. He must remember the purpose of the mission and not let mere pleasure get in its way. But then he tried to rationalize that this was part of the mission. He must find out what she knew and then decide what her fate would be. Yet he knew, if he examined what he was doing rationally, that his following her would not pass the test. Following her was unlikely to reveal what she knew. But he was enjoying what he recognized to be the pleasure of the hunt.

After that analysis he had started his car, ready to abandon the chase. At that same moment she stepped out of her front door and looked upward, arm outstretched, palm held up as though checking for rain. When he saw her bright red shirt he knew it was an omen. Little did she know, he thought, that when she was selecting it this morning she was choosing it for him. Wherever she went it would be easy for him to follow her. Twenty minutes later she had backed her car out of the drive. He let her get part way down the block before he followed.

It had been an exhilarating day. He had been close by her all day and she had had no idea. He had been a bit concerned when she had turned into the Cardinal facility. He had had to be careful and was disappointed that on the very first stop he hadn't been able to get out and follow her inside. He might be recognized there. If someone spoke to him, it might draw attention to him.

Instead he had waited across the road, positioned so that he could see up the long drive. It had been one of his shorter waits of the day. In less than ten minutes, her car started to head back down the drive. And then almost immediately it stopped. "Uh-huh," he said out loud to himself as he noted the brief tête à tête between the two women. And then reprimanded himself. He had made a rule for himself some time ago. He was not allowed to talk to himself out loud.

But that was the only self reprimand of the day. For the most part he had been highly pleased with himself. His driving skills were extraordinary. Not once, in spite of the fact she had taken the 401, as well as the busiest downtown streets, had he lost her. And then of course, there were his street smarts and intelligence, which had always held him in good stead. A psychologist once told his mother that his IQ was the highest he'd ever encountered. She flaunted that information often. At first he had believed it to be a sign that she was indeed proud of him, although in his whole life she had never told him he had done anything well. But as he grew older, he realized that it was not because of pride that she ensured people knew of his intellect, but in an attempt to excuse him.

"Well you know, my boy has an exceptionally high IQ and we all know geniuses have their idiosyncrasies," she would say.

The highlight of today had been his picking up the dropped pen in front of the Lost Camel. In handing it back his finger had briefly brushed her wrist. Electricity charged through his body. And yet she hurried away not noticing. And the irony of it all awed him. The unnoticed person who had given back her pen had the power to take something so much more important from her. If it came to that she would notice him then.

But right now he was uncomfortable. He was stiff from sitting in the car all day. He didn't like the idea that his body reminded him of its presence much more than it used to.

And now he was hungry. He had missed his lunch entirely and it was his habit to take dinner early, just about now in fact. His stomach rumbled. He did not like even the mildest form of physical discomfort and he now felt he was truly suffering. In addition to being hungry he was badly in need of a bathroom.

The woman still sat in her car. Now she had the cell phone to her ear. He was angry with her for wasting his time and causing his discomfort. He wanted to shout at her to hurry up and do whatever she came here to do. Instead, he reassured himself that she would soon be heading home anyway and it was time for him to leave her. He drove away in search of physical relief.

A small strip mall stretched the length of the next block. He saw a sign for a fast food restaurant. That would have to do. He hated using public washrooms but had no choice. He would have to cope.

He had to go to the back of the restaurant and down narrow steps to the restroom. From his experience, this was not a good sign. The best-kept restrooms were always on the main floor. The "Gents" door that greeted him was typically dirty. He used his shirt-tail to grasp the doorknob. He must remember to put it into the laundry as soon as he gets home. The room was a tiny space with only one stall and a urinal. The stall was being vacated by a young man covered with tattoos. Expecting the fellow to stop at the sink he stood back by the door to give him room, but instead the boy grunted a "'Scuse me" and pushed by him and out the door without stopping. He shook his head and almost said "Barbarian" out loud but made himself say it only in his head. How could anyone go to the toilet and not wash their hands? Well, let them get that flesh-eating disease and whatever else might be going around.

He squeezed into the stall and looked with disgust at the rust and filth that had accumulated on the bowl. Much worse was probably growing on the black toilet seat. But the churning of his bowels forced him to problem solve rather than leave. He took a piece of toilet paper and used it to protect his hands as he flushed the toilet. He waited for the tank to refill and then flushed again. That should get rid of some of the germs in the bowl should he splash on himself. Then he took strips of toilet paper as his mother had trained him and folded them just so to cover the seat. Just as he was about to sit down he brushed against a piece of his makeshift seat cover and it slid to the floor. Now in real distress, he started again and had to sit down before the seat was perfectly covered.

He had two more public restroom hurdles to get over. First, hand washing. He grimaced at the sink that was lined with greasy gray sediment. Thank goodness they had paper towels and not just those hot-air things. He pulled down a paper towel and used it to turn on the taps and push the button of the soap dispenser. Hands washed, he let the taps run until he pulled down another towel which he used to protect his hand as he turned the taps off.

After he dried his hands and carefully deposited the brown paper towel into the wastebasket, he checked his reflection in the cracked mirror. His cap wasn't quite right. He raised his left hand to the back of the cap and held it snugly while he jiggled the peak into its proper position with his right. Down just slightly, until it almost hid the blue eyes that were so pale they were almost colorless, rimmed by eyelashes so fair they were almost invisible. Much better. If one were to wear a Blue Jays cap, one must wear it properly.

Now for the last hurdle. Another paper towel to open the door, keep the door open with his foot while he tossed the paper towel back into the room into the wastebasket and let the door slam behind him. He escaped up the stairs germ-free.

He would not of course eat here. He always checked out the restroom first to determine the hygiene of the establishment. This one definitely didn't pass. He gave himself another word of congratulation as he noticed the tattooed boy with the unwashed hands behind the counter. He was always right about these things. "Disgusting," he allowed himself to say out loud as he left.

14

Not a bad day's work. Carson was pleased with what they had accomplished. They had confirmed that Richard Porter had indeed been at the dinner, which Carson had had no doubt about anyway. In addition, they discovered that Porter had been given a lift by a friend and arrived home too late to have murdered his live-in girlfriend. In fact, he had been dropped off just a few minutes before the 911 call had come in. So they could assuredly remove Richard Porter from the list of suspects. Some interesting, maybe important, stuff on the wife, Sara Porter. Unfortunately, they hadn't been able to see her personally yet, but they had enough hard information to make a good showing at the Inspector's four o'clock meeting.

They arrived at the station at two minutes past four. They would have made it on time if Kirpatrick hadn't insisted he couldn't last another hour without eating. He could feel his blood sugar dropping, he said. He had wanted to stop at some vegetarian spot but Carson nixed that. They'd never make the meeting on time. He compromised by speeding through a McDonald's drive-through, slowing down just long enough to order "whatever is sitting ready under the heat lamp," grab it, and hand the bewildered young woman behind the window a five-dollar bill, saying keep the change.

"This stuff is 99.9 percent fat," Kirpatrick grumbled.

"I thought you were worried about your blood sugar not your cholesterol." Kirpatrick was going to have to become a little less choosey or the job of a detective would become a hardship for him. Missing meals and grabbing whatever was available when one did eat were the norm.

"Simpson doesn't accept anybody being late for his meetings," Carson continued. "And believe me, if we're late, while he is carefully carving us up you will be wishing you could trade the experience for both dropping blood sugar and rising cholesterol. And then when I'm through with you, you'll never ask for lunch again."

Carson watched Kirpatrick squirm a little in his seat, unfold the rolled top of the take-out bag, wrinkle his nose in disgust and pull out the Big Mac like it was a dead thing. He gave it a "God what am I going to do with this thing" look and then took a reluctant bite or two. He probably needed a drink to wash it down but Carson hadn't stopped long enough for that. Kirpatrick slipped the rest back into the bag.

Carson couldn't resist ribbing him.

"That's not enough to help your blood sugar."

"Oh, yeah. That will do it. I feel much better already."

Carson grabbed the bag from Kirpatrick's lap and wolfed down the rest, forced an exaggerated belch, and tossed the wrappings over his shoulder into the back seat. He smiled to himself. Let the new initiate wonder what kind of a boor he'd drawn for a partner.

When they arrived at headquarters, they didn't wait for the elevator but took the stairs two at a time and slid around the half-closed door of the Inspector's office just as he began to clear his throat. Simpson checked his watch for a long second and frowned in their direction but must have decided he had more important matters to deal with. Another reprieve.

Carson tried to pant for breath quietly. Kirpatrick leaned casually against the wall and looked as though he had taken the elevator.

Each detective gave his report. Most had only routine stuff. Perkins had the forensics' garbage report to relay. He always asked to analyze it. According to him, garbage picking should be embraced as a form of psychoanalysis. "It's not what people keep in their lives that tells you most about them but what they throw away," he reminded them regularly. He had become known around the division as the garbage man, ostensibly because he was usually the one who was looking for clues in the report of the victim's debris. But those using the epithet were referring also to the garbage that poured out of his mouth.

The most thorough picking through of Diane Brooks' and Richard Porter's garbage, however, had produced little. They had had Thai food delivered recently and seemed to favor seafood; they drank expensive wine and they would not receive any award for helping to save the planet, as both wine bottles and some newspapers were in the garbage rather than in the recycling bins. Perkins had found no connection between any of this and the murder.

McNair and Stephens were next. They looked at one another, not having decided beforehand who would give their report. McNair jerked his head at Stephens indicating she should speak. Detective Constable Stephens had moved to Homicide recently from the special crimes unit. She was far from the first woman to work homicide but she had done a better job of fitting in than most. She had a serene confidence whether being tested by the men or at a crime scene. She had made no attempt to be like the guys and so had easily become one of them. Her blond hair was clipped back and she had a crisp, efficient way about her.

She and McNair had interviewed the neighbors and the housekeeper. No one really knew Brooks and Porter, as they had moved in only a few weeks before. The woman living on the south side said she had spoken to the deceased once. She had been doing some gardening in the front yard when Diane Brooks was returning from jogging one morning last week. They chatted for a few minutes and Brooks seemed nice enough, but the neighbor hadn't gotten any information from her. She said Brooks had somehow deflected any personal questions. She had the impression that Brooks wasn't the "neighborly type." The other neighbors had not even spotted the couple, let alone spoken to them.

Fingerprints in the kitchen had been confirmed as those of Brooks, Porter and the housekeeper. No others whatsoever. It looked as though they had lived a solitary existence since moving in.

The housekeeper had been off for a couple of days preparing for her daughter's wedding. She had been with them only a couple of weeks, worked afternoons and seldom saw them. Brooks did freelance writing and worked from home and so she was usually there, but, according to the housekeeper, was always locked in her office. She found Brooks nice enough but said her employer communicated, for the most part, only to give the woman instructions. She had seen Richard Porter only twice and described him as "so charming and handsome."

When she was finished, Stephens looked up briefly and gave a "That's it, what can you do?" shrug, hands turned palms up in front of her.

It was Greally's turn. Everyone else had spoken from their place. He moved up to the Inspector's desk, which Simpson always vacated during meetings, and hitched one hip over a corner. He leaned over to pick an invisible something from the leg of his navy Italian suit and straightened the yellow tie that sported a hand-painted parrot. Carson shuddered at the waste of good silk.

"Well," Greally started, "I haven't got a whole lot to add."

Not smart, thought Carson. You never start a report declaring you've got nothing. Carson mentally gave Greally a lecture: "You present the nothing in such a way as to make it look like it's something." It was a point he would expect to have to make to a rookie but not to a ten-year veteran like Greally.

Greally had been assigned to check out Richard Porter's colleagues. Only a few had met Diane Brooks. Richard seemed happier than he had in years. No one knew of anyone who would have a motive to harm Ms. Brooks. None thought that Porter had any enemies either. He was well-respected and well-liked by both colleagues and clients.

The Inspector broke in with a bellow, "Jesus. You people conducted dozens of interviews today and you're telling me you got nothing? I'm meeting with the commander and the superintendent in half an hour and I'm walking in there empty-handed? Is that what you're telling me? On top of which I am being hounded by the press and I have no doubt that the mayor will want us to call a press conference to reassure the citizens that they are perfectly safe because we are hot on the trail of the murderer. The only way I'm going to be able to say that is if I make the whole damn thing up because you people are giving me nothing. For God's sake somebody tell me you've got a morsel I can offer to stave off the vultures."

Carson cleared his throat.

"Well Carson, let's hear it. If it's worth hearing that is. If it's as useless as the rest of this stuff, don't waste my time."

Carson started by quoting pieces of the interviews that confirmed Porter's whereabouts and innocence. He took his time building up to the more interesting bit.

"We also talked with Tony Hamilton who is a friend and colleague of Sara Porter's. He has also been a close friend of Richard Porter's since university. In the interview Hamilton immediately showed signs of discomfort and with a little prodding told us about his having had dinner with Sara Porter last evening. They were at Primavera in Little Italy and Porter had quite a bit to drink. Hamilton said he had been concerned about Porter's drinking since her husband left. It apparently consistently goes beyond one or two social drinks. But it wasn't just her drinking that had bothered him but what she had said and her demeanor when she said it.

"According to Hamilton, Sara Porter is usually what he described as a nice and balanced individual. Last night, he said," Carson looked down and read from his notes, "'She was full of anger and – well – what I can only describe as hate. It was an entirely different Sara that I was seeing. Not just her words, but the anger in her voice, and most disturbing, the hate that she expressed with her eyes.' He went on to say that she told him that she had never hated anyone before but that she hated Diane Brooks. She added that she knew she would get over it eventually. However, there was one thing she would never be able to forgive, Richard Porter having a child with his new live-in."

Carson paused, waiting for everyone to remember that they had been told that Brooks was pregnant. When he could see by their renewed interest that they had, he continued, "When she said that, he said that she looked –" Carson searched through his notes again for a few minutes to find the exact word –"'ferocious.' Hamilton said the scene, and apparently it was a scene, had shaken him, because, as he said, it was so out of character.

"Ms. Porter had driven herself to the restaurant and Hamilton was concerned about her driving home. She insisted that she would have a couple of cups of coffee before leaving the restaurant and would be fine. Hamilton left her there at about nine thirty.

"We've tried a couple of times to see her but she has been away all day. Also, she has coincidently taken some leave from work, just e-mailing it in this morning. She is, however, in town. When we stopped in to see Richard Porter, he was on his way to make funeral arrangements, but he said he had spoken to her briefly. We are heading back to her place from here and then will catch the husband again a little later."

He had the Inspector's complete attention.

"Well, finally. We at least have a start." Simpson was rubbing his hands together.

"So you don't know what time she got home?"

"No, not yet but —"

"I've got some information on that," Greally interrupted. The Inspector's anger had knocked him from his perch on the corner of the desk and he wiggled his hip back onto it.

What the hell, thought Carson.

"When I was through with Porter's colleagues," Greally continued, "I had some time left and since no one had been assigned Sara Porter's neighbors yet, I thought I might as well get a start on those interviews.

"I spoke to this old guy next door. He said that he had seen two detectives earlier who had stopped at the Porter house but he said that they hadn't been interested in speaking to him."

Shit. Carson didn't allow a single body part, even a finger to respond. He conveyed nothing other than a look of mild professional interest. Kirpatrick's greenness showed as he looked down at the two size twelves that he couldn't stop from shuffling. Everyone else, including the Inspector, took a quick look in their direction. Everyone, that is, except Perkins who kept his eyes on Greally. A foul mouth but a good heart.

"So, anyway, this guy is a real talker and I've got detailed notes here. Half of it's probably useless but the key piece is that Sara Porter didn't return home last night until eleven thirty."

Simpson went from rubbing his hands together to rubbing them over one another as though washing them.

"Good work, Greally. That's the kind of initiative we need."

He stared at Carson for a full minute. "You two get that interview with Sara Porter, now." He used his pointer finger to jab the "now" at them.

Carson nodded casually, ensuring his relief didn't show. He had been sure Sara Porter was going to be pulled from them and handed to Greally. And he would have been kicking himself because he would have deserved it.

"And, Greally," added the Inspector as he checked his watch and headed for the door, "get over to Primavera and get whatever you can including the time she left the restaurant."

There had been a downpour much of the afternoon and heavy rain still fell. Carson had hastily left the car at the curb and they made a dash for it but arrived sodden. Carson's shirt clung to his chest. The car quickly became a mini steam-bath and both of them sank into inertia and their own thoughts. To interrupt the hypnotic *slap, slap* of the windshield wipers seemed to take more energy than either of them could muster.

After about fifteen minutes, the vent managed to conquer the interior mist, the rain began to let up and Carson turned the wipers down to low. Kirpatrick shook himself slightly as though kicking his mind back into gear. Perhaps it was actually the physical act of gathering courage.

"Do you think maybe we should have talked to that old geezer?" he asked tentatively.

Carson wanted to respond sarcastically but restrained himself from deflecting his self-anger onto Kirpatrick.

Instead he said, "*Hochmutt kommt vor dem fall.*"

"What?" Kirpatrick turned to him, his brow wrinkled right up to his gelled blond hair.

"It's a proverb that my German teacher in high school taught us. I'm not sure I've got it quite right but it's something like that."

"What's it mean?"

"'Pride cometh before the fall.' In this case perhaps we could stretch it to say, 'Arrogance comes before the fall.'"

Kirpatrick still didn't really get the connection but that was OK. Maybe he didn't need to get it. Maybe he would have responded to old Dempster if Carson hadn't set the lead in ignoring him.

He knew Kirpatrick had probably sat there for the last fifteen minutes wondering what the Inspector would think and whether his rising star had just plummeted earthward.

They passed a billboard advertising some kind of soft drink that read "Reach Out and Touch Somebody." Ads were crazy these days. They didn't seem to have anything to do with the product they were selling.

OK, he thought, Kirpatrick, here I come.

"Listen, don't worry about Simpson. First of all he's got too much on his mind to worry about a little slip-up. It's not one thing that counts. It's patterns he watches for. Slip up in the same way two or three times and then start worrying. Besides, he knows it was my goof-up, not yours. And finally worry more about Greally than the Inspector."

"What d'ya mean?" Kirpatrick's brow went into action again wrinkling and unwrinkling itself several times.

"Nobody else in that room would have pointed out someone else's slip-up. He deliberately dumped on us. Which may be why the Inspector seems to have ignored it. If we are lucky, it may backfire."

Kirpatrick sat looking out through his rain-streaked window for several seconds and then turned back to Carson.

"Would Greally have done the same if it had been someone else?"

"Maybe, maybe not."

"I'm assuming he doesn't know me well enough to be targeting me. What's he got against you?"

Carson was pulling up in front of Sara Porter's house for the third time that day.

"Maybe I'll tell you about it over a beer sometime," he said.

15

Words hadn't returned to Sara on the drive home. Not even enough to allow thought. The shock of Diane's death had left her mind unable to function beyond automatic pilot. But as she opened the back door, the silence that met her penetrated her stupor in a way that the sound of the pelting rain and the conversations with Chloe and Richard had not been able.

"Hi, I'm home!" she called as she had hundreds of times over the years, not knowing why she felt the absolute need to. There was of course no one to respond. The house was full of belongings but the absence of a human presence created a hollowness that even the physics of sound recognized. Her voice reverberated through the house and returned to her, not quite an echo.

She knew she was functioning mechanically but couldn't quite get beyond that mode. Drop the Drug Mart flier back into the recycling box. Take off the wet trench coat and loop its collar over a coat hook. Watch for a moment the drops merging on the floor below it to form a tiny puddle. Walk upstairs to her room and make her way between the piles of Aunt Kate's mementos that lie on the floor to the en suite. Drop her clothes, sodden from the wet weather, into a heap at her feet. Turn on the shower. Let the water run hot until steam obliterates her image from the mirror. Turn down the temperature slightly and step in.

She saw herself in Pauline's parking lot. Standing nude, face turned up to the dark sky, rain pelting against and through her body, her clothes in a soggy pile beside her.

When the shower had done what it could, she wrapped herself in her white terry cloth robe, wound a towel around her dripping hair and went downstairs.

She retrieved the morning paper from the front porch. It had escaped Mr. Dempster, and due to the plastic sleeve that covered it, the rain as well. She pulled off the wet sleeve and set the paper on a table next to the sofa in the living room.

In the kitchen she opened the wine cooler and stared at the collection of bottles, choosing one and perusing the label and then another as if deciding which would best complement a special meal. She finally selected a sauvignon blanc from Spain for no reason whatsoever. Then she reached for a glass from the shelf above. Her fingers touched a long-stemmed wineglass and then closed on a water tumbler instead. As she turned to go back to the living room, she made herself stop, returned the tumbler and took down the wineglass.

Evenings that were beginning to close in early, together with the rainy weather, created shadows dark enough to hide corners of the living room. Sara switched on a lamp and curled up at one end of the sofa, the newspaper folded in her lap. She could see only part of the headline. The letters ER and then MURD. She wasn't ready to face the rest.

She forced herself to sip, not gulp, the wine. She implemented a new technique to assure herself that she, not the wine, was in control. She counted to ten between each sip. When the glass was empty she made herself count to fifty before pouring another and forced each movement to be leisurely as though sipping iced tea on a shady veranda on a hot summer afternoon. After the second glass, the wine had begun to carry warmth to parts of her that the shower hadn't been able to reach.

A few more sips and it was time. The headline she unfolded read "FREELANCE WRITER MURDERED IN OWN HOME."

A picture of Diane was below it on the left. She glanced at it and then looked quickly away, afraid that if she paused there Diane would lock eyes with her as had the murdered girl in the clipping from the past this afternoon. If someone she didn't know and who had died so long ago could have such power, what force might Diane, freshly dead, hold?

She skimmed the article and her eyes rested on the last line in the first column. "Ms. Brooks' body was found in." She would have to move her eyes up to the top of the next column to finish the sentence but she knew she didn't have to. The kitchen, she thought. Her heart pounded and a trickle of cold sweat ran down her back. She was afraid to look at the rest of the sentence but forced herself to confirm she was right. How could she have known that? Just a lucky guess, she tried to convince herself. After all, how many rooms in a house were there? But the knowing she felt was not like a guess. She gave up her wine sipping rules and took several gulps.

The sound of a car door slamming, and then another, came from somewhere outside. A moment later the doorbell rang, startling her. She wasn't expecting anyone. It was probably someone selling something or canvassing for a charity. The worst possible scenario would be Ken or Dina, or, heaven forbid, both of them. Since she hadn't answered their calls, she wouldn't put it past them to appear uninvited and unannounced. It would be driving Ken crazy not knowing what she was planning. He would assume she had a plan. She wished she were as resourceful as he thought she was.

She couldn't cope with anyone right now. The curtains were drawn. She would simply ignore the bell. It rang again and then again with an insistence that excluded sales people or canvassers. She was sure it was Ken. After the fifth ring he seemed to have given up. She listened for car doors to slam. Nothing. She was listening so intently that when the phone rang it hit her ears with a louder than usual shrillness. By the time she got her legs unwound from underneath her and had reached the phone in the kitchen, she expected whoever was calling to have hung up.

"Hello?"

"Sara Porter?"

The caller sounded like the magazine subscription salesman who had bothered her the night before and she was tempted to say "No, Ms. Porter is not in." But she hesitated for too long and the answer was assumed.

"This is Detective Sergeant Carson, from the Toronto Homicide Division, Ms. Porter."

Oh God, it was about to start.

"Yes, detective, what can I do for you?" She adopted the voice she used with Ken when trying to feign control.

"Well, for starters, could you let us in?"

"Let you in?"

"Yes, ma'am. We're at your front door."

"Oh my God, I'm sorry. I — uh — thought you were someone else … "

She felt foolishly like a teenager who had made some silly faux pas.

"That's alright, ma'am. Please just open the door."

She opened the door to face someone she would have labeled as a Bay Street financial type. The perfect navy suit and an understated but obviously expensive tie. She had to lift her chin a few inches to see his slightly pockmarked but still handsome face.

She stood back inviting him in. A young kid followed him. Surely not old enough to be on the police force. For an instant she thought that perhaps it was "take your child to work day." She remembered James going to work with Richard once. But then the detective introduced him as his partner.

She felt awkward and distinctly disadvantaged standing there in a robe, bare feet and a towel turban that she had to repeatedly rewind to keep on her head. She excused herself and ran upstairs to pull on jeans and a T-shirt.

When she returned, the older of the two detectives had taken her place on the sofa next to her wine. Thank God she hadn't used the water tumbler.

He put down the section of the newspaper he had been perusing, not the leading article but the stock page, and stood, offering her spot back. She declined and took the wing chair by the fireplace. It was higher. She remembered a summer job she had had while at university as a consultant in a personnel placement agency. It was the consultant's job to interview people who were looking for work and match them with employers. In the training program she was taught the importance of ensuring the consultant and interviewee each used the right chair. The right chair for the consultant was the one that was two or three inches higher than the one designated for the interviewee. The consultant immediately had the advantage. Interviewees other than the exceptionally confident were intimidated and failed the initial interview. She quit within the week. But she always remembered the chair trick and although she had always seen it as a despicable technique she saw it as a fair strategy in her present situation. She didn't expect to intimidate Detective Carson but perhaps his looking up at her would help level the playing field.

The younger detective mistakenly selected a small Queen Anne chair, more decorative than functional, that had been left to her by her grandmother. It was too tiny for his six-foot-something frame and he sat clumsily on its edge, pad and pen on his lap.

Detective Carson sank back into the deep sofa where he looked perfectly at ease.

"Ms. Porter," he began, "as I am sure you have assumed, we are investigating the murder of Diane Brooks. We are interviewing anyone who had any connection with her. We'd like to ask you a few questions."

Sara nodded down at him.

"How would you describe your relationship with Ms. Brooks?"

"We had no relationship." She felt her shoulders tighten and move up toward her ears. She forced them back down.

"You didn't know Diane Brooks?"

"I knew who she was, of course, but I didn't know her." It was literally true but she was lying. She hadn't spent time with Diane but she knew her very well.

"You have never met her or spoken to her?"

"No." She had been in the same room with her though. It had been nearly two years ago but she had replayed the evening so often in her mind that even the scents were still with her. Pine, cranberry and cinnamon. Candles flickered, fireplaces burned, Christmas trees and guests sparkled. Richard's company's Christmas cocktail party was the event of the season and the guest list could pass for a who's who in North America. Sara and Richard, in the role of two of the hosts, saw little of one another throughout the evening other than to occasionally catch one another's eye across the room, Richard sending back a wink in return for her smile. As she squeezed in and out of clusters of guests she noticed a young woman she didn't recognize who was frequently in the vicinity of Richard. Everyone, Sara was sure, had noticed her. She was a stranger to this group, whose members either knew one another personally or knew to whom each person was connected and how. In addition, she was eye catching. Not beautiful, but she had a presence and wore a metallic blue low-cut backless and strapless dress that Sara had looked at several times wondering what mechanism held it in place. Sara also noticed the flirtatious smile and tilt of her head when she was around Richard. Instead of jealousy, Sara felt proud of her handsome and charming husband. Eat your heart out, honey, she had thought. She had intended to introduce herself to her but the two had never been in the same corner of the room at the same time.

The evening had ended with both she and Richard in romantic moods. Richard had brought a wine bucket with the best wine in their cellar and two crystal wine glasses up to the bedroom. He nuzzled her neck and whispered, "Remember at university we used to cut classes and spend the whole day in bed together? How about we call in sick tomorrow?"

But she had a client appointment in the morning. They moved quickly from the brink of passionate lovemaking to the midst of a passionate fight. Richard left the house and didn't return until the next morning. For the past two months she had tried, unsuccessfully, not to play the "what-if" game with herself.

"You had never met Ms. Brooks?" The detective was sitting forward, his elbows resting on his thighs and his hands folded comfortably in front between his knees. The question came gently, not as a challenge. He seemed nice. And so did the young one, although he said nothing. What had happened to the good cop, bad cop routine?

"Yes Detective. That's what I said." Her voice held more of an edge than his.

Carson cleared his throat and at the same time eased himself from her sofa. People usually struggled awkwardly to get out of its depths but he was on his feet in one smooth movement. He strolled casually over to the fireplace, leaned an elbow on the mantle and looked down at her.

"Ms. Porter, would you please describe for us how you spent last evening?"

She refused to look up at him and instead directed her remarks at his kid partner.

"I had dinner with an old friend, Tony Hamilton. And then I came home."

"What time did you get home?" Cason asked.

"I don't understand why you are asking me these questions? They sound like questions that would normally be asked of suspects." She directed her comments once again at his partner. If Detective Carson wanted to see her face, and she would assume he did — the most valuable information she collected from clients was in their facial expression — he was going to have to sit down.

"It's routine, Ms. Porter. We have to check the whereabouts of anyone who had any connection with the deceased. Could you please tell us what time you got home?"

Carson strolled over to a straight-backed chair and, before she began to answer, picked it up and carried it to a spot directly in front of her. "You don't mind, do you?" he asked.

The chair was slightly shorter than hers but with his additional height, when he sat down, he was looking her directly in the eye.

"Ms. Porter?" he prodded again.

"I'm not sure. I don't remember looking at the clock."

"Do you know what time you left the restaurant?"

She hesitated for a moment and her eyes swept to the ceiling in an attempt to trigger memory.

"I'm not sure. Perhaps ten o'clock but I don't really know." The feeling of anxiety that had started a moment ago quickly swelled to panic proportions. She really didn't know. She vaguely remembered leaving the restaurant some time after Tony but didn't have a clear recollection of coming home or getting ready for bed, which she must have done as she woke up undressed this morning.

God, think Sara think, she implored herself. But only shadows of thoughts that she couldn't get a hold of hovered at the periphery of her memory. She tried to cover the feeling of panic with a look of puzzlement.

Carson watched and waited, saying nothing.

"I don't know," she repeated. "I guess I didn't check the time at all last night. I didn't have any reason to," she said with a calculated shrug.

"We came by this morning but didn't find you and so passed by your office. I understand you are on leave."

"Yes, for a few days."

He left a silence that asked why, but she didn't respond. Too complicated to explain at the best of times. Definitely beyond her at the moment.

"We came by again later in the day." Again a question without a question. Where were you? What could she say? Trying to find a link between the murder of a young woman in the nineteen forties and the death of Judge Jamieson because their death notices both happened to be in the box of stuff her aunt had left? Had the last couple of days been as odd as they seemed when she tried to find a way to explain them or was her mind just too foggy to sort them out?

"I'm sorry I missed you. I had some errands to run." Her answer was vague but true.

"We spoke with Tony Hamilton while we were at your office. He told us that he left you at the restaurant at nine thirty. Is that correct?"

"He left me at the restaurant, yes. As I said, I didn't check the time. I would have thought it was later but I don't know." The panic attack was accelerating. Heart pounding faster, beads of sweat threatening to break out on her forehead. Nine thirty. Surely not.

"He said that you stayed behind to drink some coffee to counteract the wine before driving home."

"Yes, that's right." She hadn't ordered coffee though, but another carafe of wine. That she did remember.

Carson shifted slightly in his chair before continuing.

"Mr. Hamilton also told us that you had been rather upset."

What had Tony said? One of the files that she had squeezed into the back of her mind to be ignored for as long as possible shifted forward. Tony's look of concern and then shock. His clasping her arm across the table and telling her to settle down. But she hadn't been able to follow the sane instructions. It had all poured out, the words and the fury both fueled by wine and pain held in too long.

"He told us," Carson continued, almost gently, "that you said that you hated both your husband and Diane Brooks for what they did, but what you would never forgive would be his having a child by her."

The panic was washed away by something else. She knew for the first time what to be humiliated meant. She took a deep breath, closed her eyes, pointed her chin upward and rested the back of her head against the chair. She must look like a pathetic, spurned ex-wife. And a drunken one at that. And again how could she explain? What man would understand? Losing Richard had been bad enough. But the thought of him having the opportunity to use the learning from the mistakes they had both made with Chloe and James, and to have another shot at doing things right when she would never have that chance, hurt more than anything.

No matter what you feel inside, my dear, act as though you are in control. Aunt Kate's voice repeated a lesson she had delivered to Sara on several occasions.

Sara took a deep breath and looked the detective in the eye.

"Yes, I did say those things. I'm embarrassed but I did. I'm afraid I had a little too much to drink and too little sleep."

"You knew at the time that Ms. Brooks was pregnant?" He asked flatly as though throwing out a casual question.

"Pregnant?" She felt the blood drain from her face and then begin to seep away from her brain.

"Are you saying you hadn't heard before now that your husband and Ms. Brooks were expecting a baby?"

She shook her head. No, she didn't know.

"It was in the newspaper article you were reading about the murder." He picked up the paper and pointed to the last paragraph.

"I didn't get that far." She was starting to feel light-headed and any pretense at maintaining control was lost as she leaned forward and put her head between her knees, her still-damp hair cascading toward the floor.

Her inquisitor grasped her shoulders and asked if she were alright. Once she had managed to sit upright and insist she was fine, he said that that was all for now. They could let themselves out. As they reached the foyer, he turned back.

"Oh, by the way. We may need to speak with you again. You aren't planning on doing any traveling are you?"

Did that make her officially a suspect?

16

As he left the Porter home, Carson couldn't resist waving up at the shadow in the darkened upstairs window next door. He'd have liked to proffer one digit rather than five but restrained himself. He couldn't tell whether Dempster responded.

Night had fallen while they were interviewing Sara Porter and the rain had let up. Streaks of pale yellow and red flashed across the slick black pavement as cars swished past. He imagined them carrying their passengers home to families, children running to greet them at the door and smells of home cooking coming from the kitchen. He knew the reality for many would be kids barely looking up from a video game and ordered-in souvlaki or a pizza. His own solitary existence, he had long ago realized, was much less lonely.

They had left the car parked at the curb. As he rounded it to the driver's side, passing cars splashed beads of dirtied rainwater at his pant legs. He bent to wipe them away. Then brushed the car seat to ensure no residue from Kirpatrick's hamburger would soil his suit.

He punched Simpson's number into his cell phone as he started the car. One ring and Simpson was on the line.

"What have you got?"

"Mrs. Porter confirmed she was with Tony Hamilton last night. She admits to having had too much to drink and to having expressed her antagonism toward Richard Porter and Brooks. She didn't remember when she arrived home and says that she didn't know about Brooks' pregnancy."

"That's it?"

"Yes. All that's pertinent."

"You see her as a suspect?"

"At this point, no."

Simpson's sign off was a loud hang up. Carson could see him slamming down the receiver.

"I get the feeling the Inspector was hoping we'd give him a confession to take to the mayor," he said as he turned his attention to the road.

Kirpatrick had been quiet since they left the house and gave no response now other than a quiet grunt. Carson guessed he had been hoping for a confession as well.

"OK let's have it." Carson checked his new partner out of the corner of his eye. "I assume you're disappointed that we don't have that woman handcuffed in the back seat. And more importantly, you think that if I had handled it differently that we would have."

Kirpatrick shrugged his shoulders but said nothing. He looked intently out of his window as though searching for a landmark in the slick black cityscape that flashed by like a scene from a film noir.

The behavior reminded Carson of his second wife, Jennifer. She never said what was bothering her. You had to figure it out by guessing and then wait until she was ready to communicate again. He might have to put up with it from a wife, but he didn't feel like taking it from a rookie partner.

He raised his voice a decibel. "Hey that may have sounded like a statement but it was intended as a question. I'm the senior partner remember? How about a little respect?" His words came out louder than he had intended and the touch of humor he had meant to inject hadn't materialized. He was about to explain but Kirpatrick spoke first.

"Yeah, sorry. It's just that, what about MOM?"

"What about MOM?"

"At the college we were drilled constantly: Motive. Opportunity. Means. If those three are present you've got a very hot suspect. She spells it out perfectly and you give her an easy ride. It was obvious she was lying when you were asking her about the time she left the restaurant and the time she got home. Why wouldn't you take her in?"

Being in on the arrest in a murder case on his first assignment couldn't help but look good in Kirpatrick's file. Carson didn't blame him for his youthful ambition but didn't like his petulant tone or his too-quick move from a reticence that had suggested respect, to this familiarity that showed none.

"Let's just say that my experience told me that the tough cop act was not the way to deal with her. And you are here to watch and learn, not to second-guess me." Carson was careful to modulate his tone this time but his words conveyed firmness.

Kirpatrick opened his mouth to say something. When he caught Carson's eye he paused, mouth open for a few seconds, and then turned back to the private movie that played just outside of his window.

Sara Porter hadn't been what Carson expected. They had done the follow-up interview with Richard Porter earlier and he was understandably low key, but polished and charming, even with them. He could imagine the man's skill with women. Porter looked haggard but at the same time well put together. Manicured nails, hair just the right length, snipped by a stylist weekly, Carson suspected, to maintain the perfection and casual clothes perfectly pressed. Richard Porter had the look of someone who cared about what other people thought of him.

Carson had expected Sara Porter to be a female version of her husband. Her ensembles of robe and towel around her head and then jeans and T-shirt had surprised him. Although she had handled herself with confidence and a touch of sophistication her demeanor hadn't been applied as he suspected Richard Porter's charm was.

They had entered the interview with Richard Porter with the objective of discovering anything about him or Diane Brooks that could lead to a possible motive. They had already checked and rechecked his alibi and it was solid. There was, of course, the possibility that he had hired someone to kill Brooks but if Porter had a motive they hadn't found it.

"Could you please describe your relationship with Diane Brooks?" Carson had asked after they had offered their condolences.

"There isn't anything to describe. We loved each other, we lived together and she was apparently carrying my child." Porter's voice broke and he turned his back and walked over to the window to stare out over the city.

"I understand you weren't married," Carson continued.

"No, we weren't. I haven't divorced yet and it didn't seem important."

"Was it important to Ms. Brooks?"

Porter turned back to them as Carson had intended.

A flash of anger replaced the pain.

"I don't see that that is any of your business."

"We don't intend to pry but we have to know as much as possible about Diane Brooks and your relationship appears to have been central to her life."

Porter took a minute to douse the anger and then responded.

"Diane never mentioned marriage. And neither did I. A piece of paper wouldn't have made a difference to either of us."

"But now that she was pregnant?"

Porter swallowed hard. "Yes, that would have changed things."

"For the better?"

"Of course for the better, goddammit. What are you insinuating?"

"I'm not insinuating anything, sir. I'm asking questions that need to be asked."

Porter dropped into a chair and leaned his head back looking up at the ceiling.

Carson continued, "Did you have any kind of financial agreement?"

"You mean like a prenup without the marriage?'

"Exactly."

"No. Again we never discussed it. It was understood that I paid for the household expenses and Diane looked after her personal expenses. She had some income and her parents were generous with her."

"What did Ms. Brooks do for a living?"

"She was a freelance writer. No investigative type of journalism though if you're looking for a motive. Her work was pretty dull stuff."

"Did she have a current project?"

"She was working on something but I'm not sure what. She didn't talk much about her work."

Or was Porter simply not interested, Carson wondered.

Carson spent another half hour delving into Brooks' and Porter's lives, with Kirpatrick jotting down notes, but they had left with a sense that it had been a waste of time and paper. There was no indication that Brooks would have enemies and no suggestion that someone could have been trying to get at Porter through Brooks. Some people might not like Porter's slickness but neither the interview nor the other checks they had done on Porter suggested that anyone wished him serious harm.

They had gone directly from Richard Porter to Sara Porter. The lack of headway on the case was frustrating and Carson understood Kirpatrick's reaction to their interview with Sara Porter, even if he didn't approve of it.

Carson dropped Kirpatrick at his car at headquarters and they called it a night. It was early to be signing off in the middle of a murder investigation, but there were no new leads to follow as of yet. He expected several all-nighters ahead and suggested that Kirpatrick spend the evening with his wife. She was expecting and having a difficult time. Being a cop's wife wasn't easy at any time, but whenever anything precipitated a hormone surge, the stress on the wife increased greatly. Inevitably that meant ditto for the officer.

"What are you up to tonight?" Kirpatrick asked. An attempt to mend the tiny fissure in their relationship.

"I need to drop by my sister Maggie's place. A long-lost cousin from Britain is in town and I should at least make a showing."

"Lucky guy. Roast beef and Yorkshire pudding I'll bet."

Carson laughed.

"Not likely. My sister traded Carson for Lucciano and makes a mean spaghetti. Roast beef is considered pretty boring stuff at her house."

Carson headed in the direction of his sister's. A previously unknown cousin from Britain was visiting Toronto and had contacted them. Maggie had invited her for dinner and he had promised he would try to drop in this evening and should appear, at least for coffee. He could actually make it for dinner but knew he couldn't cope with the idle conversation and cheeriness for that long.

He'd stop at the Rose and Crown for a couple of pints on the way. That would allow him to arrive just after dinner and to be sufficiently fortified to manage to be civil for at least a half hour.

The pub was nearly full with the after-work crowd. It was noisy and warm. He worked his way through a tightly packed group of boisterous twenty-something males. They were probably just starting out in their first real jobs, but acted like cool young execs with the right haircuts, the right business suits and swilling back the right beer, whatever that was today. He realized he couldn't squeeze through close quarters as easily as he used to and managed to receive a "Hey man, watch what you're doing," when he jostled an arm that was about to pour a pint down its owner's throat and instead dribbled it down his Armani shirt. When he came out the other side he found one tiny table beside a large red "No Smoking" sticker. The sign was unnecessary as all establishments were now smoke free but the manager either hadn't gotten around to taking it down or had already classified it as memorabilia. Carson hadn't smoked for years but he still craved one every time he had a drink. Which meant he was frequently tormented.

The waitress who took his order had a Sara Porter look about her. But as she set down his beer she gave him a flirtatious smile and any resemblance disappeared. Sara Porter, he suspected, did not pass out flirtatious smiles. A damn shame though, he thought.

He'd been firm with Kirpatrick about his decision to treat her gently but had he really made the right call? Had he been too soft? It was obvious she was lying, but just as obvious to him that she wasn't a murderess. His intuition had always been right. But when did wishful thinking feel like intuition? There was something about Sara Porter that encouraged wishful thinking.

"Don't get distracted, guy," he told himself. "Don't get distracted."

When he reached his sister's suburban home he hadn't yet knocked on the door when the commotion began. The dog, which always sensed Carson's presence before he had even pulled into the drive, had alerted the household to his arrival. The dog was a black Lab and had been a puppy when its original owner, a street kid, had been murdered a couple of years ago. It had been the middle of winter. When Carson arrived on the scene he found the kid's body sprawled over a snowbank outside a Tim Horton's doughnut shop, his head bashed in with a rusted tire iron that had been tossed, sticky with blood and hair, into the snow a few feet away. The puppy was curled beside the body, whimpering and shivering. Carson tucked it inside his overcoat where it slept until Carson was off duty at dawn. He intended to drop it off at the Toronto Humane Society and even pulled off the Bayview extension and into their lot. But the warmth of the puppy was comforting and he took it back to his apartment, fed it some not-too-old bologna and fell asleep with the pup on his stomach.

He had been wakened by the pup licking his face. Pups sure knew how to find themselves homes. If it weren't for his unpredictable hours he would have kept it. Instead, he called Maggie and spent an hour talking her into taking the dog. He had to promise to dog sit if she went on vacation. He knew that was a good deal because Alberto, her husband, was a homebody and his sister was unlikely to be going anywhere.

So Maggie had taken the dog and he had visiting rights. He had dropped it off that same afternoon and he and Maggie had spent an hour drinking wine and coming up with clever names for the pup. He voted for Vino or Bacchus but when the children joined the game they had insisted on Blackie.

Now Blackie was in the hallway leaping at the door and the children were close behind screaming, "Uncle Keith, Uncle Keith."

Tony, the eldest at eleven, pulled the door open and children and dog all leaped at him. The youngest, Vincent, who had at the moment he was named become Vincie, had to tip his head back so far to see his uncle's face, that he nearly toppled backwards. Carson grabbed him and threw him in the air. Vincie wound tiny hands that smelled of chocolate ice cream around Carson's neck. Roberto, the eight-year-old, continued to shout "Uncle Keith's here, Uncle Keith's here," and Blackie barked excitedly.

"Keith, I'm out here," Maggie called out to him.

With some effort he herded the noisy bunch toward his sister's voice in the kitchen. Maggie was filling the dishwasher and she threw a smile over her shoulder with a, "Hi there."

"Hi. Where's everybody?"

"We're everybody."

"But what about the cousin and where's Alberto?"

"He's driving her back to her hotel."

"Gosh, is it that late? I thought I'd get here for coffee."

"It's OK. I know you're busy." Maggie's response was always the same. She came over and pecked his cheek. He knew she could smell the beer.

"So, what's she like, this cousin of ours?" he asked.

"Very British," Maggie laughed. "She probably wondered what the colonies did to the Carson family when she met my brood."

Carson had been amazed at his sister's adjustment from the Carson's reserved, understated household in which a wrinkled brow had denoted emotion, to this hurly-burly family in which every conversation sounded like a heated argument. She had quickly learned that her softly modulated voice was a handicap in her new world. If she continued using what their mother had referred to as a "ladylike voice" she would be a non-entity. Now she shouted comfortably over the din of her household sending key points home with arms and hands that never stayed still. The only remnants of the Maggie he had grown up with were her blue eyes, blond hair and her unconditional love for her big brother.

The children continued to bounce up and down and asked what they always asked. "Uncle Keith, Uncle Keith, can we see your gun? Please, please." Maggie shot him her usual "Don't you dare" look.

And he responded with his "Give me a break, what do you take me for?" look.

He pulled out his badge instead. Roberto was the first to grab it and ran off with the other two in hot pursuit.

"Now don't you lose your uncle's badge or you will feel my hand on your bottoms," Maggie called after them unconvincingly. He was sure they never had and never would feel her hand on their bottoms and they knew it too. The boys' screeches retreated to a back bedroom. The sudden quiet would be worth a lost badge, he decided.

The back door opened and Alberto burst in with a grin already on his face. Carson's car had alerted him that another guest had arrived.

"Keith, you made it. Welcome. Welcome." Alberto tackled Carson with a bear hug. "We don't see you often enough, but I know how busy you are. My brother-in-law the detective." Alberto slapped Carson proudly on the shoulder. "You must try my new wine. So much better than the last batch," Alberto continued without any pause for a breath.

Carson had never been able to develop a taste for the dark pithy stuff that came from Alberto's kegs in the basement. But Alberto's insistent Mediterranean hospitality usually won over Carson's weak attempt at "No thanks." He frequently left the Lucciano household with a burning in his stomach and the promise of a headache in the morning. This evening he used the excuse of having to go right back on duty to decline gracefully.

The three adults had gathered around the kitchen table and Maggie set a piece of pie and coffee in front of Carson. The inevitable conversation was quick in coming.

"So," Alberto was pouring himself a glass of wine, "you involved in this big murder we've been hearing about today?"

"Oh, just the usual. Interviewing a few people here and there."

"It's a sad one. She was a real nice lady. I met her a while ago."

"Really?" Carson was surprised. He was quite sure that the Brooks and the Luccianos were not in the same social circle.

"Yeah, our union hired her to write our history. We're celebrating our sixtieth anniversary next year and the members voted to have a book published to commemorate it. Not likely to see even another ten years with this provincial government. The damn Conservatives are anti-everything that's organized except corporations."

Carson made a quick move to steer the conversation in another direction. His brother-in-law was a true-blue union man and Carson avoided discussing the subject with him. Besides he was more interested in what Alberto knew about Diane Brooks.

"You said Diane Brooks was nice. You spent some time with her?"

"Yeah, I was one of the guys on the committee that managed the project. So many damned meetings that we could have written the book ourselves in the time it took to make the decisions about it. We hired her because she had a lot of related experience. She does, that is, used to do, centennial books for schools, hospitals, even municipalities, so she had lots of good ideas and a framework to put all of the information into. The bonus was that she was a great lady to work with. Pretty nice looking too."

Alberto threw a wink in Maggie's direction.

From what Alberto was describing, Porter was right that the kind of writing Brooks did was unlikely to get her into trouble. But it was one of the things he needed to look into further. All of her papers seemed pretty innocuous but there had to be a motive somewhere. He'd check her things again to make sure nothing had been missed. Now that his mind was drawn back into the case he was finding it difficult to stay focused on the people in the room.

He gave the kids a couple of piggyback rides and then was gone with the usual promise of staying longer next time.

17

Sara had fought her way out but now was being pulled back into the dark dampness of her dream. She stood cold and rain-soaked on a back patio looking through a French door. Although she could see little in the room on the other side of the pane she knew it was a cozy den. She could picture the huge marble fireplace to the left and struggled to make out its shape in the shadows. Below the window on the other side of the room was the window seat that had charmed her. A perfect place to sit with a cup of tea and look over the side garden. There was a bird feeder she remembered just outside that window. A wide archway directly opposite the French door opened into the warm, brightly lit kitchen. The wind blew sheets of rain against the pane of the French door and the kitchen scene was distorted as though being viewed through old, wavy glass.

The wind tangled wet leaves in her hair and warm tears mingled with the cold rain that ran down her face. That was her kitchen. It was she who was supposed to be savoring a solitary evening in the homey, comforting room. It was she who was supposed to be waiting for Richard to come home.

She pressed her face against the wet pane. Diane had sat down at the kitchen bar with her back to the French door. But Sara couldn't see clearly enough. The scene looked too dreamlike. If she could just see Diane plainly, there in the home that was supposed to be hers, perhaps she could somehow accept her fate and stop the anguish. She grasped the door handle, turned it, pushed gently and the door moved inward. She opened it just wide enough to be able to look through the crack.

A large tortoise shell hair clip gathered Diane's blond hair at the nape of her neck. Bare feet with bright red toenails rested on the rungs of the barstool. She began to slowly turn her head to look over her shoulder. Had she heard the door opening?

Sara knew she should close the door and leave quickly but her legs wouldn't move. Diane seemed to be turning in slow motion. Her head did not stop at the natural spot just beyond her shoulder but continued to swivel toward Sara. As the face came fully into view Sara could hear her own voice struggling to protest. But she couldn't speak. Two dark brown eyes locked onto hers and held her in place. She stared in horror and the face of Jane Stewart stared back at her.

She was dreaming. She knew she was dreaming but she couldn't stop it, couldn't get out. Finally the ringing of the bedside phone penetrated the blackness and pulled her back into her bed, soaking wet and heart pounding. Each throb of her heart resounded in her head. The thumping was so loud that the ringing of the phone was muffled as though coming from another dimension. She ignored it. It took all of her energy and concentration to quell the terror she still felt. She made herself take slow deep breaths until her heart was convinced that the danger was over.

Wet hair and the damp silk nightgown that clung to her attested to her struggle. She felt as though she had actually been standing in the rain. She began to feel chilled and pulled the covers up over her shoulders and curled herself into a tight ball. Twenty-four hours ago she had had a new sense of purpose. A toe-hold on life again. Now a heavy tiredness, fear, and mental numbness were weighing her down, trying to pin her to the bed. She was unable to throw them off but managed finally to will herself into an upright position carrying them with her.

Just a little longer, she thought, and she would be ready to try to face the day.

Your life's experience is not the result of what happens to you but how you respond to life's events. Aunt Kate's voice replaced the mad beating of her heart. Another of Aunt Kate's homilies. As far as Kate had been concerned we each choose the quality of our lives. We have power if we choose power. We accept the fickle finger of fate if we choose to be victims. Sara had inherited her aunt's perspective on life and wondered now how she had slipped so far from her personal life philosophy. Had Aunt Kate ever slipped or had she always been strong?

Sara regretted that fatigue and perhaps lack of sobriety had prevented her from setting the automatic coffee maker the night before. She reached for the Tylenol No. 2's, popped a couple, and then added one more to make up for the temporary lack of caffeine.

Buck up Porter. Quit being such a wimp.

Her self-lecture got her into a fully upright position but she was not quite ready to pull herself from bed. Dream segments floated in and out of her consciousness keeping the fear alive. The dream had been too real. Far too real. She needed a distraction. She leaned over the side of the bed and reached for the newspaper she had dropped on the floor last night when sleep finally began to come. She had finished reading the article on Diane's murder. Hence the dream, she was sure. She hadn't gotten beyond the front-page article, and now pulled out the business section.

She skimmed the first page. The NASDAQ was still lurching wildly, tech stocks up one day but then down for three. It was a great time to buy, claimed the analysts. The stocks were bound to come back up. Sure she thought. Wasn't that what they said in '29?

A headline caught her eye. "Union Knocks on Door of Retail Chain."

A union was making an attempt to get into the Jamieson's clothing chain. Jamieson's had been her client last year. "Those fools," she thought. "They didn't implement one of our recommendations and now look at them."

President and CEO, Patrick Jamieson, the article said, made only a brief statement: "At Jamieson's, we have always been a family and I'm sure that any overtures the union might be making will be ignored by our employees." He was either trying to improve a bleak picture or was plain naïve. The morale in their stores was dangerously low. The company might have been a family at one time but employees did not feel that they had been treated as family lately.

She had met Jamieson only a couple of times. She had worked more closely with the VP of human resources. The last time she saw Jamieson was when she had presented her findings and recommendations. Each had been earnestly accepted and then promptly forgotten when the company got caught up in expansion.

Then it struck her. *Damn, Porter, you're slow.* She reached for the folder of clippings and notes she had carried with her yesterday and pulled out the Judge's obituary and searched for the reference. *Lovingly remembered by his nephew, Patrick Jamieson.*

There could be more than one Patrick Jamieson. Tony would know. He kept much better abreast of who's who than she did. She shouldn't even be speaking to him after his talking to the police about her embarrassing scene at the restaurant. But she understood him. Tony would do anything to help her. He just couldn't keep anything inside. He was probably seen as the snitch when he was a kid. He wouldn't intend to sell out his friends. He would simply not be able to keep anything hidden. It would all spill out as though he had been given truth serum.

It was after eight thirty. She'd slept in. Tony was likely at his desk. She was glad that they had recently changed the phone system. She wouldn't have to go through the receptionist, whom she was sure was paid a bonus based on the number of useful tidbits she could pass on to Ken and Dina.

He picked up on the first ring. "Tony Hamilton here."

"Hi, it's me."

As she expected Tony immediately dove into an emotional confession. She cut him short.

"Forget it. You were a shit to do it but I know you're a compulsive confessor. As long as I'm not arrested for murder you are completely forgiven."

Tony gasped on the other end of the line.

"Arrested for murder? I didn't mean —"

"I'm joking!" Half joking, she thought.

"Tony, Patrick Jamieson, the CEO of Jamieson's. Is he by any chance the nephew of Judge Jamieson?"

"Of course. Didn't you know that?"

"I never thought about it."

The person who probably knew the most about Judge Jamieson's life and death and she had a personal link to him. Albeit a somewhat tenuous link.

"Tony," she asked. "Can you do something for me?"

Tony was even more eager than usual to be of assistance and they agreed to meet for coffee at Bloor and Yonge. Far enough from the office that they wouldn't bump into any co-workers but not too far for either of them. And they would be very close to her next stop.

When Tony had picked up the phone she had immediately felt sorry for him, sitting at his desk at Morrison and Black. She knew now with certainty she would never be back there and a sense of relief and anticipation infused her.

She felt a renewed energy and was sure it wasn't just from the codeine.

18

Mrs. Susan Ramsey had just finished a foray into the underground world at Bloor and Yonge, one of the habitats of the wealthy on a permanent quest to find one more piece of something they didn't already have. Darting in and out between the well-to-do shoppers were the workers who spent their daylight hours in the offices that were stacked on top of the expensive shopping boutiques, and who occasionally escaped from their desks to run an errand or find a quality cup of coffee. Mrs. Ramsey was one of the former. She had completed her mission. That is, she had come to the end of it rather than fulfilling it. She had spent three hours delving into every corner of Gucci, Jamieson's, and Holt Renfrew but had only one tiny package to show for her effort.

Her one purchase had been made in desperation. A pair of Perry Ellis sunglasses that she didn't need, probably would never wear, and wasn't sure she even liked. Shopping had become less and less satisfying. She feared her acquisitive senses had been permanently dulled. She felt like an alcoholic who suddenly was not satisfied by alcohol and needed something else to satisfy her addiction.

She rested on a stool of bleached wood and stainless steel in a café nestled in a corner in the lower concourse. A café latte and slice of rich pastry, selected with the intent of at least temporarily satisfying whatever was gnawing away at her, sat on the bleached wooden bar in front of her. She was calculating the number of hours in the gym that would be required to burn the calories she was about to consume. How many calories would take her from a size four to a size six?

Her self absorption was interrupted by a man who entered the café, purchased a cup of "just ordinary coffee" and sat at a table near the door. He had said nothing to her. Nor were his actions unusual. It was his very presence that caught her attention. She spent a significant amount of time on these premises. This place was what the rappers she heard screaming from her son's room would call her "hood." She knew it inside out and instinctively knew who belonged and who didn't. This man didn't. He wasn't one of the office workers or shop clerks who scampered about on breaks and lunches; he wasn't one of the professionals who passed most of their days in mahogany offices on some of the top floors; and he certainly didn't belong to her set. He was a foreign species. He was a tiny older man. His jeans and striped T-shirt looked as though they had been purchased in the children's section of Wal-Mart. The Blue Jays cap might be worn here but not as he did, pulled tightly down on his head with no sense of style. But it wasn't just his attire. He looked uncomfortable, as though he felt as out of place as he looked.

She watched as he organized himself at his table as though he were about to perform a ritual. He unfolded a paper napkin and smoothed it out on the tiny café table and set his coffee, sugar, stir stick, and second napkin in a neat line on top of it. He tore a corner from the packet of sugar with small white hands and the image of a rhesus monkey came to her. He carefully shook sugar into his coffee, stopping twice to check the amount left in the packet to ensure the exactness. When he had determined that the sweetness was correct, he carefully folded the top of the tiny packet three times and set it aside. He then opened a creamer and poured its entire contents into the cup. He set the tiny plastic container aside and placed the folded sugar packet within it. He picked up the slim wooden stir stick and wiped it with the second napkin before giving his coffee two precise stirs. The stir stick was set to the right of the other instruments of his ritual and was carefully adjusted to ensure it was properly aligned. A slight nod of satisfaction on the first sip seemed to confirm that the ritual had worked.

Although meticulous in his actions, Mrs. Ramsey saw that his attention was elsewhere. His eyes were hidden under the peak of his cap but she was certain that he was watching the woman who had entered the café a minute or two before him. Mrs. Ramsey swiveled slightly on her stool to get a better view of the woman. Fair, quite attractive, but with a little cosmetic surgery she would be striking. A tad overweight. Probably a size twelve rather than the size eight her bone structure and fashion demanded. The haircut wasn't bad and her skin suggested regular facials. Good taste in clothing. She knew what suited her and wore it well. The aubergine wool jacket worked well with her hair. It might be from Holt's but definitely not by one of the top designers. It would have been on the floor that catered to the greater masses and carried lower-end designers. Five or six hundred dollars, tops she guessed. The woman wasn't a career shopper, as Mrs. Ramsey and her friends referred to themselves with self-deprecating humor designed to forgive their extravagance. Neither was she an office or store clerk. Most likely a professional from one of the offices upstairs.

The woman checked her watch and looked up. The monkey returned to the half empty sugar package, intent on folding and refolding its empty half as though it were an extremely important task. As soon as the woman turned her attention back to the items she had taken from a plastic folder he returned his attention to her.

Mrs. Ramsey became completely engrossed in the drama that only she and the monkey man knew was unfolding. She watched as a professorial-looking man joined the woman. He kissed her on the cheek and immediately jumped into what seemed to be an emotional speech. As he spoke he focused his attention on his folded hands and thumbs that spun themselves around each other. When he looked up she was sure his eyes were moist. The woman reached across the table and gave him an awkward hug. He hugged back several times. A lovers' quarrel?

The monkey sipped his coffee and watched.

The man pulled a manila envelope from his brief case and handed it to the woman. The woman said something to him. He looked surprised, gathered his things and left. Mrs. Ramsey smiled to herself and gave the woman points. The quickest and smoothest dismissal she had ever seen.

The woman spent a half hour and two more cups of coffee perusing the contents of the envelope and making notes. She nodded her head from time to time as though agreeing with herself. Mrs. Ramsey and the monkey waited. Mrs. Ramsey was quite content. She had nowhere she had to be and something about the scenario peaked her interest. The monkey on the other hand seemed agitated. He sat, one jean-clad leg crossed over the other, the top one bouncing impatiently causing a perfectly white running shoe to tap against the table leg. He frequently reached up to straighten his cap.

The woman finally gathered her papers preparing to leave. He immediately turned his attention to the now-worn sugar pack.

The woman's bag brushed against Mrs. Ramsey as she passed.

"Oh, sorry." The woman stopped for a moment, turned and smiled at Mrs. Ramsey. Mrs. Ramsey smiled back.

The woman hurried from the café, briefcase in one hand and jacket over her other arm.

The monkey man followed.

Mrs. Ramsey had no doubt that he was following the woman. "Mind your own business." That's what Harry, her husband, would say.

19

Sara felt her two hours in the café had been productive. As frustrating as Tony could be, he was always there when you needed him. The key points from the report she had written for Jamieson's months ago were once again fresh in her mind. Even though she intended to use Jamieson's present corporate crisis as a way to get access to Patrick Jamieson for her own purposes, she wanted to get it right. She might even get Jamieson to rethink the company's management before it was too late. Jamieson's had been a Canadian institution and if it didn't change, it would self-destruct. She'd like to be able to help prevent that.

She had thought about calling Jamieson and telling him that she had been sorting through her aunt's things and had become curious about her early years. Since his uncle and her aunt had been close friends at that time and since his uncle had also passed away recently, could they meet and perhaps exchange what they knew about those early days?

It sounded a little odd but she thought she could pull it off. The problem was that Jamieson was an extremely busy man. She would never reach him directly. She would have to leave a message and they would play telephone tag. Once she got hold of him it could be days, even weeks, before he would have an opening in his calendar, and the purpose of the meeting certainly didn't sound pressing enough to urge him to squeeze her in.

She had decided that her best chance was to use business as the reason for her wanting to see him and if she wanted that to happen quickly, her best bet would be to pop in and hope for the best. She knew there was no point in trying to get access to Patrick Jamieson via the usual routes. The company's president was well protected. Without an appointment, it was impossible to get by the first line of defense, the receptionist. And then there was the even more formidable second line, his personal assistant. She needed to find a way to get into the suite of offices unnoticed. If Jamieson were in, she would make an effort to do an end run around the assistant and if he weren't she would refresh her memory of the office layout so she could find him after hours when he would be undefended by his secretary. If he kept the same routine she remembered from a year ago he tended to work until at least nine at night and was usually the last to leave.

As Sara got into the elevator, she checked her pocket for the souvenir she had accidentally taken from Jamieson's on her last visit. She had intended to return it but hadn't gotten around to it. A half hour's search this morning had found it at the bottom of the junk drawer in the kitchen. She had had to dig under the metal retractable tape measure, a roll of Scotch tape, a hoard of loose elastics and twist ties saved for emergencies that had never materialized, her library card – probably expired, an extra set of house keys, a fridge magnet advertising a now-defunct insurance broker, and a deck of Bicycle playing cards. Finding the visitor's badge with the magnetic access card attached had been a good omen. Since Jamieson's wasn't a business that required a great deal of security, and since she knew from her work with them that their systems were never up to date, she doubted whether the access cards had changed.

She paused when she got off the elevators. To the left and some distance away was the reception desk. If she remembered correctly, to the right and around the corner was another entrance to the offices that led one through the employees' kitchen. Staff tended to use that entrance, particularly in the morning, allowing them to pick up a coffee on the way to their desks. It was a secured entrance that could only be accessed with a card.

She made her way in that direction. She remembered that the offices had been scheduled for reorganization shortly after her contract ended last year. Once she got in, *if* she got in, that is, she'd have to find her way inconspicuously to Jamieson's office. Crazy Porter, absolutely crazy, she thought as she swiped her card through the slot. No green light appeared. She tried again. Nothing. She could hear footsteps coming along the hall behind her and hoped they wouldn't stop. They did.

"Hey, need recharging? These cards are really duds." A good-looking young man whose badge said he was Terry Brown was indicating for her to move aside. He glanced at the visitor's badge in her hand. "Visiting, eh?"

"Yes," she answered with what she hoped was a bright and relaxed smile. She almost added, "Doing some work with HR," but decided better of it. For all she knew he might work in HR.

Two small green lights flashed immediately in response to his card and he opened the door motioning her to go ahead.

"Have you been introduced to our gourmet kitchen?" he asked. He didn't wait for a response. "Coffee's here, exotic teas in this cupboard, and soft drinks, juice or water are on tap from that machine."

"Yes, thanks, I know my way around. At least around the kitchen that is. But the office is a real maze. Can you point me in the direction of Jamieson's office?"

"Sure. Right, left and another left and you'll bump right into Jos, guard and defender of all that's good and otherwise."

She didn't bother to question his remark, nodded thanks and headed right. The reception area, somewhere behind her and through a locked door, she remembered as sumptuous. Rich mahogany furniture on lush green carpeting. A collection of oils covered the walls. From her recollection, Jamieson's office was much the same: elegant, warm and splendid. But the terrain between the two was a hinterland of drab gray fabric screens that met one another to form what some space planner euphemistically referred to as offices. The tiny cubicles that were created allowed just enough room for a computer desk and chair. Some staff members, the most hopeful perhaps, had stuck photos of children and pets and motivational verses to the inside of the screens in an attempt to humanize their nine-to-five world. A plastic nameplate, indicating the owner, clung to the screen next to the small opening that served as a doorway. Sara shuddered at the thought of spending the better part of one's day, or worse, the better part of one's life inside one of those soft-sided tombs.

Sara displayed her guest pass prominently on her lapel and nodded casually at anyone she passed. As she reached a turn in the maze she heard the familiar voice of Martha Southern, the head of human resources. Martha had a deep masculine voice softened by her tendency to refer to everyone as "Honey," or if she were on very close terms with them, "Hon."

"Not to worry, Hon, we've got it under control. I'll raise it with Patrick at the next senior management meeting." The voice was on the move and definitely headed in Sara's direction.

Sara could explain away her presence to anyone but Martha. Martha Southern had been her main contact on the Jamieson project. In essence, Martha was the client, and no amount of creative chatter could create a plausible reason for Sara being on the premises without Martha having invited her or at least being aware of her being there.

Sara glanced over her shoulder but the path of retreat was too long. She would never make it back to the kitchen before Martha rounded the corner. Most cubicles emitted sounds of computers at work or telephone conversations. The one beside her was quiet. She stuck her head around the divider expecting to find an empty space to duck into. Instead she was greeted by the startled gasp of a young woman who quickly closed the magazine she had propped against her computer screen. When she realized that Sara wasn't the boss she raised her eyebrows in response to which Sara was about to mutter a quick "Sorry, wrong office." But Martha had picked up speed and was rounding the corner. Sara took a breath and dived into the tiny cubicle, tucking herself into a small space on the other side of the woman's chair.

An open mouth joined the raised eyebrows.

"I'm really sorry to intrude," Sara made a stab at the name. Had the plastic nameplate read Doreen or Darlene? The woman looked like a Darlene. "I'm doing a survey for the company and I was told you would be a good person to talk with, Darlene. I do have your name correct, don't I?" She spoke as softly as possible without actually whispering.

The woman nodded, already looking a little more comfortable.

"This, of course, will be completely confidential and I'd appreciate it if you don't mention our conversation to anyone. If people hear that HR is doing another survey —well you know the kind of rumors that are likely to be started."

Rolled eyes and a nodding head confirmed understanding and agreement.

Martha was gone and Sara wanted a quick escape. She rummaged through her brief case and dug below the huge report to find a note pad and pen.

"Just two quick questions, Darlene. First, how would you rate morale at Jamieson's on a scale of one to ten — one being low and ten being high."

Darlene squished up her face and bit her lip in thought. Seconds that seemed like minutes passed.

"It doesn't have to be an exact scientific response, Darlene, just a sense of what your experience is," Sara prompted her.

"A two then," Darlene answered firmly, a brief nod of her head sealing her decision.

"Alright, and on the same scale how would you rate management's sensitivity to the needs of the employees?"

Darlene again expended a great deal of energy ruminating over the question. Sara wished she had popped into the cubicle of a less conscientious respondent.

"I know you said one to ten," Darlene managed to speak and gnaw on her lip at the same time, "but could I give that one a zero?"

"Of course," Sara scribbled a zero on her paper and stuffed it into her briefcase as she made her escape. "Thanks so much for your candor, Darlene. And please remember this is just between the two of us."

"Oh, you're welcome. It was really good to talk with you about everything."

Darlene returned to her magazine and Sara left wondering about an employee who felt so burdened that uttering a couple of words constituted getting things off her chest. She was wondering even more about herself. She felt exhilarated. And yet, if found out and she couldn't come up with a really good explanation as to why she was here, her professional reputation could be at stake. Was she going over the edge?

She made two left turns in the gray maze and just as her guide had promised, came abruptly upon Jamieson's personal assistant.

Sara, who made a supreme effort to remember names, could not pull this one from her mental rolodex even though she was sure that the young fellow had mentioned it when he gave her directions. His nomenclature, "the guardian," was well chosen. The woman sat smiling but rigid behind her fort of a desk. Sara would try to make a foray into her territory but knew she would be rebuffed. What the secretary didn't know was that right now Sara would be happy having simply gathered a little intelligence. Was Jamieson in the office today and would he be working late?

"Hello," Sara smiled as she approached. "I don't know whether you remember me … "

"Of course, Sara. It's nice to see you again."

Damn, the woman had one up on her already.

"I didn't expect you to be back," the woman added, still smiling. Was this conversational only or a subtle suggestion that the work the Morrison and Black team had done hadn't been highly regarded? Sara had no doubt that, whether true or not, the innuendo was intended. A calculated move to put Sara off her stride.

"I have some information to share with Mr. Jamieson that is very important." Sara could call Patrick Jamieson, "Patrick" to his face and could refer to him as Patrick to Martha, but she knew that referring to him by his first name to the guardian would be seen as disrespectful, not only to Patrick but also, by association, to her.

The guardian was already slowly but firmly shaking her head, her smile never wavering. Sara forged ahead.

"I know his schedule must be crammed but I'm sure he will find this information highly valuable. Is he in today?"

The woman ignored the question.

"I'm afraid it's impossible. If you would like to tell me what it is about I will see if Mr. Jamieson agrees with your definition of important and if so will book an appointment for you."

She turned to her screen, tapped a couple of keys and pulled up his schedule as though to confirm her complete control over it.

What had been distant muffled voices suddenly erupted loudly into the area as Jamieson's office door opened.

"Thanks for your time, Robert." Patrick Jamieson had stepped a couple of feet outside of his door and was shaking hands with his departing guest. As he began to turn back into his office Sara quickly seized the unexpected opportunity, aware she was making an enemy for life of the woman behind the desk.

"Hello, Patrick." She stepped forward and stretched out her hand. "Sara Porter. I led the —"

"Of course I remember you, Sara. Good to see you again." Bright blue eyes lit up, energizing an otherwise tired face. "I didn't know you were back."

Sara ignored the last statement.

"Your assistant has explained how tight your schedule is," a little deference to the guardian, but not enough she knew to make amends, "but I have something that is important to discuss with you, particularly in light of the unionization situation. If you could find fifteen minutes I believe you would find it very beneficial."

"I was thinking about having a quick coffee break while I read the *Globe*. I don't think the ship will sink if I postpone reading the financial page until tonight." His smile grew wider. He stood back and motioned for her to go ahead of him into his office.

"Jocelyn, could you please bring us a pot of coffee?"

"Of course, Mr. Jamieson." Jocelyn's tone was a perfect combination of warmth and professionalism.

Sara looked back as Jocelyn picked up the phone. Ordering coffee, Sara hoped, but knew there was the distinct possibility that she was calling allies to launch an attack against her new enemy.

20

Patrick Jamieson motioned Sara to a corner of his office where a large velvet sofa presided over the other furniture that was gathered around it. Jamieson offered her the sofa and took a serious looking straight-backed chair with mahogany arms. Jamieson looked expectantly at her across the wide oval coffee table. She had to tip her chin sharply to look at him. She wondered if he had ever had a summer job at the agency that had taught her the "the power is in the height of your chair" philosophy. Surely he had.

He was the first to speak.

"I hope you're not uncomfortable. I find that sofa is a little low but I'm sorry I can't volunteer to take it myself. Wrecked my back playing rugby and I need more support."

So he wasn't playing the chair game. She was beginning to like Patrick Jamieson.

A wave of nervousness swept in and settled in her stomach. Now that she was here it struck her powerfully that everything she had to say sound terribly unsubstantial. Her palms began to sweat. Thank God they had already done the handshaking.

"Patrick, I'm sorry about the trouble you are having with the union organizers. I know that must be very stressful," she started and then hesitated for a moment.

Get to it Porter, she thought.

"However, the key action items we stressed as a result of last year's employee satisfaction assessment, I am convinced would have prevented this from happening if they had been followed."

Jamieson opened his mouth to speak but she forged ahead.

"I'm sure there are all kinds of good reasons the recommendations weren't implemented." Not so — they had, as too often was the case, gotten too busy and had forgotten about the initiative. Being too busy was a poor and often self-destructive excuse. But she had to offer a face-saving bit. "And it is obviously not my role to reprimand Jamieson's, nor am I here to say we told you so." She inserted a smile and then continued. "I'm convinced that some of the items could still be implemented quickly and relatively easily and prevent the union from getting in the door."

Jamieson inched forward in his chair. She had his attention.

"The rest can be implemented gradually and your employees need never think union again."

The penetrating blue eyes lit up again. She pulled copies of the original report from her case and gave Jamieson a brief refresher of the survey results. Then she moved into describing a quick-start program for getting the Jamieson company back into shape.

"I strongly recommend that you start by meeting with the staff as soon as possible. Meet with small groups if you can't get everyone together. It's important for people to see personally that you do care. Let people know that the values that made Jamieson's strong are still alive but admit that they perhaps haven't been shouted as loudly as they should have been the last few years."

A quick tap on the office door that was almost simultaneous with its opening interrupted them just as Sara was getting into her stride. The tap, a request for permission to enter that the immediate opening of the door acknowledged wasn't necessary but still proper, had been Jocelyn's self-announcement. She made an entrance that was at once elegant and efficient, in spite of the apparent weight of the silver coffee service she balanced. Sara watched the heels of Jocelyn's alligator pumps disappear into the plush carpet with each step of her advance.

The tray slid onto the coffee table smoothly and silently. Not a clash of silver against wood or rattle of porcelain cup against porcelain saucer.

"Shall I pour for you, Mr. Jamieson?" No acknowledgement of Sara's presence.

"No thanks, Jocelyn. I'm not terribly adept at serving but I think Sara will overlook that failing and pour for us."

With an emphasis on the word "that" and a smile in Sara's direction, Jamieson admitted he had indeed dropped some corporate balls. Sara's respect for the man leapt and so did her liking.

"And, Jocelyn," he added, "could you cancel my eleven o'clock meeting?"

Sara set aside her notes in order to pour the coffee and then went immediately back to the list of quick-fixes that Jamieson's could implement.

Jamieson did much note taking and head nodding, interspersed with an occasional pithy question. Just as she had presented her last major point about the employee engagement learning program she felt was direly needed to increase staff's commitment, he wriggled his wrist further out of the white linen cuff to check his watch.

"You'll have to excuse me for just a minute. I have to take a call.

He moved to his desk and notified Jos that he was ready.

"Hello, Martin. How are you?" His opening held the same warmth with which he greeted her.

Sara didn't want to appear to be listening and so wandered over to a collection of pictures scattered on a lovely antique table by the window. She perused the photos. Jamieson with Princess Diana, Jamieson with Harrison Ford, Jamieson with the Obamas, and with several other news-making types. In a photo of a ribbon-cutting ceremony she recognized Nathan Phillips, Toronto's mayor at the time of the opening of this Jamieson's location. The smiling man beside him must be Jamieson Senior and the woman in a feathered hat probably Patrick's mother.

"I understood that had been taken care of." Jamieson kept his voice low but its mellowness had disappeared. "Look, I've told you and the whole committee that I'm not in this to lose. It's your job to ensure we've got the support and maintain it."

Sara had moved on to what appeared to be family photos. A group on a dock. lined up with arms over each other's shoulders. The women wearing full bathing suits and bathing caps and the men in conservative trunks. With a start, Sara realized that she had gotten so involved with the Jamiesons' corporate struggle that she had forgotten her real motive for being here.

She picked up the photo taken on the dock and moved over to the window. Her heart started racing a little faster. This was the Group. Aunt Kate was at one end, easily recognizable by the pose. Her right hand rested on her hip, the hand bent under so only the top of her wrist was visible. Her chin was tilted slightly upward and there was a look of defiance about her.

In the middle between two men, Harper, she guessed and probably Teddy, was another young woman, beautiful in spite of the rubber bathing cap she was wearing, its strap snapped tightly under her chin. Even in a shot at this distance, those eyes penetrated the lens. Jane Stewart. How long after this was taken was the girl dead? And more disturbing, were pieces of that tragedy forming in the minds of any of those smiling, apparently carefree faces?

Sara found herself shivering. She moved to the other end of the table where sunlight streamed in from the window and stood in its warmth.

She had found her segue into her aunt's and Judge Jamieson's past.

"You set up what? I'm not interested in being interviewed by any smart-assed journalist out to make a name for himself. I'm squeaky clean but some of those guys could devour Snow White and turn her into a piece of shit." Jamieson no longer bothered to keep his voice low.

"Find the right interviewer or I don't do one. I want absolutely no cracks in this campaign." Jamieson didn't give his caller an opportunity to reply. He hung up the phone and tugged at his jacket sleeve as he moved away from his desk.

"Sorry for the interruption." The charming voice was back. "You may have heard that I'm running for parliament."

Sara nodded, although she hadn't actually heard but thought she probably should have. "Yes, congratulations."

"Thank you, but there is an amazing amount of road-paving to do before even entering the race."

Before Jamieson could close their meeting Sara picked up the picture of the Group from the family photo display and enthused, "Can you believe this? My aunt is in this shot."

"Really?" Jamieson joined her by the window.

"See right here on the end."

"Kathryn McPherson? I didn't realize she was your aunt. She passed away recently, didn't she?"

"Yes, just after your uncle."

After the two exchanged condolences Jamieson went on to explain the photo.

"This was taken at my grandparents' summer place. These people were inseparable. Next to your aunt is Harper; he eventually worked with our family and handled all of the financial affairs. Then there is Jane Stewart, and then Uncle Teddy. Jane Stewart met a very tragic end. She disappeared toward the end of that summer and her body was found on a deserted part of the beach not far from the cottage."

"Yes, I heard something about that." Sara made an effort to convey no more than a casual acknowledgement.

"The fellow on the end is Kendall. Don't know what happened to him but I remember he was the Group's clown." That coincided with Howard Hamilton's memory of Kendall, a man quite forgettable except that he made people laugh. Not a bad way to be remembered, Sara thought.

"Who's the scrawny kid mugging at the camera?" Sara point to a small figure that seemed to have jumped into the picture in front of the Group at the last second, before the shutter spiraled open and closed.

"That's Howie, the son of our housekeeper, Phyllis Baker. Died young, poor guy but a couple of her younger children still work with us."

Sara wanted to seize the opportunity and question him more about the Group but didn't get the chance.

A loud rap at the door announced that someone had gotten by Jocelyn. It couldn't be Jocelyn herself because the door didn't open simultaneously with the rap. Jamieson hesitated for a moment, obviously not used to being interrupted, and then responded with a "Yes? Come in."

Martha Southern strode into the office and looked not at Jamieson but directly at Sara.

Sara, what a surprise! I didn't know you were here." Martha's deep voice boomed across the room. It gave no hint of the surprise she professed.

21

Carson rested his elbows on his desk and ground the heels of his hands mercilessly into his dry gritty eyeballs. He had worked all night and his body was demanding sleep. But he had more to do and he knew from much too much experience that if he could keep going a little longer, his body would kick back into gear and he would be able to push it for several more hours if need be.

Late last night he had gone over to forensics on Jane Street in hope of getting access to Diane Brooks' personal effects. Getting access to evidence storage was not usually a slam dunk. Forensics was reluctant, and rightfully so, to risk any contamination of articles which might prove important to the Crown's case should there ever be one. It turned out, however, to be his lucky night. The officer on duty was a neighbor of his sister and his kids played with Carson's nephews. After a bit of small talk about the boys trying out for house league hockey, Carson's request to have access to the Brooks effects was granted with nothing more than a nod, a pair of gloves and a key.

Forensics too was being refurbished and the older property boxes hadn't yet been moved back to the evidence room. The last time he had been there the room had been lined with gray metal storage shelves, each shelf piled high with labeled boxes. A couple of new-looking bankers boxes were piled in a corner, and one white one labeled Brooks had been left in the middle of a boardroom-sized table of pale blond wood. Shelves had not as yet been installed. It felt sterile and the belongings of the victim looked impersonal and abandoned.

In the box, was a plastic bag that held Diane Brooks' final choice of clothing. The white blouse of soft silk had settled unobtrusively into one corner of the bag. Not until one pulled it out was the large rusty spot that caked it obvious. Purple stretch pants filled most of the bag. White lacy lingerie that competed with the blouse for softness rested in another corner. A diamond and pearl ring and a tortoise shell hair clip had completed her ensemble. The contents seemed oddly inadequate. Normally the victim's shoes swelled the bag but Diane Brooks had chosen to go barefoot that evening.

A decision that struck him as that of a free-spirited, lively individual. The thought saddened him.

Otherwise the box held only a pad of paper, her laptop, and a ballpoint pen, the kind that, as he once discovered had a tendency to leak at 30,000 feet. He had been flying to pick up a suspect who had been spotted by the Chicago police. He arrived at O'Hare with a huge blue ink spot that had spread so far across the front of his shirt that his jacket couldn't hide it.

He was just shutting down Brooks' laptop when his cell phone rang.

It was the duty sergeant, telling him there had been another murder. A teenager had been knifed at a club. Apparently a nice clean-cut middle-class eighteen-year old.

A cruiser had been immediately dispatched to the scene and the club was locked up but who knew who had left before the car got there?

Carson was barely in his car when he got a call from Simpson. This made the third murder in a few days and the Inspector's voice reflected his stress level.

"Somebody in that club has to be able to describe whoever did it. I don't want anyone to leave there, and I mean anyone, until you have something. I want you to head this up. Get Kirpatrick down there and I'll send a few more uniformed as well."

Kirkpatrick mustn't have been having a great evening at home. His voice was down when he picked up the phone but became decidedly cheerier when he heard he'd be out all night on a case.

They had spent the rest of the night at the Down Under Club, a barrack of a place that used to be a warehouse. The lights had been turned up, and it was not a place that was meant to be lit. Cobwebs hung from steel beams; tables were formica kitchen jobs that had been left over from the fifties, and barely left over at that. Chairs matched the period but that was the only thing they matched. Their chrome legs were corroded and covered with rust or dirt and torn; colored plastic seats oozed dirty cotton padding.

Altogether they interviewed over a hundred kids. Some hysterical. Many too cool, as though the murder of a peer was an everyday happening. None had seen who had done it. Carson and Kirpatrick heard only what they already knew. There had been a fight and when it was over Neil Kestler was slumped on the bar with a stab wound in his stomach.

His friends claimed he hadn't been involved in the fight but it had erupted around him. No, they didn't know who had been in the fight and no, they hadn't seen any knives.

The music had been so loud and the club so dark that many hadn't even known there had been a fight, let alone a murder.

Kirpatrick had tried every trick in the book and added several of his own in an attempt to get some kind of information out of someone, anyone. Carson understood his motivation. Kirpatrick was desperate to not be part of a team that went back to Simpson empty-handed twice in one twenty-four-hour period.

Carson had to give him credit for his effort. He tried everything from empathy, to sharing cigarettes with cool-looking kids who claimed to be eighteen but had no doubt gotten in with phony ID, to an unpracticed tough cop routine that Carson was sure had some of the kids snickering rather than shaking. If anyone had seen anything they were likely too afraid to talk. This wasn't a crowd in which you were likely to find the one or two nerdy kids who felt it was their duty to do the "right thing."

They found no weapons of any kind. It was the practice of the club's security to check everyone for hardware before allowing them in. The owner was furious that someone had gotten through with a knife. Carson suspected that this security crew would be looking for a new job tomorrow.

The night had been made more exhausting by the dense cigarette smoke and smell of stale beer that filled the place. The ventilation was either nonexistent or on the blink. The cigarette smoke would cost the owner. The whole city had been designated smoke-free ages ago.

The only good thing about the night was that he and Kirpatrick hadn't been elected to take the news to Kestler's parents. Carson had had to do it too often and was convinced that no matter how tough a cop was, the task sapped away a little of their life-force, which could never be replaced.

When the two finally left the club, they had stepped into a damp, dusky morning that could easily have been taken for evening, Kirpatrick clutching their consolation prize, a bag full of sundry street drugs, under his arm.

Both sides of the street were lined with cars. Parents waiting to pick up their children. Thank God he had never had children, Carson thought. No matter how old they were they would still be a worry and in his job he was only too aware that there was plenty for parents to worry about. Mercifully, most of these tired-looking people, pulled out of bed too early, had no idea of just how much.

The morning was spent briefing Simpson and filing reports. The coffee he had been drinking for several hours non-stop had burnt a trail down his esophagus and into his gut. He felt like he had been mainlining caffeine. His heart pounded and although his body felt exhausted, he was at the same time wound up and strung out.

Greally was the last person he wanted to deal with but he wasn't given the option. Perfectly pressed and chewing his signature wad of Juicy Fruit, Greally leaned against the entrance to Carson's cubicle. Carson had had the bad luck of drawing a workspace next to Greally's. He could think of a long list of not-so-nice criminals whom he would select as neighbors ahead of Greally.

"So, nothing from the Porter broad."

It wasn't a question but a statement. Who had Greally been talking to?

"No, nothing from the Porter woman, if that's whom you mean. Or better still, nothing from Sara Porter." Carson placed the heels of his hands back on his eyeballs and tilted his chair back against the wall.

"Such a gentleman. Never done you much good though has it?" Greally did sarcasm better than most.

Carson caught the innuendo but chose to ignore it. In fact, he chose to ignore Greally completely, hoping the rat would find someone else to gnaw on. No such luck.

"She's guilty, Carz, guilty as hell."

Carz? Christ, the nerve of the man. Marlene was the only person who had called him Carz. Greally must have picked it up from her. Carson forced himself to continue to ignore the man, but it was getting tougher.

Greally wasn't deterred.

"You know damn well she was lying about not remembering what time she came home. You know she hated Diane Brooks, hated the thought of Porter having a child by her, and was home late enough to have had time to get to their place and kill her. It's time to start putting the pressure on her."

Carson used a heavy sigh to push his chair back to its upright position. The ignoring option had been eliminated. If Greally didn't get a reaction from Carson, he would go away with his need to shit-disturb unsatisfied and would take his theory to anyone else who would listen. Greally could be very convincing. He could have been an evangelist or a politician. He somehow got people to buy what he was saying in spite of reason shouting loudly that what he was spouting was BS. If he managed to convince the rest of the unit that he was right, then everyone would start focusing on Sara Porter as the number one suspect.

He made a concerted effort to keep the exasperation he was feeling from his voice.

"Greally, the woman was drunk. I don't suppose you've ever been just a little hazy about the happenings of the night before?"

Greally continued to lean and folded his arms in his "I'm above it all and in particular above you" stance. Carson remembered that pose. It had been in a different doorway. Carson had been working late in the case room, going over all of the notes jotted on a white board. It was the middle of the night and there was no one around. He hadn't heard Greally approach and was startled as he looked up to see him there. No preamble, just: "It's time you knew, Carson. Marlene and I are together. We have been for weeks. When you get home she won't be there." And he pushed himself casually away from the door jamb and was gone.

In retrospect, Carson was surprised that Greally hadn't waited around to enjoy the shock and sadness that Carson knew he wouldn't have been able to hide.

Marlene was fifteen years younger than Carson. She had been a PhD student working part-time at the coffee shop up the street from headquarters. He had fallen in love with her youth, her energy and the quick smile that he knew she shared with every customer but that he liked to believe was even more special when sent his way. Their first date had been the annual police picnic. She had been completely at home because she knew so many of the men from their coming into the coffee shop. Greally, he remembered, had grabbed her as a partner for the three-legged race.

Carson had been married twice before and had had no intention of ever marrying again.

It had just evolved. She had spent more and more time at his apartment. He never went to hers. He liked to be in his own space and wake up in his own bed. At first she would spend one night and then it would be a weekend, then several days. It got to the point that most of her clothes and personal belongings were at his place and eventually she just stayed without either of them having stated the intention of that happening. Carson had let it happen because there was no reason not to. He loved her, she was easygoing, never placing expectations on him and secretly he knew that one of her attractions to him was that she was studying psychology. Perhaps she would understand his idiosyncrasies better than the other women in his life had, and perhaps she could even help him understand himself.

At first she had seen his odd behaviors, like throwing out a nearly new pair of shoes because they had been scuffed, as a personality quirk. Something almost endearing and deserving of gentle teasing. "There goes my Carz again," she would say, "never accepting anything less than perfection in his world. That must mean I'm pretty perfect then, huh?" She would laugh and kiss him, and on really lucky days when neither of them was rushing anywhere, would pull him into the bedroom, push him onto the bed and jump on top of him. In that space, the world really was perfect, and sometimes it would be hours before they would return to the one that wasn't.

A few months after she had moved in with him, Marlene celebrated her thirtieth birthday. That morning, before they got out of bed, she announced that it was time they got married. Once again he had no real reason not to. They got out of bed, searched the blue pages of the phone book for the number for City Hall and booked the next opening. Marlene bought a pale blue silk suit that made her eyes, the bluest eyes he had ever seen, even bluer, and he bought a new Versace tie to go with his best dark navy suit. His sister, Maggie, and Alberto accompanied them as their witnesses and after the ceremony they went back to Maggie's for a light lunch and champagne. As much as Marlene had insisted on getting married, the event itself seemed almost unimportant to her. It had hardly been a blip in their daily routine. Carson expected that talk of a baby would be next and he wasn't sure how he felt about that, but otherwise he had no reason to expect things to be any different than they had been. But almost immediately Marlene became more aware of his compulsive behaviors, or more frequently let him know she was aware of them, one or the other.

"Carz, this just isn't normal. You really should go for counseling," she would repeat on many occasions.

He would throw back, "That's just the way I am. It's only a nuisance to myself and does no harm to anyone else. So let's forget about it."

She would immediately drop the subject and find some unimportant happening at the university to talk about.

One Saturday morning he had just turned on his favorite jazz music station and settled in the living room with his coffee and newspaper when he noticed a scratch in the cherry inlaid coffee table that he had found at an estate sale. The craftsmanship had been noticeable even to one ignorant of the art of woodworking. Its stain was a rich auburn and the finish a soft satin.

The scratch across the bottom left corner began boldly, traveled for three inches and ended as a barely visible hairline. He ran his finger over it.

The response that welled inside him was as usual immediate. A flash of terrible pain at beauty lost melded instantaneously into fury. He swept the newspapers from its top, picked up the table and lugged it through the apartment door, heading for the garbage room in the basement. He carried the heavy table awkwardly as he made his way down the stairs, noisily bouncing into the wall on one side and the black iron railing on the other. Just before he reached the next landing he heard Marlene above him. He looked up to see her leaning over the banister. He knew she was speaking to him but it seemed as though the voice must be coming from someone else. There was an anger and frustration in it that was foreign to the woman he adored.

"Christ, Carz. What in the hell are you doing? You really are crazy. You know that?"

Her voice echoed down the stairwell. As it reached him, her face was already filled with regret and fear. In that instant she knew as well as he that their relationship now was marred more indelibly than the table. Her face blanched. There was no taking back the words and Carson would never feel the same about her again.

He carried the table back to the apartment, sat down and put his feet on it, read his paper and finished his coffee, leaving the mug to sit on the satiny wood. They continued to live together but the relationship had ended. It was three months later that Greally had made his announcement.

"If Sara Porter was drunk," Greally was saying, "all the more likely she would commit murder. Her inhibitions were down."

Carson shook his head, not looking up from the doodles he was drawing on a note pad. He wanted to say that his every instinct told him that Sara Porter didn't do it, but he strove to be logical.

"We just don't have a solid enough case against her."

Greally continued to lean for a few more minutes and then responded: "You're afraid I've prematurely decided she is guilty and will do whatever I can to prove myself right in spite of any evidence to the contrary. You are just as dangerous. You've decided she's innocent and are ignoring any evidence that might prove her guilty."

Greally had cleanly scored the final run of the inning.

22

Sara was glad the elevator was empty. She leaned back to steady her shaking legs. The mirrored wall felt cool through her jacket. She had been crazy to do what she had done and still didn't know for sure whether she had gotten away with it. She had managed to hold her composure or thought she had the whole time she was in the Jamieson's offices, even when Martha challenged her. Mind you, she had had some help there.

Sara had been trying to formulate a plausible response to Martha's comment that she hadn't known that Sara was on the Jamieson's premises when Patrick Jamieson responded, "I invited Sara in to discuss possible options for dealing with this union business. I meant to let you know but somehow let it slip."

Sara's relief had been mixed with something else and she had found herself biting back unexpected tears. She had been rescued. She couldn't remember the last time she had been rescued or even helped. She suddenly realized how long she had been fending for herself, in every way.

She decided her foray had been successful. From a professional point of view she was convinced that she had helped the company. As far as completing the job Aunt Kate had left her, she had made progress, even though Martha had interrupted her. Before she left, Jamieson had said that he was in the process of going through his uncle's things and there were many photos and letters dating back to the days of the Group. He thought they might be of interest to her as well. Why didn't she drop in on Sunday for brunch and they could look through them together?

She hoped he wasn't looking for a thank you for the rescue.

Sara pushed her way through the revolving doors and into the street. Indian summer had swept in during the morning. The temperature had risen several degrees since she had entered the building and now her suit jacket felt far too warm. She pulled out her cell phone to check for messages. Head down, punching in her code, she didn't notice she was moving into the path of a fast moving Gen Xer, sleeves rolled up and suit jacket slung over his shoulder, enjoying the last taste of warm weather before winter slipped into the city.

They collided and her phone clattered to the sidewalk. "Sorry," they both chorused at once and he bent to retrieve her phone. As he handed it to her, a chill overpowered the warm weather and ran from her tailbone up into her scalp. Just yesterday someone else had picked up something for her as she was coming out of the Lost Camel. An image she hadn't been aware of at the time appeared full blown. A small hand reaching up to offer her pen, the figure still bent over and only the Blue Jays cap visible. Why should it be bothering her now? Diane's murder was putting her nerves on edge. That had to be it.

Her logic and the summer temperature soon returned heat to her body. Perspiration dotted her forehead and ran in a rivulet down her back. She pulled off her jacket as she reached the car park. It was a relief to enter the cool, dark stairwell. She hoped she remembered where she had left the car. It seemed like a very long time ago that she had driven in. P3 she thought. Three levels down.

It was the middle of the day and completely quiet. No commuters coming or going. Her shoes echoed on the dirty cement stairs. She stepped over an empty rum bottle and breathed shallowly to avoid the smell of urine. A street person had probably spent the night here using the dirty steps as a bed and the alcohol as comfort.

She stopped at the first landing to readjust her load of briefcase, purse, and jacket.

She could hear footsteps on the stairs above her. Not clattering ones like her own. Muffled as though they were wearing running shoes. She thought little of it but instinctively glanced upward. Light from the entrance put the descending figure completely in shadow. Suddenly the figure stumbled and the empty liquor bottle clanked against the concrete wall. A small white hand grabbed the railing above her.

The chill of fear returned and she turned and ran downward. A collage of thoughts accompanied the pounding of her heart. It had to be her imagination. Who would want to follow her? He was likely just someone heading for his car. He couldn't be the man who picked up her pen yesterday. There were lots of people with small hands … but not small monkey hands like his.

She rummaged in her bag for her keys as she ran and thought she heard muffled footsteps behind her but couldn't be sure. She charged through the green door that read P3 and left it to slam loudly behind her. Where had she left the car? To the left or the right?

Remember!

She dashed to the right looking up and down the rows. She heard the door slam behind her. She didn't look back. There, two rows over. Her black Volvo. She ran to her left clicking her remote key as she ran. She felt relief as she reached the car and grabbed the handle and pulled. Locked. She clicked her key again and then spotted a red sweater that she had never seen before on the passenger seat. The wrong car. A twin, but not hers.

Fear was turning to panic. She scanned the area from where she had come. No one and no sound. Surely if the person behind her had been returning to their car she would have heard a door slam or an engine start. Nothing. She crouched and made her way along the row keeping as low as possible. A beeping siren exploded into the silence and was magnified by the open space and concrete walls. Sara gasped and jumped upright, hitting her head on a car's side mirror. Someone's alarm system! Then she spotted the flashing lights of the car, her black Volvo, a few rows away and closer to the entrance. He was there. He knew which car was hers. She glanced toward the exit. She could just see the top half of it above the cars parked beside it. Could she make it to the exit before him? Before she could decide the door opened a crack and a blue cap slipped through it and was gone.

Her knees buckled under her and she slipped down into a sitting position on the cold cement floor. She held herself tight until the shaking stopped. My God he was stalking her. He knew her car. But why? He must be some loony. Or maybe it was the police following her. But why would they set off her alarm? Her Volvo continued to wail for attention and she pulled herself upright and moved as quickly as her wobbly legs would allow. She held the security remote tightly in her hand but didn't use it until she was right at the car, not wanting to alert her predator of her movements in case he had not left but was waiting behind the door. Alarm off, door unlocked, she checked the back seat, scrambled into the car, relocked the door and immediately started the engine, all the time watching the exit. Did the door open a crack? She didn't wait to see but gunned the Volvo up the three ramps, ignoring the several times her tires recklessly scraped against the curb.

She didn't notice the blue Honda Civic emerge from the second level and snake its way up the ramp some distance behind her.

23

Sara emerged from the parking garage into bumper-to-bumper traffic. Normally she would have found it immensely frustrating. Now the imposed slowness gave her a chance to breathe deeply and slow the pounding of her heart. Torontonians liked to complain that constant road construction during the good weather made summer driving worse than the ice and snow of winter driving. Today they were right. It seemed the works department was determined to use the lingering good weather to pave as many feet of roadway as possible.

Sara was detoured off University. She made the turn but ignored the orange sign that instructed her to drive straight ahead. Instead she took a left and in hope of finding a shorter route made her way behind the hospital complexes that lined that main thoroughfare. She wasted ten minutes exploring dead ends before she turned around and rejoined the now longer cue that was obediently following the signs. She should have known better. Three taxis were hunkered in the almost-still line of cars. If there had been another route they would have taken it.

Use the time, she told herself. Collect your thoughts. Although her heart was no longer pounding a deafening drum roll in her ears, it was still racing. Those minutes in the underground parking were the first time she had ever experienced fear. She had been anxious before the delivery of each of the children. She had been alarmed when they discovered that James and his friends were experimenting with drugs. The thought of losing her career, her toe-hold on the world, frightened her, as did the thought of spending the rest of her life alone. But real fear, the raw terror she had felt in the garage, was a new experience.

How had she done, she wondered. Had she made the best decisions possible in the circumstance? Had she sufficiently controlled her fear? Had she outwitted him?

When she realized what she was doing, she knew that Richard had been right. She was a compulsive overachiever, marking her performance in every aspect of life, even now in a potentially life and death situation. Surely the last thought in a normal person's mind wouldn't be, "How did I do?"

She had turned north onto Bay and the traffic had picked up. The farther she drove from the car park, the less plausible the whole thing seemed. Just because someone with small hands in a Blue Jays cap picked up her pen yesterday, and a person with small hands and wearing a Jays cap was in the car park, it didn't necessarily follow that they were the same person or that the man was following her.

An earlier thought returned and sparked an anger that burned away any residue of fear. The police. They were following her. That had to be it. Damn that Detective Carson. The anger didn't grow. It exploded. How dare they follow her? Who did they think they were? If she were a suspect, tell her, goddammit!

She reached over to the passenger seat with one hand, rummaged through her bag for her cell, and called information.

"Toronto Police Headquarters, please."

An electronic operator gave her the number and told her that her call would be automatically completed. The phone was picked up on the first ring.

"Toronto Police Headquarters."

"Detective Carson, please."

"Detective Carson isn't in his office. May I take a message?"

"No, this is urgent." It was urgent to her. "Is there any other way I can contact him?"

"You might try his cell number."

The woman passed it on to her. Sara had no pen and so repeated it under her breath until she finished redialing. Damn. Was the last digit 7 or 8? Sara dialed 7 and held her breath.

"Carson here."

Carson was in the lunchroom when he took the call from Sara Porter. After the brief conversation, he pocketed his cell and resumed emptying a fresh packet of coffee into the coffee-maker's filter. With the refurbished headquarters came an automatic coffee dispenser that had been squeezed in beside the pop machine. It called itself The Coffee Elite and boasted that it brewed the best gourmet coffee on the planet. But Carson knew better. He had retrieved the ancient coffee maker just as a bunch of the detectives had been arm wrestling for it. The young guys complained that the battered machine and its coffee-grimed pot ruined the sleek new eating area. They insisted on filling their cups with cappuccino or that flavored stuff that masqueraded as coffee from the new upscale equipment. Carson's contemporaries stuck to the old pot. "Coffee you could count on," they called it.

Coffee played an important role in a cop shop. Plenty of cases had been discussed, personal tragedies shared, and jokes made, while gathered around the pot, waiting for the warm brew to drip through. Turns had been taken keeping the pot filled and those who shirked their coffee duty were in deep trouble. A report uncompleted could be forgiven but not an empty coffee pot. The coffee maker's importance came not just from the critical feature — that it made coffee that could keep the dead awake — but there was something comforting about the old pot and the ritual that went with it.

"Sara Porter," Carson said to Kirpatrick who was slouched at a table, checking out his Sunshine Girl in the morning paper. A cup of something that smelled sickly sweet like an amaretto liqueur sat at his elbow.

"Yeah, what about her?" Kirpatrick asked, not taking his eyes off of the young woman who apparently had appeal for him but left Carson cold. She was so slender she was little more than bones covered with skin. Holding her would be as exciting as putting one's arms around a wooden coat rack, Carson thought. He liked the warmth and softness that a little feminine padding brought to an embrace.

"That was Sara Porter on the phone," he announced casually.

"Oh, yeah?" Carson had his attention now. "What did she want?"

"Don't know," Carson shrugged. "She sounded not too happy about something and said she wanted to see me. She'll be here in twenty minutes."

"Damn, and I've got to leave. I promised Kathy I'd be home in time to go with her to the obstetrician for her ultrasound. She says I'm not taking enough interest in the baby."

Kirpatrick looked glum. Carson suspected it was as much the fact that he had to leave before Sara Porter got here as it was his domestic problems.

"Don't worry. I guarantee you're not going to miss a confession," Carson assured him.

Kirpatrick just nodded and left, leaving the Sunshine Girl exposed on the table. Carson ran his hand over his day-and-a-half stubble. He knew he must look like hell and found himself wishing he didn't. He poured his coffee and carried it with him down the hall to the locker room. They had removed the lockers to paint the room and had managed to mix them up when they put them back. His locker had always been the third from the end and he had had no need to remember its number. Now he looked down the row trying to remember it. Either sixteen or seventeen. He whirled the numbers on the combination lock to sixteen. It opened easily and the old papers stuffed in the bottom and the old smelly gym shoes that he hadn't worn for years confirmed it was his. His gym bag sat slumped on top of them. Otherwise it was orderly and nearly empty, with just the basics that any detective kept close at hand. A shaving kit with toothbrush, paste, shaver, cologne and deodorant. Shoe polish and brush. A freshly pressed suit and a couple of shirts crisp from the laundry still in their white paper packaging. The only thing that truly marked the locker as his were the two silk ties hung carefully on hooks on the door.

He set his coffee on a bench and stripped to his socks and briefs, rolled his stale and sticky clothes into a ball and shoved them in on top of the gym bag. A little deodorant, a fresh shirt and perfectly pressed navy suit and he felt his energy returning. He gave his shoes a quick buff before he put them on. No time for a shave. He picked up his coffee and took a couple of sips as he checked out his beard in the wall mirror. Not bad, he thought as he ran his hand over the stubble.

24

She pulled into the Women's College Hospital parking garage. Police Headquarters was just down the street. It was a nondescript buff-colored building that could have housed almost anything. Anything, that is, that was serious business. It exuded neither warmth nor welcome but that, she supposed, was appropriate considering the people and issues that entered here.

The sergeant at the desk changed her impression.

"Good afternoon. How can I help you?" His smile convinced her that it truly would be his pleasure to be of assistance.

"Detective Sergeant Carson is expecting me."

The sergeant called Carson on his cell and, with another smile, told her Carson would be down to meet her right away.

Sara paced back and forth between the information desk and one of the pillars, using the movement to help grow an attitude of indignation that she hoped would carry her successfully through the meeting.

When Detective Carson arrived he made a couple of forays into the world of small talk on the way to the lunchroom where he had apparently thought they should meet. The suddenly hot weather. How was the traffic? Sara answered, but just, trying to maintain an "I've got a bone to pick" persona. She found it more difficult than she had expected. There was something paradoxical in this man that she found attractive. There was a mixture of the toughness and distance that one expected from someone in his profession with a sensitivity and empathy that were less expected. The slight hint of good cologne she detected as they squeezed into the crowded elevator together was distracting as well.

Carson offered her coffee, reading aloud the numerous choices from the front of a futuristic-looking coffee dispenser. When she responded, "Just regular Colombian would be perfect, thanks," his smile suggested she had just moved up a notch on his approval rating scale.

He led the way to a corner table that was directly above the busy College

Street and she wished for a moment that she was still down there in traffic, heading home.

"Well, what can I do for you?" Carson asked as soon as they were seated. He looked directly and earnestly into her eyes. A sincere personal habit, she wondered, or police lie-detection training?

"Why are you having me followed?" she asked, looking intently at him in return.

The hint of surprise that briefly washed his face triggered her fear once again. If not the police then …?

"We are not having you followed, Ms. Porter. Tell me why you think someone is following you."

Carson's tone had softened slightly. Had he seen the fear arrive? Sara took a breath and tried not to show the quivering she felt inside. She thought for a moment, looking for details that would explain her fear and prevent her from looking like a hysterical woman.

"Yesterday I was in a café on Queen Street West. I was sitting by the window, watching people go by. I noticed a Blue Jays cap that would appear at the corner of the window from time to time. I had the impression that someone was lingering outside but didn't think anything of it. When I left the café and was a little ways up the street I dropped my pen and a man picked it up. He handed it up to me from a crouched position but didn't look at me. All I saw was his hand, white and very small for an adult but too well-used to be that of a child, and his Blue Jays cap."

Now, sitting in the sunlight that beamed through the lunchroom window, with her hands wrapped around a cup of coffee, the event suddenly seemed increasingly absurd. Her planned indignation and the momentary fear both disappeared. She paused for a moment.

"Go on," he encouraged.

She shook her head and looked down into her coffee. "This sounds ridiculous and I'm feeling rather embarrassed."

She hoped he would echo that the whole scenario was very unlikely but instead he said, "I've met little in police business that to the average sensible citizen wouldn't seem ridiculous. Please tell me the rest."

Her uneasiness returned and she continued hurriedly.

"This afternoon I was on Bloor Street and was entering an underground parking garage. I was on the stairs and I heard someone above me. When I looked up they were in shadow but a small white hand was grasping the railing. It frightened me and I ran down to my parking level. I was disoriented and went to the wrong car and a few moments later I heard the alarm of my own car. Someone must have set it off but I didn't see anyone. It was difficult to see between the cars."

She decided to leave out the detail of her crouching down and crawling between them.

"Then when I looked toward the exit I saw the door open. I could only see the top half but I saw someone leave. He was short and wearing a blue baseball cap."

Carson stared pensively at her for a few minutes saying nothing and then suggested they move to his office so he could take some detailed notes.

She had to walk quickly to keep up with his long strides. They had walked by several mini offices, created by dividing open space with fabric screens, when he stopped short in front of one, stood aside, and motioned for her to go in. Someone spoke to Carson and he stopped outside to speak with him.

At first she thought the display on his desk was a colorful collage. And then the individual pieces separated themselves from the whole. Several colored 8 by 10 photos were scattered across the desk. Each a different view of the same subject. The body of Diane Brooks taken from every conceivable angle.

Carson was barely through his office door when he shouted, "What the hell?" and quickly began gathering the pictures into a confused pile. The photo from which Sara could not remove her gaze was the last he collected, giving her enough time to unwillingly commit it to memory. Diane slumped over the kitchen bar. A dark blotch covering the left upper part of the white shirt that was neatly tucked into purple pants. Diane's blond hair falling across her shoulders, gathered at the nape of her neck by a large tortoise shell clasp. Her right hand still holding a pen.

Nausea overtook Sara and she ran from the office, down the hall to the bathroom she and Detective Carson had passed moments ago. Once in the restroom, she let the water run cold and splashed it on her face until the nausea passed. She patted her face dry with a paper towel and leaned forward, resting her forehead on the cool mirror.

It wasn't the dead body that had made her ill. For the first few seconds she was able to look at the photo with a surprising detachment and curiosity. What sickened her was the realization that the Diane in the photos was the Diane in her dream last night. Diane had been sitting at the kitchen bar, had been wearing a white shirt and purple pants. Even the tortoise shell hair clip was the same. She had dreamt the scene exactly as it had been. Acknowledging the implications of that brought another wave of nausea.

But the matching of the photos with her dream hadn't been her brain's first response. As soon as she saw the photos, words from Aunt Kate's notebook had come to her.

God she still has style, she thought, hatred overpowering any other emotion.

That was exactly her own immediate reaction to the photo of Diane in death. She shuddered at the callousness and egocentricity of the words. Surely no normal person could react with so little feeling.

"Greally, what the hell were you thinking?" Carson held his hands clenched tightly at his sides as he strode into the space next door.

"What's your problem?" Greally made no effort to conceal his pleasure at his own cleverness.

"You did that intentionally didn't you? You spread those damn things all over the desk because someone told you she was coming in." He'd hit Greally once before and was struggling against a repeat performance.

"Yeah, and it worked. Look at her reaction." Greally walked to the door and glanced down the hall, checking that Sara Porter had not emerged from the ladies' room. "She's as guilty as hell. You're just postponing the inevitable and making us all look bad in the process."

Carson said nothing but glared his anger at the other man.

Greally needed no encouragement to continue.

"You're getting soft, Carson. I hear they're offering early retirement packages to some of you old farts. Maybe you should go for one while you've got the chance." He shoved past Carson and headed down the hall toward the Inspector's office. Carson had no doubt what the topic of conversation would be.

25

Sara spent the entire afternoon at police headquarters. Cason apologized for the photos having been left on his desk, probed her memory for details about the little man in the Blue Jays cap and explored the issue of whether Richard had had any enemies that might be getting back at him through the women in his life. No, she said, she couldn't think of anyone who didn't not only respect but also like her husband, or rather, estranged husband.

Carson told her he was going to have a couple of the patrol officers keep an eye on her and he could guarantee they wouldn't be wearing Blue Jays caps, so should she notice one lurking around her she was to call him immediately. He gave her another card and this time put his cell phone number on the back.

They didn't discussed her reaction to the photos. He must have assumed it was a normal response to the sight of a murder victim. She let him think that.

As she left the building, she realized that she wanted to avoid going home. She hated the way the closing of the door echoed through the house when she went in, mirroring her own feelings of emptiness. She had always looked forward to going home to their warm, beautiful house. It had been a haven for her. But since Richard left, she felt she had to pull herself into the house. Her routine was to linger at the door to muster the energy that entering required, then take a deep breath and plunge into the mudroom at the back entrance, as though diving into a backyard pool that had seen no sun. And, although she had been ready to move when she and Richard had been together, she now couldn't bear the thought of selling the house Chloe and Jamie had grown up in.

Today she wanted even less to go home where there would be nothing to stop her thoughts from forging ahead to destinations she wasn't ready to reach. She pulled out her phone on the way out of the station and punched in Chloe's number.

"Hello." The voice was that of someone not yet awake.

"Sorry, Chloe. I didn't expect you to be asleep."

"That's OK, Mom. I didn't get much sleep last night with the thing about Diane and everything. I've got a mid-term paper due too."

"Why don't you go back to sleep. I just called to see if you had time for a coffee. Nothing urgent. I'll talk to you soon."

"Mom, are you OK?" Chloe could always read her better than Sara, at times, would have liked. Wasn't it the mother who was supposed to sense the daughter's problems?

"Perfectly."

"You sound a little funny."

"No, it's just hot and I'm talking while I'm walking."

"I've got time for a coffee if you have," Chloe offered, obviously not accepting the lame explanation.

Sara counted her blessings. Having children who cared and seemed to like spending time with her was something she knew many people would envy.

They met at the Starbucks at the end of Chloe's street. Chloe sported a pair of light green cotton pants that looked like, and probably were, operating room scrubs. A sleeveless black T-shirt acknowledged the warm temperature and her dark, naturally curly hair had been sprung into action by the humidity, forming a thick, unruly cap. Sara remembered trying to get a comb through that hair on hot summer days when Chloe was a child. Chloe's squealing, foot stomping and wiggling inevitably led to Sara giving up on her task. Chloe would run out the door, hair flying behind her, half of her head reflecting some effort at grooming and the other a tangled mass. Eventually Sara gave into the fact that that beautiful hair had to be shorn.

A small silver bone that looked as though it had speared itself through the lower part of her right nostril completed Chloe's ensemble. Sara decided not to react to the new piece of jewelry but she rested her eyes on it for just a second too long, trying to figure out how it had been inserted since both ends were bulbous.

"Damn, I meant to take it out but I forgot." Chloe frowned as she rummaged in her canvas bag for change.

"I would have noticed the hole anyway," Sara smiled.

"You haven't for the last couple of months," Chloe grinned back.

"OK, you got me." Sara laughed.

"My treat. What can I get you?" Chloe had gathered a handful of coins from the bottom of her bag.

Once settled at a corner table, Sara asked Chloe about Richard.

"I'm worried about him, Mom. I don't think he's sleeping or eating, but I guess that's normal under the circumstances. Hopefully the police will arrest someone quickly and then maybe he'll be able to get himself together."

"He'll be OK." Sara made a feeble attempt at reassuring Chloe. Her energy was concentrated on pushing aside the picture of Diane's body that kept floating into view.

Sara realized meeting for coffee hadn't been a great idea. She tried to make conversation. How were Chloe's classes? How were she and Craig getting along?

Neither wanted to talk about the murder and yet anything else seemed too trivial to hold their interest.

Chloe ventured a conversation about her brother Jamie. "Have you heard from him lately, Mom?"

"No, it's been over a month I think." Thirty-three days to be exact but she didn't want Chloe to know she was keeping track. "He's probably surfing somewhere without access to phones."

"That would be very rare today, Mom. He should be more considerate. Even if he had to travel miles to the nearest phone he should do it. He must know you worry."

Chloe, Sara knew, would never go a month without being in touch. In fact, she wouldn't go a week. But Jamie was a free spirit. He had often been off in his own world even when he was living at home. There was definitely a selfishness in his makeup that frequently hurt. Was it genetic? Right now she could readily accuse Richard of having passed on that trait. But perhaps he had been spoiled as the younger one. Chloe was right but Sara still felt a need to defend. Probably a sign that she had indeed spoiled him.

"Jamie just gets into his own world and I suspect doesn't realize we worry about him."

Chloe's shake of the head confirmed she didn't agree but took the discussion no further.

After they had made a few more unsuccessful attempts at normal conversation, scraped the last bit of foam from their cappuccino cups with wooden stir sticks and licked them clean, they nodded to each other that it was time to go.

It was early evening before Sara arrived home.

The Indian summer had brought with it a humidity that drastically dampened the effusive welcome everyone had given it earlier in the day. Her thought of having supper on her back patio quickly dissipated when she stepped from the Volvo. It would be too uncomfortable. There was not even the slightest breeze. The heavy clinging air begged for a storm. Besides, if she sat outdoors she risked Stephen Dempster spotting her, and he would undoubtedly have something to lecture her about. She thought of the scolding he gave her when she didn't take enough interest in his concern about the fellow delivering fliers. As much as she hated to give him any encouragement by showing the slightest interest, considering the happenings of the last couple of days, she supposed she should ask him whether the fellow was wearing a baseball cap. She turned toward his door but knew she didn't have the energy to cope with him now. She'd ask him tomorrow.

The coolness of the central air system enveloped her as she entered the mudroom.

She dropped her portfolio and suit jacket, and peeled off her sticky silk blouse, dropping it on the bench under the coat hooks. She kicked off her shoes as she unzipped and dropped her skirt and then struggled out of the clinging panty hose. There were some advantages to living alone.

The cold tiles felt wonderful under her feet. She had picked up some poached salmon on the way home. She would add a light dill dressing, a salad of tossed greens, and a glass of white wine, and she would have the perfect warm weather supper.

She had her hand on the fridge door and then decided to check for messages first. Tony had called. He wanted to know whether anything was wrong. She seemed to have been in such a hurry when they met that morning. Was she still angry with him? She deleted it. Let him stew just a bit. She had forgiven him for sharing her embarrassing outburst with the police, but it still hurt.

The next was from the gas company. They wanted to book an appointment to do the annual tune-up of the furnace.

She felt herself stiffen at the next message.

"Sara, call me immediately." It was Ken. "I've had a call from Martha Southern at Jamieson's wondering what new contractual arrangements we have made with them. She wasn't aware that you had started a new project until she bumped into you there this morning. And embarrassingly, neither was I. What the hell … "

Oh, stuff it. She pressed the pound key to skip the rest of the message. Exhaustion from the day's events locked Sara's eyes in a stare as she listened to the irritating message guardian announce the messages that were about to be deleted, when they had been left and by whom. It took several seconds before her distracted and tired mind caught up with her eyes and registered the object caught in her stare. An empty milk glass sat in the middle of the kitchen island. Odd. She hadn't left it there. She didn't even drink milk. Neither did Chloe. Besides Chloe hadn't said anything about having been home and, in any event, the glass had been used too recently. Fresh milk trails still lingered inside the glass. It must have been Richard. He was the only member of the family who actually liked milk. Maybe he had needed to pick up something; many of his things were still there. She sometimes thought he was treating his new life with Diane like an extended vacation, something he would enjoy intensely but would return from. She knew the more likely reality was that he wanted a completely fresh start and felt no need for anything from his past life with her.

She turned her mind back to her messages but the milk glass kept distracting her. She punched the star key to escape from the message guardian, pressed the button to hang up, and then dialed Richard's cell.

He picked up immediately.

"Hi, it's me."

"Yeah, how are you?"

"Fine. Are you doing OK?"

After nearly two months apart she felt a ridiculous need to make small talk before getting to the point. After asking about the funeral arrangements and whether she could help, she finally asked whether he had been in the house.

"No. Why?"

"I was just wondering because I just came home and someone has been here drinking milk. There's an empty glass sitting on the island and you are the only —"

"Get out of there!" Richard's cell was breaking up but it was evident he was shouting."

"But —"

"Just — get the hell out now. Go around to the front of the house. I'm a few blocks away. I'll be right there. Get out."

As she hung up, a familiar squeak came from the front hall stairs. The children had learned in their early teens that the third stair from the bottom squeaked no matter how carefully one tread.

She swallowed the words "Who's there?" before they escaped, and ran across the kitchen through the mudroom to the back door. As she grasped its handle she remembered she was dressed only in panties and bra. She ran the few steps back to the clothes she had discarded and grabbed her skirt and blouse.

Her trembling legs made it difficult to balance as she stepped into her skirt and she stumbled into the bench, banging her right shin. Skirt half done up, she pulled on her blouse as she darted out the door thinking how foolish it would be to die because of modesty.

A few days ago the thought of anyone killing her would have seemed entirely over the top. Now she wasn't so sure.

Sara avoided Dempster's side of the house. If he saw her walking down the drive in a suit skirt and bare feet he would be out there in a second. She chose instead to walk around to the front of the house on the lawn that ran between her home and the neighbor on the other side.

When she reached the front she positioned herself out of view of Dempster's upstairs window. The fading early evening sunlight made the whole thing seem foolish. She realized it wasn't the first time today she had felt this way, which reminded her of Carson. Hadn't he promised he would have a patrol car keep an eye on her? She looked up and down the street but saw nothing that looked like a police car, marked or otherwise. The only vehicle was an older blue Honda Civic parked on the street several doors down.

Richard's BMW sped into view and pulled into the drive with a recklessness that brought him to a stop with the right wheels resting on the carefully manicured front lawn. Not something the meticulous Richard she knew so well would ever have let happen in the past.

He charged out of the car and half ran, half strode to her side.

He looked haggard and older than the last time she had seen him. His face was lined, pouches underscored eyes that were circled with black, and his dark brown hair had become a candidate for the "before" in a Grecian Formula ad. Could mourning and stress do that to someone in a couple of days?

She quickly repeated her story emphasizing that there was probably an explanation for the milk glass.

Richard said nothing, just moved past her toward the house, pulling out the set of house keys he still kept.

"You wait out here," he instructed. His take-control attitude hadn't been affected by his tragedy.

Richard worked the inserted key and then tried again. He looked over his shoulder at her and asked, "Did you come out this way?"

She shook her head.

"Well it's unlocked." His accusatory, "You're unbelievably careless" tone was also still intact.

Sara felt herself slipping into a familiar defensive mode. She hadn't left it unlocked. She hardly even used the front door.

"You stay here," he repeated over his shoulder, each word spoken slowly and deliberately, as though his instructions might not have settled into her slow brain.

"Shouldn't we call the police?" she asked as he moved into the darkness of the foyer.

Richard returned to the light.

"A lot of good it will do, but here." He tossed her his phone and retreated into the house.

Sara moved onto the porch to stand by the open door. Richard had started his inspection in the living room and when he passed back through the foyer she knew why. He carried the heavy brass fireplace poker in his right hand, grasping it just below its lion head handle. A corner of her mind noted that Sophie, the cleaning lady, had apparently been overlooking the fireplace tools.

"Be careful," she whispered feeling the need to make some sort of contribution. He ignored her.

He walked quietly but she could visualize his path through the dining room into the kitchen, across the kitchen to the family room, and then emerging back into the hall that ran into the foyer.

Sara dug into her skirt pocket for the card that Detective Carson had given her. As she dialed his number she watched Richard reappear in the foyer and make his way cautiously up the stairs to the second floor. She noted the creak as he put his weight on the third step from the bottom.

"Yeah," Carson answered on the first ring again. He obviously didn't carry his cell in the bottom of a purse like she did.

Sara explained what had happened and that Richard was checking the house.

"Tell him to get out of there and look up the street. There should be a patrol car not far from you."

She told him there was no car unless it was a blue Honda Civic.

She thought she heard a muffled "shit" and then, "I'll be right there."

She leaned into the doorway to call the detective's instructions up to Richard but his voice reached her first.

"Oh God, no!"

It was a cry of anguish and it was coming from their bedroom. Sara propelled herself across the broad foyer and up the stairs. What horror could he have found? Had something happened to Chloe? No. Impossible, she had just left her. Jamie? No, he was in the South Pacific. Having mentally accounted for everyone who was important to her, she felt more under control as she reached their bedroom.

"Richard?"

He responded with a retching that came from the en suite. He was on his knees vomiting into the toilet.

"Richard, what's wrong?"

"It's that bastard. It's him," he managed before beginning to heave again.

She waited until he stopped and handed him a towel to wipe his mouth.

"It's who?" she asked, although she was afraid she already knew the answer.

"Whoever killed Diane. He's been here."

"How do you know?"

"I — I can smell the bastard. The same sickly sweet scent that was hanging around when — when I found Diane."

Richard put his arm across the toilet seat, dropped his head into his arm and sobbed.

Sara acknowledged his pain by a brief touch to his shoulder and then did what she knew he would want, left him alone.

For a brief moment she convinced herself he was imagining things but as she walked back into the bedroom, no longer running on adrenaline as she had been when she had first entered, she smelled it too — a strong, too-sweet smell of cologne. A scent — no, too sickly sweet to be called a scent — a smell, that didn't belong there and yet it was somehow familiar.

None of this made sense. It was hard enough to imagine who might want to murder Diane, but then to have them break into her home with who knows what intent? It surely couldn't be the same person.

The potent perfume reached her pain centers and they immediately responded with a pressure that began building deep behind her right eye. She opened the doors to the balcony and turned back to look around the room.

Aunt Kate's memorabilia were still in carefully organized piles all over the floor but there were two bare spots. The piles for 1946 to 1948 were gone.

26

It was well after dark when Carson emerged from the Porter house but the heat was still powerful enough to deliver him a blow. He automatically glanced up at Dempster's upstairs window and for a minute thought he caught the shadow of a figure. Surely the old guy wouldn't be at his perch at this hour. The house was in total darkness. Carson should check whether Dempster had noticed anything unusual earlier. If he had he probably would have called the station anyway. Carson had discovered, on mentioning Stephen Dempster in front of one of the dispatchers, that he was one of their several regulars. He was a self-appointed neighborhood watch of one.

He should also go back to the station and file a report but exhaustion was getting the better of the caffeine that had kept him running for the past thirty-six hours. He'd phone in a short report. The full version and Dempster would have to wait until the morning.

He had the car door open and was about to slide in when the memory of the humiliation he had felt yesterday worked its way through the numbing exhaustion. Greally had embarrassed him once for not getting what he needed from Dempster. Even though the chance of a repeat performance was nil since Greally was off tonight and wouldn't know about the Porter intruder, Carson knew he couldn't leave without knocking on Dempster's door. He forced his heavy legs to carry him along the front walk that weaved its way from the driveway across a huge expanse of lawn to a door with what, in the shadows, appeared to have a lion's face for a knocker, and a small peep hole above it. He ignored the knocker and instead pressed his finger long and hard on the button mounted on the right hand side of the doorframe. After ringing the bell several times he walked around the house to the back door. No response. Dempster must be out for the evening.

"Thank you, God." Carson glanced heavenward. If there was a god, he was being kind tonight.

He nodded at the patrol car parked two doors up on the other side. Damn. If the car had been assigned to Sara when he had asked, they might have had the stalker and perhaps even the murderer, if they were one and the same. Tomorrow he'd find out why it hadn't been given the priority he had asked for. He had no doubt that Greally was involved somehow.

A corner of his mind noted that he had just thought of Sara Porter as just Sara, not Sara Porter, not Ms. Porter. He was too tired to consider the implications.

He headed for home via the Bayview Extension, which wound south into the industrial eastern end of the downtown core. His usual route would have taken him as far as the River Street cutoff and into a mottled part of town where here and there, renovated fixer-uppers were surrounded by less desirable rooming houses. But his rumbling stomach pointed out to him that the weakness he was feeling was not due only to lack of sleep. He couldn't remember having eaten anything other than a bagel since yesterday. He took the first turn off the extension onto Pottery Road and wound his way up the escarpment to the Dairy Queen perched at its top. A hamburger, fries, and a chocolate shake should, between the fat and the sugar, quickly alleviate any feeling of weakness.

He could have satisfied his need for junk food at any number of restaurants on his route home but none other offered the quiet contemplative view over the city. Carson sat on the concrete picnic table, put the cardboard food tray beside him and rested his feet on the concrete bench that had been molded as part of the table. The hazy darkness of late evening had been replaced by an inky blackness that showed off the half moon that hung over the city skyline. The illimunated downtown bank buildings and the CN Tower created a spectacle just as beautiful as the moon and the cluster of stars that formed the city's backdrop.

A few hours ago, the narrow patio, squeezed between the parking lot and the edge of the cliff, would have been lively with families, couples, and groups of teenagers all with one thing in common — a need to distract their attention from the heat with a cone of soft ice cream, or for those who believed they deserved an extra reward for putting up with the uncomfortable out-of-season humidity, a banana split. Now only one couple, two tables down, shared the shadowy space. They were wasting the view quarreling over something the man had purchased.

A very subtle breeze, no more than a couple of degrees cooler than the cloying air, brushed Carson's forehead. He set down his burger and turned his face upwards in search of another.

He had spent over two hours with the Porters, checking the house and getting them to replay everything from beginning to end several times. A loose screen at the back was the likely point of entry and the intruder had almost surely exited boldly by the front door while Sara was scrambling to get out the back. He had called the guys in to dust for prints but hadn't expected them to find anything. There were unknown prints on the screen but Sara had had the windows cleaned the week before and they probably belonged to the workers. Some were also smudged which could indicate someone handling the screen afterward with gloved hands.

Richard Porter was convinced that the intruder was the same person who had murdered Diane Brooks. It seemed farfetched since there seemed to be absolutely no link between the two women other than Porter himself and any checking they had done suggested this was a man with no enemies. Although Carson wasn't completely sold on that.

He saw Porter as a man with a charming manner that cloaked a hard and self-centered core, someone who expected the world to move in his orbit. These were characteristics that could create enemies when transferred to the business world. Carson found that during the two hours he had spent with them he had come to like Richard Porter less and Sara Porter more.

He was worried about her. There was no doubt in his mind that she was being stalked by someone, maybe, maybe not, Diane Brooks' murderer. He was afraid that if the stalker didn't get her, his colleagues would. And now, Richard Porter's claim about the sweet scent was likely to make matters worse for her. He could hear Greally now: "So Richard Porter smells the cologne of the murderer again. And where? In Sara Porter's bedroom where one would expect to smell cologne. The cologne of Sara Porter herself."

The fact that Sara's were the only prints on the milk glass and that they were fresh and perfectly clear wouldn't help either. That her prints were there wasn't a problem. She would have taken the glass out of the dishwasher. But the lack of any other prints or even smudges of her own suggested that no one else had touched the glass. If they had they were very canny and had handled it very carefully by the rim, the area least likely to be touched when it was taken from its upside down position in the dishwasher. What was also odd was that there were no lip prints on the glass, as though someone had filled the glass and then poured it out, without actually drinking from it. He was inclined to believe that the intruder had simply used the milk glass to flaunt the fact that he had been there. He wanted Sara to know that he had the power to intrude into her life as personally as he chose. Carson had met many men like him but the thought of the insidiousness with which their minds worked still made his skin crawl.

Greally would say that Sara Porter had invented a stalker to deflect attention from herself. So far, the investigation had found nothing to suggest that anyone had been stalking Diane Brooks and yet Brooks and Richard Porter spent every evening together. The night Brooks was murdered was unusual. How would the murderer have known Brooks was alone unless he'd been watching her? And yet, if the stalker was the murderer why hadn't he murdered Sara? She was alone. The opportunity was definitely there.

Carson gave the skyline one last long look and wiped mustard from his mouth with a paper napkin. He gathered the remnants of his meal, none of them edible, into the paper tray and stuffed it into an overflowing trash can next to his car.

He found the old adage of "sleeping on it" frequently worked, and he headed home to do just that. Although this sleep, he thought, might be too deep to produce any results.

27

As soon as the detective had closed the door behind him, Chloe had leapt to her feet from the oversized living room chair she had curled up in earlier to contain her fear. Sara noted that the two glasses of scotch her daughter had used to settle her nerves had more than done their job.

"Nice ass," Chloe grinned, her eyes still on the door.

"Chloe!" Sara wasn't in a joking mood and would have preferred her daughter choosing another word. What had happened to buns, bottom or behind? But she managed a return grin.

Her daughter was right. The posterior view of Detective Sergeant Keith Carson was definitely appealing. She had noticed and liked the way his clothes hung on him. There was something about well-tailored clothes of fine fabric that, ironically, made you ignore them and focus more on the body that wore them.

Richard had left as soon as Carson had given him the nod. No question to Sara as to whether she would be alright. Chloe was her father's complete opposite in every way: size, fashion sense, and most importantly, heart.

She tried to convince her mother that she should stay overnight to keep her company but Sara adamantly refused and called a cab for her daughter.

Chloe shook her head, "Stubborn, just like great Aunt Kate."

"Will everyone stop telling me I'm like Aunt Kate? I'm nothing like Aunt Kate. She was a strange, domineering, manipulative, maybe even wicked, woman. I'm not her!"

Fear shot the response from Sara's mouth. Fear that much more than stubbornness had been passed down from Aunt Kate.

Chloe stared at her, mouth open, but uncharacteristically, nothing came out. She had no idea how to react to an outburst so unlike her mother.

After a few seconds she managed, "Where did that come from?"

Sara shrugged and smiled weakly as she steered Chloe down the walk and into the waiting cab.

The innocuous gray police car sat at the curb on the other side of the street, two doors up. She could vaguely make out two figures in the front seat.

Carson had insisted another pair be assigned to her backyard and had done a lot of arguing and voice-raising with whoever had been at the other end of the phone to convince them that the extra surveillance was needed.

Although the two in the backyard definitely made her feel secure, having them there also felt intrusive, as though they were house guests. She felt she had to offer them some hospitality.

She made her way through the kitchen and out the back door to the garden. She searched the darkness and just as she spotted the light from a cigarette by the pool, one of them called to her.

"Mrs. Porter? Do you need anything?"

Immediately the cigarette glow disappeared.

"No," she answered as she strolled toward them. "I was actually wondering if you would like anything before I go up for the night. A cold drink or coffee perhaps?"

"No, thank you, ma'am." They stood up as she approached. Like Carson's partner, whom she had met the day before, they seemed awfully young. Too young, she thought, to protect anyone other than their kid brother or sister. They chatted for a few moments and assured her that she should call should she hear anything at all.

Sara sat on the back steps for a few moments looking for a breeze. She took a few deep breaths and enjoyed the moon and its entourage of stars. In spite of today's entry into a foreign world of fear she felt something being lifted from her as though drawn by the moon's magnet. She explored a feeling that was vaguely familiar but nearly forgotten. It was unfetteredness, and she worked to articulate its source. The pain she had been burdened with since Richard had left, was gone. Seeing Richard today for the first time in weeks, she realized that she no longer needed him. Since he had left her she had been totally consumed by the fact that someone had taken what had been hers, and in that state, she had seen that lost possession as perfect and essential. She had focused only on Richard's charm, his good looks, and his success. She had chosen for years to ignore the less attractive characteristics that lay underneath.

She shook her head at the months wasted being depressed about something that long ago had been a *fait accompli*. She simply hadn't stopped long enough to realize it.

The lightness she felt dissipated as she headed up to bed and stepped on the squeaky stair that had signaled the prowler's presence this afternoon. Her nervousness grew as she approached her room. She thought about sleeping on the sofa in the family room, but that would mean the intruder had power over her and she refused to give him that.

She sat on the chaise and perused the piles of Aunt Kate's history and contemplated the two bare spots. Why did he take those two particular piles?

It couldn't be just coincidence that those years were the time of the Group and the investigation into the murder of Jane Stewart.

Sara rubbed the goose bumps from her arms. What ghosts from the past had been released from that box? Who would be interested in a sixty-year-old murder? And how could there be a link to Diane's murder? It seemed preposterous and yet if Richard were right and Diane's murderer was also her intruder, there must be some connection.

And why take the clippings? What was he looking for?

Then it dawned. Perhaps he wasn't looking for anything. Perhaps he wanted to prevent her from having the information. Well he was too late for that. She had pulled the most interesting pieces from those piles and what she had left she had listed with a brief description on her yellow notepad.

Perhaps she should have mentioned the clippings to Carson but the discussion had focused so intently on how the intruder had gotten in and what she and Richard had seen and done that it hadn't occurred to her.

She pulled the clippings and notes from 1945 to 1948 from her portfolio and turned again to Kate's notebook and entries headed "Summer, 1948."

We spent much of the morning lolling around trying to think of something interesting to do. Teddy came up with the brilliant idea of packing a picnic lunch and going up the road to the river. Mrs. Baker put together an amazing basket of cold turkey sandwiches, hard boiled eggs, sweet pickles, freshly baked brownies and such, and then, of course, Teddy added his touch — chilled wine and crystal glasses. We swam in the river and I came out with several bloodsuckers clinging to my leg. Jane and Harper both squealed and stood back taking the role of spectators. (How Jane ever expects to be a nurse I don't know.) Kendall, of course, thought it was a hoot and dear Teddy took charge. He ran and got the saltcellar from the picnic hamper and poured the entire contents on the little beasts and they shriveled up and dropped off like dead things. Harper had the audacity to complain that there was no salt left for the eggs.

Jane has been making googly eyes at Teddy. What's worse, Teddy is reciprocating. I know Teddy is only playing but I'm furious with both of them. Perhaps I am most angry with myself for wasting emotional energy on a fantasy.

Jane and Teddy snuck off by themselves to the dock tonight. I have no doubt he was being a gentleman and keeping her warm. She hasn't figured out yet that she will never get more than a kiss on the cheek. Sometimes I think I'll tell her just to see her reaction but I'd never do that to Teddy even if he is being an ass. I'm stuck with …

Sara fell asleep before she finished reading the entry.

28

If Bill Coombs had known that this would be the last morning of his life he might have approached it differently. He might have gotten up at five and washed the windows and swept the verandas of each of the ten cottages in his care so that people would be able to say, "That Bill Coombs. The best property management guy on the lake. You always knew your place was in good hands with Bill."

Or perhaps he would have driven the thirty miles to the nursing home that housed his wizened and sour father whom he hadn't visited in three months, so that he could die guilt-free, at least in the parental care department.

Or maybe he would have gone up to Casino Rama and tried the black cherry machine one more time. He always said he was going to win that damn jackpot at least once before he died.

But Bill didn't know what the day had in store for him, so he slept until eight thirty. He had watched a couple of early morning wrestling matches on satellite TV and would have liked to have slept later but the neighbor's dog had started barking. One of these days he was going to prepare a tasty piece of steak for that damn animal.

Now he sat at the kitchen table eating strips of too-limp bacon folded in an under-toasted piece of white bread. He washed down each bite with a slurp of instant coffee. He stared at the folded newspaper that rested on the table beside his right arm. He no longer bothered to go through the motions of opening, rustling, and refolding the paper. He had never read it. He had adopted the morning paper as a safety measure. As long as he was staring intently at it, his eyes would not inadvertently wander to his wife.

"You never look at me when you talk to me," she complained.

He didn't look at her at all, if he could help it.

At least once a day, however, he would catch her stomach in his peripheral vision. It hung over her belt like a pouch of dough and on each glimpse he marked its resting place on her thighs. Daily, it seemed, it continued its kneeward descent. In a man, a stomach like hers was a beer belly. Not terribly attractive, but acceptable. In a woman it was disgusting. He didn't have the vocabulary to articulate, even to himself, what that hanging sack of fat represented to him. Words like slovenly or sloth hung at the corner of his mind, but he wasn't sure they were right. Whatever it was, anger flared in him every time he mistakenly looked at her. He would immediately take the anger and fling it at her in a sharp complaint about the meal in front of him or about nothing at all. What he did know was that he threw the anger at her because he didn't know how to direct it at himself.

Too long ago he had married this woman, not for love but for lust. A lust easily aroused in a nineteen-year-old. One that the layer of fat that had already started to pad her stomach could not deter. She had carefully fuelled his passion with practiced movements he still remembered. On hot summer days, the lifting of her shoulders that would tug the front of her blouse already stretched tight across her breasts, until the top buttons popped open revealing the deep moist cleavage that had to be explored. The caressing of his own lips with the soft pink tongue that would suddenly transform into a hard, hot prod as it darted into his mouth.

He was angry at the stupidity of the young man he had been but even angrier at the man he was today, inexplicably unable to leave this slug of a woman even though she sickened him.

This morning she was rustling around the kitchen, taking a quick swipe here and there at the greasy counter. Just enough, he knew, for her to be able to respond to his complaint about the dirty kitchen with, "What do you mean, I just did the counters this morning." He could see without looking, her dirty pink once fluffy, now matted, slippers shuffling across the linoleum. He tried to remember what color the floor had been. He remembered when his father had laid it, and his mother had been so proud of it. Green, he thought, or possibly turquoise. That was over forty years ago, and now only the black rubber backing remained other than in the occasional spot that got no traffic. He let his eyes wander to a corner to check the color, but even there it was too faded to discern. His wife never complained about the worn linoleum. Probably because the black tar paper didn't show the dirt that caked it.

She had insisted that the warm weather was too nice to waste and had propped the door open with a brick. Now a drowsy fly buzzed around his head. He took a couple of swats at it with the newspaper and wondered if you could still buy flypaper. His mother used to have a sticky coil hanging right over the table. He and his sister used to bet on which of its buzzing victims would be the first to stop struggling. He didn't remember having to swat flies then.

He was about to head down to the lake to do his morning tour of the cottages in his care when he heard a car crunching over the gravel driveway toward the house. It wouldn't be any of the property owners. Not at this time of year. And they never had visitors. Bill Coombs felt uncomfortable. He did not like surprises. He hoped it was just someone using his driveway to turn around.

His wife, however, always ready for a diversion, headed toward the open door.

"Geez, woman, what are you doing? Get back here. You're not even properly dressed."

The slam of the car door destroyed any hope that the visitor would not stop.

His wife had ignored his order.

"Someone from the city. Don't recognize her though."

"How do you know she's from the city?"

Bill headed for the door.

"You can always tell when they're from the city."

About that she was right.

Sara took a deep breath as soon as she stepped out of the car onto the gravel drive, looking forward to the smell of fresh country air. Instead, she was met with a waft of fried bacon. It reminded her stomach that she hadn't eaten and it raised a rumbling protest.

This must be the right place. Ralph Jefferson had told her that he couldn't give her a key to her aunt's cottage but had added, "This is completely unofficial, of course, but you could try Bill Coombs, the fellow who manages your aunt's property up there. I met him when I went up to check things for her. His is the last house before you reach the cottages."

The back door of the small frame house stood open. A large man moved out onto the stoop, tucking the tail of a rumpled dress shirt, rolled up at the sleeves, into the waist of his green work pants.

"Nice day," he said by way of greeting as Sara approached.

Sara agreed and explained who she was and that she wished to check out the cottage, adding that her aunt's lawyer had told her that she might ask him for his help. She didn't lie and say that Kate McPherson had left her the cottage but that conclusion could easily be taken. Bill Coombs took it and she didn't correct him.

"I was sorry to hear about your aunt. Hadn't seen her for a couple of years since I guess she took ill, but she used to come by at least once a year. She would walk around the property and maybe spend a couple of hours. Never went inside though." His fleshy brow wrinkled and he paused as though asking himself why. After a moment he answered his own unspoken question. "Too many memories I guess."

"She was an elegant lady and always real nice," he added a moment later, ensuring he had paid the dead woman sufficient tribute.

He must have seen her aunt only on her good days, Sara thought. Elegant, always. Nice, too seldom.

Sara asked if she might have the key and expected him to go back into the house for it. Instead he pulled on the metal chain that drooped from a belt loop to his pocket and a bunch of keys appeared. The keys looked very much alike to her but he immediately chose one and worked to open the clasp to the key ring to release it.

"It's a top-notch cottage. Of course, not as modern as the others now. But it won't take too much fixing. It's been kept in perfect condition. Never so much as a leak and I check every fall for any openings that mice or squirrels might get through. It's a shame though that it hasn't been used. Never could figure out why she let it sit here if she didn't want to use it. Thought maybe she was waiting for a hot real estate market but we've had several of them and she just didn't seem interested. Even had an offer for her one time. Some people were up here visiting and liked the look of the cottage and I gave her a call. She didn't sound very happy to hear from me."

It seemed that Bill did remember a time when Kate wasn't so nice.

The clasp was stubborn. Bill continued to work at it.

Sara wished he would stop talking and focus on what he was doing. She didn't feel like chatting. But Bill did.

"You know it's been over sixty years since it's been used. I was only eight the last time your aunt had it open. I remember because it was the same summer that girl was murdered. But you wouldn't remember that."

Sara had turned partially away from him, trying to catch a glimpse of the lake between the trees at the end of the road. She pivoted back. It hadn't occurred to her that Bill Coombs would have been around here that long ago.

"Now that you mention it, I do remember something about that."

The attempted casualness came out awkwardly but he had no reason to take note.

"What do you remember about it?"

She tried to insert a tone of ghoulish interest.

"I was pretty young but something like that you keep thinking about it afterward and it kind of paints a permanent picture in your mind. It doesn't sound very nice, but that girl's murder was the most exciting thing that has ever happened at The Point. For sure in my lifetime. I was one of the kids who found her." There was still pride in his voice.

Bill had managed to open the clasp of the key ring and extricate the key for the McPherson cottage, but he didn't look at Sara as he spoke. Instead the focus of his attention seemed to be her stomach. She looked down to make sure she hadn't spilt the coffee she had been sipping on the drive north.

"Got our pictures in the Toronto papers," he continued. For the first time his eyes moved up to her face. They were dark brown and too innocent for a man of his age. When he squinted into the morning sun that bathed Sara's back, his eyes became slits in his beefy face.

"The key sticks a bit. Maybe I should come down to the cottage with you."

"Tell me more about finding the body. That must have been frightening for an eight-year-old," Sara encouraged him.

They started to walk downhill over the uneven, patchy lawn toward the cluster of cottages that sat on The Point.

"Scary for sure, but exciting too. The police had been looking for her for a few days but I wouldn't say they scoured the area. I know," he laughed, "because my friend Howie and me was behind them every minute. They used to shoo us away but we'd be right back.

"On the second or third morning after they started looking for her Howie came to our door first thing and says, 'OK, Billie, let's go.' I asked him where we were going and he says, 'To find the body of course.' Like, what else would we be doing? So I told him he was crazy. I said she wasn't even around here. 'Oh yes she is,' he says. He's got inside information."

Bill stopped to enjoy a string of guffaws that came out like a drum roll.

"Inside information." Bill shook his head. "Howie always tried to make people think he knew stuff that nobody else knew. His mother was the Jamiesons' housekeeper and he seemed to think that gave him some special status. He used to lord it over me because my parents were just the caretakers for all of the cottages, just like me and the wife today.

"I didn't believe he really knew where to look but what eight-year-old wouldn't be game for a search for a dead body. Howie went right to the spot though. It was in a reedy spot on the shoreline that wasn't easy to get to. It was an overgrown scrubby area that had been used as an unofficial garbage dump by the locals. There was rusty cans, smashed crates and a rusted bicycle wheel and, right at the shore, an old rowboat lying upside down. The body was under the rowboat. Insects and rodents had already started to do a job on it but no big animals had got to it. I guess the rowboat was too heavy. As soon as I saw it I hightailed it out of there, but when I looked over my shoulder Howie was just standing there staring at it. He was like that. Real cool. When I got home, my mother called the police and they were pulling up in our drive by the time Howie got back. I guess that was my fifteen minutes of fame."

Sara detected a touch of sadness in his voice, a recognition that his life had peaked at the age of eight.

Sara was still moving at her city pace and Bill puffed a little in his effort to keep up. His work boots plodded on the ground beside her and his bunch of keys jangled with each step. A bee buzzed persistently, circling his head and then hers. Otherwise there was complete silence. It had been months since Sara had been outside of the city and she had looked forward to the quiet. But this was more than she had imagined. Not only were there no people and no traffic, but the boats that provided a lazy drone in the summer had also disappeared for the season. She wondered if one could suffer from noise withdrawal.

"Is the spot where you found her close to here?" she asked.

"Not far, but it doesn't look the same any more. Some new cottages were built on the land adjacent to The Point on the north side. The beach at the second cottage in, the Pickfords', would be about where we found her."

They had reached her aunt's cottage. Its impressive two stories looked over Lake Simcoe. A screened porch was wrapped around two sides. The white paint on the siding showed only slight signs of peeling and the glossy green paint on the porch and shutters caught the reflection of the sun. It looked in good repair but at the same time uncared for. Its flower beds were empty but for a few sturdy plants. Two gold chrysanthemums were still in bloom having somehow squeezed life from the dry clay soil that cracked around them. In each window a pair of gray curtains drooped on either side of faded shades rolled half way up.

He saw that she was looking at the windows.

"The curtains and blinds don't look so good. The wife washes them but they're starting to fall apart. Your aunt didn't want anything changed. There are even some canned goods left in the pantry. It seemed strange, but the murdered girl was one of your aunt's group. They were all real close. I guess she wanted things left as they had been in happier times."

Sara turned her attention back to the porch. "Tell me, Bill, did the porch and trim used to be a different color?"

"Sure was. Blue. I should know," he laughed his guffaw laugh again. "I scraped every bit of it maybe twenty years ago. Your aunt decided to go with green then, and stuck with it ever since. It was the only thing she ever changed."

Sara didn't hear the memory Bill was sharing. The word blue took her to her aunt's notebook and the description of finding a dead girl's body—*She could feel the dampness of the wood of the door jamb that supported her shocked body and she concentrated on the pattern made by the cracks in its blue paint.*

Bill's noisy wiggling of the key in the lock refocused her attention. He had selected the front door of the cottage that opened off the porch. He wiggled the key some more then pressed his shoulder against it and pushed hard. He left the door slightly ajar, pulled the key from the lock and handed it to her.

Sara moved toward the door and the darkness behind it but wasn't ready to go in. Instead she thanked Bill and turned toward the lake. A few minutes sitting in the sun would renew the resolve that had been so strong last night. But last night she wasn't sure a girl had been murdered in that cottage. Now she was.

She started down the steps to the dock and then stopped to call after the figure that lumbered away from her. "Bill, do you know where the murdered girl was staying?"

He was happy to have an excuse to linger and walked back toward her.

"That's hard to say. There was a group of five or six friends all summer long and more on the weekends. They often stayed at the Jamiesons' but it seems to me they moved back and forth between the two cottages sometimes, depending what other guests there might be at the Jamesons'. They were real social people."

Sara looked over at the elegant summer home next door to her aunt's. Although they were all impressive summer residences, the Jamiesons' seemed to hold court over the other cottages and they were diminished in its presence. Its two windowed turrets watched over the lake, and in turn were the landmark used by boaters looking for The Point. The house sprawled over a wide lawn that rolled down to a huge boathouse with a guest apartment perched on top. Its flowerbeds were still full of bloom as were the veranda's hanging baskets that swayed in the breeze. Although closed for the season, one expected at any moment to hear squealing children run out of the cottage, slamming the screen door behind them.

A smaller cottage sat behind the main one. It had no turrets or veranda but otherwise looked as though it had been parented by the larger building. Its green trim matched that of the larger house and the border gardens that surrounded it were just as neat.

"Is that a guest house?" Sara asked.

"Nope, that's the staff house. That's where the Bakers have always lived in the summer months. Howie's younger brother and his sister still work for the Jamiesons. Poor Howie passed pretty young. Too much booze they say. Not long after my little brother Donnie. Only he got killed by some drunken driver. But I guess one way or the other alcohol killed 'em both."

One more question had to be asked and she felt nervous about posing it. He would surely wonder why she would ask such a question and she was fearful of the answer.

He waited, sensing she needed something else.

She picked at the stairs' railing, pulling off slivers of weathered gray cedar to reveal new wood below. "You don't by any chance remember what the dead girl was wearing?" she finally asked.

"Of course I do, like it was yesterday. Black pants, a silky red blouse and red sandals."

It was an hour before Sara was ready to enter the cottage. She first explored The Point and the cluster of new cottages next door. Still thought of as new by the locals, the cottages on the adjacent property were at least twenty years old. Each had a single story with wide picture windows, a screened porch at one end and a deck, almost as big as the cottage itself, overlooking the lake. The only distinguishing feature was the exterior color the owner had chosen and the prerequisite sign that hung at the foot of each driveway to assure guests that they had found the right cottage.

Sara chose the property identified by a highly varnished piece of wood that hung from a rough wooden post. A loon was carved in a corner and the names Bunnie and Lorne Pickford below. The letters were crudely chiseled and a repair had been made to one of the loon's wings that gave it the appearance of a mutant, a loon with a third wing sprouting from its back. Perhaps a proud gift created in a son's shop class. The choice of pink for the cottage's exterior had surely been rued as it flaunted dirt and age much more readily than its dark green and brown neighbors.

Its beach was a short stretch of clay shoreline. It faced east, having traded evening sunsets for moments like this when it could bask in the warm morning sun. A floating dock bobbed lazily a few feet off shore. Small piles of gray, fine sand that rested in the crevices between tree roots and under fallen tree trunks along the shore attested to someone's attempt to create a sandy beach for children's play. But the weather and waves of Lake Simcoe had fought to keep it in its natural state and had gradually dragged most of the sand into the lake.

Sara picked up a stick and wrote her initials in the damp clay and wondered how long it would take for her mark to be washed away. She knew she was avoiding thinking about the reason for her trip here and forced herself to get to business. She had timed the walk from her aunt's cottage. An easy ten minute stroll. What might it have been like in the dark on a September night in 1948? She pictured two people carrying a dead body awkwardly between them. One carrying her feet, the other holding the dead girl from under her arms, stumbling from time to time as they worked their way through the uncut brush, laying the body down from time to time to catch their breath or to get a better hold on the slipping body, and finally maneuvering their burden over and around the trash that littered the shore. It would have been difficult but possible, physically possible at least. But emotionally? Could her aunt have carried her friend's body down here and then given it over to an overturned rowboat?

Perhaps, she decided, depending on the motive. Would love for Teddy Jamieson have been sufficient motive for her aunt? Had her aunt been capable of an even more sinister role? Sara shook her head to dissolve the thought.

A sudden rustling sound in the brush startled her. As she turned, a chipmunk scuttled from a tangle of dead branches, a winter night's dinner in its mouth.

She strained to listen. Conditioned to shut out the noise of the city she had to concentrate to tune in the soft scudding sounds and snaps around her. The warm, soothing beach suddenly felt remote and lonely. She started back to The Point at a brisk walk. As the rustling noises behind her grew, the walk turned into a sprint.

Now Sara stood on the cottage porch in front of the door that Bill had left slightly ajar. One more thing to be done and then she would have run out of excuses and would have to go inside.

She rummaged in the brown leather carryall she hung over her shoulder and pulled out Aunt Kate's notebook. She gently turned the yellowed, brittle pages until she found the passage Chloe had read the other day.

The stench assaulted her as she opened the door of the empty summer cottage. 'My God, there has got to be a dead raccoon in here,' had been her first reaction. After years of helping her parents open their cottage every spring she was used to finding carcasses of animals that had sought a sheltered place to die. But never before had she experienced a smell so piercing that it immediately carried a pain to her head.

Her companion's only response was to turn on a dusty lamp whose dull yellow light revealed the shape of a chair beside it. The chair had been draped with a sheet to protect it over the winter. Apparently oblivious that the chair was not meant to be in use, a shriveled body lounged in it. Its body fluids had oozed from it, releasing an odoriferous death announcement. A rat, poking its nose from under the chair where it had scampered when it had been interrupted, confirmed that the announcement had been received. White shiny spots glistened on the ankle where the rat had visited.

She could feel the dampness of the wood of the door jamb that supported her shocked body. She concentrated on the pattern made by the cracks in its blue paint. As the nausea subsided she found herself hypnotically focused, not on the horror, but on the body's determined effort to deny death. The head was quizzically cocked to one side, red lipsticked lips parted as though about to challenge a companion's argument. Dark shiny hair fell over the shoulders of a red silk shirt, a tanned arm was tossed casually across the broad arm of the draped chair and legs hidden by black slacks were neatly crossed to one side. Toenails painted bright red matched the strappy sandals.

'God, she still has style,' she had thought, hatred suddenly overpowering any other emotion."

Sara closed the notebook and carefully tucked it back into her satchel using the time to gather her resolve. She placed the palm of her hand on the door just above the knob and pushed. It swung slowly inward. The narrow windows carried too little light into the room in front of her and it took her eyes a few minutes to adjust to the dimness. The smells of the room emerged before its shapes. A damp mustiness assaulted her but quickly moved past as though happy to find an escape.

She avoided the objects directly in her line of vision and let her eyes wander around the room. The doorway in which she stood entered directly into the living area. A huge stone fireplace commanded the far end of the room. A deer's head, its antlers draped with fine cobwebs that caught the light from an upper window, hung above it. Bulky sofas draped with yellowed sheets slumped on either side of the room. Dust mites were caught in the stream of light that shot through the east-facing window on the right-hand side of the room.

Her eyes were drawn upward by sunlight coming from above. The ceiling arched two floors above. The second-floor hallway leading to the bedrooms looked over an ornately carved railing into the room in which she stood. A large floor-to-ceiling window overlooked the lake. The light pouring in played on the wisps of cobwebs, which moved gently in the current of air her entrance had created. Bill had done a reasonable job of keeping up the outside of the house; Mrs. Coombs apparently didn't take as much pride in her work.

Finally Sara let her eyes move to the objects that sat in a dark corner directly in front of her. The largest shadow gradually developed into an armchair covered by a sheet. The smaller shadow became a lamp perched just behind one of the chair's shoulders.

She had been right. Kate hadn't been writing fiction. Sara could easily imagine the body of Jane Stewart lounging in it. She shivered. After a moment's pause she let the cottage draw her inside but took care to leave the door wide open.

29

Bill Coombs rummaged in his back shed. He found the bucket and the spray bottle of window cleaner. Now all he needed was a rag. The ones he had found lying in the corner were pretty dirty and had stiffened into a wadded ball from being left crumpled when damp. He'd thrown them back down. But he couldn't find any cleaner ones and besides did it really matter? He bent and picked up one of the balls again and slapped it against his leg in an attempt to turn it back into a rag.

A shadow filled the shed's small doorway.

"Whaddya doin?"

That damn woman. No brains that he'd been able to find in forty-five years, but never missed a thing.

"I'm going down to clean some windows."

"Oh sure you is. Taking a look-see at that woman is what yer up to."

"Don't be so damn stupid, woman." He dropped the rag and the bottle of cleaner into the bucket, pushed past her, and started down the hill toward the cottages. He was angry that she had the ability to invade the private corners of his mind and embarrassed by what she saw there. He shouldn't be embarrassed, he reasoned. He wasn't going to do anything really bad. He just wanted to watch the woman for a little bit. He thought he should be able to take a peak at her through one of the windows and then if she happened to see him he could pretend he was cleaning the windows. That was all. Nothing really bad. He wouldn't even think any bad thoughts when he watched her. He'd just imagine standing behind her and pulling her against him and running his hand over her flat stomach. That was all. He wasn't a bad man.

He'd have to check each of the windows until he found which room she was in. Hopefully she was spending some time in one room going through some things. He started at the back of the cottage and worked his way through lilac bushes to get to the window, trying to minimize the snapping of branches. He had to shade the right side of his face from the glare of the sun and lean close to the glass to see in. The kitchen was a tiny room with a table, some open shelves, an icebox — he could remember old Harry Martin delivering ice before the cottagers had refrigerators — and a sink whose pipes were hidden by a piece of faded gingham that was tacked around the sink's edge and fell to the floor. It reminded him that he had set a mousetrap under there ages ago. One of these days he should see if it had caught anything. He hoped there was no stench from a rotting mouse.

She wasn't in the kitchen. He would work his way around to the side to check the dining room and then the living room. He was beginning to turn the corner, preoccupied with pulling a couple of twigs from his thick gray hair when they nearly collided. They both registered an instance of shock and then the other became completely composed, slowly shook his head and sighed. It had been many years but Bill remembered that look in his father's eyes and the message it had sent.

"Billie, why are you so stupid? Why do you put yourself in these situations? Why do you always make me do this?"

The pain didn't surprise him. That look had always been followed by the lash of a belt or a kick of his father's boot. This pain though was much sharper and took his breath away. He crumbled to the ground. "I'll just lie here," he thought, "until the pain passes."

30

It looked as though everything had been left untouched, just as Bill had said. If it weren't for the dust and the covered furniture one could easily imagine the Group gathered around the fireplace last evening playing games. A chessboard and its ivory men sat on a games table to one side of the fireplace. Shelves on the other side of the fireplace held boxes of cards, a cribbage board, a Monopoly game and an Ouija board. Sara sat on the floor to explore the shelves' contents. A pile of magazines showed a preference for *Good Housekeeping* and *Look. Good Housekeeping* articles focused on the secrets to being a good wife. They implored women to create an oasis for their husbands' return in the evening. They were to prepare a perfect dinner, ensure the house was tidy, keep the children quiet and have their husbands' slippers waiting. "Don't talk about yourself," one article insisted. "What you have done during the day will be very trivial compared to the serious matters he has been dealing with." She wondered if articles like that had sealed Aunt Kate's decision not to marry.

Look seemed much more the type of magazine she imagined her aunt being interested in, touching on current affairs, Hollywood figures and generally who's who. She was struck by the number of uniformed figures that populated its pages. The Second World War and its memories would have at that time still have been very much part of the lives of the members of the Group.

The games had been well used. The lids of boxes had split corners and playing cards were dog-eared. A crossword puzzle was half completed. A bridge scorepad was nearly full. It looked as though Teddy and Kate were usually partners and usually won.

It was evocative memorabilia. But nothing that provided any clues as to what had happened at the end of the Group's last summer together.

What had she expected she wondered? To find a murder weapon lying on the floor? Perhaps it was just the need for a distraction from her own life, and not Aunt Kate, that had brought her here.

As Sara pulled herself to her feet, the dust she had disturbed retaliated and a series of sneezes overtook her. On the last sneeze a button from her blouse popped off and rolled under a shelf. "Damn," she thought. It was a one-of-a-kind button. It was square and within the square were smaller squares of alternating red and blue. The buttons matched the red and navy trim on the blouse's collar. She wouldn't be able to find a replacement. After several minutes on her stomach brushing her hand over the dust-carpeted hardwood under the shelves, she gave up the search, resigned to a new set of plain white buttons.

Sara wanted to explore the rest of the cottage but she was loath to move farther away from the front door that she had left standing open. The daylight and fresh air it drew into the room were reassuring. The fear she had felt yesterday when she had heard the creaking of the step in her own home still lingered, ready to leap into full-blown panic if provoked.

She slung her satchel over her arm ready to leave and then shook herself. *Come on, Porter, no wimping out.* She looked over to the stairs leading to the bedrooms and forced herself to dash up them. At the top she realized she was holding her breath and stopped for a moment to gasp for air, checking over her shoulder as she did. Then she made a quick tour of the upper floor, popping her head in one bedroom after another. Each of the five was similar: a double bed with a wooden headboard and no bedding, only a mattress cover, a bed table and lamp, a dresser and chair. Each was stripped of any personal belongings like a vacated hotel room. Only one room revealed that someone had once spent time there. Sara noticed it only at the last second as she pulled her head from the room. A shadow hinted that something had been left under the bed.

Sara pulled out a dusty box and realized that it was a portable writing desk.

She sat on the bed to examine it. The bed creaked as she sat down and the mattress sank so low that the wooden frame dug into the back of her legs. She wiggled to find a comfortable position.

The box was of gray cardboard with a slanted top that provided a writing surface. The lid was hinged with gray corrugated ribbon. Inside the box were a bottle of blue Pelican ink, a green marbled fountain pen, gray writing paper tied with a gray ribbon and matching envelopes. Two intertwined initials, J and S, at the top right corner of the paper announced the quality of the paper and the good taste of its owner. Jane Stewart had left something behind, Though it didn't appear to have anything to tell. None of the paper had been written on. She took out the pen and ink and turned the box upside down on the bed. Nothing was written on the bottom. When she lifted the inverted box the packet of paper and the envelopes remained on the bed. The sheet of paper that had been sitting on the bottom now rested on top. It had been written on.

Sara hesitated for a moment, feeling she was invading a dead girl's privacy. Perhaps it was a love letter or the last letter to her parents. But the address suggested she wasn't going to have to deal with guilt but disappointment. It had been written to the Dean of Osgoode Hall. It was only a business letter not a personal one. It was an incomplete draft. Many words had been stroked out and sentences rewritten.

Dear Sir,

~~Something has come to my attention.~~

As difficult as this is for me, I believe it is my duty to inform you of one of your student's deviant behavior. Mr. Theodore Jamieson has been in an ~~unnatural~~ ungodly and unspeakable relationship with another man for some time.

Instead of surprise, Sara felt confirmation of something known but previously not recognized. Sara opened her satchel and pulled out the plastic envelope that carried what she sensed were the most important of Aunt Kate's collection. She shuffled through the odds and ends until she found the photo of the Group that had nagged at her every time she looked at it. Her aunt wasn't in this candid shot. It must have been taken by Kate. The rest of the Group was sitting on a rug on the grass, with a picnic basket, wine glasses and a bottle of wine. Jane Stewart and a boy with a cherub face were looking toward Kendall and laughing. Perhaps at one of his practical jokes. But Teddy and Harper had been looking at one another. They seemed oblivious to the rest of the Group.

Now she understood what she hadn't been able to read in that photo before. Teddy and Harper had loved one another. It explained Kate's frustration at Teddy's inability to return her affection. That made perfect sense to her but this letter didn't. She felt as though she had been duped by a good friend. She had become attached to Jane Stewart and had imagined her as a vibrant innocent young woman. Now Sara saw another side of her. Could she have been that vindictive? Sara looked for an excuse for the young woman. Perhaps this note was just a means for Jane to vent her hurt and anger and was never meant to be sent? But if anyone else had seen it, would they have thought that?

She could imagine the searing anger her aunt would have felt toward Stewart had she found that letter. It wasn't difficult to imagine because Sara was certain that it would be akin to the all-consuming fury and hatred that Diane Brooks had kindled in her. What was harder to confirm was how well either of them had kept those emotions in check.

That, she realized, was what was really terrifying her. Not the sick little man who had invaded her life, or this haunting murder from the past, or even the fact that Diane had been murdered. But the possibility of what she herself were capable.

She had found that the best way to disperse emotion was to dwell on something to which one had to apply logic and she tried to do so now. Had Stewart finished and mailed the letter? Not likely. Jamieson had definitely graduated from Osgoode Hall and, even considering his family's reputation, it was quite possible he would not have been allowed to continue at law school had this come to light. Not in 1948. Had her letter been discovered and had that letter been motive for murder?

How different the lifelong friendship of Teddy and Harper looked given this new dimension. How difficult it must have been for them to continue their relationship safely at a time when homosexuality was not accepted in mainstream society. And yet, they had apparently succeeded. Teddy was very successful in the most conservative Canadian establishment and, as far as she knew, no one suspected their relationship was anything more than that of old school boy chums and business associates.

But there had to have been times when their lives were painful. Harper had never been able to overtly share any of Teddy's successes. She looked at the picnic photo once more and imagined the look of love between them was tinged with sadness.

Sara put everything away and decided to take the writing box with her. What she would do with it she wasn't yet certain. She steeled herself to check one more thing downstairs before escaping into the sunlight.

She approached the armchair from the back. The sheet covering it hung to the ground. Jane Stewart was either murdered in this chair or had been placed in it after she was killed. Would the sheet be the same one that had covered it over fifty years ago? If Bill's mother had been as averse to housekeeping as his wife then it likely was the same.

Sara lifted the sheet from the back of the chair, curious to see the fabric underneath. The sheet had served its purpose well. The yellow and blue flowered chintz had held its color. As she replaced the sheet a dark stain on its underside caught her attention. She carried it over to the window to find better light.

As old as the stain was, she recognized it immediately. That summer day when Chloe and James were barely school age flashed into her memory complete with colors, scent and tastes. The sweet scent of the freshly mown lawn mingled with the perfume of the pink peonies that flanked each side of the front steps. The day had been hot and the children had insisted on setting up a Freshie stand. A few kind neighbors dropped a dime in the box the children were pretending was a cash register and swallowed in one gulp the sickly sweet grape drink. The children's clothes were splattered purple.

But that wasn't all that was stained that afternoon. The children soon grew bored with their Freshie stand and asked to take an old sheet outside. The plan was to drape it over the lawn furniture to make a tent. But that couldn't keep their attention for long either. Soon they were taking turns lying on it, and pulling each other across the lawn. Grass stains that even a miracle detergent couldn't remove had streaked the sheet and she had allocated it to the bed linens' equivalent of the glue factory, the ragbag.

That's how Aunt Kate and Teddy had moved Jane Stewart's body to the beach. They had dragged it on this sheet.

As Sara moved away from the window she realized that she shouldn't have had to take the sheet to the window to inspect it. Before she had gone upstairs, the sun had moved enough to throw light through the open door and across the chair as though it were in center stage under a spotlight.

Her senses went on full alert. Her eyes darted to the door. It was now firmly shut. But she hadn't heard it bang closed as she would have, had it been caught in a gust of wind. The sudden sound of an acorn bouncing noisily across the roof of the veranda shot an extra dose of adrenaline into her system, snapping her into flight mode. Her olfactory glands were also attempting to send a message, but her body wouldn't let her delay to tune into it.

She scooped the writing box from the floor beside the chair and ran from the cottage, her heart pounding and the sheet trailing behind her. She didn't notice as she ran by the bare lilacs, the still finger of Bill Coombs that protruded from under the bushes, crooked as though beckoning her in.

31

Carson's alarm woke him at six a.m., several hours short of what he needed. His habit was to charge immediately out of bed, but he couldn't make his body respond to that idea today. He managed to kick at the sheet and blanket until they were scrunched at the end of the bed and stretch out. He listened to the traffic swishing past under his window. He couldn't imagine not being part of the city. He loved its sounds, its smells, its energy. He was never happier than when completely in the midst of people noisily living their everyday lives. He wished he'd been born years earlier when newsboys cried out the headlines and street vendors loudly hawked their wares.

Although most people chose a Queen Street address because its busyness made it less desirable, and therefore cheap, Carson had chosen it precisely because it was busy. He could live comfortably without ever leaving the block he lived on. It provided everything he needed in supplies and services, as well as company. The sign on Wing's shop downstairs promised "Vegetables, fruit, cigarettes, groceries and patent medicines." Vegetables, fruit and cigarettes, yes. The odd can of soup constituted the groceries, and as for patent medicines, one or two dust-covered bottles of aspirin tried to fulfill the owner's claim.

Wing called Carson Mr. Detective and, frequently popped an extra mango or bunch of grapes into his bag. Carson was sure that the shopkeeper felt it never hurt to be on the good side of the law, but after having exchanged pleasantries, several days a week for a dozen years, Carson hoped the little gifts represented something more.

A couple of doors down from Wing's was a delicatessen with the best bread, croissants, cheese and cold cuts in town. Next to it was the neighborhood pub where everyone really did know your name. Strung along after it: a hardware store, dry cleaners, and a Money Mart that advertised, "Cheques Cashed," and they were, at a premium that would bring only the most desperate poor buggers through its doors. The neighborhood was this side of trendy and Carson hoped it would stay that way. Although some committee that had put up fancy signs on lampposts declaring the area "Broadview Village" obviously didn't agree with him.

Carson lingered in bed, listening to Wing chatting to people waiting for the streetcar as he filled his produce displays.

Mr. Detective rolled over to replay a dream before its fragments dispersed. He had been driving his Mustang and Sara Porter sat behind him in the back seat. He watched Sara in his rearview mirror. She smiled politely when he apologized for the mess in the back seat, but he could see her pulling old McDonald's containers and pop cans out from under her.

He still felt the embarrassment he had experienced in the dream. Although chances were slim that Sara Porter would ever be in his car, it was time he got his act together, and his car was as good a place as any to start. Although it would take huge self-discipline to follow through with it, he would put cleaning his car on his to-do list for the day. It had been nearly two years since the door of his car had been dented in the shopping mall parking lot and, other than to fill it up, he had ignored it ever since. Maybe he should just sell it, get a new one and start with something pristine again. "No way Carson." The little voice in the back of his head that he thought of as his better self was awake too. "You've got to quit taking the easy way out and start coping like a sane human being."

"OK, OK," Carson grumbled as he pulled himself upright and swung his legs over the edge of the bed. He'd done enough reading on compulsive disorders to know that he would likely benefit from medication. But the thought of taking anything scared him. On a rational level there was a good reason for that. Should the cop docs catch him on anti-depressants or whatever was prescribed for whatever was wrong with him, he could be off the street in a heartbeat. That would mean taking early retirement from the force because he couldn't cope with being chained to the routine that a desk job ensured. But beyond the career risks, he was afraid that taking medication would mean losing control. He didn't like the idea of some chemical running around in his brain and affecting his reactions to life, although one might argue that he frequently let alcohol do that anyway.

The digits on his clock slipped from 6:09 to 6:10. He pulled off the boxers he'd slept in. It was the third day of the Diane Brooks case and so far nothing. He was convinced that the longer it took to solve the case, the greater Sara's danger. That thought woke him sufficiently to get him to the shower, where its pummeling beads did the rest.

By seven he was in the office. As usual he had planned his day on the drive to work and arrived frustrated by the little he had put on his mental to-do list. He and Kirpatrick would see Dempster first thing and he still wanted to double check Brooks' belongings, but otherwise he had no leads to follow. Everyone related to the case had been interviewed and re-interviewed. Hopefully something useful had transpired overnight. He checked the reports from the fellow who had watched Sara's house. No activity at either the front or the back of the house. He leafed through a stack of phone messages and related notes. They had been prioritized. At the top was a call from a neighbor of Brooks and Richard Porter who had seen a car that didn't belong in the neighborhood on several occasions the week before the murder. The follow-up had already been assigned to Greally and Perkins. At least that was a possible lead. The rest sounded like the usual crackpot calls. They would eventually be followed up but wouldn't be treated with urgency.

He tried calling Dempster but there was no answer. Dempster didn't have voice mail. That seemed to suit what Carson knew of him. Dempster wouldn't want anyone to intrude into his life in any way, even with something as innocuous as a recorded message.

He and Kirpatrick headed for Dempster's in the hope that he might be there by the time they arrived, but mainly because they felt driven to accomplish something and nothing better was in the offing.

They banged at Dempster's front door, banged at his back door and looked through the kitchen windows, which were the only ones close enough to the ground to allow a glimpse inside. Everything was neat and tidy.

They asked a couple of neighbors if they knew whether he had gone away or when he would be back, but it seemed Dempster was adept at learning everyone else's business without revealing any of his own. He would have knocked on Sara's door but noted her car was gone.

Carson called in and assigned a constable to get on the phone to check whether any other Dempsters in the city were related to Stephen Dempster and, if so, if they had any information on where they might find him.

The spurt of energy he had experienced at the beginning of the investigation was being replaced by grinding frustration. He felt it necessary to articulate the obvious.

"We've got to figure out the damn motive."

Kirpatrick nodded agreement.

Carson did his best thinking on his own. "Look, you've got plenty twenty-four-hour shifts in your future. And there's not much we can do right now. Why don't you take the rest of the morning off?" he suggested. "I'm going to try to get a little more background on Diane Brooks. If anything comes up, I'll call you."

"Thanks. I wouldn't mind going home for a couple of hours. Kathy was crying when I left. My new job and the pregnancy together seem to be too much for her."

Kirpatrick colored slightly at having shared an intimate detail of his life to a superior and one he didn't yet know well.

Carson had hoped Diane Brooks' laptop would give up something valuable, but it didn't appear so. They couldn't find even a daytimer. Carson thought that odd. He called Richard Porter and left a message. Within five minutes Porter called back.

"You've found something?" Porter's voice was urgent.

"No, I'm sorry, Mr. Porter. I have nothing new to share with you but I need some information from you."

"What is it?" Richard Porter switched from urgent to tired and impatient.

"We haven't been able to find a daytimer for Ms. Brooks. Do you know where it might be?"

"No. She had a large one that should have been in her office or with her in the kitchen. She liked to work there. She found it cheerful."

The sad irony in that made them both pause for a moment.

"One more thing, Mr. Porter. You said you didn't know what she was working on. What about her past projects?"

"She had done quite a few centennial books for communities or institutions. She did one for the Toronto Public Library and for one of the hospitals. I forget which one. And also for a county somewhere in eastern Ontario. That's about all I can tell you."

"Thanks, Mr. Porter. Sorry to have had to bother you." Porter had hung up before Carson finished his sentence.

Carson checked the laptop again. Nothing. If the murderer had taken her daytimer and wiped out her electronic schedule he must not have wanted anyone to know whom she'd met with recently. It seemed more and more likely that Diane Brooks' murder was tied to her work. But how?

Carson headed up the street to the public library to see if the library had anything written by Diane Brooks. He waited while the only librarian on duty, or at least the only one in sight, tried to explain to someone how to find references on dinosaur fossils. The learner, a grimy fellow somewhere in his thirties, nodded throughout the lecture and rubbed a dirty hand mechanically against an equally dirty pant leg. It was obvious to Carson that his interest in dinosaurs was nil, but his interest in a comfortable place to pass a few hours was high. The libraries were clamping down on street people using them as a daytime shelter. This guy was one of the smarter ones and came in with a manufactured purpose.

After watching the librarian futilely dispose of ten minutes of all of their time, Carson interrupted. He was doing her a favor but she didn't recognize it. Her first response was a crisp, "I'm sorry, but you will just have to wait your turn."

When he explained who he was and what he needed, she directed her student to a web page, apologized that he would have to wait for one of the much-in-demand computers, and left him. The unintentional student was quicker at grasping a favor. He nodded a thanks at Carson and ambled past the computers to a comfortable easy chair.

Once the librarian had looked up Brooks' name and gotten more information from Carson about her writing, she explained that the type of books Diane Brooks wrote weren't generally available to the public. They were privately published and sold by the organization that had commissioned her. Carson interrupted her again, just as she was beginning to warm to her new lecture topic. Would he be able to at least find a list of Brooks' books? Within another five minutes he left the library with the list as well as copies of two of Brooks' books, *St Patrick's Hospital: 1900 to 2000* and *Harley Public School: A Hundred Year History,* which the librarian had discovered in the archives that recorded the city's history.

Carson spent the next couple of hours skimming through the books.

Brooks wrote well and wove interesting anecdotes through historical data, which on their own could have been pretty boring stuff. She had an ear for an interesting story and seemed to be able to draw people out. He felt he knew more about Diane Brooks but no more about a possible motive.

His body was in a solve-the-crime-mode and pent up adrenaline that had no outlet was making him jittery. He needed to get out and needed to do something. He remembered his early morning commitment to wash his car and decided he could think doing that as well as he could sitting in the evidence room, probably better.

Carson climbed into the Mustang and headed for the car wash. He stopped on the way at a Canadian Tire auto shop to pick up leather cleaner, air freshener and new floor mats. If he was going to do it, he might as well go all the way.

As he pulled into the car wash the irrational anxiety he had felt since deciding to tackle his car crept closer. There was no line-up at the car wash to use as an excuse to turn around and he drove right in. The sound of the spray and slapping of the strips of chamois on the windshield were soothing. His panic dropped a notch. He had learned a long time ago, but seemed to continually forget, that anxiety was caused by the anticipation not the doing. Once he did whatever it was he was compulsively avoiding, the panic eased.

Carson was almost looking forward to tackling the interior. He pulled up beside a vacuum cleaner and got out. He was proud of how well the bodywork of the Mustang had held up. The dent in the door where the steel had been exposed had begun to rust but the rest of the red paint job still shone like new. A few age spots had eaten their way into the chrome on one of the mirrors but otherwise the outside was in pretty good shape. Ironically, the layer of dirt must have protected it from the road salt that covered Toronto streets in winter.

The owner of the car parked next to him eyed him as Carson pulled out trash that filled the last third of the garbage can closest to him, and then blatantly stared at him as he started filling his neighbor's can as well. He found a couple of lost items — a Ludlum novel whose cover was only a little greasy from a half-empty container of fries that had been sitting on it, and a CD of the Gypsy Kings. They were the only two items that weren't trash-worthy. The last piece of paper he pulled from the crack between the rear seat and its back was a grocery list Marlene had written. Smoked salmon, capers, rye bread, cream cheese and white wine. That had been their favorite Friday evening supper when he was lucky enough not to be working. He hesitated for just a minute before crumpling it into a ball and tossing it.

Just as the paper found the mouth of the green trash can, his cell rang.

"Detective Carson?"

He recognized Sara's voice immediately but there was something different about it. This must be her professional "let's get down to business" phone voice. He could picture her behind a desk speaking with a client.

"Ms. Porter, what can I do for you?"

"I was wondering if I could have an hour of your time. It has nothing to do with the — with Diane Brooks. I'd like your opinion on some information I've found amongst some of my aunt's things."

He should ask for more information to see whether he was the person who could actually help her but he chose not to.

"Sure. I'd be happy to help you." He didn't want to appear too anxious but he did have an excuse to pass by there this afternoon. "Actually I need to talk to your neighbor, Stephen Dempster. Would you be home around five thirty?"

Sara explained she was calling from her car and was just north of the city, but should make it home before five thirty. Carson had an hour and fifteen minutes to finish the car, check in with headquarters and drive the twenty minutes to Sara's Lawrence Park neighborhood.

Carson returned to his car cleaning. The vacuum took all of the coins he had dug from his pocket and the ashtray. Those he found under the seat stretched the time just enough to suck the dirt from the last corner. By four forty-five he had finished. He used the polishing rag to give his shoes a quick buffing, smacked the dust from the knees of his pants with his hand, checked his tie and hair in the side mirror, and gave himself a nod of approval.

As he pulled into the traffic he realized that he was whistling. When was the last time he had whistled? Months ago, years ago? He had no idea.

32

The drive home from The Point was calming. The harvested fields were a patchwork quilt of browns and golds on either side of the highway and the traffic was lighter than usual. The snake of bumper-to-bumper cars that carried their owners down to the city to work and back to their commuter communities had taken a Saturday break. Once Sara had placed the call to Detective Carson she began to feel much more in control.

She needed to share her theory about Stewart's murder with someone who had some expertise in police work and who would not immediately dismiss her as a nutcase. Any of the police on the force who had had access to Carson's interview with her about the night of Diane's murder would likely see her, at best, as a drunk. She had decided Carson was her best bet. Although he had asked tough questions, and his firmness when suggesting she be available for further questioning told her she was certainly on his list of suspects, something in his tone and in his eyes told her he believed her. When it came to non-verbal communication she usually interpreted correctly. In fact, her clients told her frequently that she had an uncanny ability to pick up on the key issues in an organization without anyone actually speaking of them. She wondered why her intuition had been shut down when it came to Richard.

"Well, Kate," she thought. "I've given your box my best shot. If I've blown it by calling Carson, well —." She could hear her aunt repeating one of her favorite quotes from Churchill: *We can never say that we have done our best; we must do what has to be done,* and felt a swelling of annoyance.

"Well, you come up with something better then," Sara mentally retorted.

She knew there were branches of policing that dealt with old cases. Did forensic evidence last fifty years? She had no idea. She had gathered considerable knowledge: where the body had been left, a very likely motive for the murder and almost surely who had disposed of the body. Perhaps an expert could actually identify the murderer. It would be a relief to pass whatever she had discovered about Stewart's murder on to someone else. But at the same time she had been tempted to hold onto the conundrum and to continue poring over the musty letters, the cracked photos and haphazard scribbles in notebooks that made up its pieces. As long as she kept herself immersed in Stewart's murder she could avoid thinking about Diane's.

At some point soon she knew she would have to force herself to delve into the files that were stored at the back of her mind and somehow retrieve the night of Diane's death. The image from her dream of Diane on the kitchen barstool, her back to Sara, kept slipping into her mind bringing a cold sweat with it. And then, fast on its heels, the scene in Carson's office. The photos spread on his desk: Diane, dead, from every possible angle. Diane sprawled over the kitchen bar. Diane barefoot and wearing the purple pants and white shirt, just as in her dream. She forced her mind back to the rolling countryside, the cattle conferring lazily under the trees, the small mountain of orange pumpkins waiting to be carved into Halloween lanterns and baked into Thanksgiving pies.

By the time she arrived home she had all of the information that she planned to share with Carson organized in her head. As she pulled her bag from the car something fell to the drive way. The cottage key. Locking the cottage hadn't been a consideration when she ran outside. She had been too distraught to even think of giving the key back to Bill. She just wanted to get into her car and get back to the familiar as soon as possible. She couldn't see any harm in leaving the cottage open but she supposed she should call Bill and tell him she had the key. Perhaps later. Carson would be here soon.

The phone was ringing as she entered the house. After seven rings it would go into the voice mail. Seven would seem annoyingly long to her callers, but she had found that seven allowed her to get to one of the extensions from the house's most distant points, the laundry room or the back patio. She grabbed it on the seventh.

It was Tony. She wished she hadn't rushed to reach it. She didn't feel like talking. At least not to Tony and besides she didn't have time. He spoke slowly in his low, carefully modulated voice that she imagined a psychiatrist might use when assuring a patient that being a raving maniac was not out of the ordinary. "Sara, we miss you." Tony might have been a mother speaking to her runaway child.

She pulled an emery board from her bag and started to work on her nails. She could start to get ready while she was talking. "What's up, Tony?" She really hoped he wouldn't answer with a blow-by-blow description of a day at Morrison and Black but knew it was inevitable. Could a different question have led him elsewhere? Unlikely. Morrison and Black seemed to be his life. Amazingly, although she spent an average of sixty-five hours per week working on their behalf, she didn't feel that way at all.

Sara made commiserating noises as Tony talked about the client who insisted on M&B doing more work than had been contracted for but was angry when it was suggested that the fee would have to be increased. She waited for him to end his story so that she could slip in with, "Oh, Tony. Sorry, got to go. I left something on the stove. Talk to you soon."

But he foiled her, moving into his next subject without even taking a breath. "Everyone's pretty down around here."

"Oh, how so?" She took care not to sound too interested, hoping to get an abbreviated version of whatever was to come.

"Ken has warned us that the bonuses are not going to be what we all had anticipated."

In spite of her effort to remain disinterested he had hooked her. "What? Don't you believe a word that slimy weasel says," she warned him.

"That metaphor doesn't work."

"What?"

"Weasels aren't slimy." Tony chuckled at his own cleverness.

"OK, slimy slug. Is that better?"

"Perfect."

"Tony, I'm serious. Don't believe him. The firm must have earned more than it has in any year in the past ten. I alone charged out as much as the whole firm was earning a few years ago."

"God, I knew you were busy, but I didn't know you brought in that much."

"Well I did, and others did reasonably well too, so don't let him hand you any line about poor earnings. If he continues, ask to see the books."

"Sara, are you crazy? Ken would be furious. If he does keep those little score cards like everybody says he does, I'd be scratched from the game."

"It's the staff's right, Tony. The bonus is part of the pay package. You have every right to see the books."

"Well, why don't you ask him when you get back?" Tony suggested.

Sara felt a surge of annoyance. She was tired of always being the front battalion sent into the war zone at Morrison and Black.

"Tony, will you please stick out your own neck for a change instead of borrowing mine? Besides, I don't know when I'll be back." And then a quick final warning, "Don't let him walk all over you." She hung up before Tony could answer. She regretted it immediately. She knew that she had just guaranteed another conversation with Tony so that he could "clear the air." Those would be his exact words and he wouldn't be able to sleep until he was sure she was no longer annoyed with him.

Damn short-sighted, Porter. Besides she felt guilty. Tony was basically a nice guy and it was probably too late in life for a personality makeover. From wimp to Mr. Assertive was not in the cards. She remembered him saying once that his father had had a temper that flared over everything when he was young and he had avoided conflict ever since. In addition, her own anxiety was making her petulant, and Tony always seemed to be there with his most irritating behaviors when she was least able to handle them. She remembered Kate's frequent hurtfulness and how it was one of the characteristics she liked least about her aunt. She renewed her commitment to be kinder to Tony.

She glanced at her watch. Just barely time to shower and change before Carson arrived. She adjusted the shower to its fullest force and as hot as her body could take and let its needles massage her for a full ten minutes — her back, her breasts and her stomach. She used to dash in and out of the shower as quickly as possible. Now the steaming water soothed and renewed her. She had to force herself to turn it off. If Richard had been there he would have been shouting at her to quit wasting the water.

She rubbed her now-rosy pink skin dry with a heavy white terrycloth towel and then stood staring into her closet a little longer than usual. She selected a soft blue turtleneck that was purported to bring out the blue in her eyes and pair of charcoal gray slacks that the saleswoman who sold them assured her took at least one size off her hips. There were times when one chose to be taken in, and that had been one of them. She brushed her hair vigorously until her scalp hurt and then caught it back loosely at the nape of her neck with a silver barrette. It wasn't one of her better hair days but at least she wouldn't answer the door with a towel around her head this time.

By five o'clock she had the clippings, letters and scribblers containing Aunt Kate's disjointed notes and Jane Stewart's writing box spread out on the granite top of the kitchen island.

When she heard a car pull in she checked the driveway from the window over the kitchen sink. The bright red Mustang surprised her. It certainly wasn't police issue. Perhaps it wasn't Carson. But the car had barely come to a stop when the driver's door opened and Carson unfolded himself from the front seat and smoothed the front of his jacket before heading down the drive toward the front door.

Sara tapped on the window and motioned him toward the back door. He greeted her with a grin he hadn't used on his other visits. When he entered the mudroom he carried with him the scent of an earthy man's cologne mixed with the smell of leather polish. It was a surprisingly appealing combination and she wondered if she could sell the formula to Dior.

Sara pulled stools up to the kitchen island and used the opener she had promised to avoid, "You will probably think I'm crazy but —." She had intended to sound in charge, but the insecurity she'd been fighting slipped to the forefront. She could have carried it off with confidence with someone else, but something about Carson was disarming. She truly did not want him to think she was a crazy lady.

He interrupted her with another grin: "Why don't you just tell me about it?"

It was a longer story than she had expected. Receiving the box from her aunt, an overview of the story of Jane Stewart's murder, her aunt's mementos which were somehow linked to the death, the people she had visited, the information she had gathered, and her trip to the cottage at The Point.

As she told her story, she made a pot of coffee and served it. Carson said nothing, other than sharing the important information that he took his coffee black with one sugar. She had expected him to interrupt her with questions or comments. Surely if he were taking her seriously he would. She began to feel embarrassed and started to rush through the details.

Carson didn't miss it. He interrupted her now. She wasn't sure whether she was pleased or unnerved by his ability to read her. "Hey, slow down. I am taking this seriously and I'm not in a rush. Take your time with the details. It's often the little things that are most important."

And so she talked of the photo of Teddy and Harper, what she guessed and what she believed Jane Stewart's letter confirmed about their relationship. She repeated Bill Coomb's story of finding the body. She described the Group as she pictured it in 1948: Teddy, good-looking, very wealthy, apparently an all-round nice fellow, enrolled in Osgoode Law School: Aunt Kate, a student of English literature at the University of Boston, bright, beautiful, self-centered, caustic, and likely in love with Teddy; Harper, a business student, sensitive and likeable, probably Teddy's lifelong partner; Howard Hamilton, the sometimes Group member; Kendall, the practical joker, had been in the business program with Harper but dropped out to work in the family business; Jane Stewart, a nursing student at Toronto General Hospital, likely in love with Teddy, apparently a woman not to be scorned, murdered at twenty-two.

She pulled the sheet that she believed had been used to drag Jane Stewart's body from the plastic grocery bag in which she had stored it and showed Carson the grass stains. There was only one piece of information she had decided not to share. The piece of black hair tied with red threads. It was too personal. If it did belong to the dead woman she didn't want it dumped in an evidence box to be handled like a piece of paper. If at any point it were critical to the case she would let Carson know about it.

Her eyes frequently searching the ceiling, Sara pinned down and sorted through every detail that had been flitting haphazardly through her mind over the past several days. She selected the most meaningful and wove them into a tapestry of friendship, invincible youth, love, hate and murder. The whole was much more dramatic than the pieces had been.

Finished, she folded her hands on top of Jane Stewart's writing box and looked expectantly at Carson. Carson said nothing. The kitchen tap dripped into the stainless steel sink. She'd either have to learn how to change washers or find herself a handyman. They both sipped their coffee and Carson picked through the pieces of her aunt's life that were spread in front of him.

Being with someone, and at the same time being perfectly quiet, was soothing. She felt no need to fill dead air with forced small talk. Carson was obviously comfortable too. But she expected silence was normal for him. The detective had a detached air about him that suggested a solitary nature that found conversation an intrusion.

The silence was broken by a rumble, like a long drum roll, that escaped from Sara's stomach. It was too long and too loud to be ignored and they both laughed.

"I think I just got reminded that I haven't eaten all day. If I put on a pot of spaghetti, will you join me for an early dinner?" It was a spontaneous thought and she wasn't sure whether she hoped he would accept or decline.

Carson said nothing for a moment and continued to peruse the notebook he was leafing through, head bent over it. Sara noted three or four white hairs vying for attention amongst thick dark brown waves. He's deciding how to refuse politely, she thought. Having dinner with a suspect is probably against regulations.

He glanced up briefly, barely raising his head. "Yes, sure. That would be great." His eyes went back to the notebook and then flashed back up with an afterthought, "Thanks."

She made an attempt to appear casual as she rummaged frantically through the cupboards in search of tomato sauce. She never cooked any more and had no idea whether she had the ingredients to produce the dinner she had offered.

"Why do you think he took some of this stuff?" Carson was focusing on the newspaper photo of Jane Stewart now. Sara wondered whether the dead girl had locked eyes with Carson as she had with her.

"Who?"

"Your intruder yesterday. I wonder why he took some of this stuff."

"I don't know. Maybe just to prove he'd been here?" She didn't believe it.

"Maybe." Neither did he.

Sara reminded herself of the rationale she had created for sharing these things with Carson. "Do you have people who look into old cases?"

"Sure. They have a pretty good success rate too. Science has come a long way. If Stewart was murdered in your aunt's cottage, and since it sounds as though it has been left pretty much as it was, there could be some useful evidence there."

"I guess I shouldn't have touched anything. I may have disturbed some things." Sara felt a spurt of frustration with herself. You'd think that anyone who even occasionally watched TV would know better than to blunder through a possible crime scene. But she'd been too curious to stop and think about it. Besides she hadn't really expected things to have been left untouched.

"Yes, you might have ruined any evidence that was left." It apparently wasn't Carson's style to cushion people from the reality of their own mistakes. Carson looked up and focused intently on her face. It was the first time she understood the idea of being pinned by someone's eyes.

"You've explained everything you've discovered. But what made you start looking to begin with? Why did you think there was anything significant in this box? The clippings about the murder weren't unusual. Her close friend was murdered. They were young and it was likely a very dramatic event in her life. It would make sense that she would save the newspaper accounts."

Sara sorted through her reasons and started with the one that was the most subtle but at the same time most definitive. "Aunt Kate would have hated people to see most of the things in the box. They weren't like her. At least not like the person she had created in later life. Some are simply romantic mementos of a young girl but most are shallow and insipid. And some are society notes about who did what, where, and with whom. Aunt Kate became a successful and prominent businesswoman. Her galleries were known in art circles around the world and she had a high profile in both the art world and the business world. She would not want to remind anyone, family or otherwise, that a great part of her life had been spent frivolously. And she certainly wouldn't want even the hint of any scandal to be connected in any way with the McPherson name before or after her death. I think a murder, however old, could fit into that category of scandal. Aunt Kate was a very private person. Leaving this box behind allowed people to see parts of herself she had kept well hidden for years.

"There had to be a purpose for her to leave it at all. There definitely had to be a purpose in leaving it to an individual. Me, as it happens. If it were unimportant, she would have gotten rid of it long ago or just left it in a closet in the expectation that after her death it would be seen as junk and thrown out. Which very likely would have been the case."

"What about this clipping of Judge Jamieson's death? Why do you think it's here? It looks like she hadn't put anything in the box for over twenty years. And now this." He waved Jamieson's obituary over his coffee.

Sara felt a thrill of confirmation. "You noticed that too."

"Hey, I'm not a detective for nothing you know."

"That's the other thing that told me that Kate left the box for a reason. The obituary tied the past to the present. The box contained some sort of unfinished business. Maybe there was a link between Jamieson and Jane Stewart's death. Or … " Now she was certain he would think she was wacky.

"Or?" he prompted.

"Or Jamieson was murdered, and my aunt suspected that that was the case and that his death is somehow linked to that last summer at her cottage."

He didn't smirk or even look skeptical. She told him about her conversation with Pauline Williams and the judge's comment that both he and her aunt had made decisions that once acted upon couldn't be changed.

When she finished, Carson only nodded pensively, his lips pursed. He gathered up all of the pieces, put them in the manila envelope he had asked her for and wrote Kathryn McPherson diagonally across it in blue ballpoint, set it to one side of the island and set Jane Stewart's writing box on top of it. He left the grass-stained sheet on the floor in the black garbage bag into which she had stuffed it.

A very orderly man. Not too orderly she hoped or he wouldn't be able to handle being around her for long.

"I'll make sure these get looked at," he assured her. "But I can't guarantee when. The team that works on cold cases is off on some DNA training right now and, in any event, I am not sure how they assign priority to cases. I don't want to get your hopes up because although this stuff looks interesting it may not lead anywhere, and if it does, it could be a long time, months, even years from now."

Sara nodded her understanding. What he said was not surprising but she felt disappointed just the same.

Sara began to open cans and Carson decided to drop in on Dempster before dinner. She took the opportunity to attack the freezer a little less nonchalantly than she had done a few moments before. Her search of the cupboards had turned up a can of crushed tomatoes, tomato paste, Italian seasoning and dried spaghetti. She could get by with those ingredients, but she guessed that Carson was a Bolognese kind of guy and would definitely miss the meat.

The freezer was half empty but ground beef had always been a staple. Surely at least part of a package lingered somewhere. Yes. Under the turkey that had been on sale after the holidays two years ago. Gray from freezer burn the flat oblong brick could have been ground anything but the sauce would take care of any inadequacies. She had just put it in the microwave and pressed defrost when Carson returned.

"That was quick. I guess that means Dempster definitely wasn't home," Sara said.

Carson got the subtle joke at Dempster's expense. "No he wasn't and I'm sure if he'd known the police wanted to talk with him, that he would have high-tailed it home from wherever he was."

Sara told the neighborhood stories about Dempster interfering in everything from newspaper delivery to composting. Carson was enjoying the humor until she told him about Dempster warning her about the flier delivery boy.

The vertical line between his brown eyes became a furrow and his eyebrows merged into one line. "Sara, you should have told me about that."

She noticed that he called her Sara. She knew that that was quite a trivial observation in light of the fact they were discussing the person who was likely stalking her, but she reflected on it for a moment anyway.

He asked where the flier was. She took him to the mudroom and pointed to the folded drugstore sales sheet lying on top of the pile of newspapers in the blue recycling box. Carson picked it up from the recycling box by slipping a ballpoint pen under its fold, balanced it carefully and slipped it with smooth expertise into the plastic bag he had asked for.

She decided not to tell him his efforts were useless, that she had put it in the recycling box, taken it out, taken it in her car, leafed through every page and returned it to the recycling box. If there had ever been anything useful on it, that was unlikely to be the case now.

After Carson had secured his evidence, conversation moved from Dempster to the more personal. They had both grown up in the city and had attended neighboring high schools. Soon they were playing the inevitable "Did you ever know so and so?" game. Carson was saying, "If you went to Northern you must have been at the championship game that year at Varsity Stadium … " when his voice faded.

She had pulled a knife from the knife holder on the counter to chop onions and froze when she looked down at her hand gripping the long steel blade. The hand seemed entirely separate from her. A chill of fear scampered up the back of her neck and prickled across her scalp.

Suddenly Carson was no longer on the barstool but standing beside her, his hand on her arm. "Are you OK, Sara?"

She hesitated for a moment. *Act as though you are in control. That, my dear, is the key to life.* She heard Aunt Kate so clearly she couldn't help looking toward the doorway. Sara quickly followed the advice.

"Yes, I'm fine. Low blood sugar from not eating, that's all."

The furrow appeared between Carson's eyes again. She wasn't sure he believed her.

"Why don't you open some wine for us?" She worked to keep her voice light and chopped frantically to hide the trembling of her hands.

"Wine and you're light headed?"

She attempted a laugh. "Choose something that's not too dry and the sugar will take care of it."

The warmth of the wine, the spaghetti and Carson's company sapped the terror from her leaving only a residue of anxiety, like that of a forgotten nightmare. Before he left, Carson had gone through the house checking that all windows and doors were secure. He'd called to confirm that a car was being sent to watch over her again. She got the sense that he had had to do some convincing to get it. She apparently wasn't very high on the endangered species list of whomever Carson had talked to. She wasn't sure whether that was reassuring or otherwise.

33

Sara watched Carson drive away, and then flicked on the television. She flashed through its 101 channels, turned it off, ran a finger over her CD collection, pulled one out, slipped it into the player and turned the volume up several notches. The Phantom of the Opera vibrated through the house. She did the circuit from the kitchen to the family room, the living room, dining room, and back to the kitchen, and then turned around and completed it backwards.

The knife incident was still bothering her. That wasn't the only time over the last few days that handling a knife had brought on a panic attack. It had happened a couple of times when she had picked up a knife. And what about this stalker? Was he real or a figment of her imagination? Who would stalk her for no apparent reason? And who would murder Diane for no apparent reason? A psychopath?

She needed to talk with someone.

She ran up to her room while Colm Wilkinson's Phantom bared his soul.

Where had she jotted Patty's new number? On the back of an envelope, she thought. White or buff? She visualized white with a coffee stain that had been left behind when she had used it as a coaster. With all of the piles of paper, including envelopes from Kate's box, covering every previously empty space in the room, picking out a single envelope wasn't as easy as it might normally have been. She finally spotted it on Richard's highboy dresser.

It was just after ten eastern time, seven in California. Patty would likely be home from work. She and Patty had spent four idyllic years together in college where the greatest crisis was no date on a Friday night or maybe a tough exam, though that usually ranked a distant second. Porter, you were shallower than Kate at that age. Maybe. But there were days when she'd love to be so shallow again if it meant the only tears were from uncontrollable laughter, as had been the case back then. Their room had always been full of people drawn by the laughter and not wanting to miss the fun.

The McPherson family had for generations sent their children to college in Boston. No one seemed to know why Boston but it had become not just a tradition but an obligation, and so Sara had done her duty. Patty had been assigned her roommate in residence and at first glance the match was an impossible one. Patty was a generous, gregarious New Yorker with no regard for rules and an IQ that relieved her from any need to study. Sara was the stereotypical polite Canadian who waited for the lights to change before crossing the street even if there wasn't a car in sight and had just scraped together the grades to get accepted at Boston U — albeit because she hadn't been working hard enough. They found, however, that the old adage, opposites attract, applied just as well to college roommates as to life partners. Soon Sara was climbing out of dorm windows after curfew and picking up a New York accent, which people still commented on, although she thought any trace had long ago been left behind. Patty's generosity extended to sharing not only her clothes and the flock of boyfriends she herded mercilessly wherever she went, but her knowledge as well. As a result of Patty's largess, Sara not only discovered a different self but had learned how to learn and graduated in the top five of her class.

She carried the envelope with Patty's number down to the family room and curled up on the sofa with the phone in her lap. Patty and she both had studied psychology and Patty had gone on to do post-graduate work in criminal psychology. She had taught criminal psych at a college in New York for several years and then had an opportunity to train at Quantico, the FBI academy. She had recently landed a job as a criminal profiler with the LAPD.

Please be home. She was and Sara felt better as soon as she heard her voice.

"Wow, Sara, where are you? At a bloody opera?"

"Oops, sorry. Just a sec." Sara had forgotten the music was blaring and ran across the room to turn it down.

Patty hadn't changed. She didn't miss a beat. "Something tells me you are in need of some psychological counseling, Hon. Miss Efficiency, that being the normal you, takes three days to return a phone call and is so distracted she doesn't notice that the Phantom is being staged in her living room. What's happening up there?"

She could picture Patty nibbling on the eraser end of a pencil as she waited for the answer. Eraser ingesting had been her friend's trademark. Patty must have eaten a whole rubber tree in the time Sara had known her. They had decided that Patty's preference for pencils and Sara's for pens marked their most striking personality difference. Sara was decisive and action-oriented, seldom changing her mind, while Patty liked to try different scenarios, erasing each until she found the one that fit.

Sara was too distracted to take the interest in Patty's personal life that she normally would, but she managed to ask the right questions about her new job and her love life. The first was going like gangbusters, according to Patty, but the latter would make a better operetta than the Phantom. It was nice to know that some things didn't change. Patty had long ago adopted Neil Diamond's *Love on the Rocks* as her personal theme song. She was always erasing a relationship and trying another but managed to ensure that it was always the guy who dropped her.

"He just couldn't handle a long distance relationship," Patty was saying of the man she'd lived with for six months in New York and on weekends during her training at Quantico. Which is precisely why you took a job in LA; Sara kept the thought to herself.

Patty had a long list of unresolved personal problems. But then, all of the few psychologists Sara knew seemed to have chosen their profession as part of a search for their own answers.

"But what's happening up there?" Patty repeated.

Sara answered her with a brief overview of Diane's murder and her own private stalker experience. She didn't bother to talk about the box. It would take too much energy.

"My God, Sara. What happened to Toronto the Good? You should come down to LA where it's nice and safe."

Sara steered the conversation to the topic she needed to talk about. "Bump into many psychopaths in LA?"

"Probably, but at first sight you'd never know. They are usually full of charm." Patty paused, probably stopping for a quick nibble on her pencil, and then continued, "I'm assuming this discussion is going somewhere?"

"Yes." Sara tried to sound nonchalant, "I was thinking that the murderer and/or stalker would have to be a psychopath and then I realized that I didn't really know what one was."

"Hey, you've forgotten Psych 101 after only twenty-five years?"

"Apparently. All I remember is that Skinner box with mice running around in it."

"That's because it's so akin to the rat race you've adopted." Patty took every opportunity to reprimand her for her crazy working hours.

"OK, Mom. Now, what's a psychopath?"

"He or she is basically a cold bastard who doesn't experience emotion or have empathy like most people do. As a colleague of mine likes to say, 'The words are there but there is no melody.' If you really want to depress yourself by studying this stuff, a guy named Hare has done some of the most in-depth research on psychopaths. A fellow Canadian of yours actually. He developed the PCL-R that's generally accepted as the psychopathy bible. It's a checklist of the characteristics of a psychopath. The more boxes with little ticks in them, the scarier the person gets."

Sara tightened her grip on the phone. "Uh huh. So what are some of the characteristics?"

"I can give you a web address where you can find info about the instrument if you want to check them out but I don't think it will help you. You have to spend time with the person to identify the characteristics. Even for professionals it takes some intense interviews and some serious checking into their histories to identify all of the characteristics. It can be particularly difficult because, like I said, one of the characteristics is charm. Psychopaths have been known to wind the best in our business around their little fingers, even convincing them they have seen the light, that they are devastated by the horrendous nature of their acts, and that early parole would be just the thing so they could get busy repaying their debt to society. They instinctively know exactly the right buttons to push to put themselves onto someone's "my favorite people" list. Next thing you know they've killed their best friend and probably the poor shit of a psychiatrist as well."

Sara shivered.

"But I'm making them sound more dramatic than they are," Patty continued. "There is also your everyday garden variety psychopath who hasn't murdered anyone, at least not yet. That's the guy who wants to get to the top but doesn't want to bother climbing the corporate ladder. He'll do whatever is necessary, including lying, cheating and defaming others' character to jump on a high-speed elevator to success. Or the woman spurned who intends to get even and doesn't care who gets hurt in the process. Or the guy who abuses his wife and kids."

Sara ticked off four candidates while Patty was talking, with Ken Morrison at the top of the list. She put a mental question mark beside Aunt Kate's name.

Patty gave Sara the web address for the Hare instrument and apologized that she had to go. Someone was holding a reception for her to introduce her to the department.

"I wish we could talk longer. I know you're not giving me all the goods, Sar. Let's talk tomorrow."

Sara couldn't let her go without asking her final question. "Just one more sec. I've one more question. It won't take long."

"Sure." The word was drawn out and laden with concern. Patty had always chided Sara for never wanting to inconvenience anyone and Sara realized that asking her to take time for another question had just upped Patty's concern.

Sara paused to gather her courage and to think how she might word it and what she would say if Patty asked why she wanted to know.

"Sar?" There were never gaps in their conversations.

"I was just wondering. Could someone do something horrendous, something criminal, and have no memory of it?"

Now Patty paused. Sara knew she was debating whether to ask her why she wanted to know. Instead she answered the question as though quoting from one of her lectures. "Criminal amnesia can be triggered by shock, alcohol or other drugs. Some murderers have even claimed they walked in their sleep and had no knowledge of their acts. It could certainly happen. But in my experience, evidence suggests that whether one remembers an event or not, most people will not carry out an act in any kind of an altered state that they would not ordinarily be capable of."

"What about those hypnotist acts? You know, the ones where you get hypnotized and fall in love with a chair and don't remember a thing afterwards."

"Hypnotism can remove inhibitions and allow you to do things you would feel foolish doing otherwise, but experiments with hypnotism during the cold war had little success in turning mentally healthy individuals not normally capable of murder into assassins. But yes. It is possible for the mind to block out an act that is too shocking for the mind to cope with."

"Hmm. Interesting." Sara attempted to sound detached as if the whole discussion was a purely intellectual one.

She knew Patty wasn't fooled. "Listen, Sar, as a friend and as a psychologist, I'm not feeling good about this conversation. I want you to call tomorrow. Hear?"

Sara promised. There was some slight reassurance in what Patty had said. That is as long as she wasn't by nature capable of murder. Before Diane Brooks had come into their lives it would have been a definite no. But what if Aunt Kate was a garden-variety psychopath and she had inherited the genes? Could the right trigger have turned her into something worse?

She wanted to check out the web address Patty had given her but first she had to call Tony before it got too late. He was thrilled she had called; it made his evening. He knew she was stressed out. What were friends for if not for dumping on when one needed to unload, and "Let's have coffee this week." It was a five-minute conversation. She contributed two sentences, but at the end they both felt better.

Sara headed for the computer in the den. She stopped in the kitchen on the way and checked out the wine bottle they had opened for dinner. Empty. She considered opening another but settled for a can of iced tea instead.

The site Patty had recommended had plenty of information on the PCL-R. It appeared that one couldn't get direct access to it. Probably a wise move to prevent people like herself, who didn't know what they were doing, from using it. Several articles, however, listed some of the characteristics that Hare had identified. One click of the mouse and they would disappear before she could read them. That would be the sensible thing to do. Everyone knew that whenever you read a list of symptoms for any illness that you would immediately identify with at least half of them and could quickly produce the symptoms for the other half. But just maybe, there would be definite no's and she could relax and go to sleep.

1. Charming, particularly when it is useful to be so. A definite yes right off the bat but surely that one could be rationalized. Didn't most people feign charm when it was convenient to do so?
2. Lying. Regularly to Ken Morrison, when it was necessary for self-preservation. Did that count?
3. Manipulation. She had done a pretty good job at Jamieson's office and gotten herself invited for brunch tomorrow so she could snoop into the judge's things.
4. Narcissistic. Did buying pants because they made her hips look smaller count?
5. Easily bored. Definitely. She thrived on change.
6. Impulsive. Going into Jamieson's was pretty impulsive. She was getting a definite maybe. If she had been scoring for Aunt Kate, it would be a definite yes. She scanned down the page. "Although psychopathy has not been proven to be familial, a combination of genes can create a predisposition."

She hit the power button on the computer and her screen snapped to black. She knew she would be reprimanded the next time she used it with a message reminding her that her computer had not been properly shut down.

She felt even less in control than she had an hour ago. Well so much for the old saying that knowledge is power, she thought.

34

Patrick Jamieson might have been strolling across the lawn at The Point sixty years ago. He wore timeless brown wool slacks, a brown tweed jacket and open-necked shirt with a green and gold ascot knotted neatly around his neck. He could also have been entertaining half a century ago. He was the perfect host with the touch of elegance that had gone missing today from all but the most formal events.

He had greeted Sara personally at the door, although she had caught a glimpse of at least two people who seemed to be household staff scampering about as he led her to the back of the house and Theodore Jamieson's den. "Since this is where most of Uncle Ted's papers are and it has always been one of my favorite rooms, I thought I would ask Mary to serve brunch in here," he explained while pouring her a glass of orange juice and champagne.

She accepted the glass, a little disappointed that the aroma of coffee she had homed in on as they walked through the house hadn't materialized into a cup of much needed caffeine. Sara had struggled to go to sleep last night and reconfirmed the well tested fact that trying to force sleep was counterproductive. She had even resorted to counting sheep. But she had never managed to get more than eight sheep to clear the rail fence she had constructed for their exercise before her mind wandered to enumerating the characteristics of a psychopath instead.

She had looked at the clock every half hour until four thirty a.m. and then her body's tiredness overtook her still-running mind. She wasn't sure how her mind and body were going to handle the champagne.

She understood why Patrick was fond of this room. Floor-to-ceiling bookshelves lined two walls. A library ladder hung from the top rail on one side. The sofa and several chairs were of well-worn but still rich looking leather. Most were a dark green but the odd tan piece haphazardly placed here and there refuted any suggestion that this was a space that had been created by design. The room was cluttered, bordering on, but not quite, messy. Tidy would not have worked for this room. It needed the stacks of books and papers that sat precariously on every end and coffee table, as well as much of the floor.

At one end of the room was a large marble-faced fireplace. Patrick or one of his household staff had lit a fire early enough to ensure it was now confident and crackling. There was no need for scented potpourri to create a mood. Theodore Jamieson's years in this room had created his own scent. The smell of sweet pipe tobacco mingled with leather, old books, and burning wood.

Jamieson's huge mahogany desk sat at the other end of the room in front of a set of wide French doors flanked by windows on either side. Although a masculine den, Teddy Jamieson hadn't created a dark corner, but one full of light. His desk overlooked a huge back lawn and garden. Two gardeners were busy preparing the yard for winter. The piles of raked leaves that dotted the lawn suggested they had awoken long before Sara. One of the men deftly wound burlap around a rose bush as though wrapping a mummy.

"You like the room too." Patrick broke the silence that Sara hadn't even noticed.

"If I were ever to design a room perfect for curling up in this would be it."

"You're welcome any time." Although his face showed no expression, his blue eyes smiled at her as they had in his office. Patrick Jamieson was a comfortable person to be with.

He cleared books and papers from the coffee table in front of the fireplace and gazed around the room looking for a spot to put them. Unable to find table or shelf space he shrugged his shoulders, set them on the floor and shoved them under the table with his foot. Now here was a man who was not compulsively neat.

"I thought we'd eat and then go through those things." He nodded to a file box sitting beside one of the highback chairs that sat in front of the fireplace. He took the chair next to the box and gestured to her to take the other. They were barely settled when the door opened. A woman struggled into the room carrying an oversized tray laden with eggs Benedict, pastries, fruit and thankfully a large silver urn of coffee. The woman, whom Patrick introduced as Mary, was tiny with a pinched face. She wore a hair net that plastered her dark hair to her head. The woman must have been over sixty and Sara guessed that every few weeks she spent an evening in her bathroom with Miss Clairol.

Mary arranged the brunch on the coffee table and then went back to the doorway and spoke to someone who lingered there. She returned balancing a dark wooden tray that carried a silver place setting, white linen napkin, and a rosebud floating in a tiny crystal bowl. She placed the tray on Sara's lap and then made one more trip to the door for its twin, served it, and left.

They ate companionably with no urgent need for conversation. The only sound other than the occasional snap of the fire was the distant scratching of a rake across the lawn.

Languid, Sara thought. That was how she felt. Languid. The heat from the fireplace combined with the champagne put her into a state of deep relaxation. Even moving from the chair would take enormous determination. Mental exercise had even less appeal. She had no interest in turning her mind back to murder either old or new. Jamieson seemed to be in no rush to turn to his uncle's belongings either. They chatted about theatre, the chronic financial problems of the Toronto Symphony, of which Jamieson was a board member, and the Blue Jays' chances of winning the World Series.

"Kate and Teddy would have been surprised at our brunching together," Jamieson smiled at her.

"I think they'd be pleased." Sara paused for a moment to enjoy the last bit of hollandaise sauce that was lingering on her fork. "I gather they were very close at one time and I got the sense that they were always dear to one another, even though they weren't in touch a great deal the last few years."

"Definitely. In fact it was always assumed in our family that Teddy and Kate would marry. I was too young to remember them well during the summers at The Point but I can remember, years later, my grandparents being concerned that Teddy hadn't married, and they would always say, 'What's wrong with you? Kate is the perfect woman for you and she has never married. She's just waiting for you, you know.'"

"I wonder if she was."

"Perhaps she loved him enough that she never found another man who could replace him. But I suspect she knew him well enough to realize he would never marry her or any other woman."

The subject of his uncle's lifestyle didn't seem to bother Jamieson so Sara pushed a little further. "I had wondered whether he and Harper were life partners."

Jamieson looked genuinely surprised and then curious. "How on earth did you figure that out? I don't think our family even knew, or wouldn't acknowledge it if they had any suspicions. It only struck me a few years ago when alternative lifestyles became more open. They didn't change their behavior but I guess I simply read it differently than before.

"Teddy and Harper had been best friends since high school. When Harper graduated from university, Teddy talked my grandfather into hiring him as his financial manager. My grandparents even provided him with a small apartment upstairs and he lived as part of the family. Any free time Teddy had, which was little during his years in law, was spent with Harper. They even traveled together. Teddy was devastated when Harper died."

Jamieson clasped his hands together and turned them into a church steeple, and rested his chin on the point of the steeple. He looked at her expectantly, waiting to learn how she had discovered the men's relationship.

Sara had no intention of mentioning Jane Stewart's letter and so responded sparingly. "I guess it was mostly intuition. I noticed them looking at each other in a very caring way in some of my aunt's photos and I knew Harper had been a close companion to your uncle all of their lives." She ended with a shrug.

"Well, you were spot on. Too bad they weren't able to enjoy one another openly. For all of his success I always felt there was a sadness in Uncle Teddy and I now suspect his and Harper's restrained relationship was the cause."

"Your uncle died suddenly didn't he?" Sara ventured into the other topic she had come to explore.

"Yes, he did. Although he had had a heart condition. Actually I found him, over there," Jamieson nodded toward the desk, "slumped over his desk." And then his face became one of concern. "Sara, I'm so sorry. How insensitive of me. I shouldn't have told you that or else shouldn't have had brunch served here. We can move to another room if you like?"

Sara waved away his concern. "No, I'm fine. It doesn't bother me at all." Which was true if the judge had died a natural death. If he had been murdered she wasn't quite so comfortable. "I hope it wasn't a painful death?"

The question was a weak attempt at keeping to the discussion of his uncle's death. To her ear it sounded like either an obvious attempt to keep the topic open or an inept attempt at conversation. She hoped he heard neither.

"If it were, I expect the pain was short. It was a massive heart attack." He paused for a moment, and when he spoke it was at a slower pace that allowed for contemplation. "It's amazing how you can see someone almost every day and not actually look at them. As I waited for the ambulance I truly looked at him for the first time in perhaps months or even years." His tone was one of regret. "He looked so old. I didn't realize he had aged so. His face was not only lined, but full of broken blood vessels and his fingertips were blue. That I suppose could have been due to the heart attack though." He shook his head as though attempting to release a sticky memory. "I'm sorry for being so morbid. Let's take a look at his happier times."

Patrick reached for the box and was about to open it when the housekeeper rapped and darted in. "Telephone, Mr. Jamieson. It's Mr. Fellows. He said it was important." She bobbed back out as quickly as she had come in.

Patrick nodded but didn't move from his chair. He opened the box and perused its contents for a few minutes. Patrick finally decided that he had kept his caller waiting long enough. It had been so long that Sara was certain he was making a point to the caller. He slowly pulled himself to his feet and excused himself, setting the box in front of her.

"Here, why don't you get started?"

The box was full of photo albums and she had barely opened the first when he returned. As brief as the call had been, it caused him to change his demeanor as swiftly and automatically as a chameleon changed its color. His innate graciousness was still there but he had turned from host to the competent executive who was tired of suffering fools.

"Sara, I am terribly sorry. I'm going to have to leave. This politics business is taking its toll already. I'm beginning to think I am surrounded by a group of incompetents."

He suggested that she either take the albums with her or she was welcome to stay and go through them here. In fact, why didn't she do that? He would ask Mary to bring her fresh coffee. The decision was made and he was gone before she could accept. But she was happy with the plan. She had no desire to cart any more memorabilia into her home. So far they had brought only distress with them.

The first album had a padded red cover with "Photo Album" written in gold, just in case anyone didn't know what it was for. The covers and the album's leafs were held together by what looked like a long black shoelace that was threaded through a set of perforations. The pages were of a heavy black paper. The black and white photos with edges that looked like they had been cut with a dressmaker's shears were held in place by tiny gold picture corners that were glued to the pages. Many fasteners had lost their power and several photos had slid loose among the pages.

The album, dated 1945, included many shots of the Jamieson family. Two young men in uniform — Sebastian, who would have been Patrick's father, and his cousin Sam — appeared frequently. The Group seemed not yet to be fully formed. She could find only Teddy's, Aunt Kate's, and Harper's faces occasionally peaking over family members shoulders, and she spotted her father in a couple. Her grandparents would still have been alive and the family would have spent the summer at the lake.

Among the 1946 photos she was able to find all of the Group members, but it didn't appear they were all there all of the time. Some photos included a couple of them, usually with Jamieson family members. There was also a fellow with a chubby cherub-like face who appeared occasionally. None of the photos pictured the Group together.

In the 1947 photos, things changed. There was only an occasional glimpse of a family member. Jane Stewart's beautiful eyes and Kendall's practical jokes, like bending to show his derrière to the camera, were added to the antics of Kate, Harper, and Teddy. The Group had emerged with an identity of its own.

There were few candid shots. The group seemed to enjoy posing and clowning for the camera. Arms and legs flailed and faces were contorted. They also enjoyed writing what they must have thought to be clever captions. A shot of Teddy, Harper and Kendall had "The Three Musketeers" written under it. One caught the Group as a shaky pyramid, Aunt Kate perched like a gamine on top. It was captioned, "Queen of the Hill." Teddy had neatly written "The Love Birds" under a picture of Jane Stewart on the front steps of the Jamiesons' cottage with the fellow with the cherub face beside her, his cheeks dimpled by his smile. The date on the back was August 1946. It had been placed in the wrong album. She couldn't find the young man in any of the photos taken the following summers. It must have been a short-lived romance.

A photo of her aunt in a formal gown posing confidently, aware of her beauty, and Teddy in black tie, his arm around her, toasting the camera with a glass of champagne, was captioned "Percy and Gus." When she turned it over she understood the reference. The note on the back read July 1947, followed by what must have been a popular rhyme or line from a song: "We never miss a society fuss. No function's complete without Percy and Gus."

That one picture summed up a great deal. Kate and Teddy were definitely a couple on some level and they, and probably the whole Group, saw themselves as witty and clever people-about-town.

A tall, thin, serious looking fellow, whom she guessed was Tony's father, appeared occasionally in the later photos. Otherwise the 1947 and 1948 photos were more of the same. Seemingly endless idyllic days at The Point with nothing more to worry about than where they should picnic next, who would push whom into the lake or whether someone would have to go to town for Schweppes for their gins and tonic.

Sara had a sudden pang of nostalgia for those days of innocence even though she hadn't lived them. The "lovebirds" photo drew her back to it and she imagined sitting on the steps with them, feeling completely at home. She felt as though she knew them. She gently tugged the photo from its tiny corner fasteners and put it in her bag.

Sara closed the last album and pulled herself from the chair and into a stretch. She wandered along the bookshelves dragging her fingers across the spines. There were many leather-bound collections of the great authors. Shakespeare and Balzac appeared to be the most read, their leather spines soft and creased with opening. All of the books were alphabetically arranged from Abercrombie to Zola. The piles of books around the room seemed inconsistent with the meticulously ordered shelves.

She admired the ornately carved ivory box and matching letter opener that sat on the judge's desk. Had he had a moment to appreciate them once more before he had died? A black leather agenda with the initials TJ in gold in the bottom right corner rested in the middle of the desk. Opening it seemed an act of ghoulish curiosity and she would be embarrassed if anyone caught her perusing it. Mary was likely to come in to clear things away. However, if she stood in front of the desk and turned the book just slightly, she should be able to read it, but at the same time have it well enough hidden to be able to close it unnoticed if someone came in before she was finished. The word cunning from Hare's psychopath checklist popped into her mind.

She flipped through the pages until she reached September. The name Kate was scrawled across a page at least twice a week. She had no idea he visited her aunt so regularly. She flipped to the week of his death. He had two doctor's appointments, an eye check-up and an another appointment. That last entry read "specialist — Ferguson." She thought Ferguson was a cardiologist.

The last day the judge had seen her aunt was the day of his death. The day before he had several appointments. She glanced over these entries and then moved on wondering what appointments he had made for a future that had never unfolded. The day after his death caught her attention. Lunch with Gord Simpson. Simpson was the Inspector of Homicide. Any residue of inertia she'd felt earlier disappeared. Her heart began pounding a little faster. Just a social lunch? Or had he decided it was time to get rid of a burden he had carried for over fifty years? As she was closing the book, the day before his death caught her attention again. The last appointment was squeezed into the tiny square. It looked like "Dr. Brooks, here," but the "Dr." was written on top of the last name. Her first thought was that the judge had a lot of doctors and at least one made house calls. She turned it to the light for one last look before closing it and the overlapping letters popped into their proper order: "D. Brooks, here." An adrenaline rush sent her heart pounding against her ribs as Jane's and Diane's murders collided in her mind. Diane had met with the judge, probably right in this room the day before he died.

Sara was about to close the calendar when the door opened and Jamieson charged back in. "Got halfway downtown before I remembered that I forgot my cell phone."

Sara stepped too quickly back from the desk feeling like the proverbial child caught with a hand in the cookie jar.

Jamieson hurried over to the desk where his cell lay not far from the judge's calendar. He stopped for a moment and perused the open page, then closed the calendar, letting his hand rest on it for just a moment.

"Enjoy the photos," he said nodding toward the box on the other side of the room as he turned to leave.

Sara got the message and felt her embarrassment swell until it reached her cheeks.

Well you deserved that one. She had taken advantage of Jamieson's hospitality. Aunt Kate would not have approved. Whether of the etiquette breach or having gotten caught, she wasn't sure.

As she gathered up her jacket and bag she noticed that she had forgotten to return the last album to the box. She had left it on the floor beside her chair. As she picked it up something escaped from its empty back pages and fell gently toward the brunch's remains on the coffee table. A lock of black hair tied with red threads settled on a crumpled white linen napkin.

35

"It's day five and you're telling me we have nothing new other than Sara Porter is being stalked and her home was entered by someone, probably the stalker." Simpson was massaging his temples as though getting his brain to work better would somehow improve the quality of the information he was receiving.

Simpson had pulled anyone on the Brooks' case, who wasn't smart enough to be out of the building, into his office for an update meeting. Greally was an easy find since he made a point of staying within Simpson's viewfinder whenever he was in the building. Perkins heard Simpson telling Greally he wanted to round everyone up and he had just about made it into the stairwell with his mug of coffee when Simpson lassoed him with a shout from his office doorway. "You can get that smoke later Perkins. See who else is around and get them in here." Perkins caught up with Carson and Kirpatrick in the front lobby heading at full speed for the door. They suggested that he hadn't really seen them at all but Perkins wasn't playing.

"If you think I'm going to spend the next half hour by myself watching Greally suck up to Simpson, you're dreaming in technicolor." And so one keener and three reluctant participants had gathered in the Inspector's office.

"No, I don't think that information's quite right." It was Greally, leaning against the door jamb, hands in his pockets.

"Oh, how so?" Simpson took his fingers from his temples, repositioned his head to one side and put on his "tell me more" expression.

"Sara Porter is *supposedly* being stalked and *supposedly* someone broke into her home. I don't see any real evidence of either." Greally always spoke with the kind of confidence that could turn people from Missouri into believers. "You don't have any actual signs of forced entry, other than a loose screen, which someone could have entered through or which Sara Porter could have loosened herself. An empty milk glass with no prints whatsoever, including lip prints, suggesting to me that Ms. Porter poured the glass of milk and then poured it down the sink. Papers missing from upstairs? Who says they are missing? Sara Porter of course. Richard Porter is convinced it was Diane Brooks' murderer who entered the house. Why? Because the scent he noticed when he found Brooks' body was also evident in his wife's bedroom. It seems to me it would be quite likely that the scent of Sara Porter's own cologne would be in her bedroom, and I can't believe that no one collected her perfume before she had a chance to dispose of the one she was wearing when she murdered Diane Brooks."

The "no one" he referred to was, of course, Carson.

"That's crazy. If the cologne were one that Sara Porter wore regularly, why wouldn't Richard Porter, who had been married to her for years, have recognized it? Carson's impatience slipped in spite of his best effort to restrain it.

Perkins kept his mouth closed. He probably didn't want to position himself on one side or the other.

Kirpatrick was looking back and forth between the two sparring veterans, a single frown line appearing just below his blond hairline. "I don't get it. Why would Sara Porter lie about being followed and having her house broken into?" Kirpatrick didn't know Greally well enough yet to realize that he was manipulating everything to fit his "Sara Porter did it" theory.

Greally slipped into his coach's mode just like Carson imagined he slipped into his shiny Italian suits. "Listen, Kirpatrick, don't be naïve. The number one rule is don't take anything a suspect, or anyone else for that matter, tells you at face value. Ask yourself 'How do they benefit from that?' With Sara Porter the answer is obvious. The stalker story creates a possible suspect, other than herself, for the murder of Diane Brooks. Otherwise, Sara Porter is the one and only, and she's getting just a tad nervous."

Carson watched Kirpatrick give a slow nod, move his gum to the other side of his mouth and casually lean his chair back against the wall in a two-legged balancing act as though looking for a more seasoned posture that would rebut Greally's "naïve" remark.

The Inspector was back to rubbing his temples. As much as he would like to be the one to offer a morsel to the hungry Simpson, Carson wasn't ready to table the information Sara had shared with him last evening about the Jane Stewart murder. In fact, at this point there wasn't any reason to, as the only possible link between the two cases was the fact that Sara's stalker had taken some of her aunt's papers that related to the Stewart murder. And that was a link only if the stalker was also Brooks' murderer. Besides, a sixty-year-old murder and a group of well-to-do university kids who grew into prominent citizens as suspects? Greally would have a heyday with that. He would use it as another example of Sara trying to come up with anything, however outlandish, to direct police attention away from herself.

Carson had looked into a couple of things related to the information Sara had gathered: Judge Jamieson had, according to the death certificate, died of a heart attack. The only way they could get any more information would be by exhuming the body and to make that happen he'd have to have something a lot more concrete than a sixty-year-old murder, and the fact that the judge's obituary had been placed in a box of ancient memorabilia.

The Jane Stewart case had never been resurrected as far as he could tell. It had taken him two hours to find the box that contained the file from among the stacks of cartons waiting in limbo. The thousands of reports that sat there had been marked to be saved digitally but with the tight budget there was a good chance they would disintegrate before anything was done with them.

Toronto Police had been invited to take over the case, as the Ontario Provincial Police responsible for the area had never run into a murder case before. In 1948, Toronto Police didn't see many themselves.

The case was contained in only two manila folders. Either there was little information to gather or no one had tried very hard. Carson suspected the latter. The last report was dated Oct. 15, 1948. It concluded, "After exhaustive efforts on the part of Detective Bruce Jones and Constable Ben Williams," Carson shook his head as he read on, "the lack of motive, evidence or leads suggests that the crime was committed by a transient who unless linked with another crime in the future is unlikely to be identified."

An earlier report documented the first stages of the investigation and included interviews with the Group.

Miss Jane Stewart, it said, had been staying with the Thomas Jamiesons at their summer home at Oak Point, better known by locals as "The Point," on Lake Simcoe. After the name Jamieson was the notation, "Important: Jamieson Senior is a liberal Member of Parliament and owner of the Jamieson's Department Store in Toronto." That was the kind of information that today no smart cop would forget but wouldn't write it blatantly in the file either.

She was reported missing the evening of September 4 by her parents Mr. and Mrs. John Stewart. Miss Stewart had been last seen the previous evening and two young boys, Billie Coombs and Jimmie Baker, discovered her body a few days later, on a deserted piece of beach, commonly used as a garbage dump, next to The Point.

The interview notes made no effort to suggest objectivity. "Mr. Theodore Jamieson was most co-operative and anxious to help. Miss Stewart had been a frequent guest at the Jamiesons' summer home for several seasons. It was his belief that she had left for Bradford in the early morning of Sept 3 to catch a train to Toronto. He had offered the evening before to drive her, but as Mr. Theodore Jamieson and his houseguests were up until approximately three o'clock in the morning playing board games (and, although not stated, it was suggested that some conservative drinking had taken place), she insisted that he not get up but that she would hire a taxi from Bradford. When he awoke at noon, she had left. Mr. Jamieson assumed that she had returned to Toronto.

"Miss Kathryn McPherson, of Toronto, daughter of the late James McPherson, barrister, is a very self-possessed and charming young woman. The McPherson cottage is adjacent to the Jamiesons' and the young people had spent several summers together. Therefore Miss McPherson knew Miss Stewart well. Miss McPherson had closed her cottage for the season (both of her parents having died tragically in an automobile accident last year, Miss McPherson inherited the cottage) and returned to the city the weekend before Miss Stewart's disappearance. Therefore she had little information to share. She knew of no one who would want to harm Jane Stewart."

Other interviews with the houseguests repeated the same information. Too much the same, Carson thought.

Carson was anxious to get out of this meeting with Simpson. They still hadn't identified the motive for the Brooks murder but it had to lie in her work. Her missing agenda must be significant. Since Richard Porter professed to know nothing about Brooks' current project, they had to track it down somehow. Again her laptop had had nothing to offer. Her electronic files contained nothing dated within the last six months. Prior to that she had saved copious notes on all of her projects.

Two short rings came from Carson's breast pocket. "Oops, sorry. Forgot to turn it off." Simpson frowned at the interruption. Carson pulled out his cell, punched send and moved a few feet away from the huddle.

It was Sara. If he had been given the opportunity to select the person he would most like to hear from this morning she was the only candidate he could think of.

She went straight to the point. Either she was not a small talk kind of person, the kind he liked, or she wanted to send the message that their relationship was purely business, which he wasn't so sure of. She told him she had just spent time at the Jamieson home and had discovered that the judge had met with Diane Brooks the day before his death and that he had an appointment scheduled with Simpson for the day after his death.

Greally had turned slightly toward him, straining to hear, Carson was sure, while pretending to be absorbed in whatever Simpson was saying. Carson wanted to shout "Yes!" but instead said only, "Interesting." He knew the "interesting" would get Greally. "I'm in a meeting and can't talk now. I appreciate the call."

Greally looked at him expectantly as he returned to the group. "My sister. Reminding me about Sunday dinner." Carson threw it out casually as though to the group at large. He and Greally were playing games again. He handed

Greally a lie that Greally knew was a lie and knew that Carson intended him to know was a lie. Greally glared at Carson, his complexion reddening slightly. Carson had delivered a "f — you" and Greally had signed for it.

Carson needed more before he shared the new information, even with Simpson.

"And, Carson, what about you and Kirpatrick? Where are you heading?" Simpson was checking for next steps.

Carson spoke deliberately so that the few steps he was ready to share might sound like a grand plan.

"There's Dempster, of course. He's been away for the weekend. We still need to catch up with him again. I also want to check out Diane Brooks' home office again to make sure we haven't missed anything."

"Waste of time." Greally shook his head. "We've had three teams go over it. We picked up all of her files and went through them with a fine-tooth comb. We even went through her grocery lists. What we need to do is bring in Sara Porter."

Greally looked expectantly at Simpson.

Carson's stomach tightened.

Simpson shook his head. "This isn't a street person we're talking about. If we arrest Sara Porter it's going to get plenty of attention. Our case has to be iron clad. I don't intend on being embarrassed by any half-assed investigation. We're not arresting her until you get me something solid."

"OK, guys, let's get it!" Greally bellowed and punched a fist into the palm of his other hand.

Startled, Perkins spilled his coffee on a rumpled pant leg and made his only contribution to the meeting, "Shit, Greally."

Carson hated it when Greally played cheerleader.

It felt good to get outside. The humidity of the Indian summer had been swept away by a cold front that had moved down from the north bringing more seasonally crisp autumn air with it. The new station was positioned on the corner of two busy main streets, but in spite of the exhaust fumes, the earthy smell of dried leaves made it to his sense centers. Fall, not spring, was for him the season of renewal. Perhaps just more evidence of his perversity or a hangover from school days. While spring held only a tickle of joy at the end of a long winter, fall made his heart take little leaps that some people would call a feeling of happiness. It was more he thought a feeling of hope or expectation. Each autumn, better days became possible. Fortunately, the fact that the possibility was often not fulfilled did not prevent the spurt of subdued excitement from returning the following year.

Kirpatrick, too, seemed to be re-energized. Suggesting he spend yesterday with his wife had paid dividends. His wife must have been smiling when he left this morning for his good mood was evident. But Carson was learning that there was a downside to Kirpatrick's good moods. The happier he was, the more he talked. And Carson's newly cleaned Mustang gave him something to talk about.

"Holy. Look at that. There was a real beauty under that dirt. I don't suppose you cleaned her up in honor of your new partner?" Kirpatrick's jesting suggested a new level of comfort with his senior. In giving him the much needed time off yesterday, Carson had given him a peek at the human under the quirky and unpredictable exterior that had previously kept Kirpatrick in a constant state of discomfort.

Carson magnanimously tossed him the keys when they reached the car.

"I get to drive? I think I should be recording this somewhere. Two firsts in one day. Sure you're OK. Sarge?" Kirpatrick grinned and climbed into the driver's seat.

Carson directed him to Richard Porter's address, hating every minute in the passenger seat. There was a reason he always drove. He couldn't stand not being in control.

The impressive Victorian house was still empty. Carson wondered whether Porter would ever move back in. He didn't think he would be able to in the same circumstance.

Carson had found nothing useful among the papers that had been collected from the kitchen where Diane had been working when she was murdered, or from other corners of the house, including her office and the bedroom. He wanted to check her office more carefully. He didn't expect to find more files but few books had made it to the evidence room and if she were a writer of history it would make sense that she would have books on whatever it was she was researching.

They found Diane's office at the top of the stairs, a bright yellow room that barely qualified as an office. Its sofa and chairs, each positioned to catch the sun, were wrapped in slipcovers of blue and yellow cotton. A vase of four large yellow sunflowers sat in the middle of a coffee table, a dish of dried rose petals beside it. It was the kind of room that seduced you into playing hooky and spending lazy afternoons with the perfect novel and unending cups of tea. Carson would add Arrowroot cookies for dunking. He could picture Diane Brooks barefooted, curled up in the biggest chair by the window, her dark hair falling forward as she dipped her head into her book. What would she have been reading if she had been here now, he wondered.

The room was perfectly tidy. It was a room that looked as though it took neatness for granted although the forensic team would have helped by removing any papers and files.

"It looks like Greally was right. There isn't much here." Kirpatrick was the first to break the soft spell of the room. Or perhaps he hadn't felt it. "But it's a good idea to take another look," he added quickly, and got busy opening drawers and looking under the desk.

A small desk and swivel chair were the only concession to an office. He rolled the chair over to the white painted bookshelf that ran under the window and stretched to either wall. Diane Brooks had been an eclectic reader. Spirituality, the popular fiction of John Grisham and Elizabeth George, *Little Women* and *Lord of the Rings, Beauty Tips from the Stars, Eating For Your Body Type, The Memoirs of Jimmy Carter, The History of the Simcoe Area* and *Unsolved Murders in Canada.*

He pulled out the last two, both library books. They had been taken out last month and the library's system would be busily logging overdue fees which would never be paid.

The book on Lake Simcoe recorded its history until only 1945. Before Jane Stewart's murder. But it did prove that Diane Brooks had an interest in the area. Carson's heart began to race a little faster and he recognized the homestretch feeling. It must be how racehorses feel when they are heading to the finish line. They know they are nearly there. They just have to keep doing what they are doing and make sure they don't break stride.

Unsolved Murders in Canada had only a two-page description of Jane Stewart's murder. Like the police investigators, its author seemed to have had difficulty finding anything to report. Perhaps Brooks had been more tenacious. Several Post-it notes had marked the two pages with arrows pointing to various sentences. Diane's neatness was apparent even in her handwriting. She preferred black ink on green stickies. The tiny letters were a meld of script and print, each looking as though it had been painstakingly formed. The small black arrows were complete with feathered shafts.

An arrow pointed to the sentence "Miss Stewart had been staying at the summer home of the Thomas Jamiesons." Diane's note on overlapping Post-it notes read, "Were the Jamieson family and their friends ignored as suspects because of their position in society and no one wanted to take the risk? Or were they ignored because it was assumed as upstanding members of society, they could not be involved in such a crime?"

The question, "Did anyone check whether her bed had been slept in?" was posted beside the sentence, "According to her host, Theodore Jamieson, it was assumed that Miss Stewart had arisen early and taken the train from Bradford to Toronto." Another Post-it note read, "How was she supposed to have gotten to Bradford? Did anyone check with the local taxi company?"

There was no indication that she had come to any conclusion. The questions suggested nothing other than the murder of Jane Stewart had piqued her interest.

Two spiral bound stenographer's pads were tucked between the two books. A title was neatly penned on the blue cover of each. *The Oak Point Centennial Project — Book One* and *The Oak Point Centennial Project — Book Two.* On the first page of *Book One* was the list of interviewees. Three entries had an asterisk beside them. The reference at the bottom of the page said simply "info on JS murder." The remaining pages contained what appeared to be a synopsis of the interviews she had done. He skimmed through all of them, finding nothing more interesting than memories of the first corner store; winters in which the weather was so merciless that people were housebound for days on end unless they ventured out on snowshoes; and the early cottagers who would come from the city by train, their household staff having arrived earlier by horse and buggy and carrying everything from good linens to the silver tea service. Each interview contained several headings, one of which was "J.S.'s Murder." The notation under it was usually "was too young to remember the incident" or "remembered it well but no useful information to add."

Finally, Carson turned to the first of the three interviews that had earned an asterisk:

Miss Molly Madisons. Local schoolteacher from 1946 to 1976. Invited me to browse through her diary with the comment "Alas I have no scandalous secrets to hide." A delightful woman, still very sharp, never married. I noticed a notation in her diary dated September 3, 1948:

"Walked Laddie tonight as usual around The Point. It was a perfect late summer evening. I so enjoy this time of the season when cottagers begin to return to the city and give us our wonderful lake back. As I strolled across the lawn that stretches between the Jamieson and McPherson cottages (Laddie had taken off ahead of me after a raccoon most likely) I heard what sounded like a vicious argument at the smaller cottage and there was a dim light on in the living room. Odd, as I'm sure Dorothy Coombs told me that she was through cleaning there for the season as Katherine had closed it early and gone back to the city. I should be reprimanded for my nosiness but I must admit I did make an effort to hear the conversation. I couldn't make out a great deal but after several minutes of raised voices a woman laughed, more, I believe, in derision than in joy. The laughter was followed by a male voice yelling 'You really are despicable,' and then the voices became muffled again. And that is my big excitement for today. I am so bored that I'm becoming a Nosy Parker."

I asked if she still remembers this and she said yes she does because of it being just the week before they found the body of JS. I asked if she told the police and she said no. When I asked why she said because she was sure it was nothing. The Jamiesons and McPhersons were fine people and she didn't want to cause any trouble for anyone. She had always been taught that one should mind one's own business, although she admitted that over the years she has wondered whether she should have said something.

The second interview that was asterisked was headed "Interview with Mr. and Mrs. Bill Coombs." Diane Brooks recapped Bill Coombs' story of finding the body and then continued.

When I asked him if he could remember anything unusual about the activities around the cottages the days immediately before the body was found, he said no but he remembered his mother, Dorothy Coombs, who was the cleaning lady for the cottages (his father was the caretaker), saying that something was odd about Mr. Teddy Jamieson, saying he thought Miss Stewart had taken the train the morning she went missing. because Jamieson had asked Mrs. Coombs the previous day if she knew anything about the train schedule from Bradford to Toronto and she said there wasn't any train before one in the afternoon on Wednesdays. She knew because her sister had physiotherapy treatments in the city every Thursday morning since she had been partially paralyzed by polio. Her sister had to travel the day before, on Wednesday, as it was an early morning appointment and she always took the first train that left Bradford station at one o'clock. She wondered why he would say he thought she had left early in the morning to catch the train when he knew there wasn't a morning train. But she warned us not to say anything. "Those are the people that put the bread and butter on our table and if anyone in this house says one word of this to anyone they aren't going to get any water let alone bread and butter for a month. Ya hear me? Besides they're good people. It must just be some mix-up or other."

The final asterisk rested beside the name of Judge Theodore Jamieson. Most of the interview contained anecdotes about his parents buying the cottage from the Jeffersons, who were the first people at The Point, and about a rescue of a several fishermen who had been caught a ways off The Point when Lake Simcoe, which had a reputation for its unpredictable waters, suddenly became rough and turned on the people it had beckoned to. Two were drowned and two made it close enough to shore to be rescued by the judge's father, Thomas Jamieson.

Under the "JS's Murder" heading there were only a couple of lines.

When I enquired what he remembered about the murder, he said only that of course it was very sad, Jane Stewart had been a friend and the family felt a certain responsibility for her death since she had been their guest.

When I mentioned that my research suggested that perhaps the case hadn't been thoroughly enough investigated, he said only that it had been a long time ago and he saw no benefit in raising again something so tragic. He then ended the interview although we had booked for fifteen minutes longer. He did however suggest that I call again in a couple of weeks??? Is he debating about what he should tell me?

According to Sara, that interview had taken place the day before his death. He hadn't discounted anything Sara had said the previous evening but the idea that her aunt's box of stuff held clues to a sixty-year-old murder had seemed a little far fetched. Now it seemed that not only was that quite possible, but in addition, the sixty-year-old murder might be a motive for Diane Brooks' murder. It didn't make much sense though, since the key players were dead. But his instincts told him that this was it. It was the tiny thread that was the beginning of the solution in every complicated case. If one found it and worried at it until one could get a hold of it and pull it gently, it would eventually unravel the entire puzzle.

"What's that?" Kirpatrick was standing over him. It was time to update his partner. He was going to have to officially submit these things as well as the material he'd collected from Sara's last evening as evidence and it wasn't fair for his partner to be out of the loop. Not here though. They had already intruded too long in Diane's personal space. He glanced around the soothing room once more, inhaled a breath of rose petals and jerked his head toward the door.

"Let's go. I'll tell you about it outside."

They sat on the back steps of the Victorian wraparound veranda. Kirpatrick's already ebullient mood went up another notch when he heard they had something to offer Simpson. At the same time he was either slightly incredulous or afraid to hope that this new direction might actually lead them somewhere productive.

"Do you really think the two murders could be connected?"

"Don't know." Carson shrugged his shoulders under his navy blue suit. But what he did know was that anything was possible. He had investigated murders whose motives were the usual; money, passion, or spousal abuse. But there were just as many that were harder to fathom, and definitely harder to crack. There was the case in which an attractive fifteen-year-old schoolgirl was murdered by her psychotic neighbor because he believed she was the devil sent to tempt him. He murdered her, he said, to prevent himself from sinning.

In another case, a middle-aged man appeared to die from sleep apnea but was actually killed by his wife who couldn't take his snoring any longer. She put a pillow over his head and sat on it. She got off on a plea of psychological trauma brought on by sleep deprivation. One of the first things he had learned in the homicide division was to not depend too heavily on logic. Motives for murder were often not based on the average man's sense of reason.

Kirpatrick had wandered across the lawn, cell phone in hand, to call his wife.

Carson rested his elbows on the step behind him and dropped his head back so that he could feel the sun on his face. He tracked a puffy white cloud as it scudded across the bright blue sky. The slight chill that was in the air when they left headquarters was becoming more definite. He'd soon have to get out his winter topcoat.

He pulled himself upright and leaned his arms forward on his knees. He had an urge for a cigarette. Usually he associated smoking with coffee, beer, or sex, but these few moments of quiet time-out also called for one. He distracted himself by looking more closely at the yard. Trees and bushes were stark pen sketches against a brown and gold carpet of leaves. No one had raked yet.

The spot of white was conspicuous in the autumn tableau. Something had gotten tangled in a clutch of dead leaves that were packed tightly in the branches at the base of a naked forsythia bush He strolled across the lawn, knelt on one knee beside the bush and reached below. It was a stretch but he could just reach the base and came out with a handful of dark, decomposing leaves and one piece of damp white paper. He took it back to the steps and smoothed it out. The dampness had roughened its surface and lifted most of its ink.

It was obviously a receipt and probably of little use. It could have blown from anywhere in the neighborhood. The bright sunlight reflecting on the white surface made the faded type even harder to decipher. He tried cupping his hand around it to shield it from the sun. The name of the establishment emerged and next to it the date. Not clearly but strong enough not to be denied. His stomach flipped and his morning coffee burned in his esophagus. Primavera Ristorante, dated the evening Sara and Hamilton had had dinner there. The evening Diane Brooks was murdered, just feet away on the other side of the French doors behind him.

The books he had taken from Diane Brooks' shelf were piled on the step beside him. He opened the book on the history of Lake Simcoe and tucked the receipt in the back. He played with the white edge that protruded from the book for a few seconds and then grasped it and pulled it out again. He stretched out one leg and worked the evidence Simpson and Greally were waiting for deep into one of his pants' pockets.

36

Sara drove home from Jamieson's, the Jane Stewart photo captioned "the Love Birds" on the passenger's seat beside her, the lock of black hair tied with red thread resting on top of it. It was identical to the lock of hair she had found in her aunt's box. The locks of hair created a mix of curiosity and repulsion. Rather like the appeal of shrunken heads. But at least with shrunken heads one knew little about the donor. Now that two locks of hair had materialized she was even more sure to whom they had belonged. Perhaps she should have told Carson about the hair. But to what end? They could identify the DNA but had no other sample to compare it to.

And then there was Diane's name in the judge's appointment book. It was too much of a coincidence. There had to be a connection. Yet, if there were, it was mind-boggling. Had the same woman who had taken her husband from her also uncovered a murder in which her aunt was involved? How could this woman, to whom she had never even spoken, insinuate herself so powerfully into her life? She wondered if there had ever been a hurricane named Diane. She remembered a hurricane striking the Caribbean a few years ago, just after she and Richard had left St Martin, one of their favorite vacation spots. The island had been broadsided by the storm. The preferred beach they had spent their days on, where grape leaf trees provided the perfect shady spot for reading or sipping a piña colada, had been washed away. People had lost their homes and the beautiful resort at which she and Richard had stayed was now derelict. Chunks had been taken from people's lives and shock and pain left in their place. But destruction also made way for renewal.

If Diane Brooks had never appeared, she and Richard would still be together living half-lives and she wouldn't even have realized it. If Diane hadn't appeared, raising her stress level, she would have been better able to handle Ken when he announced that she was being relocated to a cubicle, and she'd still be struggling for a partnership instead of…? What, she didn't know, but whatever it was it would be a vast improvement over Morrison and Black.

OK, Porter. None of that damn glass half-full stuff. You've still got a few major problems. Among them was the fact that she couldn't remember the night of Diane's murder. And the awful shock that the murder scene, including what Diane had been wearing and where she had been sitting, was exactly as in her dream. And then there were the panic attacks that knives had begun to induce.

The chills of fear returned, leaving cold pinpricks as they ran up her back. Her conversation with Patty last night hadn't brought the relief she had been so desperate for.

And then there was her maybe-stalker. As much as she didn't relish it, she had to speak with Dempster. If the fellow who had claimed to be delivering fliers had been wearing a Blue Jays cap, that would clinch it.

She wondered too about Patrick Jamieson. Why had he stopped to check the page she had been looking at in Jamieson's calendar? Was he concerned about what she might have learned? It was evident that securing a place in the political arena was important to him and his telephone conversations suggested he intended to do whatever was necessary to win. What might he consider necessary? Sara liked Patrick but had learned from Richard's leaving her that you could never know what was going on in someone else's head, or even who they really were.

Sara pulled into her drive and nosed the Volvo from the sunlight into the dark garage. She could make out the shadow of an old bureau lurking in a corner. She had intended to give it to the Salvation Army but hadn't gotten around to calling them. She turned off the ignition and had one leg out of the door when she heard a rustling sound. Her internal alarm system wailed as she quickly pulled herself back into the car and locked the door. She strained to listen but her pounding heart deafened her. She started the ignition and backed out into the sunlight and stopped several feet from the garage.

She stared into the garage looking for movement. Nothing. She had been leaving the garage door open and leaves had blown in. Perhaps the rustling had only been a squirrel working its way through them.

"Damn you, whoever you are!" she yelled, ridding her system of the adrenaline that had been pumped into it. She would not be terrorized, she told herself. She had little hope that the police would find the stalker. They were busy with more important cases and had little information to go on even if it were a priority. She'd better start fending for herself. She got out of her car and headed toward Dempster's back door with new resolve.

As she knocked on the back door she constructed a response to the verbal attack she knew would greet her. Dempster had meticulously raked his leaves last week, leaving not even a crumbled corner of one behind. She, on the other hand, hadn't gotten around to hers and her leaves were now blowing onto his lawn. She knew that a mere murder and a stalker would be considered weak excuses. She'd be better to just apologize before he could say anything. A good plan. Pre-empt the attack.

No answer. Perhaps he wasn't back yet. A pawing sound on the glass panel next to the door caught her attention. It was his calico. Odd. Mr. Dempster doted on his cat. She couldn't imagine him leaving her alone over a weekend. Sara bent down to tap on the panel, the cat pawed back. This didn't feel right. Mr. Dempster was elderly. He could have had a heart attack or stroke. She knocked louder and waited. Only the soft pawing and mewing of the cat answered her.

She tried the door handle. It turned but the door didn't open easily. She put her shoulder against it and pushed it inward. There was definitely something wrong. Mr. Dempster, the Neighborhood Watch poster boy, would never go out and leave a door unlocked.

The back door led directly into the kitchen. She stood for a minute looking around the tired fifties-style kitchen. Turquoise painted cupboards, black and white tiled floor, and a turquoise table on the far side of the room beside the window, set for one. It appeared that Dempster didn't even let meals interrupt his surveillance. The house was quiet except for the meow of the cat and a loud hum of a refrigerator that looked to be the same vintage as the rest of the kitchen. Dempster was reputed to be wealthy. Likely, she thought, not because of what he earned so much as what he didn't spend.

"Mr. Dempster?" she called not expecting an answer but looking for confirmation that her entering farther into the house was indeed justified. The cat's long plaintive meows had turned to short impatient ones that she recognized as a demand for food. It rubbed itself against her legs and followed her as she moved across the kitchen, poking the back of her ankle with its nose.

"In a minute," she whispered and realized she was creeping through the house. She felt like an intruder but a very nervous one. Perhaps she should call for help. She had promised Tony that she would take a St. John Ambulance first aid course with him but had never gotten around to it. What good would she be if something had happened to the old fellow?

The house was spotless but exuded a musty smell. A combination of old belongings, an old body, and an insistence on keeping the house tightly shut. According to Dempster, energy was wasted if one opened a window even a crack. As she moved into the front hall a strong metallic smell cut through the mustiness. The hallway she had entered ended in a foyer about twenty feet ahead of her. A huge puddle of dark stuff had been spilled on its mottled gray marble. Cat footprints walked away from it. A dark trail on the pillar beside the puddle pulled Sara's eyes upward to an upstairs hallway that overlooked both the foyer and the street. Mr. Dempster was sitting at his post by the window, but leaning against the wall, the back of his white shirt as dark as the puddle below him.

Her first thought was that a first aid course wouldn't have helped. Then the smell and horror overtook her. She gagged and looked for the quickest escape. The front door was now only a few feet away but she would have to cross the puddle of blood to get to it. She turned and ran back the way she had come, escaped out the back door and dropped onto the back steps, her head between her knees.

She was back in grade twelve English class. Mr. Murdock, her favorite teacher was directing an impromptu reading of *Macbeth*. She had been thrilled that he had asked her to read Lady Macbeth. "Who would have thought the old man to have had so much blood in him?"

He had said she had read it perfectly, with just the right amount of sangfroid. She had had to look "sangfroid" up in the dictionary and then made herself use it ten times in the next week to make it her own. People had looked at her strangely that week as she had worked "sangfroid" into every possible conversation.

A cat was trying to intrude from another world, meowing and nudging her arm. She would just ignore it until it went away and let her be. But the person shaking her shoulder and calling her name wouldn't be ignored. When one shoulder didn't work he shook her by two.

"Sara, are you alright?"

She forced her head up from her knees. Carson was kneeling in front of her, one hand on each of her arms. Concern had furrowed itself into his brow and took the light from his green-blue eyes. She managed to say her line before the body-shaking sobs took over.

He had known it all in an instant. As soon as he saw her sitting on Dempster's back steps, her head on her knees, the cat winding itself around her, and the back door standing wide open, he knew. He knew Dempster was dead. He knew that Dempster had been dead when he had knocked on his door Friday evening. He knew he had been dead last night when he left Sara's warm kitchen to knock on his door. He knew Dempster had probably been dead when he had arrived at Sara's Friday afternoon in response to her call about the break-in. As Sara had gone out her back door that afternoon, he was sure the intruder had gone out the front, around the far side of Dempster's house to the back and in the back door or window. Dempster had approached the intruder the day he was checking out Sara's house and pretended to deliver fliers. He had made sure that the neighborhood snoop would not be able to identify him. While Carson was inside the Porter house interviewing Richard and Sara about the break-in, the murderer had slipped out of Dempster's. The only consolation for Carson was that he could have done nothing to prevent it.

At first he couldn't get Sara to respond and when she did she was hysterically quoting Shakespeare and crying. It wasn't exactly standard police procedure but she needed holding, so to hell with Kirpatrick looking on. He pulled her close to him and called instructions over her sobs.

"We need to get her settled down. Go into the Porter house and find some liquor. There's a wine fridge in the kitchen if you can't find anything stronger." He pried Sara's keys from her clenched fist and tossed them to his partner.

Kirpatrick returned on the run with a bottle of Chateau Mouton Rothschild and a glass. Carson wasn't going to debate whether Kirpatrick's choice was the most appropriate for medicinal purposes.

The shaking in Sara's body had lessened and he was about to offer her the wine when she pulled herself abruptly away from him and looked in the other direction hugging herself. "I'm so sorry. I didn't realize — . Mr. Dempster's dead. I think he's been murdered — like Diane. There's blood all over his back and … "

"It's OK." He heard a gentler voice than he remembered himself using in a long time. "Drink this and Kirpatrick and I'll check things out." She took the wine with one hand and wiped the tears from her face with the back of the other.

Kirpatrick had already gone into the house. Carson followed him and immediately detected the scent of death. Once you smelled it you never forgot it. The odor also confirmed for him that his theory was probably right. Dempster had definitely been dead at least a couple of days.

Kirpatrick was in the front hall staring up at the alcove in the upstairs hall.

"Geez, dead on his perch." Kirpatrick was slowly shaking his head.

If the time of death Carson was betting on proved to be correct, there had been a shadow in that window Friday night just as Carson had thought. Only it hadn't been the shadow of nosy Dempster, but that of his corpse.

Kirpatrick was heading for the stairs to the next level. "Hey," yelled Carson "We can't go up there until the crime scene guys have checked everything. Let's get this called in."

Kirpatrick went to the car to make the call although his cell would have worked just fine from the house. Carson understood his need to get outside. He too went back into the sunshine and immediately took a deep breath of fresh air to compensate for the shallow breathing mode that had automatically kicked in as soon as he had detected the scent of death. The cat on her lap, Sara was sitting on the bottom step, pouring herself a second glass of wine.

He needed to take an official statement from her and suggested they go to her house. She picked up Dempster's calico and took it with her.

They settled once again on stools in her kitchen. A faint scent of spaghetti sauce lingered but the event next door had erased last night's warmth. He wished he could spread the items he had found at Diane Brooks' home out on Sara's kitchen bar. He wished they could companionably peruse and discuss them as they had the Stewart material that Sara had shared with him last night.

Instead Sara recounted her brief story. How she went to Dempster's door, noticed the cat, tried the door, entered the house, and saw the pool of blood and the body upstairs. She hadn't noticed anything out of order and hadn't touched anything.

She seemed much more distant than she had the evening before. Perhaps it was the shock. Perhaps she was embarrassed that she had been hysterical. Perhaps she was embarrassed that he had been holding her. Probably all of the above.

She held the calico while they talked and petted it with the same precise rhythm one would use working worry beads through their fingers.

He suggested she call someone to stay with her but she declined.

As he left by the back door, she called after him.

He looked back and she said nothing for a moment and then simply, "Thanks. I'm glad it was you who was here."

So was he, but he just nodded and headed across the drive to Dempster's.

37

Within thirty minutes the activity had begun. Police cars, uniformed and plain-clothes officers, and an ambulance filled the two driveways that ran between the Dempster and Porter properties. Yellow police tape cordoned off Dempster's property. Cameras flashed. The crime scene folks dusted for prints, vacuumed the carpets and checked Dempster's clothes for fibers, while other officers scoured the property.

Curious neighbors milled about on the front sidewalk. Those who had arrived first updated others on what they had missed. People introduced themselves to one another by their street number, "Hi. I'm John. Number 22?" A question mark at the end allowing for the slight possibility that the person to whom they were speaking already knew who they were or at least the house in which they lived. People in shirt sleeves, whose curiosity had taken them to their front doors and then gradually lured them to the growing block party, stood rubbing their arms for warmth but couldn't bring themselves to retreat to their homes. That Dempster, the one person everyone in the neighborhood knew, was dead, was accepted as a fact. How he died, no one knew, but the police activity told them it was not a heart attack.

"Poor man." One woman shook her head.

"Poor man nothing." A man was gripping a brief case. "If anything criminal happened to the old geezer I'll bet you ten to one it had to do with his damn busy bodying."

A private man like Dempster would be incensed by this intrusion. No. More than that. The intrusion would be painful.

The members of the various teams ran about busily and unemotionally. Some focusing on their jobs so they wouldn't have to think about the victim. Others, detached because they had become immune to death and tragedy over the years.

Carson made a point at every murder scene investigation of taking a few minutes to reflect on the victim as a person. He or she would become a statistic quickly enough. His emotional response to Dempster's death was different from his response to most. For Diane Brooks he had felt sadness at the tragedy of a young and attractive woman dying too young. Sadness at what might have been but would now never be realized, was his most common response. But with Dempster, he felt a sense of loss even though he didn't know the man. Dempster was a nuisance but he was also a character. And characters make the world a richer place.

Both deserved to have their murders solved and Carson forced his mind back to the task.

Carson kept checking messages, looking for anything that would take them to the next step. But there was nothing.

After he had learned that there had been a connection between Brooks and Judge Jamieson, he had tried to contact the judge's nephew, Patrick Jamieson, but so far had had no luck. Patrick Jamieson hadn't returned since he'd left home that morning. Carson had gone by the estate hoping to at least interview the Jamieson staff but hadn't gotten an answer to his pounding on the front door, side door, or two back doors of the huge house. When he enquired at a neighbor's he was told that that the staff was off from Sunday afternoon until Tuesday morning. No one knew where they might go on days off or even their last names; they were just Mary and Jimmie.

Greally and Perkins had followed up with Brooks' neighbor who had seen a strange car in the neighborhood several times recently. The woman knew nothing about cars. They had shown her pictures of several models and she guessed maybe a Toyota Corolla or a Honda Civic but added that she really had no idea. She was more definite about color. She was positive, she said, that it was green, blue or gray. Greally and Perkins didn't believe this indecisive woman's information was of any value but Carson remembered Sara's reference to the car that was parked up the road the day someone had broken into her home. He suggested they focus on a blue Honda Civic but that alone was of limited use. Forensics would have nothing to offer about the Dempster murder for several hours. Carson felt like he was trying to turn over the engine of a stalled car. They urgently needed to get somewhere but they were stranded. The murderer was way ahead of them and Carson was afraid he was heading for Sara.

He had managed once more to get overnight protection for Sara but not without another altercation with Greally. Since in Greally's mind, she was the murderer, he saw no need for her to be protected. "So," Carson had answered, "consider it watching a suspect if that makes you feel better."

Simpson had asked forensics to put a special push on the reports. The homicide team would meet back at headquarters at ten o'clock that evening. Carson decided they would wait until then to share what they had discovered in Diane Brooks' home office. By then he might even have had a chance to talk with Patrick Jamieson.

A damp fall night was closing in when they left Dempster's. Carson could see Sara sitting at her kitchen window. He waved even though he knew that she wouldn't be able to see him in the dark.

Knowing this was likely to be an all-nighter, Carson suggested Kirpatrick go home for a couple of hours. Carson dropped Kirpatrick at his car and pulled back out into the street going nowhere in particular. He slipped a Spanish guitar CD into the deck and his mind into automatic pilot and let the car cruise through the dark city streets. When it hit the Yonge Street strip he took control and headed south. Theatergoers, druggies, young bar hoppers, prostitutes, and panhandlers wove in and out between one another, each completely at home. Carson rolled down the windows to let the city in. Perhaps it would bring inspiration with it.

38

Sara watched for a while from her kitchen window. She wasn't curious like her neighbors. She already had much too much knowledge about what had happened in that house. But the power to function well enough to pick up the phone or even make a cup of tea seemed beyond her. So she sat on a kitchen stool staring at the frenetic activity that swarmed Mr. Dempster's home. But she registered little.

She should call Chloe. Chloe would be upset when she heard about Mr. Dempster. Would something like this get on the news immediately? She assumed the police had to try to first contact next of kin. She didn't think he had any close relatives. He and his wife had never had children and he was an only child so there wouldn't even be nieces or nephews. She thought she remembered him visiting a cousin in the UK a few years ago. Not only would Chloe be worried about her but she would feel badly about Mr. Dempster. She was the only person Sara knew who was genuinely fond of the man and had been since she was a child. When he would reprimand her for running through his flowerbeds to retrieve a ball, Chloe would smile her impish smile and say sorry and then stay to chat rather than scurry away like the other children did. When he came out into his yard, instead of avoiding him, as she would have if she had followed her parents' example, Chloe would call over to him and then skip across the driveway for a visit. What they talked about Sara never found out. When she asked, Chloe would shrug her shoulders and answer, "Just stuff." Mr. Dempster would reciprocate by hurrying down from his window perch to be the first to buy a glass of Freshie when she and Jamie set up their stand on hot summer days.

"Now that one has impressive entrepreneurial instincts," he said to her once, nodding toward Chloe. It was the only time she could remember him ever saying anything positive.

The calico jumped onto her lap and startled her back to the present. Suddenly she realized that the space between her house and Dempster's had disappeared in darkness. She had missed the dusk. Evening had dropped quickly. She cupped her face against the window to see better. A few vehicles remained in the driveway. The ambulance was gone. They must have brought out the body but she hadn't noticed. She was just as glad. The house was fully lit and she could make out figures moving through rooms. Many bent over as though examining something, others carrying boxes, some standing in conversation. The backyard was illuminated as brightly as the house. The scene could easily be mistaken for a movie crew at work.

The phone rang and she shooed the cat from her lap, stepped down from the stool and nearly fell. One leg was numb from sitting for too long in one position. She limped across the kitchen, grabbing the counter as she went, and reached the phone just one ring before the voice mail would have kicked in.

"Hello." She sounded in pain and she was.

"Mom, are you alright?"

"I'm fine, Chloe. What are you up to?" she tried to lighten her voice.

"Nothing. Just checking on my favorite mother."

"I'm glad to hear I still hold the title." Sara managed to add a smile to her voice.

"Chloe, I need to tell you something."

"What's wrong?" Sara could see Chloe's body stiffening, preparing for the blow.

"It's OK, sweetheart. At least it hasn't anything to do directly with us."

She could hear Chloe sniffle when she told her about Mr. Dempster.

"He was one of my favorite people."

"I know."

"The murderer isn't the same person who murdered Diane is it?" Chloe spoke slowly as though not wanting to finish the question so as not to have to deal with the answer.

"I don't know. The police probably aren't sure yet. They are still going over his place."

"Oh, poor Mr. Dempster. He wouldn't like that."

"I know."

"Mom, I'm coming over. You're not staying alone. It could be the same person who broke in on Friday."

Sara insisted it wasn't necessary and Chloe ignored her.

"I just have this paper to finish. It'll take about an hour and then I'll be over. Craig is away for a few days and I'm alone anyway. By the way, I guess considering everything this shouldn't be a priority, but I'm starving and I doubt you have a thing in the house. How would you like to order in Chinese?"

Chinese seemed like a good choice to Sara. No knives required.

Sara had promised to call Patty. It was only six thirty, three thirty on the west coast, and Patty wouldn't be home yet. She hesitated to bother her at the office, but if she waited until Chloe arrived she wouldn't get to talk to her. At least not about what she wanted to discuss. Sara moved to the phone beside the sofa in the family room, the calico meowing behind her. She first ordered the Chinese and then dialed Patty's new number.

Sara needn't have worried about disturbing Patty. Her immediate response was, "Thank God. I've been worrying about you since last night. I decided if I didn't hear from you by seven tonight I was calling you."

"What? I didn't sound that crazy last night did I?"

"Absolutely certifiable. Just give me the goods. I'm swiveling around to look out the window so I won't be interrupted by the paper that everyone seems to feel is their responsibility to pile on my desk. OK, girlfriend, give it to me. And don't spare the details. You hear?"

After fifteen minutes Sara was feeling breathless and relieved. She had shared everything that had happened in the last week reiterating bits that she had shared the evening before. She told Patty about becoming suspicious about the contents of Aunt Kate's box, the sixty-year-old murder of Jane Stewart, her suspicion that the judge had been murdered, Diane's murder, her maybe-stalker, her trip to the cottage, what she had shared with Carson last night, and the murder of Mr. Dempster. The only thing she wasn't ready to talk about was the blank spot in her memory the night of Diane's death. She had never put it all together before and she was stunned by the magnitude of what she had experienced in a few short days. Patty's uncharacteristic momentary silence confirmed her own shock.

"My God, Sar. When I said last night that you'd be safer in LA, I was half kidding. But not now. You pack your bags right now and get out here. You're living in crazy land. There is definitely some psycho loose in your world."

Sara wasn't ready to pack up and leave, although it was tempting, so she chose to ignore the comment. "Patty, about the judge. He was supposed to have died of a heart attack. His nephew, who found his body, noticed a couple of things that he saw as old age or related to the heart attack. His fingers were blue and there were broken capillaries on his face. Are they consistent with a heart attack?"

"Blue fingertips and broken capillaries are both associated with asphyxiation. The blue fingertips could be because of poor circulation and nothing else. But both of them presented together suggests that you might be right about his death not being natural."

"He was suffocated?"

"Possibly."

"Shouldn't the capillaries have caught the attention of whomever pronounced him dead?"

"Not necessarily. Elderly people often have broken capillaries. They might not have paid much attention. Particularly since he hadn't been well and his death wasn't unexpected. But since his nephew noticed them, that suggests they weren't normal for the judge."

"But Diane and Mr. Dempster were stabbed. At least I think Mr. Dempster was stabbed. If the judge were suffocated would that mean that his killer wouldn't be the same person?"

"Not necessarily. Some killers use different methods although most have a favorite. My guess would be that your guy *likes* to stab people. Although he may have some other motive, he enjoys the killing. If he didn't, he'd find a less personal method. He could have suffocated the judge because he needed it to look like a heart attack. And if this whole thing is somehow linked to the Jamieson family or friends, then the killer may have known and been fond of the judge. Maybe he wasn't looking for a high from the act. It was probably just something that in his mind simply needed to be done."

"From the little I've told you, can you identify any likely characteristics of the murderer?" Sara was hopeful but didn't expect much.

"It's tough to do if you haven't got details about the murder scene. But let's try this. At Quantico they go by an FBI system that develops a profile based on whether the person is organized or disorganized. If I asked you whether you think this guy is likely organized or disorganized what would be your gut feel?"

Sara didn't hesitate. "Organized. Definitely."

"Why do you say that?"

"Well, he easily got into all three houses: Diane's, Dempster's and mine, if it was the same guy in each case. So easily and quietly in fact that he was able to come up behind Diane and Dempster without their knowing it. As far as I understand, they were stabbed from the back and there was no struggle."

She turned to look over her own shoulder. The reflection of the lighted room against the darkness of the sliding glass doors prevented her from seeing beyond it. Was that movement behind the glass or just the shadow of a tree branch? A spark of fear propelled her to the curtains' pull cord and she quickly drew them tightly shut.

She moved to an easy chair that was positioned against the wall and continued, "He left no finger prints here or at Diane's. If my stalker is the same person, he was darned good. Yes, he seems organized to me."

"I'd ditto that. Good analysis by the way. Maybe you should become a profiler."

"Why not?" Sara laughed. "I am definitely in the market for a new career."

"So anyway." Patty was audibly chewing on the end of her pencil between words. "If this guy is an organized killer, according to the FBI's system, he is likely to be intelligent, to be or have been in a professional job. He has a fairly high need for structure. He likes routine. Although, as I mentioned, he enjoys the killing but he will have what he sees as a rational, justifiable motive for each of them."

"Interesting, but I guess you can't give me the guy's name, address and phone number?"

"Not quite. Profiling can direct you to someone, perhaps on the periphery of a case that you might not otherwise consider or can be used to narrow down a list of suspects. If you have more than one person with motive, means and opportunity, profiling allows you to zero in on the right person. However, when I say *you*, I don't mean you personally. Don't start playing sleuth, Sar. It looks like you are in more than enough danger as it is. Leave it to your detective."

"*My* detective?"

"Yeah, your detective. The minimalist picture you painted of your tête à tête over wine and dinner last night was a sure give-away. So, is he a hunk or what?"

Sara laughed. "Well according to Chloe he's got great buns."

"And according to you?"

Sara could hear voices on the front porch and then Chloe's key in the lock. She was going to get out of answering the question she wasn't ready to even broach with herself.

"Chloe's just arrived. Why don't you say hi to her? I'll call you soon."

Chloe burst into the family room bringing the smell of Chinese food with her. She had met the delivery boy on the front porch and the large red paper bag was wedged between her chin and the bag of laundry that filled her arms.

On hearing that Patty was on the phone she dropped everything onto the sofa and gave Sara a quick kiss on the cheek as she took the phone. Patty was Chloe's godmother and one of the few people Chloe talked *with* rather than at. When Chloe hung up the phone she was smiling.

"I can't believe Patty is your age, Mom. She seems so young."

"Thanks." Sara screwed up her face in mock pain.

"I'm sorry. I didn't mean that you're old. It's just that she is just like … "

"I know, I know," Sara broke in. "No need to explain. Patty will always be the same, whatever age she is."

As Sara tore open the stapled bag of Chinese food, it occurred to her that Patty and Chloe anchored her life. She couldn't imagine the essence of either ever changing and she felt a sense of relief at the recognizing there were at least some things she could always count on.

They sat on the floor on either side of the coffee table and ate from the containers. Once again their conversation skirted the most obvious topic as they tried to find comfort in the mundane. Instead of murder they talked about Craig's passion for politics, the prof who gave Chloe's last political science paper a D, obviously not recognizing the brilliance of her thesis, and Sara's acting as foster parent to the calico.

"You should keep it, Mom," Chloe suggested, her mouth full of a whole chicken ball covered in red sweet and sour sauce. "Mr. Dempster would like someone he knew to have it. And besides you should have a pet. Under the circumstances a Rottweiler might be a better choice, but I can't see you going for that. The calico would at least be good company."

"I don't need company. And now that I am finally," Sara emphasized the word finally, "what demographers call an empty-nester, I really don't want to be responsible for anyone's or anything's well-being. And this one is incredibly demanding. She jumps up on my lap constantly and insists on being petted. It's affection on demand."

"Maybe she's not demanding affection. Maybe she realizes that *you* need it."

One of Chloe's insightful zingers skillfully delivered.

"Well, you at least have to give it a name," Chloe continued, apparently not expecting a response to her last remark.

"No way." Sara waved a chopstick in protest. "Once you name an animal, it's yours."

Chloe had started yawning part way through dinner and Sara encouraged her to go to bed. As Chloe kissed her on the cheek Sara felt a sudden sense of panic. Why had she agreed to Chloe keeping her company? She hadn't been thinking clearly. What if she were putting her daughter in danger?

Sara peered through the kitchen window to check that her protectors were in the backyard. A cigarette glowed and one shadow waved at her. A look through the living room window confirmed the police car was sitting two doors up on the other side. She tugged at each window and door several times until she was satisfied that she had controlled as much as she could and then outfitted herself for a long night. She made her way upstairs with a large serving tray laden with a pot of mint tea, a bag of not-too-stale jujubes, a thick but light novel, her cell phone with the number of one of the constables in the backyard already punched in, ready to send, and the calico under her arm. She paused part way up listening for unfamiliar noises. Nothing.

Chloe had left her door ajar and a wedge of light was painted across the floor. Her gentle snoring matched the purring of the cat. The house felt like a home again. It struck Sara how much less vulnerable a home felt than a house. Perhaps she would get some sleep after all.

39

The newly decorated meeting room at police headquarters was sterile. Gray walls were a backdrop for chrome chairs covered with fake black leather and arranged around a black chrome-legged table. Someone had tried to warm up the room with motivational posters celebrating teamwork and picturing groups of children and collections of dogs, each supposedly working together for some common good. The prerequisite fluorescent lighting accented the worst features of everything in the room, including Simpson and his three team members who were each selecting and trying out one of the new chairs for the first time. Even Kirpatrick, twenty years younger than the rest, looked haggard. Black smudges sat under Greally's eyes, and jowls that Carson hadn't before noticed hung from Simpson's jaw. Carson assumed he didn't look any better than the rest.

Perkins had the night off as he had just completed a thirty-six hour stint working on a suspected Asian gang killing as well as the Brooks case. Budgets were tight, and working only one case at a time was a thing of the past. A young woman had been shot in a parking lot behind a Shoppers Drug Mart. Whether she was the intended victim or just in the wrong place at the wrong time still wasn't clear.

Simpson tossed a file folder on the table as he sat down, automatically choosing the head of the table. "Looks like the same guy. According to the autopsy report, Dempster died of a knife wound to the back in precisely the same spot as the one that killed Diane Brooks. According to the Doc, too identical to be a coincidence. Not only that, but to hit the exact spot that would ensure immediate death took some knowledge. Whoever our killer is, they may be crazy but they know what they are doing. Dempster was killed some time Friday, possibly around the time of the purported Porter break-in."

Damn. He'd been right about when Dempster had been killed. Carson also didn't like Simpson using the word "purported." Yesterday, until Greally had put a different spin on things, Simpson was referring to the break-in as fact. Now he was suggesting possible doubt. Greally was getting to him.

Kirpatrick didn't move his head but Carson saw him slide his eyes toward him to check out his reaction. He gave none.

Simpson continued. "There are no fingerprints. In fact the only unusual thing, other than the murder, is the fact that there is only one set of fingerprints in the whole house. Dempster's. No one else had apparently been inside that house in recent history. Not even a sign of a housekeeper. He must have been an oddly anti-social individual."

Carson thought of his own apartment and realized that it too, on inspection, would be devoid of any sign of human presence other than his own. No one had been there since Marlene had left.

"Well, that does it. This has got to give us enough evidence to arrest Sara Porter." Greally was moving into the outside lane trying to take control again.

"How so?" Carson asked in his calmest voice.

"It's obvious. Sara Porter murdered Dempster because he knew something that would tie her to the Brooks murder. She then faked a break-in so that we would assume that whoever had broken into her house had also murdered Dempster."

"But she discovered the body," Kirpatrick interjected.

"She probably figured she had to, since *we* obviously weren't going to." Greally looked blatantly at Carson. "She was getting nervous that there was no suspect for the Brooks murder other than herself and she wanted to get us looking in another direction."

"Before we start jumping to conclusions," Carson moved on quickly so that Greally couldn't rebut his comment. "Kirpatrick and I have other information that needs to be considered."

Kirpatrick sat up straighter, as though proud to be included. Simpson looked hopeful and nodded to Carson to go ahead.

"Here's the overview. We can go into more details later. Diane Brooks was a freelance writer. While researching the history of a summer community up on Lake Simcoe she came across an unsolved murder of a young woman named Jane Stewart that dates back to 1948. Brooks kept her research including her interviews in a set of notebooks. All of her files had been cleared out but the books on her bookshelf had been left. The notebooks were among the books.

"The community she was researching is called Oak Point or The Point as the locals call it. The Jamiesons, that is the family of the late Judge Jamieson, as well as the late Kate McPherson, who is Sara Porter's aunt, had cottages, really summer homes I guess, there in the forties. The Jamieson family still does."

Simpson's eyebrows shot up.

"Teddy Jamieson? He died last month. In fact he called me a few days before he died to arrange a luncheon meeting. We never did get to have it. I didn't know him very well and I wondered why he had wanted to see me. Anyway nothing related to this I'm sure. Carry on, Carson."

Carson wasn't so sure that Simpson's invitation wasn't related to the Brooks murder, but wanted to take things further himself before he broached that subject. So he carried on. "Diane Brooks had had an appointment with the judge the day before he died. I don't know whether she was sharing information with him or getting it from him. There is also a link between the Porter break-in and the Stewart murder. The intruder took clippings and other memorabilia that had belonged to Kate McPherson and which were dated around the time of the Stewart murder. There is some evidence that suggests Jamieson and McPherson had a hand in at least covering up the murder if nothing else. Sara Porter recently visited her aunt's cottage, which has been closed since the death of Jane Stewart, and brought back a letter that suggests a possible motive for the Stewart murder as well as other evidence related to the crime that may or may not be relevant. All of this new evidence suggests a strong link between Diane Brooks' murder and her investigation into the murder of Jane Stewart in 1948."

Greally had been arrogantly shaking his head the whole time Carson was speaking. Simpson was mentally sorting through what he had heard. "So you are suggesting that someone did not want Diane Brooks to discover or reveal information about a sixty-some-year-old murder?"

"Yes, exactly." Carson nodded confidently but was acutely aware the whole thing sounded fantastical.

"Come on. Give me a break. Whoever committed that murder would likely be at least seventy-five today, more likely dead. Are you suggesting some old geezer or a ghost knocked off Brooks? I don't buy it. All I see is another motive for Sara Porter. If her aunt were implicated in the murder of this Stewart woman, then saving the good old family name could be as good a reason as any to kill Brooks. Particularly if she were looking for an excuse anyway."

"Greally, you obviously didn't hear me when I said that much of the Oak Point evidence came from Sara Porter herself. She's hardly going to present us with a motive that points to herself if she were guilty."

"That's where you're wrong. Or at least," Greally corrected himself, "that's one of the places where you are wrong. Here's how I see it. When Porter realizes she is our numero uno and numero only suspect she tries, as I said before, to create company for herself. So first there is her intruder and then there is this Oak Point deal, some ghost from the past. She figures if she is suggesting the motive of covering up a sixty-year-old murder to us we would never think of it as her motive but would go off looking for someone else. She's desperately carving decoys and floating them in front of us."

Simpson moved his chair back and put both palms on the table to push himself to a standing position. He had been hounded daily by his superiors, the media and the Brooks family, and the fatigue was showing. "Sara Porter is smack dab in the middle of this however you look at it. I hear what you're saying, Greally, but I'm not moving from the position I took yesterday. We don't arrest Sara Porter unless we have more than circumstantial evidence."

As Carson and Kirpatrick headed toward the underground parking, Carson fingered the piece of paper resting deep in his right trouser pocket.

Kirpatrick was unusually quiet. As tired as Carson? Preoccupied with his home life and becoming a father? More comfortable with his new partner? Perhaps his talkativeness had been only new-job jitters. That would suit Carson just fine.

Before Carson could break the silence his cell phone did it for him. Perkins didn't bother with salutations.

"Hey, can you hear me? It's God awful noisy here." Perkins' voice was raised over a background of laughter and the jumbled hum of multiple conversations layered over one another.

"I don't suppose that's the sweet sound of the bar? I thought you'd be in bed."

"Yeah, soon. But first got to reward myself for my long dedicated hours. Let me get outside so I don't have to do any more damage to my vocal cords."

The din gradually faded, Perkins greeted someone, a door opened and closed.

Carson waved an absent-minded good-bye to Kirpatrick and continued toward his own car.

"OK I'm back. Here's the thing. You won't believe what I picked up tonight."

Perkins paused for a breath. He must have been rushing. Carson could picture him taking the opportunity to haul up his trousers.

"I was sitting with a couple of uniforms," he continued. "They started talking about having caught a call to a place on the Bridle Path. They were talking about it being over the top, an indoor swimming pool and the works. It's owned by Charlie Ramsey. You've probably heard him of him. He's a big developer. The guys said the call was a waste of time but seeing the house had almost made it worth their while. So I asked what the call was. It turns out that the other day the lady of the house saw what she was sure was a guy following a woman. The woman fits Sara Porter's description and guess what?"

Perkins paused for effect. "The guy wore a Blue Jays cap."

Thank God. Now he had a witness who could confirm that Sara was being stalked.

Thank you Mrs. Ramsey, whoever you are. The immediate sense of relief and elation washed away the anxiety he had begun to feel; his attraction to Sara hadn't impaired his professional judgment.

As Carson pulled away from headquarters he pushed a Rolling Stones CD into the player, turned the volume high, and shouted with the band as he drummed the beat on the steering wheel.

I can't get no satisfaction. 'Cause I try and I try and I try …

40

Carson felt sluggish. The energy that had been generated by Perkins' news the night before had almost dissipated. The tiny piece of paper that he had transferred from yesterday's pants pocket to today's weighed him down. What he was doing could have serious consequences. It would be seen as withholding evidence and the reprimand would be severe, perhaps even terminal. In reality he had no intention of withholding anything. He respected the profession to which he had given over twenty years of his life far too much to do that for anyone. He was simply postponing logging it. His hope had been that they could find another likely suspect, or better still, the actual murderer before he shared his find. He knew if he added the restaurant slip to the list of evidence on the "Sara Porter did it" list that everyone would stop looking for anyone else. He feared that that had already happened but at least it wasn't official. But he couldn't keep it much longer. Something had to be accomplished today.

He had asked Perkins to get a copy of Mrs. Ramsey's statement describing the fellow in the Blue Jays cap following Sara. As much as it had relieved Carson to know that someone other than Sara had reported someone following her, the reality was that that alone was unlikely to get them closer to the killer. He would have liked to release a description of the man to the media but he knew that without being able to link the stalker to the murder, Simpson would never approve it.

It was still dark as Carson headed up the Bayview extension into midtown. He picked up his cell to check for messages for the third time since he had pulled himself awake at five a.m even though he knew he hadn't missed a call. As he was about to press Kirpatrick's number, the desk sergeant called.

The constables watching Jamieson's home had just called in. Jamieson had returned. Kirpatrick would be called to meet him there and instructions would be passed to the constables on site to go to the door right away and let Jamieson know that Carson would be there shortly and needed to speak with him. Carson expected Jamieson wouldn't be too receptive to the interview anyway, considering he had been out all night, presumably without sleep.

Letting him get into bed and then waking him would make him even less likely to be co-operative.

The day hadn't yet begun to appear on the horizon when he reached Jamieson's. Kirpatrick arrived just as he did.

A constable was manning the front gate that, when opened, revealed a circular drive that passed through a portico at the front entrance. The house was large but the windows Carson could make out seemed too few and too small for the size of the house. He guessed that most of the house would be dark on even the sunniest of days. One window at the front of the house burned with a dim orange light. He pulled up to the front entrance and Jamieson opened the front door before Carson could get out of the car, and waited, arms folded, at the entrance. Even in the dark entrance way Carson could see that Jamieson was a man craving sleep. As Carson had expected, Jamieson did not greet them like a welcoming host.

"What could you possibly want from me that would bring you here at this time of the morning. I don't suppose it matters to you but I haven't slept in nearly twenty-four hours."

"Detective Sergeant Carson, Mr. Jamieson, and Detective Constable Kirpatrick." Carson did not bother to offer a hand that he knew was unwelcome. "I apologize for the hour, sir, but we have been trying to reach you since yesterday afternoon."

"Well I assure you I haven't been lying on a beach. I have been holed up in an infernally unproductive all-night political meeting. Now what can I do for you?"

"We are investigating the murder of Diane Brooks and would like to ask you a few questions."

"I don't know how I could possibly help you." Jamieson's words were clipped but he appeared to have resigned himself to the intrusion. As he spoke he shut the door behind Carson and Kirpatrick and headed down the hall toward the one lit room. He offered no invitation but apparently expected the two men to follow him.

The room was a small den just big enough to accommodate two oversized chairs in front of the fireplace and a writing desk facing a circle of leaded glass that looked over the drive. The light Carson had noticed from outside came from a small Tiffany lamp with an amber shade that sat on the desk. Jamieson waved reluctantly toward one of the chairs. His upbringing forced him to offer at least this modicum of hospitality. Kirpatrick stood, notebook in hand, and when Jamieson noticed, he pulled out the hard, backed chair from behind the writing desk and then seated himself in the more comfortable chair across from Carson.

"Did you know Diane Brooks?" Carson began.

"No, not at all. I saw something about her death in the paper. I can't imagine that I would have any information that is useful to you." Jamieson unknotted an ascot from around his neck as he spoke and stuffed it into his pocket, a signal to Carson that he was soon retiring, whether Carson liked it or not.

"I understand," Carson continued, "that Ms. Brooks visited your uncle shortly before his death. Would you know why she met with him?"

"How do you know that she met with my uncle?" Jamieson jockeyed for control of the interview.

"It's just one of the pieces of information we've gathered during the investigation." Carson avoided telling Jamieson that his brunch guest had been a snoop. "Do you know why they met?" he asked again.

"Yes, as a matter of fact I do. She was doing research on a cottage area on Lake Simcoe called Oak Point. I understand that she had been contracted by the community to write a centennial book for the anniversary next year. Our family owns a summer home there."

"Do you have any idea of exactly what information she was looking for?"

"Not for sure. I didn't ask but I assumed she was collecting residents' memories of The Point. Uncle Teddy had been going there since he was a baby."

"And you also spent summers there?"

"Of course. Every summer until I was working full time in the family business."

"But that would have been some time after Jane Stewart's murder?"

Jamieson looked startled, and then puzzled, but refrained from asking a question and simply answered what had been asked.

"Yes, of course."

Although Jamieson hadn't asked the question that had sparked the quizzical look, Carson decided to answer it. He knew unanswered questions tended to block people's openness.

"Ms. Brooks' notes suggest she had some interest in the death of Jane Stewart."

Jamieson couldn't hold his next question back. "You don't think the two deaths are connected?"

It was Carson's turn to ignore a question. "Can you tell me what you know about the Stewart murder? I presume your family would have talked about it."

"I don't know a great deal. I remember my parents and my grandparents talking about it once. They felt some sort of responsibility because she had been a young woman and their house guest. But nothing was discussed in detail. In fact they simply referred to the event as "the tragedy" and for years I assumed she had drowned. I remember being curious and wanting to know more but knew it would upset my parents if I asked questions, so I didn't."

Jamieson's eyes left Carson's face and focused on a news magazine that sat at his elbow.

"I don't know how I came to find out that she had been murdered but at some point I did. That summer was a dark spot in the family history and no one ever referred to it again that I remember. I never felt that it was avoided because they were bereaved but more because it was an embarrassment."

Jamieson's tone had become reflective. It was as though he was no longer answering Carson's question but working things out in his own mind. Then he looked back at Carson and continued with increased energy.

"The whole thing wasn't nice. That I can tell you."

To say that a murder wasn't nice, Carson thought, was a bit of an understatement but he understood what Jamieson meant.

Carson changed directions. "You live alone here, Mr. Jamieson?"

"Yes, I do now, since my uncle's death. Except for the servants, of course, but they don't actually live in the house. They have apartments over the stables. It's now a garage but it used to be a stable and we still call it that. Old habits die hard."

"How many servants do you have?"

"Just two, Mary and Jimmie Baker. They have been with us forever. Their mother was our housekeeper until she passed away."

"I'd like to talk with them as well."

"A waste of time. If I can't tell you anything they certainly can't. They're on their days off but will be back tomorrow evening if you must see them." Carson felt like he had another Richard Porter on his hands, deciding what was useful and what wasn't. He swallowed the irritation that was climbing up from his stomach. "Do you know how to reach them?"

Jamieson drew a book from the drawer of the writing table, leafed through it until he found what he wanted, jotted down an out-of-town number and handed it silently to Carson. "Mary is visiting her sister. I don't know about Jimmie."

"I was sorry to hear about your uncle's death." Carson was visualizing a couple of moves ahead and how he would get there.

"Thank you."

"I understand he died of a heart attack?"

Jamieson nodded.

"Was there anything at all that might suggest to you that it wasn't a natural death?"

Jamieson, a man who presented himself as one who was never surprised, looked startled. "No, of course not. What are you suggesting?"

"I have to ask. Your uncle died not long before Diane Brooks, who was murdered and who was investigating Oak Point and the murder of Jane Stewart, which your uncle may have had knowledge of."

"You're not suggesting … " Jamieson was almost to his feet.

"Mr. Jamieson, I am not suggesting anything. Your uncle was at The Point when Jane Stewart was murdered. She was a house guest. It is likely he had some knowledge."

Jamieson sat back down and stared again at the magazine. Carson guessed it was a habit he had formed as a CEO to prevent anyone from reading him as he formulated a response.

"Was there anything at all unusual about his death?" The repeated question was a gentle prod.

"Nothing that I would normally have thought of but I'm stretching to answer your question." He hesitated for a moment and then continued. "My uncle had seemed very well in spite of his heart condition. He had been planning a cruise. When I found him — he died at his desk you know — it struck me that he had a lot of broken blood vessels and his fingertips were blue, but the doctor didn't seem to see anything unusual. Nothing else I can think of."

Carson switched back to the Stewart case. "Do you know of anyone who would not want Jane Stewart's murder to come to light again?"

Jamieson shook his head. A few strands of blond hair mixed with gray slipped from their place onto his forehead. Jamieson ignored them. "No, other than it might be painful for her family." Jamieson made a tent with his fingers and rested his chin on them as though the action would trigger his thought process. "But even then the pain, I would think, would be slight. Her parents would have died long ago. I believe she was an only child. At one time in my teens I became curious about the murder and looked up old newspaper articles at the library. I have it in my mind that the police concluded that the murderer was a vagrant, possibly a tramp passing through the area. If so, he would likely be dead as well. If not, the chances of finding him now would be even less than then."

"What if your uncle was somehow implicated in the crime?"

Jamieson switched from thoughtfulness to anger. "What nonsense." Jamieson was on his feet. "I understand that you are under pressure to get the Brooks murder solved with the mayor and the chief of police bragging at every public event about the reduction in crime." Even when angry, Jamieson apparently had a need to appear fair and reasoned.

"But dredging up something as ancient as this and then implicating respectable people who can no longer speak for themselves is despicable." His voice rose with each sentence as though working toward an orchestrated crescendo. "Believe me, I will not take any slandering of my uncle's name lightly."

"Hey, hey." Carson had pulled himself onto his feet as well and used an open palm gesture to temper Jamieson's attack. Hitting hot spots could be useful. People often shared more than they intended when angry. But if it happened too early the individual might shut down before they reached the most important topic. "I'm not suggesting your uncle was an accomplice to the crime but what if he had knowledge he chose not to divulge?"

"My uncle was on the bench for thirty years. No one respected the law more than he did. The idea is preposterous." Jamieson lifted a decorative box from the mantle for no apparent reason other than to slam it back in place. A small brass hinge flew from it and skipped across the hardwood floor. The brief release of emotion appeared to allow his rational self to take charge once again. "Suppose, and I really believe it's ludicrous, but suppose my uncle did decide to protect someone. Where are you going with this?"

"We need to discern who, if anyone, would not want that knowledge made public."

"My uncle's companion is dead, my sister lives in New York with her family and the Jamieson name means very little to her now. That leaves me. Of course I would prefer it not be made public. If it turned out to be true, I suppose I'd grieve a little, try to understand why he did what he did, and move on. I certainly wouldn't carry on any cover-up."

"Not even considering the fact that you are attempting to revive your political career and in a very high profile role at that? I would think a tarnished Jamieson name could be a death blow to any bid for party leadership."

Jamieson's body went rigid, arms tight at his side, fists closed as though restraining himself in an invisible straight jacket. "Detective Sergeant, remember what I said about slandering my uncle." His words were slow and forced, as though the tightness of the invisible jacket were making it difficult for him to speak. "The same applies to me. I will take any attempt to drag the Jamieson name into any of this very personally. If a word of this becomes public without absolute proof, you had better have a very good early retirement package. I don't wield power lightly but believe me, Sergeant, I do have it." He raised his voice slightly and added a sharp "Good night."

Even in the dim light the whiteness of Jamieson's fists and the area around his mouth were evident. Beads of perspiration had materialized on his forehead. Carson wondered whether heart disease ran in the family. He considered asking whether the man was alright but he could see no evidence of physical pain. Carson needed nothing more and so accepted his dismissal with a nod, signaled Kirpatrick to follow him and made his way down the dark hallway to the front door.

Jamieson had clearly answered the question that had been foremost in Carson's mind. Jamieson would go to some lengths to protect the family name. The question left unanswered was just how far would he go.

41

Sara's hope of sleep had been fleeting and she spent most of the night keeping as vigilant a watch as the men outside. She dozed off around five a.m. Chloe had already left when she awoke at ten. A note scribbled on the back of a grocery slip sat on the kitchen island next to a dirty cereal bowl and coffee mug. It read, "Call you later. Don't forget to buy food for Calico. I gave her some milk, but in spite of what the cartoons suggest, I don't think cats can really live on it. Love, Your First Born."

The calico didn't seem to think so either. She was meowing her sharp "I'm hungry" meow. Sara scooped up the cat and held it facing her. "OK, cat. This is a temporary living arrangement but as long as you are here these are the rules. I decide what you are eating and when. Your plaintive noises will not move me. You will not, in even the smallest way control my life. I am the master. You are the pet. Understood?"

The calico had locked her eyes on Sara's face in a cat stare that was either complete indifference or rapt attention. Since it immediately took up its irritating chorus again, Sara assumed the former.

Sara held out until she had ground some fresh coffee beans and turned on the coffee maker. Regrettably she hadn't set the coffee maker in her room last night and was starting the morning with a heavier head than usual. Once she had a mug of coffee in her hand she began rummaging through her cupboards for a tin of tuna. The phone rang just as she had begun to open the can. It was Tony and he didn't bother with salutations. "Sara, you're not going to believe this. Ken and Dina haven't shown up this morning. You know they always have the door open before eight. At first we just thought they had gone away for the weekend and had gotten back late, but by nine o'clock we knew something was wrong. Someone called Ken's house and there was no answer and there wasn't at Dina's either. We're all lined up in the hall wondering what to do. Calling the police because someone's an hour late seems a little overboard but this is highly unusual behavior. What do you think we should do?"

"Take the day off." Sara was trying to open the can and had cradled the phone between her shoulder and ear. The cat continued to chant as it circled her ankles.

"Is that a cat? You don't have a cat do you?"

"At the moment I do but this is going to be a short relationship."

"Anyway, seriously. What do you think we should do? It was a unanimous decision to get your opinion."

Instead of feeling complimented, as she knew Tony had intended, she felt annoyed. Couldn't anyone think for him or herself? Everyone seemed to look to her for everything and she wanted a sabbatical from the role of the wise one. She realized that she had always accepted that role, perhaps even welcomed it. At work, with family and with friends. It had become part of her identity. Sara will have the answer. Sara will figure it out. But now the thought of providing anyone with guidance exhausted her. She made an effort not to let the exhaustion she was feeling show in her voice.

"Get the key from the superintendent. I know they are really sticky about handing it out but if he's hesitant have him call me. Ken gave me official access to the key a couple of years ago when he still had some hope of charming me into becoming one of his groupies. The super should have my name on file. If you don't hear anything from Ken by noon call the police and leave it up to them, whether they are willing to do anything at this point. I'm sure it would be too soon for a missing person's report, but since the circumstances are so unusual they might take the initiative. They can at least tell you if they have been reported in an accident."

Sara placed the opened tuna can on the floor and the cat gave a "humph" of satisfaction.

Tony was relaying her comments to the group gathered in the hallway outside of Morrison and Black. "Sounds good. We concur. Everybody says hi. I'll keep you posted."

Sara could see Tony now. He would be putting his cell into the outside pocket of his tweed jacket and starting off down the hall in the loping run he used when a semblance of urgency was required.

Odd about Ken and Dina. As much as she disliked a great deal about both of them, she felt concern. Ken was meticulous about his routine to a point of near compulsion. He would never miss having the office open by eight unless something serious had happened. Even then, if physically able, he would have called someone. Or, more likely, have had Dina call them. Something was definitely not right.

Sara planned her day to keep herself too busy to notice the pictures that floated through her mind like corpses bobbing downstream. She made a short shopping list. Cat food, litter, and litter box. Since she had to shop anyway she might as well pick up some things for herself. Next time there was an opportunity for a spontaneous dinner for two she would be better prepared. She jotted down ingredients for coq au vin and added a selection of cheeses, fruit, and biscuits to the list.

Today would be strictly a "me" day. She wouldn't think about murder past or present. In fact, she'd get her hair done, have a facial, treat herself to lunch, and buy a good book and a new Diana Krall CD. It sounded like what under normal circumstances would be a near perfect day.

Other than a call to her cell from Tony, she had several hours of uninterrupted personal indulgence. Tony called to let her know that they had contacted the police. One of the consultants who frequently had coffee with Dina had found her behavior a little strange on Friday.

"I had told him," Tony said, "what you said about demanding to see the year's financials to verify that the bonus we are getting is accurate. I guess he mentioned that to Dina and he said that she looked very strange, told him it was a very distrustful thing to do and left with her coffee barely touched. Then she made a phone call and left the office. That was the last time anyone saw her."

"What about Ken? When was he last seen?"

"He was out of the office Friday afternoon and didn't come back either. Dina called and asked one of the consultants to make sure the doors were locked when they left."

"Tony, I think you better get someone to check the books immediately. Call Frieda Black." Frieda was Ken's deceased partner's wife and still a major shareholder. "Let her know what's happening and see if she can expedite things. Ethically we all have a right to see the books but we don't have the authority to ask to see them."

"You don't think that Ken ran off with the store do you?" Tony's voice conveyed the incredulity of a child who's been told that Santa, not the Grinch, stole Christmas.

"I don't know but I think it would be prudent to check."

She hadn't heard anything since. It was late afternoon before she returned home with groceries, a red nose from a too-strong facial peel and a new haircut that in the salon mirror had looked ultra chic, but in her car mirror looked more like a bad idea. The calico was waiting for her at the kitchen doorway and reprimanded her with a set of sharp meows. What for, Sara wasn't sure. But it was apparently quick to forgive. As soon as Sara sat down on the family room sofa with her new book the cat leaped on her lap, lay on its back and gave a languid stretch. It was asleep before completing its stretch, paws hanging in mid air. Sara couldn't remember ever having been that relaxed, even as a child. She followed the cat's example and stretched herself and then snuggled as deeply as possible into one corner of the soft sofa, taking care not to disturb the calico. She was barely settled when the phone rang. The soft voice asked for Mrs. Porter.

"Pauline is that you?" Sara asked.

"Yes, ma'am. I hope I'm not bothering you at all."

"Of course not, Pauline. How is your daughter?" Sara could picture Pauline on the sofa in her bright living room with sweet, spicy smells coming from the kitchen. It had only been a few days since she had visited her but it seemed much longer. That day was in the time she had begun to think of as BE, before everything. Before Diane was murdered. Before she had her own personal stalker. Before she had become a suspect. Before she realized that there were things she couldn't remember and wasn't sure she wanted to. Before she became afraid of knives. Before she realized she had wasted months grieving the loss of a relationship that had been over long ago. And before Mr. Dempster was murdered. It had been a completely different age.

"She's fine. She's doing her homework. Thanks to God it's a real good girl that I have."

"I would say thanks to you as well, Pauline."

Pauline ignored the compliment. "Mrs. Porter, remember you asked about whether your aunt had visitors and I didn't have anything to tell you?"

"Yes, Pauline. Have you remembered something?"

"Not exactly about a visitor but we were talking about someone on our coffee break today and I thought maybe I should tell you about him. This fellow used to come with Judge Jamieson. The judge treated him nice, but more like an employee than a friend. He might have been his driver. He would come up to your aunt's floor with the judge and get him settled in a chair next to your aunt's bed and then the judge would tell him he could leave. He would leave but I saw him around the doorway a couple of times and I thought he was trying to hear what they were saying. But that could have been my imagination. He was a very helpful fellow. Claimed he had medical training and would often help the aides lift or move patients and he did seem to know what he was doing. But the bad part was, and that's what we were talking about today, was his cologne. We called him Sweet Pea. It was so strong that some people got headaches after he'd been there, and we had decided to ask him to quit wearing it if he was coming to the Cardinal but then, of course, we didn't see him again."

Goose bumps covered Sara's arms.

"Mrs. Porter. Are you still there?"

"Yes, Pauline. I was just thinking about something. Pauline, could you describe him for me?"

"Yes, easily. It wasn't just the cologne that matched the Sweet Pea name we gave him. It was his size too. He was really small for a man. Little hands and these little running shoes. He must buy child's clothing. And he always wore a baseball cap."

"What kind?" asked Sara, although the answer was inevitable.

"What kind of a baseball cap? It was a blue one. A Blue Jays cap."

Before she could dial Carson's number to pass on the information, the phone rang again, wiping out any Pollyanna idea she might have had about this being the best day she had had in awhile.

42

Carson felt time taunting him as the day flew by. He had arrived at headquarters just as the birds began to chirp one another awake. He checked with the fellows who had watched Sara's house as they came in at the end of their shift. Nothing more exciting than a man sneaking out the back door of a home up the street from Sara's when another man went in the front. He passed on the job of tracking down the Jamiesons' household staff to Graves and Stephens. Since they had been the first officers on the scene when Diane Brooks' murder was reported he liked to keep them involved. What the servants would have to offer he wasn't sure. Perhaps an overheard conversation that might reveal something of what the judge knew about Jane Stewart's murder.

He wrote his report on his inauspicious meeting with Jamieson and then forced himself to tackle the other tedious administrative paperwork that went with the job. It was at least a distraction from the frustration of having nowhere new to go with the case. His clean desktop always created the impression that he was up to date. Only his crammed bottom drawer and Sally, the civilian support staff member who had unluckily drawn his name and had to constantly hound him to get even the timesheet she needed, knew how much of an illusion his clean desktop was.

By afternoon, his body was demanding sleep and he dropped onto one of the cots set up in a back room for exhausted people who didn't have time for more than a quick nap. He woke at four, less than refreshed, and headed out to interview a couple of Dempster's neighbors, whom the constables who were helping them out hadn't been able to contact. It had been a dull day and already the evening, lengthened by the arrival of fall, was starting to slip in.

As he merged into a stream of traffic heading north through the city his phone rang.

"Carz?"

It was Marlene. He hadn't spoken to his ex-wife since she had left, other than one brief and formal "Hello, how are you?" at last year's Christmas party. He couldn't think of how to respond and so tried, "Marlene?"

"Uh-huh. How are you, Carz?"

"Just great. You?"

"Yeah. Fine."

There was silence. He waited.

"Carz?"

"Yeah?"

"Carz, I need to tell you something. It's about Greally."

Marlene had always called all of the cops, even her husbands, by their last names.

"Yeah?" She seemed to need coaxing.

"Greally has it in for you." She said it in a rush as though if she didn't, she would back down.

"I appreciate the scoop. But he's made that pretty clear for some time."

"No, this is something specific. It's about the case you're on. He's going to dunk it."

Carson swerved into a spot at the side of the road so he could concentrate. A woman who had been planning to reverse into the same spot gave him a tirade with her horn but must have taken his scowl for road rage and pulled away shaking her head. "Keep talking."

"That woman involved in the case. The one married to the guy whose girlfriend was murdered?"

"Sara Porter."

"Yes, that's her. Well he just got a call. Apparently there was a murder Saturday someplace up north. Some guy who is a caretaker for a bunch of cottages was stabbed. No one was on the property the day of his death but his wife and … " God, he knew what she was going to say. "… Sara Porter. Greally said that clinched it. Her husband's girlfriend, her nosy neighbor, and now this guy. He's going to get a warrant for her arrest. He tried to call Simpson, but he was in a meeting. He says you've blown the case and he's going to shove the arrest up your — well anyway, that's the gist of it."

He felt cold. Not because his career could be going down the drain but because his instincts might be. Motive, opportunity, and means. Sara had a possible motive for the first two murders at least, an opportunity to commit each of them, and the means. A knife wasn't difficult to come by. Plus, the big one, the restaurant receipt that placed her at the Brooks murder scene. The facts were too great to ignore. Was Sara that clever a woman to give not one sign of guilt? Or was he just too distracted by her to notice any? *Bloody hell!* His horn bleated as he slapped it with the heel of his hand.

"Carz, are you OK?"

"Yeah, fine. Thanks for telling me."

"God knows why I felt I had to."

What could he say to that? He waited.

"Greally's not really so bad, Carz. It's just that, as ridiculous as it may seem under the circumstances, he's really jealous of you."

He was tempted to keep her talking even if he didn't like the topic. She had a deep, soft voice that turned any conversation into phone sex. It had only been within the last few months that he had broken his habit of playing her voice over in his mind. But this wasn't the time for virtual dalliances with ex-wives.

"Yup, well I guess I'd better get going before your husband turns me into a fossil."

"Carz?"

"Yeah?"

"Carz, I'm pregnant."

He had to work to swallow hard before he could speak. "That's great, Marlene. That's great."

Carson disconnected and reached for the plastic water bottle on the seat beside him. He poured some water from it, splashed his face, and then patted it dry with a corner of his shirt tail, heaved himself up to tuck his shirt back in place and pulled out into the traffic. He wasn't sure why the news of Marlene's pregnancy had hurt. Was he still in love with her? Perhaps his reaction was simple mourning for things that might have been.

Whatever, he had to focus on the immediate. Sara's arrest. Whether he had been a fool and Sara was guilty, or whether his instincts were right and she was innocent, she was going to be arrested. If Greally made the arrest he would bring her into the station like a trophy, like a hunter with a deer on the roof of his car. If she had to be arrested, Carson was the one who was going to do it.

First he punched in Perkins' number. Perkins was the operator at the switchboard of the station's grapevine. Whatever was going down, whether related to a case or something personal, Perkins knew about it.

"Have you heard anything about a murder up north that was linked to Sara Porter?" Carson asked as soon as Perkins answered.

"Yeah. We just got a call about a half hour ago for Greally from the Bradford detachment of the OPP. It's a town on highway eleven, just before you get to the beginning of the cottage country around Lake Simcoe." Perkins had assumed Carson wouldn't know where Bradford was. He was right. When Carson went anywhere it was to another city. "Quaint" had little appeal. It was one of the reasons he hadn't joined the Ontario Provincial Police himself. They were responsible for the jurisdiction outside of the main municipalities.

"One of the guys up there is apparently an old pal of his," Perkins continued. "Some guy was stabbed to death up that way Saturday afternoon.

The time of death coincides with the time his wife says Sara Porter was there checking out her aunt's cottage. Somebody linked her name with the case down here. I called Greally at home. He's on his way in."

"Does Simpson know yet?"

"Nope. He's still in a meeting with the commander and left a message not to be disturbed."

"Do me a favor. Go in there and tell Simpson he has to call me immediately."

"Christ, Carson, I'm already on Simpson's shit list. What are you trying to do? Get me to the top of it?"

"Come on, Perkins. You owe me one." He wasn't really sure that Perkins actually owed him anything, but Perkins had so many close calls with Simpson that he owed almost everybody something. Besides he and Carson went way back.

Perkins was still thinking.

"Look, Perkins. I want to get to Simpson before Greally does. I'm going to arrest Sara Porter."

Greally had put Perkins down several times and particularly enjoyed doing it when Simpson was around. Carson knew that Perkins had no desire to see Greally made the star of the department.

"OK." Perkins sighed a big one. "He's just down the hall. Give me two minutes."

In less than two Simpson was on the line. "This had better be good."

"I'm heading for Sara Porter's. I'm bringing her in."

"What have you got?"

He told Simpson about the restaurant receipt and gave Greally his dues by adding that someone had called Greally with information about another murder linked to Sara Porter. He gave Simpson a quick overview. Thank God Simpson was too excited to ask details about his finding the restaurant receipt.

"Good work, Carson." Simpson's voice suggested more relief than elation.

"I'm going to send Kirpatrik in to pick up a warrant and have him meet me at Ms. Porter's.

"It'll be ready."

Now for the hard call. The one to Sara. He wanted to prepare her rather than arrive on her doorstep and have her welcome him with her great smile. It would be hard to get from there to where they had to go.

43

He wiped his mouth carefully with the red-checkered cotton napkin, then refolded it and placed it neatly beside his plate. His lunch of cold cuts, fried potatoes and onions, and sliced tomatoes had been satisfying. He hadn't used his knife and spoon, so he would leave them neatly beside the napkin, ready for his next meal. He carried his plate, glass and fork to the sink, washed each and put them away on the single shelf mounted beside the sink.

He was pleased with his planning. He had decided that if he set out immediately after lunch he quite possibly could be back in time for dinner. However, just in case his wait was longer than he anticipated, he had prepared two sandwiches that would fit nicely into his belt pack. They certainly wouldn't be as healthy as a proper meal but one occasionally had to make sacrifices and at least he wouldn't have to suffer the discomfort of an empty stomach.

He fastened the navy nylon belt pack around his waist and tucked the long length of belt that remained down a trouser leg. He then removed the dish soap and cleaning powder from under the sink and lifted a board from the bottom of the cupboard. The shallow space between the bottom of the cupboard and the floor had been just deep enough to store his knife. He removed the hunting knife and then put everything neatly back into place.

His father had given him the knife on one of his rare and awkward visits. It had been summer, he remembered, and they had been at the cottage at the time. Although he still carried his and his mother's hatred of that man, he had always thought the hunting knife in its tooled leather case was quite beautiful. His mother had told him to throw it away but that had never made any sense to him. What did it matter where it had come from if it were something he liked? He told her he had tossed it into the lake when he had gone out fishing but really he had hidden it with his magazines behind the woodpile in the back shed.

Some people said life was a battle of good versus evil. He knew it was guilt versus pleasure. He considered himself lucky that guilt was something he had seldom had to contend with. On the rare occasion it had tried to limit him, he had easily subdued it.

He attached his knife to his belt and then took his windbreaker and cap from the coat rack in the corner of the kitchen and put it on. He reached high, then sideways and then bent as though picking up something. The jacket, he was satisfied, covered his knife completely. Finally, he put on his cap and walked over to the mirror that hung over the sink to check his reflection. He stood on tiptoes and took his time adjusting his cap until it was positioned just so.

Before he opened the door he looked cautiously out the window to check that no one was around. He went outside and stood on the small porch for a few minutes. Satisfied that he was dressed perfectly for the weather and that he would be neither too hot nor too cold, he locked the door. Before he started down the stairs he checked his pocket. Yes, it was still there. He had been worried that he might lose it. At first he had wrapped it in a Kleenex and then put it in his pocket. But he frequently emptied his pockets of tissues as he didn't like dirty ones lingering about and he had feared that he might accidentally discard the wrong one. So now it rested naked at the bottom of his pants pocket, small, smooth and cool, waiting to play its role in the next step of his plan.

44

Carole Anne Williamson had had carrot red hair and a spattering of freckles across her nose. She and Sara had become friends when they sat beside one another in grade two and dared one another to taste the white glue they used in art projects to see whether it really tasted like peppermint. Sara's most powerful memory of Carole Anne was her habit of describing the events of her life as "surreal." When she was named homecoming queen she had gushed that it was "just so surreal." When she had confided to Sara that she had let Kenny Parker "do things" to her behind the bleachers after cheerleading practice, she said it had been surreal. Sara could picture her now, eyes wide, arms out to the sides and palms raised saying, "It was just soooo surreal."

Although, she knew Carole Anne exaggerated, Sara had always wished she could experience something that would legitimately qualify as surreal. As she looked at her neighbors' homes through the front window of the unmarked police car, noting who had finished their lawn clean-up for the winter and who hadn't, she knew that this was it. This was surreal. Here she was: Sara Porter, relatively successful professional and separated mother of two grown children, with little else of significance that she could think of to mark her life, now under arrest for the murder of her husband's lover.

Aunt Kate, she thought, you wouldn't have let this happen to you. Guilty or not, you wouldn't be in my position. For the past week she had wanted to be as little like her aunt as possible. Now she wished she had acted more like her. Aunt Kate would have taken the incident of Tony telling the police about her drunken blathering on the night of Diane's murder much more seriously. Sara had realized that that had put her into the suspect category but hadn't really believed that it would go any further. Aunt Kate would have hired a criminal lawyer, and instead of playing amateur sleuth and examining a sixty-year-old murder, she would have hired a private detective to investigate Diane's murder. In fact, she'd probably have hired an entire battalion of them and the real murderer would be tracked down by now, or if not, Aunt Kate would have an ironclad alibi.

Sara was angry with herself. She knew what should have been done. Why hadn't she done it? Too stressed? Too depressed? Probably. But they were good excuses, not good enough reasons. She hammered her fist against the passenger's door.

"What's wrong?" Carson spoke for the first time since he'd put her in the front seat. At least she hadn't been stuffed into the back. Kirpatrick had looked surprised when Carson had suggested he sit in the back, but had said nothing.

"I'm mad as hell. That's what's wrong." Her voice was loud enough to be heard two car lengths ahead if the windows had been open.

"At me?"

"No, not at you." Now she was yelling. "At me, goddammit. How could I be so stupid as to allow myself to get into this situation?"

He was glad to see her angry. She had been too subdued. Over-the-top anger wouldn't do either but she needed to keep the adrenaline flowing to keep herself sharp. He knew Greally would be part of the interrogation and anger would work better with him than submission. Any sign of weakness and he would go in for the kill.

She had shown him her vulnerability back at her house before Kirpatrick had arrived.

"Keith?" she had asked tentatively preparing her thoughts. His heart did a quick flop. She'd never called him Keith before. He wished she hadn't chosen that moment to do so. The whole thing was getting tougher.

"Keith, do you really think I could have murdered Diane?" she then asked.

Her voice was shaking and uncertain. The sudden realization of what she had been going through stunned him. She wasn't frightened that she was mistakenly being taken for the murderer; she was afraid that she actually had murdered Diane Brooks. She couldn't remember the night of the murder and so thought that perhaps she had done it. She was terrified at the thought. His first instinct was to console her and tell her that of course she wasn't guilty. But he couldn't. His role wouldn't allow it. Even if it had, he wouldn't give her false hope. The evidence against her was strong and there were no other contenders for the position of number one suspect. In fact he had never worked a case so bereft of suspects. He was struggling to find a response when she saved him.

"I'm sorry. I shouldn't have asked that. I put you in an awkward position." Her voice had regained its control and she was the professional addressing a client.

Kirpatrick hadn't arrived yet and she excused herself to get changed. She already looked great to Carson. Smart gray pants and a white sweater with a large cowl collar. She returned dressed in a navy business suit that was fitted at the waist and flared nicely over her hips. The single strand of white pearls and matching earrings softened the look. She was a woman in control but with no hard edges either literally or figuratively. Sara understood the power of appearance. She had plenty of smarts and would need to use them all.

After her outburst of anger in the car Sara was quiet other than her audible breathing. She stared straight ahead and seemed to be collecting herself.

Her back was ramrod straight and she turned to him. "Detective Carson, I have some information that you need to act on immediately."

"Ms. Porter, it would be wise not to talk about anything until your lawyer is present." he told her. The formality they had both adopted felt uncomfortable, like wearing clothing that wasn't one's personal style but appropriate for the occasion and so had to be suffered.

She discounted his comment by waving her hand as though stopping a pesky mosquito from buzzing around her face.

"I had a call from one of my aunt's nurses at the nursing home. I met with her a few days ago to find out more about my aunt's last days. I asked her whether my aunt had any visitors. At the time she had said no and then later remembered a man who wasn't actually a visitor but he had accompanied the judge on visits to my aunt. He was small, wore a Blue Jays cap and cologne that was so strong it gave people headaches."

Carson quickly assessed the new information. The description was consistent with the sketchy description Sara had been able to offer of the stalker and Richard Porter had insisted the killer and the stalker had left the same strong scent behind.

"Christ." Now it was Carson's turn to raise his voice. He looked at Kirpatrick in the rear-view mirror and saw his surprise at Carson losing his cool in front of an arrestee.

Expletives while on duty were definitely against department regulation. Carson tempered his voice. "Call in and check whether anyone was able to track down Jamieson's household staff."

Kirpatrick placed the call and waited while someone tried to locate them. Carson had been driving barely at the speed limit, postponing Sara's delivery into the hands of the system for as long as possible. Now, as the new information pumped adrenaline into his body, he pushed his foot down on the accelerator.

"Yup. OK. Thanks." Kirpatrick had his information. "They couldn't get a hold of them directly but they finally reached their sister. Apparently she had just returned from dropping the housekeeper at the bus station. The bus should arrive here at about six o'clock. But she said the brother, Jimmie, hadn't been there. She doesn't know where he spent his days off."

Carson's heart began pounding a little harder. As much as he worried about Sara's arrest perhaps she was better off at the station than at home. He continued his instructions to Kirpatrick via the rear-view mirror.

"As soon as we get to headquarters I want you to grab a car and Perkins, if he's around. If not, any experienced detective you can find." Carson wouldn't risk handing this to two rookies. "Get over to Jamieson's immediately. See if you can find the guy. Jamieson said the help lives over the old stables. If you don't get an answer get Jamieson to let you in. If this guy Jimmie is there, detain him whether or not he fits the description and call me. If you can't find him give the housekeeper and Jamieson the description and let me know if it matches him. If it doesn't, find out from Jamieson who was likely to accompany his uncle to visit Ms. McPherson. Got it?"

Kirpatrick nodded back at Carson's reflection and pulled himself to the edge of the seat, ready for action.

Carson got Pauline Williams' address from Sara and called the desk sergeant. The Williams' address was in a tough part of town and he knew there would be a car in the vicinity. He asked the sergeant to track down a team for him, give them the address and have them call him on his cell en route. He wanted a more detailed description and would possibly need the woman's help in getting a sketch of the guy if they didn't find him quickly.

Carson squealed the car to a stop in front of headquarters and Kirpatrick charged out of the rear shouting at Perkins who was just coming back from a restaurant down the street. Perkins was carrying a brown paper bag that showed the giveaway grease spots of hamburgers and fries. As Kirpatrick ran over to him, Perkins frowned, raised the bag and then gave a visible sigh of resignation at another meal destined to be eaten on the run.

Once they got into the elevator and were alone Carson turned to Sara.

"Look, this is good news. But you aren't out of the woods yet."

"I know." Sara made sure neither her eyes nor her voice showed the fear that still sat in the pit of her stomach. She knew she could show her real self to Carson, but needed to practice for whatever lay ahead.

45

Carson left Sara in a small meeting room with harsh fluorescent lighting that made her feel cold and headachy. It was a spare room. Just a table, a few chairs around it. The walls were bare, perhaps, she thought, to ensure that the room remained inhospitable so that suspects didn't get too comfortable.

Carson returned with two men. One, whom he introduced as Staff Inspector Gordon Simpson, was composed but had darting eyes and a ready smile that she recognized as eager anticipation. She had seen the same expression on the faces of clients when they were bargaining with their union and could see a deal in sight that was mostly in their favor.

The other, a Detective Greally, was a man containing his anger. His face was grim and he had his arms folded across his chest and spoke aggressively in short, loud sentences. His anger, she sensed, was directed at Carson but his greeting when introduced to her, a jerk of his head and a scowl, made it clear that in his mind she was already convicted. For a moment she shrank inside but then her anger began to grow once more. Who was he to assume her guilt? She stood up, nodded, looked him in the eye and reached out her hand, not pulling it back when he did not immediately respond. Eventually, he touched her hand for an instant and then pulled away again. She then turned to the Inspector with her hand outstretched, "Inspector Simpson."

Simpson didn't hesitate to respond. "Ms. Porter," he answered, returning her brief but firm handshake.

"Gentlemen," Sara began before any of the three could begin to speak. Her tone was that of a chairperson opening a meeting. "I seem to find myself in rather a difficult situation. Although I am certainly not guilty of murdering Diane Brooks," — she sounded more sure of that than Carson knew she actually felt — "I think it would be prudent for me to leave any discussion until my lawyer arrives. I spoke with him before I left home, but he was in consultation in a judge's chambers when I reached him. I don't expect he will be here for another half hour. I hope that is not going to be a problem for you."

Greally and Simpson glanced at one another and Carson took a step backwards so they wouldn't see the look of satisfaction he was trying to erase. None of them would be foolish enough to interview her without her lawyer. Too many guilty people had gotten off because of carelessness. But Sara immediately taking control disrupted the usual police-suspect dynamic and sent the message that neither she nor her guilt should be taken for granted.

Simpson nodded. "Of course, Ms. Porter. It is not our habit to interview people without their lawyers present. That is beneficial to none of us. Who is your lawyer by the way?"

"Dean Hoffmeyer."

Hoffmeyer's firm had been a client of Sara last year and she had become friendly with Dean and his wife, who was also a partner in the firm. He was shocked when she told him her story over the phone and anxious to, as he said, "clear up this ridiculous mess."

Simpson nodded recognition of the name. Hoffmeyer was one of the country's best-known criminal lawyers. His record was the gold standard in Canadian jurisprudence. Simpson's look at Carson said, "You'd better have a damn solid case."

"We'll leave you until Mr. Hoffmeyer arrives." Then he turned to Carson and Greally. "I have a call to make. I'll see you two in my office in five minutes."

The three turned to leave the room.

"Detective Greally, could you do something for me?" The three stopped, and although she had spoken to Greally, they all looked expectantly at her. "I'm getting a headache, Detective, and I wonder if you would have time to get me a cup of coffee before your meeting?"

Careful, Sara, Carson thought. He knew what she was doing and he was enjoying it. She was being perfectly polite, almost personable with Greally and putting him in the position where he had to respond in kind. She was playing the "you're not putting me down" game. Greally's antennae were up but he didn't know Sara well enough to read her. If he thought for a minute she was playing with him he'd give her an even harder time than he was already planning.

Greally mumbled, "I'll find someone to get it for you."

"Oh Detective —" Greally's only response was pausing halfway out the door. "Just a little milk would be perfect. Thanks very much."

Carson wanted to throw her a look that said, "Christ, Sara, you have been arrested for murder so take it easy." But he didn't know how, so he avoided looking at her and followed Greally and Simpson from the room.

Once the three had left, Sara let the shaking that had been of earthquake proportion in her stomach escape to her hands. Hold on, Porter, she told herself, as she clenched her hands in her lap. As angry as she felt about

Greally's rudeness and evident assumption about her guilt, she was sufficiently sane that fear was her strongest emotion. She had no alibi for the night of Diane's murder. But much worse, she couldn't even remember a non-alibi like, "I was alone at home watching TV." She still had no idea what she had done after dinner with Tony. Deep in her heart she believed she couldn't have killed Diane. It wasn't in her nature. But drinking herself into oblivion hadn't been in her nature before Richard had left either. She didn't like the person she'd become over the last couple of months. Impatient with Tony, who always meant well, lying with ease to Ken and Dina, and harboring fierce anger at Richard and even hatred toward Diane. Stress and depression were definitely the reasons. But who was the real Sara Porter? The best-she-could-be daughter, friend, wife, career woman, and mother? Or was that person just an ideal role she had created for herself and portrayed well when times were good? Was the real Sara the one who was being revealed now, when things were too stressful to keep a mask in place? Had she been living Aunt Kate's advice, "Act as though and you will be," her entire life?

She paced the room, circling the small rectangular table in an attempt to relieve the tension and control the shaking. Someone might come in any minute with her coffee. She had to get herself together. She sat back down and folded her now-quieter hands in front of her on the table, just as Greally opened the door. He must not have been able to find anyone else to fetch her coffee. He came directly to the table, set the coffee down without looking at her and walked out.

She offered a "Thank you" that sounded as though it had been given in response to a smile. She had to stand up to reach the coffee. He had set it as far away from her as possible. She wrapped her hands around the oversized white mug that sported the Toronto Police logo. She should be drinking mint tea, rather than coffee, but the warmth was soothing.

She had already briefed Dean Hoffmeyer on the phone, and had used part of the drive here to go over in her mind anything else he should know. She needed to find something to think about to keep her mind busy and in control, so she could function as sharply as possible. She pulled her cell phone from her bag. No one had taken it away. She guessed the "one-call rule" she had seen in police dramas didn't apply here. She should phone Chloe so she wouldn't worry if she couldn't reach her mom. With everything that had happened over the last week Chloe had become extraordinarily protective. Sara had to think of something to tell her daughter other than the truth.

First she checked her home voice mail for messages, not really expecting any. One from Tony. No one had yet heard from Ken and Dina. They had called Mrs. Black, as she had suggested, and an accountant was looking at the Morrison and Black books as he spoke. Another from Chloe. "Hi, Mom.

Thought you might call, so wanted you to know I've got a headache and so I'm going to disconnect the phone." Her voice was full of her usual exuberance in spite of apparently not feeling well. And then, "Mom, you won't believe this. Remember that new blouse you bought a while ago? The one with the square buttons that match the red and blue trim of the blouse? When I got in this afternoon I found one of them on our kitchen counter. I don't ever remember your being here wearing that blouse, and anyway, how would it get on the counter? How's that for weird? Anyway, I'm going to bed. I've got a headache."

Sara had quit listening part way through the message. The fear she had been feeling turned to cold terror. Her entire body shivered and cold perspiration trickled from her armpits. There was only one way her lost button could have gotten into Chloe's apartment. The stalker had been in the cottage with her when she lost it and now had gotten into Chloe's apartment to deliver her some kind of a sick message via her daughter. Perhaps he had been there when Chloe called. *God not Chloe! Please not Chloe!*

46

Sara's terror escalated. She had Chloe on her autodial. She punched one number and Chloe's phone rang. Once, twice, three times. Chloe please, please answer. At the end of the fourth, Chloe's voice message answered. "Hi, it's Chloe and Craig but we can't take your call. You know what to do next. Talk to you soon." Her first instinct was to run out into the hall screaming for Carson to get to Chloe's immediately. But that would waste time. They would ask her to explain and then would take time deciding what was to be done and who was to do it. And if they did get there quickly they would barrel into Chloe's apartment and who knows what the madman would do to Chloe, if he hadn't already.

She grabbed her coat on the way to the door and then decided to leave it behind. If she saw Carson or either of the other two she would act as though she were going to the washroom. She remembered the ladies' room she had run to when she had been ill in Carson's office the other day. It was between this room and the exit. Keep cool, keep cool. Chloe, please be alright. Chloe, please.

She walked into the hall making a supreme effort to look as though she were someone casually heading for the washroom, rather than the frantic woman she actually was. A female officer approached and Sara asked in passing, "The ladies' room. It's this way, isn't it?"

The woman was focusing on a clipboard and glanced up briefly, "Yes, the third door on your right."

When Sara reached the door of the washroom she glanced over her shoulder to ensure the officer wasn't looking and then moved on, trying to hold herself back from running. She wouldn't take the elevator. The stairs seemed safer and the red exit sign was only a few feet ahead. She pushed through the door, checked to ensure the stairwell was empty and broke into a run, taking the steps two and three at a time. She twisted her ankle on the bottom landing and limped into the first-floor entrance. There was a large expanse of tiled floor between her and the front entrance, and overseeing the space, someone in uniform. She realized the person at the desk was not the sergeant who had been there when they had come in. This fellow was much younger. Probably covering for his superior while he took his break. She worked to hide both her limp and her desperation as she headed for the door.

He was looking toward her. If he knew she had been under arrest, there was nothing she could do to prevent him from calling upstairs. If he didn't, she had better act naturally. She turned toward him and gave him a nod.

"Have a good evening."

"You too, ma'am. It's getting chilly out there. I hope you don't have far to go." He had noted her lack of coat.

"No, my car's right around the corner. Every fall I put off wearing a coat as long as possible. I guess it's time to give in." She gave a slight wave and pushed herself through the heavy doors.

A cold wind threw icy rain hard into her face, taking her breath away. She cursed the weather. Traffic would be slow. Chloe lived only five or six minutes from here in summer driving. The now slick pavement would make it precious minutes longer. As she got to the bottom of the steps she saw Dean Hoffmeyer pulling around the corner. Should she get his help or would he slow her down, advising that what she was doing would put her in a much worse position and that the police were the ones to be helping Chloe? She ducked her head and walked quickly in the other direction, sheets of rain hitting her one after another. In a few minutes she would be missed. There were no cabs cruising on College. She continued running toward busy Yonge Street where she should be able to find a cab easily. But it was rush hour on a nasty evening and everyone else was thinking the same thing. She balanced on the edge of the curb scanning up and down the main thoroughfare. Cars swooshed past, splashing her legs with dirty cold water and throwing yellow and red streaks of light on the wet pavement. Every cab that passed was dark, the shadow of a fare huddled in the back. Finally the white light of a Co-Op cab turned the corner. She and a heavy set man with an overcoat and huge briefcase, who had been standing beside her on the curb, both sprinted toward it chorusing "Taxi!" Even with his extra load he beat her easily. He was almost into the back seat when she caught up and grabbed his arm. He glared over his shoulder at her.

"Please, please. This is an emergency. I really need this cab," she pleaded.

He looked at her wet hair plastered to her head, water running down her forehead, suit jacket already soaked through and pumps that had all but disappeared in a gutter of oily black water. He said nothing, shrugged, stepped back and walked away shaking his head.

She hurriedly gave the driver Chloe's address and started to ask him to rush when he interrupted her, "I know, lady, I know. It's an emergency." He spoke as though that was the excuse everyone who got into his cab used. But he darted into the stream of traffic and seemed happy enough to demonstrate his driving prowess.

Sara mentally pushed the car forward, past closing shops, past the university buildings on College Street, past a homeless teenager hunkered down over a grate, protected from the driving cold rain by only a light sweater and sheet of plastic. Sara noted the absence of the pity she normally would have felt for him. Please, God, please, let Chloe be alright.

Three more blocks to Chloe's. It should be safe to call Keith now. If she called too early they would find her and stop her before she reached Chloe.

She tried his cell. He answered on the first ring, his voice tight with stress.

"Yeah, Carson here." There was a hubbub of voices behind him.

"It's Sara. I need your help quickly." She tried to control her voice but knew it conveyed her near-hysteria.

"Hold on a second."

She heard a door close and Carson was back, his voice a hoarse angry whisper.

"Christ, Sara, what in the hell are you doing? Do you have any idea what you've done to your chances? What's going on?"

"Keith, just listen. It's Chloe. He's been in her apartment and he may even … " She had to take a deep breath and force herself to continue. "He may even be in the apartment now. I can't reach Chloe by phone. I'm almost there." She gave him the address.

"Listen, Kirpatrick, just called in. We think we've confirmed his ID. There'll be a car at Chloe's right away. Just stay outside and —" The cab was pulling up in front of Chloe's apartment house and she pressed "End" before Carson finished his instructions. She shoved a business card at the driver and opened the door before the car came to a stop.

"Reach me at that number." She called as she jumped out of the cab. "I'll pay you well."

"Lady," he shouted, "what the fuck is this?"

She heard his tires skidding on the wet pavement as she darted through the front door of the old graying building.

Chloe lived on the third floor of an old walk-up. Once an elegant address, it was now occupied entirely by students who had chosen it for its cheap rents, not its history or high ceilings and wrought iron balconies. Sara ran up the first two flights, her feet automatically finding the hollow in the center of each marble stair that years of footsteps had worn. Music that she could not identify blared from behind a door on the second floor. A young man with a pizza overtook her and continued up to the third floor.

Sara slowed her ascent, looking upward, as she began the third flight. Dread of what she might find pushed against her chest, holding her back. But only for a moment. She took the rest of the stairs two at a time.

Chloe's apartment, number 17, was at the top of the stairs. The door, while partially closed, had not been tightly shut. Sara's fear spiked once more. Never would Chloe leave the door open. It was always securely locked.

Sara pushed it open a crack. If he were inside she didn't want to alert him by having light from the hall fall into the apartment. She widened the crack just enough to allow her to slip through and quickly closed it, but not tightly. The apartment was dark and Sara could make out little but she knew she was standing in the room that served as sitting room and dining room. The kitchenette was to her right. The window facing her from across the room looked into the inside courtyard and allowed little light at night. She could see a light from the apartment on the other side of the courtyard. To her left was the bedroom where Chloe should be sleeping. She crept along the wall toward it. As her eyes adjusted to the dark she could make out Chloe's and Craig's bikes hanging on the wall. Practical storage in a tight space or art on a budget, she had never been sure which.

At first it was her instinct that told her he was there. Then halfway to the bedroom a hint of the sickly sweet smell that had lingered in her own room reached her. *Oh dear God no!* What could she do if he had a knife? She needed a weapon. She remember that Craig kept his golf clubs leaning in the corner of the room just past the bicycles and just before the bedroom. She slipped off her shoes and continued to work her way forward, her feet squishing in cold, wet stockings. She could barely make out the golf bag and used touch and feel to find and choose what she thought was an iron. She carefully slipped it out of its place. She gripped it firmly, rested it on her shoulder and crept to the edge of the bedroom doorway. She moved forward far enough to allow one eye to check the room.

The bedroom faced the street and Chloe had joked that they saved on electricity because the neon light from the chicken deli next door was strong enough to read by. A slight exaggeration, but a rectangle of yellow light did fall across the room and Sara followed it to the bed. A shadow with no definition other than a peaked cap, sat on the edge of the bed, leaning over it like someone checking on a sleeping child. At that moment Sara stopped thinking.

"Nooooo." Sara screamed as she ran across the room, the iron raised like a baseball bat. The shock of metal against skull shuddered up the shaft and through her body. The figure fell sideways and a groan came from somewhere.

"Chloe? Chloe?" Sara pawed at the bed. Where was her daughter? She fumbled with the bedside lamp and managed the switch as it fell to the floor, casting a light upward with little more power than that from the window. She could make out no figure in the bed. She furiously pulled back the bedclothes searching, as though Chloe could have somehow pressed herself into the mattress.

Still clutching the golf club, Sara ran through the apartment calling her daughter's name and flicking on lights as she went. She pulled open closet doors and shoved clothes aside. She picked up the open packet of migraine medication that sat on the kitchen cupboard and put it back down. She ran back through the bedroom to the bathroom. The door was closed. Sara shifted the club and covered her mouth with her hand to stifle the fear that was trying to escape with a sob. Chloe had to be in there. There was no other place. Sara slowly opened the door and found herself calling "Chloe" as softly as she had when trying to awaken her daughter from nightmares when she was a child. Sara held her breath as she ran her hand down the wall, found the light switch and flicked it. The bright overhead light instantly exposed black and white tiled floor and walls. The red shower curtain was pulled closed around the bath. It was only a few steps to the curtain but Sara had to struggle to make the distance. She grasped a fold of the heavy plastic and closed her eyes as she yanked it open. Still holding tightly to the curtain for support she forced her eyes open. Empty. Dear God, thank you. She clung to the curtain for support. She couldn't think. For a moment she felt paralyzed, her eyes locked on the dripping tap and the rust that the persistent water had painted around the drain. She shook her head trying to put her body and mind back into gear. Where was Chloe? Renewed strength surged into her muscles and she ran back into the bedroom.

"What have you done with my daughter?" she screamed. The intruder lay on the other side of Chloe's bed and Sara could see only the tip of one sneaker.

"She's not here." He spoke as though Chloe had seriously let him down. The voice was childlike and petulant. Could she have struck a child? But what would a child be doing here? She cautiously edged around the bed until the owner of the voice was in view.

He lay on his back. The baseball cap askew but still on his head. A large hunting knife lay beside his right hand. Blood dribbled from his right temple and had begun to form a small puddle beside his head.

He was as small as Pauline had described. His face was line-free and the pale skin looked soft, as though never toughened by a razor. Only a wash of gray at the temples suggested an aging man rather than a boy. What looked like the remnants of a picnic lunch, a half eaten sandwich, a paper napkin and the sandwich's wrapping, lay beside him, apparently tossed from the bed when Sara had pulled back the covers. And she had thought this afternoon was surreal.

He was staring up at her intently. "You hurt me." His voice and expression registered surprise and grave disappointment that she would do such a thing to him. He waited as though for an apology.

"Where is my daughter?" she repeated, feeling quite sure now that he didn't know but needing to somehow find that answer.

"She left. I thought she was going to go to bed like she told you on her message but she went out instead." He was annoyed. A plan gone awry. Then he added, "I was in the closet and it's very stuffy in there. She didn't know I was here." Now he spoke as though reassuring her. Don't worry, he seemed to say. Your daughter wasn't frightened. He reached for the knife with one small hand and rolled over to his other side taking the knife with him. He pulled an elbow underneath him and began to leverage himself into an upright position.

Sara stared at him, still gripping the iron, not knowing what to do. Could he get up and attack her with the knife? Did she need to hit him again? Could she hit him again?

She didn't have to decide. Two uniformed police officers kicked Chloe's door open and came charging into the room guns drawn and shouting, "Drop your weapons."

She didn't think of herself as having a weapon until one of them glared at her and yelled, "Now." The iron bounced off the dull hardwood floor, any mark it made obscured amid many years' worth of gouges.

Carson and Greally were close behind. One of the officers kicked the knife away from the man on the floor and Carson shouted orders.

The little man had lain back down on the floor and when the hubbub quieted for a moment he lifted his arm and pointed at Sara. "She hit me with that golf club," he whined as though tattling on a playmate in the schoolyard.

"Do you want to tell us what this is about, Ms. Porter?" Greally threw the question at Sara like a hardball he knew she could never catch.

"He was going to kill my daughter."

"And where is your daughter?"

"I don't know."

"She's not here but you literally clubbed this man because you were afraid he was going to kill her."

"I thought she was here."

"You couldn't see that she wasn't here?"

"It was dark."

Sara liked this man less and less, but decided it wasn't the time to try anything smart. Sara could see Carson pull himself away and begin giving instructions to the two constables. Had he given up on her or did he feel that if he interfered it would look like he was protecting her?

Carson looked down at the man on the floor. "Hello, Jimmie."

"Hello, Officer."

Greally was still busy getting even with Sara. "So you bash this guy on the head, not even knowing whether your daughter was here or not? Now if you'd killed him I suppose you'd be telling us he was Diane Brooks' murderer?"

"Greally." Carson glared at him. Greally had crossed the line.

Greally pulled out handcuffs. "Ms. Porter, it seems you've forgotten that you are under arrest for the murder of Diane Brooks." The satisfaction in Greally's voice was evident.

The little man on the floor tried to sit upright. He looked back and forth from Greally to Carson. Greally started to move Sara Porter toward the door.

"She didn't do that. She would never have had what it takes. I did." Credit where credit is due, his tone said.

The sense of relief was so powerful that Sara couldn't remain upright. She felt herself crumpling and made it to the edge of the bed before her muscles went limp.

47

Sara sat by the kitchen window, the newspaper resting on the sill and her leg propped on a stool. The pain in her ankle had lessened but it looked like it belonged to a three-hundred-pound stranger.

Chloe was still asleep upstairs. Sara had slept little. She had spent the first part of the night getting up to check on Chloe. There had been no need. Chloe was fine. Her headache had lifted quickly once she had taken her medication and she had decided to spend the evening with a friend. Jimmie was in custody. Chloe was perfectly safe but the terror of losing her child had clung fiercely to Sara and would not be shaken off by mere reason. She had spent the first part of the night hobbling back and forth between her room and Chloe's, gently tugging the duvet over her daughter's shoulder, kissing her forehead and inhaling the scent of her child. Once, Chloe had stirred and mumbled, "I'm fine Mom, go to sleep." Finally Sara had given up trying to leave her side. She wrapped a blanket around herself and curled up in the oversized basket chair that Chloe, as a teenager, had insisted was a must have. Sara had awakened at seven, stiff, cold and still tired, but her nerves were taut and she knew it was pointless to try to go back to sleep.

A large part of Sara's world was in the morning paper. One of the *Star*'s lead stories read "Head of Prominent Consulting Firm Absconds with Company Funds." She hardly needed to read the article. Tony's news flashes and minute-by-minute updates could put CNN to shame. Ken and Dina had bolted with all of the company's cash and were thought likely to be somewhere in South America. Dina had secretly called her sister, telling her that Ken would kill her if he knew she had contacted home but she didn't want her family to worry. Whether Dina meant the phrase "would kill me" to be taken literally wasn't clear. The sister thought she could hear Spanish being spoken in the background and Dina had complained of the heat. Dina's sister had called the police because she was certain her sister could never do anything criminal and had been forced into the escapade against her will by Ken Morrison. How little we know some of the people closest to us, Sara thought.

A headshot of Ken that had been taken for publicity purposes when

Morrison and Black re-invented themselves a few years ago was next to a candid photo of a cluster of people. According to the caption they were members of Dina's family. Dina was third from the right and the only one posing for the camera. If Dina had been seeking attention she had finally achieved it.

Tony reported that Ken had been startled into flight by the rumor that not only was the staff going to insist on seeing the firm's financials, but the Canada Revenue Agency also wanted a look. An Agency team had arrived midday Monday to do an audit. Apparently they had called Ken on Friday telling him to have the files ready for them.

To Sara, the matter had been surprising but not shocking. If asked in advance if she thought either of the two were capable of such a thing she would have said without hesitation that yes, in her view, they both were.

The other big story was headed "Murder Suspect Arrested." James Baker, it said, had been arrested for the murder of Diane Brooks. The police were still investigating possible links to the murders of Stephen Dempster and William Coombs. James Baker, along with his sister, had been a member of the late Judge Theodore Jamieson's household staff and, until his arrest, had still been employed by Patrick Jamieson, president of the Jamieson's chain and nephew of Theodore Jamieson. Not the greatest publicity with which to relaunch a political career. She felt badly for Patrick.

Sara hadn't expected to find anything in the article that she didn't already know but the reporter surprised her. He had done some good digging in a short time. James Baker had attended nursing school in the seventies and had trained at a local hospital. He was dismissed for undisclosed reasons. During the two months before his dismissal the number of deaths in the emergency ward where he was assigned had increased dramatically. Three families had asked for an inquiry but the hospital had managed to avoid one.

No wonder he knew exactly where to plunge the knife. And Patty had been close in suggesting that he would likely have a profession.

Calico leaped onto her lap and kneaded her thigh with its paws, looking for comfort. The "the" had gotten dropped from "the calico" and it had become just Calico. So much for her determination not to give it a name.

A cloud moved and pale tepid sunlight fell through the window and onto her shoulder. The icy rain of last evening had turned to unusually early snow and had laid a soggy white blanket over lawns and bushes. The temperature was rising again and patches of dark wet leaves had begun to appear.

Movement at the corner of her eye caught her attention and she turned to see Carson, Gucci loafers slipping and sliding, attempting to hurry up her drive. She banged on the window and waved to him. He looked up and grinned. That damn grin.

She hobbled to the back door to greet him.

"Had breakfast?" were his first words.

"If coffee and half a grapefruit count."

"No way. I'm talking a real breakfast. Bacon, eggs, fried potatoes and a side of pancakes."

It sounded like more fat than she normally ate in a month. It also sounded good.

Carson had a favorite breakfast spot, the Big Taste on Yonge Street, which was only a few minutes away. Around since the fifties, it was one of only a few restaurants that could still qualify as a "greasy spoon." When they opened the door, the smell of fried bacon wafted out, like smoke from a bar once did. The smell reminded her of Bill Coombs and the morning she met him in front of his home. Poor man. He had been a gentle person whom she guessed hadn't seen a lot of happiness.

A long counter ran down the left side of the Big Taste. Stools in front of it, an open grill behind. Sara and Carson worked their way toward the back, Sara limping to avoid putting weight on the sprained ankle. The cook flipped eggs and pancakes, made toast and carried on lively chit-chat with the regulars at the counter without missing a beat. They squeezed by an ample man whose buttocks enveloped his stool. He was attacking an oversized piece of coconut cream pie as though it were his usual breakfast fare.

In the back corner they slid into a booth with worn red leather seats. A plastic-covered menu was propped against the wall behind the ketchup and sugar cellar. They didn't need the menu.

Once the gray-haired waitress, who looked like she might have been the restaurant's first employee, had taken their order and poured their coffee, Carson slipped the elastic fastener off the cardboard portfolio he had carried with him from the car.

"I thought you deserved to know what we've learned from Jimmie."

"Is he alright?" Even though she had personally felt the man's evil, she had worried that she might have killed him. She didn't know how she would feel if she killed someone, even a murderer, and didn't want to find out.

"He'll be fine. He spent a few hours under observation in emergency last night. That's where we got most of his statement. He asked us to call Patrick Jamieson and explain to him 'his predicament,' as Jimmie called it, and ask if he could 'borrow' the Jamieson family lawyer. Jamieson seemed to be shocked by the whole thing but agreed without hesitation to get the family lawyer down to the hospital. Turns out his lawyer is also Dean Hoffmeyer, so he wasn't unemployed last night after all. It was hard to keep Jimmie focused though. He was more concerned about his head hurting than being under arrest for murder and wasn't very happy that the nurse wouldn't give him anything for the pain."

Sara was frowning.

"You said that Patrick Jamieson *seemed* to be shocked. Do you know of any reason why he wouldn't be shocked?"

"No, but we have no proof that Jimmie acted alone, although he insists he did. He has been with the Jamieson family for his entire life and Patrick Jamieson would have as good a reason as anyone for wanting to let sleeping dogs lie, since he plans to get back into politics, and at a high level."

Sara poured sugar from the large sugar cellar into her coffee. She usually didn't take sugar but felt she needed an energy boost. It poured faster than she expected. She stared at her coffee for a moment considering her dilemma. Maybe if she didn't stir it, it wouldn't be too sweet.

"I can't imagine Patrick being involved. I really like him."

Carson said nothing.

"Could you get into trouble for sharing this information with me?" she asked.

He shrugged.

"Not likely. Who's to know? And everything will be public once it comes to trial. In the meantime I know you'll keep it confidential. Besides, as I said, you deserve to know."

He looked into her eyes for a moment too long and she looked away. He pulled a sheaf of papers from the portfolio and tapped the end on the table to straighten them.

"Jimmie is some sick puppy alright but I guess that's no surprise. He readily admitted to murdering the judge, Diane Brooks, Bill Coombs and Stephen Dempster, only he never used the words murder or kill. He said he was responsible for the *necessary acts*. When I asked why they were necessary he gave us a lecture on loyalty."

Carson leafed through his stack of papers, pulled several and turned them around so Sara could read them. They were a copy of part of Jimmie's statement:

> *Most people wouldn't understand anymore. At one time they would have. It was about loyalty and pride and doing for others what they can't do for themselves. I'm the third generation of our family to be employed by the Jamieson family. My grandmother used to say we were beholden to the Jamieson family. They hired her in 1934. "Imagine," she used to say, "if I had been employed by some middle-class family with little wealth and no position in society. Imagine what our lives might have been then. We are who we are because of the Jamiesons and don't you forget that." The family is almost gone*

but the Jamieson name is still one of the most respected in the country and when Mr. Patrick gets back into politics the Jamieson family name will be in the papers everyday just the way it used to be.

"'Doing for others what they can't do for themselves.' What did he mean?" she asked.

"Don't know. I asked him to explain but he wouldn't say any more. My guess is he was referring to Patrick Jamieson, that Jamieson didn't have the stomach to kill anyone to save the family name and his career. So Jimmie did it for him."

"But that doesn't necessarily mean that Patrick was party to it."

Carson paused for a moment before he agreed.

Sara pushed the papers aside and slowly shook her head. "Jimmie had no identity outside of the Jamieson family, did he?"

"None whatsoever. He claims he did what he did for the family, but I suspect it was really for himself. He couldn't stand the thought of the Jamieson name being tarnished. In addition, I suspect he enjoyed the killing. In fact, we're checking the cold case file. People don't usually start murdering at his age. It's likely he's convinced himself it was necessary in the past too."

Sara shivered. She remembered Patty saying something similar.

"So he killed the judge because he was ready to talk about the murder of Jane Stewart and he killed Diane because she was ready to bring it into the public eye again after all of these years?"

"That's what it looks like. He may even have thought she knew about the cover-up and even who the murderer was. He's not prepared to share details. But you were right. As absurd as it seems, the judge's and Diane's deaths were tied to a sixty-year-old murder.

"Then he murdered Stephen Dempster because the old guy had seen him the day he snooped around your house pretending to deliver fliers, and he suspected that he also saw him when he came out your front door the day he broke in. So he just dropped in to Dempster's to ensure the old fellow wouldn't be able to identify him."

Carson paused to drain his coffee cup and signal for more.

"And, finally, he killed Bill Coombs. Coombs knew him, of course, from the Jamiesons' spending summers at The Point. Apparently, Jimmie felt Bill would realize that he had been following you. I suspect Jimmie could have explained away his presence but either panicked or grabbed the opportunity to kill again. Probably the latter, although he may not even realize that himself. "

Sara was shaking her head and frowning.

"What's wrong?"

"Me." Her voice showed impatience, not with him but with herself. "It never occurred to me," she continued to shake her head, "to even enquire about the Jamiesons' staff."

"Are you always so hard on yourself?" he asked the question not lightly, but as though he were working to understand her.

She shrugged and was saved from self-analysis by the arrival of their breakfast, steaming hot bacon and eggs exactly to order. Two sunny-side up for Sara and three over easy for Carson.

Carson turned his attention from murder to food. Sara wasn't able to do so as easily. She poked toast corners into an egg.

Neither spoke for several minutes. When Carson had nearly completed his mission he looked up. "Sorry. I'm really not a glutton. I haven't eaten since yesterday morning."

"And when was the last time you slept?"

He pulled up his suit sleeve and checked his watch.

"Other than a few winks at the office, I've been up for about thirty hours, but I'm OK for another few."

He picked up his coffee cup and clipped hers as though making a toast.

"Keith?"

"Yeah?"

"What about Aunt Kate? Pauline said she committed suicide, but could Jimmie have killed her as well?"

"Not according to Jimmie. And having confessed to four murders, he had no reason to deny another."

"I'm glad. I like to think she was in the driver's seat when she left us. I'm not as sure now as I was about why she did it though. At first I thought it was determination to control how she would die, even if she couldn't control how she lived the last few months. She had certainly been preparing to take her own life. She'd been saving the sleeping pills she was given each night and, according to Pauline, she had told the judge about it.

"But I'm convinced she hadn't planned to die that night until she saw the judge's obituary. They were still close. Perhaps she was even still in love with him and chose not to live once he was gone."

Sara focused on her paper napkin. She had folded it into a tiny triangle. Now she unfolded it, rested it on the table, and smoothed outs its wrinkles.

"Or perhaps," she continued. "she guessed the judge had been murdered. It's likely he told her he intended to fess up. In fact, Pauline heard him say something about how they both had things they needed to do and there could be others who would want to prevent them. Imagine the irony, and the tragedy, of having the evil that you kept hidden in the past lead to the murder of someone you cherished in the present."

Sara wiped a tear from her cheek. Carson said nothing. After a few minutes of refolding her napkin, Sara took a deep breath.

"I've got to know," she said.

"Got to know what?"

Sara had begun to shake and wrapped her arms around herself. "Why didn't he kill me? And would he have killed Chloe if she had been there?"

He reached over, took one of her hands, pulled it to him and briefly rubbed it between his two palms. "I'm not sure whether he would have killed Chloe. I don't think he knows for sure himself. You, however, had protection, but protection that I think was beginning to wear thin. As he put it, he couldn't allow himself to hurt you and he would only have done so as a last resort. Loyalty was both his reason for killing the others and his reason for not killing you."

He stopped for a moment to wipe his plate with the last corner of cold toast. "You were doubly protected. First, as Kate McPherson's niece, he saw you as a member of The Point family, and so a member of the extended Jamieson family. In addition Jamieson invited you to the house for brunch. That settled it. Patrick liked you and Jimmie wouldn't do anything to someone Patrick cared for. He was, however, desperately trying to scare you off and I have no doubt he enjoyed the sick games. Which, by the way, the button trick was one of."

"But, if he couldn't kill me, how could he have killed the judge?"

"I think that was difficult for him. In fact, he cried when he talked about it. He claims he simply did what had to be done to save the family name. He knew from overhearing the judge's conversations with your aunt that the judge had decided to unburden himself of the Jane Stewart incident. He also convinced himself that the judge was suffering with his heart condition and that he was saving him from pain and disability."

Carson gave his coffee a couple of stirs and continued. "He did make the death as painless as possible. He spiced the judge's lunch with a few tranquilizers and once the judge nodded off at his desk, he suffocated him."

"It sounds like he's casting himself as a pint-sized Kavorkian."

"He'd really like that image, but I'm afraid a mercy killing scenario doesn't fit the rest of the deaths.

"Oh, I nearly forgot." Carson paused for a moment to wipe the last bit of egg from his plate with the last morsel of toast. "I asked Jimmie about the mysterious print-free milk glass. I said something like, 'You thought you were pretty smart with that milk glass, eh Jimmie?' I was trying to get a rise from him but he just looked at me coolly and said, 'I was clever.'" Carson was chuckling. "And then he went on to say he had, of course, and he emphasized the 'of course,' been wearing gloves and he poured the milk because his stomach was upset. But when he went to drink it, it smelled as though it wasn't fresh. Sour milk, he said, sits unhealthily in the stomach, so he poured it down the sink. He added that people who live alone tend not to keep their food fresh. He should have known better, he said."

Sara smiled at the joke on herself.

Their waitress cleared away their plates and poured more coffee, living up to the restaurant menu's claim of a bottomless pot.

"OK, Keith. I'm waiting."

"For what?"

"Who killed Jane Stewart?"

Carson shrugged. "I don't know. Jimmie says he knows nothing about it other than Teddy Jamieson and your aunt had, as you guessed, moved the body. Jimmie wasn't even born when Stewart was murdered but his older brother Harvey seems to have been a bit of a groupie and followed your aunt and her friends everywhere. One night he followed Kate and Teddy, thinking they were maybe going to smooch on the dock. Instead, he watched them drag Jane Stewart's body to a deserted piece of the beach. Jimmie's brother had told the story many times. The cover-up is what Jimmie says the judge was going to fess up to, not the murder."

Carson rummaged some more in his folder. "The only information we have tied to the likely night of Jane Stewart's murder is from a diary of a local woman whom Diane Brooks came across in her research." He pulled out a photocopy of some of the notes he had found in Diane's office and paraphrased them for Sara.

"The woman was walking her dog on The Point and as she passed your aunt's cottage she heard an argument between a man and a woman. She describes the woman as laughing 'in derision more than in joy.' Then she heard a male voice say 'You are despicable.' She assumed he was speaking to the woman but the voices were muffled and there could have been more than two people there."

Sara was pensive for a few minutes. "So that must have been Jane Stewart and her murderer. It seems that she was the only woman still at The Point at the end of the season, other than Mrs. Baker, who would have been helping to close up."

"Yes, as far as we know. But Teddy and your aunt lied about a lot of things. It's possible that your aunt hadn't gone back to the city or had returned to The Point. The woman's voice could have been hers."

"Jane's apparent plan to inform the law school about Teddy and Harper's relationship could certainly be described as despicable." Sara had developed affection and sorrow for the man she had never met and there was anger in her voice. "Teddy would not be the only suspect if that were the motive. Harper and my aunt both loved him and no doubt would have protected him."

"We'll keep working on Jimmie," Carson promised. "But unless he knows and he talks, chances are slim we'll ever discover Jane Stewart's murderer."

A few days ago Sara had believed her aunt had left her something to complete. Perhaps her aunt had not been asking her to delve into the past, but to stop more death in the present. Perhaps that was it. Box closed.

Sara glanced at her watch. It was nearly eleven. Tony had said he would drop by to see her late morning. She should get home.

Carson gathered the papers together, used his balled up paper napkin to wipe a bacon-grease stain from one, and stuffed them back into his portfolio.

But neither moved. They both waited for the conversation they hadn't yet had but neither knew how to start. Sara stirred cold coffee and Carson's knee gyrated up and down like a drill searching for oil. Sara knew she was the one with the greater need and so made a beginning that came out abruptly. A shot from nowhere.

"I was there, wasn't I?"

Carson didn't need to ask where "there" was. He just nodded.

"I still don't remember." She gave the coffee that would never be drunk another deliberate stir as though it mattered. "But I dreamed about Diane sitting at the kitchen bar, white shirt, purple pants, bare feet, hair clipped back. Just as she was in your crime scene shots. It terrified me. How could I have dreamt that without having been there? And if I had been there… ? Deep down I knew I couldn't have killed her but at the same time I was so afraid I had. Who knows what one can do when one hates enough and is drunk enough?"

The memory of the cold fear with which she had lived shot tears to her eyes. She blinked them away and continued. "I even became afraid of knives. Remember the night you had dinner with me and noticed something was wrong? I had just picked up the chopping knife, and seeing myself hold it triggered a panic attack, which then of course only made me more afraid that I had killed Diane. If not, why my sudden fear of knives? I thought."

Another nod from Carson. She didn't need a conversation; she needed to share the weight she had been carrying and he understood that. She felt a surge of gratefulness and the hint of another emotion following close behind, which she ignored. Carson took her hand again and gave it a quick squeeze, not taking the chance of lingering too long and being unwelcome.

"The receipt from Tony's and my dinner at Primavera that you found in Richard and Diane's backyard, was it enough to convict me?" Now she was looking for that conversation.

Carson shrugged. "It was definitely enough for an arrest. With the receipt, your not having an alibi, and worse, not remembering that evening, and then Hamilton's account of your behavior in the restaurant, it's possible you could have been convicted."

Straight talking Carson. Just the facts. There was no "But I knew you weren't guilty."

"Jimmie saw you there," he continued. "He said you were standing on the back patio in the pouring rain, peering through the French doors. You pulled them open a crack and then left."

Sara remembered in her dream not being able to see Diane well through the rain that streaked the glass of the doors and feeling that if she could just see her clearly, at home in her life with Richard, that somehow she would be able to better accept things as they were. She missed a few of Carson's words and then tuned back in.

"Jimmie wiped your fingerprints off the door handle. He played sadistic games with you and protected you at the same time."

Now it was Sara's turn to simply nod. She folded her paper napkin and wiped the corners of her mouth, checking for dried egg, although little had entered her mouth.

"I've got to get home," she announced, crumpling the lipstick-stained napkin and leaving it on her still nearly full plate.

As she climbed into Carson's red Mustang she noticed a bag of refinishing materials, wood stripper, sandpaper, and wax in the back seat.

"Do you do woodworking for a hobby?" she asked.

"Not really. In fact I've never done it before. I've got a coffee table that looks so bad it's disgusting. But there is some beautiful wood under those coffee rings. I thought I might try to find it again."

Should she or shouldn't she? Why not. It couldn't be riskier than what she had been through the past week. "I've refinished some of my parents' old furniture. So if you need help … ?"

Carson had begun to reverse the car from its parking spot. He stopped, ignoring the car that was honking at him, and turned to look at her. "I'm sure I'm going to need lots of help."

Tony was waiting on her doorstep with one of his big bear hugs and a bag of lunch-makings: croissants, cheese, cold cuts, and a couple of Labatt Blue. She didn't have the heart to tell him that she had spent the past two hours pushing a cold fried egg around a greasy plate and couldn't bear the thought of food.

They picnicked at the kitchen counter. Sara forced tiny pieces of croissant and cheese into her mouth and swallowed them with the help of the cold beer. She knew why Tony had come and knew he was anxious to get to his agenda but he forced himself to make small talk first. How was Chloe? Had she heard from Jamie? How did he like the Far East? Did she need help getting the patio furniture in for the winter?

As he wiped crumbs from a pudgy cheek he said, "I tried to reach you several times last evening. What were you up to?"

"Oh, nothing much. I was arrested for Diane's murder."

"What! But they got the murderer. You mean that they arrested you first?"

Sara nodded, watching his face for a reaction.

"Oh, God. You mean they arrested you because of what I…?"

His face reddened and perspiration flowed freely down his forehead. Sara was sorry she had been flippant. She was afraid he was pushing his blood pressure sky high.

"It's OK, Tony. It wasn't just what you said. Anyway it all worked out. Really, forget about it." She said it as though the matter were trivial. As though perhaps he had forgotten that he promised to give her a lift somewhere.

Sara moved to the conversation that she knew would take his mind off his guilt and hers off last night. "My guess is you brought this gourmet meal in order to seduce me into getting involved in some wild plan for the late Morrison and Black."

"Well, not exactly a wild plan."

Tony mopped his brow, and relief that he was obviously forgiven and they could move on triggered one of his ear-to-ear smiles. A deep dimple momentarily poked into each cheek and Sara watched them fade as his smile dwindled. "Oh my God," she thought and her mind went back to Stewart's murder.

She realized Tony was talking and she had missed what he was saying. "Sorry Tony, what did you say? I was just remembering that I had told Chloe that I'd call her around lunchtime." Not true, but white enough to be harmless.

"I was saying that we took a vote and it was unanimous. Everyone wants you to head up the firm. It will be a different firm of course. We can't operate under Morrison and Black. Poor Frieda Black's got nothing left. The company's kaput financially and reputation-wise as well, with Ken's capers all over the news. But we have several contracts on the go and several monthly retainers. If we can keep them with us that would keep us going until we can attract new business. With you at the helm we'll do really well. And we can all make a heck of a lot more than we did when Ken was around."

He was right. They did have the business and she could bring in more. She could also do a darned good job of managing the firm and she would enjoy mentoring the new grads they had brought into the firm in the spring and whom Ken had left to flounder. There was much they could accomplish and plenty of opportunities for her to use her strengths. With the client base they had now they could build a firm even more successful than Morrison and Black.

Usually Sara weighed decisions carefully. This one she didn't have to. The answer was shouting from deep in her gut.

"No, Tony. Thanks, but no." What she was going to do career wise she didn't know, but whatever it was it would move her forward, not back.

She spent the next hour convincing Tony that they could do it without her. She described a rough plan and promised to work with them for a few weeks until they got organized.

"And then what?" asked Tony.

Sara looked at him quizzically.

"Then what for you, I mean," he explained.

Sara hadn't had enough peace of mind recently to think about it before. But the answer came to her immediately.

"LA."

48

For the past few weeks Sara had worked long hours helping Tony and the others get the new firm organized. Every evening when she arrived home she lit a fire and spent an hour in front of it, going through the keepsakes in Aunt Kate's box for the last time. Each piece she perused once more, trying to absorb some of her aunt's history as she did, and then threw it into the flames.

She had thought about keeping everything. But only briefly. The items in the box reflected bits and pieces of the person Kate McPherson was at different moments in her life, but none had any relevance to the woman she had ultimately created, or, Sara was certain, to the woman Kate would want others to remember.

By the last evening all that had been left were the newspaper clippings about Jane Stewart's murder and the notebook Aunt Kate had kept at the time. They sat abandoned at the bottom of the battered and age-stained box. The box's lid lay flat on the hearth, corners splayed, as though exhausted from the responsibility of containing such secrets for so many years.

Sara had picked up the clippings and studied them once more. On top was the photo of Jane Stewart that had locked eyes with her the first time she looked at it. Now, it was no more than a lifeless yellowed photo torn from an old newspaper. Each piece seemed to welcome the flames and was quickly consumed. And finally the box. As the flames danced around the box inviting it to join them, Sara had steeled herself for the feeling of sadness she expected to wash over her. Instead, as the box disappeared she had felt a sense of renewal.

Now, the four last pieces sat on the hearth. She had begun to drop them on the fire last night and then pulled them back. This morning she would have to decide what to do with them.

Sara's suitcase sat open on the bed, ready for any last-minute items she might remember. Patty was thrilled that Sara was coming to visit her in LA and Sara had bought an open ticket. She was luxuriating in her new freedom. No one else and no schedule would determine where she would be or when.

Keith had been in the States for a few days at a police conference. He had called from there suggesting dinner when he returned. "Sure," she had answered. "How about the Blue Dolphin?"

"I don't know that one. Where is it?"

"In LA," she laughed.

"You're kidding. You're going to LA?" He sounded disappointed.

"Yes, but not forever. I'll call you before I leave?"

Patty had insisted that Sara wasn't actually traveling to see her but was running away from a relationship with Keith Carson. Not true. At least not completely true.

Coat on and ready to leave, Sara now sat on the bed beside her suitcase and surveyed her room. She had been busy every minute of the past little while. Days spent with the new consulting group and evenings putting everything here in order. The room seemed empty without the clutter of Aunt Kate's things on every flat surface. It also felt open and free. She had not only divested herself of Aunt Kate's archive but had cleaned out every closet. Anything she hadn't worn for over a year she decided she didn't need. She had added to the pile of giveaways several expensive evening outfits that she didn't expect to wear again. Richard's success was intertwined with constant social events to which she had dutifully tagged along. Now she was looking forward to a much quieter life. Besides, every gown reminded her of a particular occasion at which Richard was the center. She had also cleaned out Richard's closets. He had only taken his best business attire and what she thought of as his sexy clothes with him. Left behind were old suits, baggy sweatshirts and socks with thinning toes. They had formed a substantial pile in the middle of the bedroom floor. When she added a dozen pair of fading jockey shorts to the pile it occurred to her that she should have become suspicious when he started buying expensive designer briefs. She had squeezed a dozen large bags into the Volvo and had lugged them off to Goodwill.

Finding an outfit in her closet had always been a chore. She had had to do battle with unruly clothes that fell from hangers or got tangled with others and blocked her access to whatever she was looking for. Now the large double closet sat gaping open with only a dozen winter garments and a few empty hangers occupying one end.

She reached for the items she had left on her bedside table last night. She moved Calico who had settled on top of them and the cat gave a sharp meow of annoyance. As she picked them up the phone rang. It was Patrick Jamieson. He had by now heard the details of how Jimmie had involved her in the horror story he had created and Patrick was calling to say how sorry he was.

"Jimmie was always a bit of an oddball," he said, "but I guess we had just gotten used to him. I feel terribly responsible that I didn't notice anything.

But there was nothing that suggested to me he was actually —," the word seemed to literally stick in his throat. "He was actually capable of murder. It's still difficult to grasp. I'm so sorry for the pain you must have experienced."

Sara was touched by his call and thanked him. Could Patrick Jamieson have been party to Jimmie's "necessary acts"? She chose to think not.

"Will this affect your plans? Political ones, I mean?" she asked.

"Not from my perspective, but we'll see if the party members feel the same way. Speaking of which, I am going to have to start attending more formal dinners again. Not my favorite part of a political career. I was wondering if you would mind if I called on you from time to time to accompany me. It would certainly make them more enjoyable."

Sara said she would be happy to have him call but after she hung up it occurred to her that she might have sounded distracted. She had been thinking about the gowns she had just given to Goodwill.

She turned to the photocopies of Diane's notebooks that Carson had given her.

She flipped through the pages until she found the passage she was looking for. It was from Diane's interview with Bill Coombs.

He had told her that his mother thought that there was *something very odd about Mr. Teddy Jamieson saying he thought Miss Stewart had taken the train the morning she went missing because Jamieson had asked Mrs. Coombs the previous day if she knew anything about the train schedule from Bradford to Toronto and she said there wasn't any train before one in the afternoon on Wednesdays. She knew because her sister had physiotherapy treatments in the city every Thursday morning since she had been partially paralyzed by polio.*

The doorbell rang. The limousine had arrived.

Sara picked up the other three articles and tucked them into her coat pocket. She would leave the copies of Diane's notebook for Chloe on the kitchen island beside the cat's traveling kit, bag of food, bag of litter and litter box, with instructions to give the notes to Richard.

She was locking the door behind her when she heard the phone ring. Why not let it go? Two minutes later and she would have left. But she couldn't. Maybe it was Chloe needing something. She got to the phone just before the voice mail kicked in.

"Hello?"

"Could I speak with Sara, please?"

"Yes, speaking."

"Oh, Sara. I didn't recognize your voice. It's Ralph Jefferson."

Aunt Kate's lawyer. Now she wished she had let it ring. It would be some administrivia to do with her aunt's estate.

"It's about your aunt's estate, Sara. It was quite complicated and it has just been settled. As you know almost her entire estate is to go to a home for retired and financially needy artists. But, in addition, your aunt left instructions that were a little odd." He cleared his throat. "Your aunt instructed that one piece of her estate be directed elsewhere on one condition."

There was silence.

"Yes?" Sara prodded him.

"Sara, this may seem like an odd question but have you visited The Point since your aunt died?"

"Yes, actually I have."

He cleared his throat once more and continued, "In that case I can confirm you have fulfilled the condition, I can now inform you that your aunt has left you the cottage." He paused. "I'm sure none of this makes little sense to you, but …"

"Oh, but it makes perfect sense, Ralph." Sara laughed.

"Oh, oh. Alright then. I'll just make up the deed transfer forms and you can call me when you would like to come in to sign them." He hung up quickly.

Now he'll think the whole family is crazy; she smiled to herself.

But then her vision blurred as tears filled her eyes. She pictured the cottage as it had once been. Perhaps she could fill it once again with the laughter that had been there when the McPherson family had enjoyed it together.

49

Carson was kneeling in the middle of his living room floor when his cell rang. By the time he pulled himself to his feet, dusted the sawdust from his Calvin Kleins and jogged across the room it was one ring away from voice mail.

"Yup. Carson here. "

"Hi, it's me … It's Sara."

"I know," His voice smiled.

"I'm on my way to the airport. I thought I'd call to say good-bye."

"I'm glad." He tried to picture her. Designer jeans and a tee, or business suit? Hair in a sophisticated chignon or the blond streaks hanging sexily over one eye? He went for the jeans and sexy hair.

They had been able to get together only once since the Brooks case closed. He had travelled to an international conference on criminology in Amsterdam and tagged on some vacation time. He had always regretted not studying art history and when he learned about a two-week program in Florence, he booked immediately. He would never regret the two weeks spent with the masters in his favorite city but sure regretted the timing. When he got back he was immersed in another case and he and Sara had managed one quick dinner at Canoe, a restaurant where a quick dinner was a horrible waste.

"You sound like you are in a good mood." Her voice was upbeat and he could picture her tucking that sexy piece of hair behind her ear.

"I am. Kirpatrick's wife had their baby and his excitement is contagious. I'm happy for him."

"That's really good to hear. What are you up to?"

"I'm tackling my coffee table. It's taking a lot more stripping than I thought. But you know what? It's looking pretty good."

"I wish I could talk longer but I have to go. I have a stop to make before the airport." Sara hesitated for a second and then added, "Don't finish the table before I get back. I want to at least help with the polishing, OK?"

"I'm going to hold you to that."

He wandered back to the coffee table, ran his hand over the silky finish of the newly revealed wood and took in its scent.

It looked like it would be a while before he and Sara got together again. But that was OK. In Carson's experience the anticipation always made the main event even better.

Sara had struggled with how to handle this visit ever since she had lunched with Tony in her kitchen weeks ago. She had called Howard Hamilton to tell him she would be dropping in and he had asked her to come to the back entrance. It was a mild, soft, winter morning. When she pushed on the gate in the high wooden fence that surrounded the garden, it squeaked like Calico when she was angry with her. The jarring of the gate disturbed a pile of wet snow that had accumulated on the top and it plopped to the ground on the other side. Now the small mound hindered the progress of the gate's swing, and she had to push hard against its gray wooden slats to open it far enough to pass through.

Howard Hamilton sat in the backyard at the same small table they had chatted across on her last visit. Only then, there hadn't been snow on the ground. He had already brushed the snow off the table and a tray, with a pot of tea, two cups and saucers and a plate of plain biscuits, sat precisely in the center, a newspaper beside it. He wore a worn gray tweed overcoat and a red scarf tied around his neck. The squeaking gate had alerted him to her arrival and he was looking expectantly in her direction as she appeared. He smiled a wan smile and pulled himself to his feet as she approached.

"I hope you don't mind our having tea out here. It may seem a little strange." His soft chuckle, no louder than the first low growl of a wary dog, barely reached her.

"I love the garden and the summer is so short." He continued, "Sometimes I think it's more beautiful in the winter. It's quite mild today and the garden is sheltered. I don't think you'll be uncomfortable."

He limped around the table and whisked the snow off the wrought iron chair that was meant for her. He pulled a section from the *Globe* that was lying on the table and set it on the seat. After testing it with his hand he decided another layer was required and added the entertainment section. Finally satisfied, he said, "There, that should insulate you from the cold metal."

This, Sara thought, could compete with any tea party that Lewis Carroll had ever dreamed up. But Mr. Hamilton was right. The garden was beautiful. Heavy clumps of snow bent evergreen branches downward and prepared themselves for their imminent slide to the ground. Red berries dotted several bushes and, as though ensuring Howard Hamilton and his garden were totally color co-ordinated, a bright red cardinal settled on a nearby bird feeder.

Mr. Hamilton poured tea, the steam even steamier in the cool air. He looked frailer than she remembered him, as though the wind could scoop him up with the few autumn leaves that lingered and send him scuttling across the snowy ground with them.

Sara searched for the right words to begin and found none. Instead she took the photo of the two lovebirds from her pocket and hesitantly set it beside Hamilton's cup. He looked down at Jane Stewart and her companion, whose dimples perfectly matched Tony Hamilton's, looked back at him.

He showed no surprise. "She was beautiful, wasn't she?" he asked as though they had been leafing through a family album and had paused for a moment at this photo.

"It wasn't just my youthful hormones." The faint chuckle again. "She truly was beautiful. It was those eyes that caught me and wouldn't let me go." He looked at Sara now and tears had filled his eyes. He blinked them away. "Drink your tea, dear. It will keep you warm while I tell you what I'm sure you came to hear."

Sara put the cup to her lips and then hesitated for a moment.

When he saw her hesitation his eyes brimmed with tears again and he shook his head.

She took a deep sip of the aromatic Earl Grey.

"When you first visited," he continued unprompted, "and brought the photo of the Group, I wondered if you would find more pictures and recognize the earlier me with Jane. We had had several photos taken together the summer before I became sick."

"You had polio didn't you?" Sara asked.

Hamilton nodded. "People say Tony looks just like I did before I was ill, the chubby face and the dimples, so I feared, or perhaps hoped, you might discover me."

Sara nodded. "I was a little slow but Tony and I had lunch a while ago and he smiled in exactly the same way you were smiling in that picture."

A sparrow swept down and pecked a cookie crumb from the table.

"The story is short and sour," he continued. "I fell in love with Jane the summer this picture was taken. I was never really part of the Group but Teddy had invited me to spend weekends at The Point. That summer was to me like something from the movies. The Jamiesons had wealth beyond anything I had ever experienced and their summer home was full of beautiful and charming people."

Hamilton picked up the photo and gently caressed Jane's face with one finger. "I imagined that she loved me too. That my wit and charm somehow compensated for my lack of good looks. Love can create grand illusions."

Hamilton lapsed into silence, his eyes still on the photo. The muffled silence that snow brings filled the garden. The only sound was the drip of the melting icicles that hung from the eaves of the veranda a few feet away and it pulled Sara into her own memories.

"Don't play under those dang things," her father would warn her and her friends when they played outdoors in winter. "If one of them falls it'll go right through your head." They stayed away from the perimeter of the house until spring.

Hamilton was the first to return from reverie. "That fall we each went our own way. I wrote to Jane a few times but she said she wasn't a letter writer so I stopped. And then I caught polio, which consumed my life for the next year and left me with this." He slapped the leg that refused to work and lapsed into silence as though his story had ended.

Surely not. Could she have been wrong? "But you did go back to The Point," Sara said with more surety than she felt.

He nodded an affirmation and continued, "I lost touch with everyone but still fancied myself in love with Jane. The next summer I contacted Teddy and found that the Group was at The Point again and I finagled an invitation to join them."

Suddenly Hamilton's voice faded as though it were coming from a distance and Sara sensed he was back at The Point in the summer of 1948. Soon his words had pulled her there with him.

She watched as the Group played croquet on the lawn and swam off the dock. She heard Jane flirtatiously tell Hamilton how much more handsome he was now that he had lost weight. She saw her aunt close her cottage for the summer. She felt Hamilton's trepidation as he gathered his nerve to propose to Jane. She saw Teddy wink as he gave Hamilton the key to her aunt's cottage. She stood beside the fireplace with Jane and Hamilton as he awkwardly proposed. Then she heard Jane's derisive laugh as she rejected him and suddenly Sara didn't want to know any more.

But Hamilton wouldn't let her leave the world he was reliving until his confession was complete. And so she felt his humiliation and fury. She saw his raised hand. She heard Jane's head crack against the mantle.

Although the sun still shone, the garden seemed colder. Sara was shivering and her fingers, clutching the tea cup, had begun to numb. Hamilton sat silently and watched the sparrow return for a second helping.

Sara reached into her pocket for the last two items. She set the two locks of black hair wound with red thread on the newspaper that fluttered on the table. She anchored them with two fingers so that the breeze would not carry them away.

Hamilton did not appear to notice. Perhaps they held no meaning.

With no preamble Hamilton jumped back into the middle of his story. "Your aunt, of course, had to make the decision about what should be done. She was the one who was always in charge. Teddy drove down to Toronto the next day to fetch her and I had drunk myself to sleep before they returned.

"When I woke around midnight I heard their voices downstairs. I went down to join them and found them drinking scotch. I remember because your aunt hated scotch. Teddy said everything had been taken care of and should be forgotten. Your aunt said no, not forgotten."

Hamilton paused and pulled a folded tissue from his breast pocket. He opened it and lifted out a lock of black hair tied with red thread and set it beside the other two.

"She had cut a piece of Jane's hair and pulled threads from her silk blouse to make these three talismans. She said that if we got away with it, and we would, in time it would all become something we could push to the back of our minds. She insisted that we each carry one of these so that we would never forget what we had done. She didn't say what Howard had done. She said what *we* had done."

Sara felt a surge of pride. It was the same feeling of pride she'd experienced when she had heard of Kate's suicide. Kate took control and made tough decisions based on her own values. Perhaps not values everyone would agree with but Kate knew her own true north.

Sara had the answer for which she had been searching since she had first begun to sift through her aunt's mementos. Yet there was one more question she felt compelled to ask. "Why did Jimmie Baker visit you?" She felt cruel, as though prodding an already injured animal.

Hamilton had been in the middle of precariously pouring more tea with shaking hands. He stopped, the pot trembling in the air, his expression a blend of surprise and pain.

Sara pushed herself to continue, "The day I visited you someone came to see you. A workman, you said. I heard him refer to you as Mr. Howard. Jimmie called Patrick Jamieson, Mr. Patrick. The coincidence seemed too great."

Hamilton had managed to pour the tea, spilling only a little. He took several deep sips as though to give himself the strength to respond.

"I had known Jimmie's mother from The Point days and had called her years ago when I needed a handyman. She sent Jimmie and he has been helping me from time to time ever since.

"The day you were here he had come by to reassure me that no one would know my secret. Jimmie has always had a need to remind you of his helpfulness. But he had visited me earlier, toward the end of the summer. He had heard Teddy tell your aunt that he was going to go to the police and unburden himself about what we had done. It would destroy the Jamieson family name, Jimmie said, as well as Patrick's chances for a political career and it was inevitable that my name would also come out. But he told me not to worry because he wouldn't let Mr. Teddy, as he called him, do anything to ruin the family."

So Jimmie had lied to Carson, Sara thought. He had known Howard Hamilton had murdered Jane but had protected him.

Hamilton put his face in his hands and sobbed but only briefly as though accepting that no amount of tears could heal the irreparable. He blew his nose in a thin gray handkerchief and continued. "I suspected what Jimmie was going to do. But I convinced myself that he couldn't do such a thing because I knew I was too weak to stop him. My mother use to deride men with 'no stuffing.' That has been me all of my life. No stuffing."

They sat silently for a few minutes. Sara took a last sip of now cold tea. She had forgotten that she had a limousine waiting. She would miss her flight if she didn't hurry.

"If you decide to talk about this officially, here is a good person to call." She placed Carson's card beside the photo.

Sorry Tony, she thought. She regretted the suffering Tony would have to endure should his father take this last opportunity to prove that he did indeed have "stuffing." As she started to open the gate she looked back. Mr. Hamilton was staring at the photo of the two lovebirds.

A heavy sadness was hanging about her and she didn't want to take it with her. She stood for a few minutes longer and Mr. Hamilton looked up. "Sara, you are like your aunt. You know what has to be done and have the courage to do it. Thank you."

As she left the garden she felt the sadness being pulled from her as though it had been caught on a bush and left behind.

It was finished. It was a horrible story, but it was over. At least her part in it was.

Sara leaned back in the limousine appreciating the luxury of a completely empty mind. There was absolutely nothing she needed to mull over, analyze or decide upon. She let her mind wander at will. It stopped in Kate's parlor, she and her aunt standing over the jigsaw puzzle, its thousand pieces scattered on the games table. She remembered Kate admonishing her, "Don't start something you can't finish."

"Well, Kate," she whispered, "I've finished."

Lightning Source UK Ltd.
Milton Keynes UK
UKHW011019230622
404818UK00002B/8/J

9 781450 233224